D.H. Lawrence, Science and the Posthuman

Also by Jeff Wallace

CHARLES DARWIN'S 'ORIGIN OF SPECIES': New Interdisciplinary Essays
(*editor with David Amigoni*)

RAYMOND WILLIAMS NOW: Knowledge, Limits and the Future
(*editor with Rod Jones and Sophie Nield*)

GOTHIC MODERNISMS
(*editor with Andrew Smith*)

D.H. Lawrence, Science and the Posthuman

Jeff Wallace

First published 2005 by
PALGRAVE MACMILLAN
Houndmills, Basingstoke, Hampshire RG21 6XS and
175 Fifth Avenue, New York, N.Y. 10010
Companies and representatives throughout the world

PALGRAVE MACMILLAN is the global academic imprint of the Palgrave Macmillan division of St. Martin's Press, LLC and of Palgrave Macmillan Ltd. Macmillan® is a registered trademark in the United States, United Kingdom and other countries. Palgrave is a registered trademark in the European Union and other countries.

ISBN-13: 978-1-4039-4232-6 hardback
ISBN-10: 1-4039-4232-3 hardback

This book is printed on paper suitable for recycling and made from fully managed and sustained forest sources.

A catalogue record for this book is available from the British Library.

Library of Congress Cataloging-in-Publication Data
Wallace, Jeff, 1958–
    D. H. Lawrence, science and the posthuman / Jeff Wallace.
        P. cm.
    Includes bibliographical references and index.
    ISBN 1-4039-4232-3
    1. Lawrence, D. H. (David Herbert), 1885–1930 – Knowledge – Science.
2. Literature and science – Great Britain – History – 20th century.
3. Science in literature. I. Title.
PR6023.A93Z9427 2005
823'.912–dc22

                                                                    2004065058

10   9   8   7   6   5   4   3   2   1
14   13   12   11   10   09   08   07   06   05

Printed and bound in Great Britain by
Antony Rowe Ltd, Chippenham and Eastbourne

To Nina and Robin

We wait for the miracle, for the new soft wind. Even the buds of iron break into soft little flames of issue. So will people change. So will the machine-parts open like buds and the great machines break into leaf.

D.H. Lawrence, The Symbolic Meaning

Contents

Acknowledgements   ix

List of Abbreviations   x

Introduction   1

Part I: Science   **9**

1 Thinking Matter   11

   1. Biological knowledge   11
   2. D.H. Lawrence and science   16
   3. Lawrence, science and humanist criticism   18
   4. Posthumanism   26

2 Science, Ideology and the 'New'   34

   1. 'Born scientific'   34
   2. Religious crisis and the New Theology   36
   3. Science and socialism: *The New Age*   41
   4. Science and gender: the New Woman   48

3 Writing Matter: Science, Language and Materialism   58

   1. 'Alert' and 'didactic' science   58
   2. Darwin, origins and the arbitrary   66
   3. Herbert Spencer: thinkability   72
   4. Ernst Haeckel: the language of substance   80
   5. T.H. Huxley: honeyed words   86
   6. William James: reality in the making   92
   7. Coda   96

Part II: The Posthuman   **99**

4 Posthuman D.H. Lawrence?   101

5 Animals   119

   1. Anthropomorphism and the meaning of animals:
     Coetzee and Lawrence   119
   2. *The White Peacock*   123
   3. *Women in Love* and *St. Mawr*   128
   4. *The Fox* and *Kangaroo*: 'non-human human being' 141
   5. Real encounters: porcupines and frogs   146

6 Humans   152

    1. Eugenics past and present   152
    2. The solar plexus   158
    3. Cultures   166
    4. Sensual riches: the posthuman in *Sons and Lovers* and
       The Rainbow   190

7 Machines   202

    1. Luddite Lawrence   202
    2. Mechanical and organic   207
    3. Deleuze and Guattari's Lawrence   211
    4. *Aaron's Rod, Kangaroo, The Plumed Serpent*: anti-capitalism
       and the posthumanistic   218
    5. 'To live beyond money': *Lady Chatterley's Lover*   227

Postscript: On Abstraction   233

Notes   241

Bibliography   251

Index   259

Acknowledgements

In one form or another, this book has been a long time in the making. For their advice and constructive criticism in the early days of research, I thank David Amigoni, Roger Ebbatson, Rod Edmond, David Ellis, Graham Hitchen, Graham Holderness, Mark Kinkead-Weekes, Laura Marcus and Andy Mousley. With those days in mind, I would also like to dedicate the book to the memory of Kate Westoby, Ian Gregor and Graham Martin. More recently, Anne Fernihough and Rick Rylance know what a great deal I owe to them. A special word of thanks is reserved for Rod Jones; the value of his ideas and intellectual companionship over the years has been incalculable. I am also very grateful for the support and advice of Simon Dentith, Hywel Dix, Dominic Head, Kevin Mills, Andrew Smith, Diana Wallace, Martin Willis and John Worthen. Paula Kennedy and Helen Craine at Palgrave Macmillan have been very helpful, and I acknowledge with thanks the initial support of Emily Rosser. Andy Goldsworthy gave his very kind permission for the jacket image, and thanks are also due in this respect to Jill Hollis at Cameron Books. This book has been made possible by a grant from the Arts and Humanities Research Board, and by the financial support of the School of Humanities, Law and Social Sciences, University of Glamorgan. Finally, for their constant encouragement and forbearance, I would like to thank my wife Frances and my children Robin and Nina – not forgetting Paddock, of course. None of them will be sorry that we are, at last, in a post-posthuman phase.

List of Abbreviations

Works by D.H. Lawrence

A	*Apocalypse*
AR	*Aaron's Rod*
CP	*The Complete Poems of D.H. Lawrence*
EP	*Etruscan Places*
FU	*Fantasia of the Unconscious* and *Psychoanalysis and the Unconscious*
K	*Kangaroo*
LI	*The Letters of D.H. Lawrence, Vol. I*
LII	*The Letters of D.H. Lawrence, Vol. II*
LIII	*The Letters of D.H. Lawrence, Vol. III*
LCL	*Lady Chatterley's Lover*
MM	*Mornings in Mexico*
P	*Phoenix*
PII	*Phoenix II*
Poems	*Complete Poems of D.H. Lawrence*
PS	*The Plumed Serpent*
RDP	*Reflections on the Death of a Porcupine and Other Essays*
SCAL	*Studies in Classic American Literature*
SL	*Sons and Lovers*
SM	*The Symbolic Meaning*
StM	*St. Mawr and Other Stories*
STH	*Study of Thomas Hardy and Other Essays*
TI	*Twilight in Italy*
TN	*The Fox, The Ladybird, The Captain's Doll* (more commonly known as *Three Novellas*)
TR	*The Rainbow*
WL	*Women in Love*
WP	*The White Peacock*

Other works

AAR	Jane Harrison, *Ancient Art and Ritual*
ATP	Gilles Deleuze and Félix Guattari, *A Thousand Plateaus*
AV	H.G. Wells, *Ann Veronica*
A-O	Gilles Deleuze and Félix Guattari, *Anti-Oedipus*
CE	Henri Bergson, *Creative Evolution*
CMT	Vivian Phelips (Philip Vivian), *The Churches and Modern Thought*
E	Samuel Butler, *Erewhon and Erewhon Revisited*

EC	J.M. Coetzee, *Elizabeth Costello*
EGP	John Burnet, *Early Greek Philosophy*
FP	Herbert Spencer, *First Principles*
GMN	Robert Blatchford, *God and My Neighbour*
IH	Wilfred Trotter, *Instincts of the Herd in Peace and War*
LA	J.M. Coetzee, *The Lives of Animals*
LH	Samuel Butler, *Life and Habit*
MaM	Henri Bergson, *Matter and Memory*
MPN	T.H. Huxley, *Man's Place in Nature*
NT	R.J. Campbell, *The New Theology*
OS	Charles Darwin, *The Origin of Species*
PC	E.B. Tylor, *Primitive Culture, Vol. I*
PP	William James, *Principles of Psychology*
PR	William James, *Pragmatism*
RU	Ernst Haeckel, *The Riddle of the Universe*

Introduction

'Quadruped. Graminivorous. Forty teeth, namely twenty-four grinders, four eye-teeth, and twelve incisive. Sheds coat in the spring; in marshy countries, sheds hoofs, too. Hoofs hard, but requiring to be shod with iron. Age known by marks in mouth.'

Charles Dickens, *Hard Times* (1854)

A horse is not a mere dead structure: it is an active, living, working machine. Hitherto we have, as it were, been looking at a steam-engine with the fires out, and nothing in the boiler; but the body of the living animal is a beautifully-formed active machine, and every part has its different work to do in the working of that machine, which is what we call its life.

T.H. Huxley, 'The Present Condition of Organic Nature' (1863)

The phalanstery can be characterised as human machinery. This is no reproach, nor is it meant to indicate anything mechanistic; rather, it refers to the great complexity of its structure ⟨*Aufbau*⟩. The phalanstery is a machine made of human beings.

Walter Benjamin, *The Arcades Project* (1999)[1]

All students of literature know the significance of *Hard Times* (1854) by Charles Dickens. Bitzer, the obedient pupil, has been taught not to see anywhere what he does not see in Fact; to discard the word Fancy, and never to Wonder. The owner of his school, Mr. Thomas Gradgrind, 'a man of fact and calculations', believes human nature to be 'a mere question of figures, a case of simple arithmetic'. We know that this is the novel's critique of util-itarianism, a philosophy underpinning early industrial capitalism which is closely associated with the methods of mathematical science. Science here is identified both with an economic system which oppresses multitudes within the newly-emergent industrial working class, and with a way of thinking which diminishes what it is to be alive, whether as a horse or as a human. In this sense it also becomes closely associated with a certain inter-

1

pretation of the word *materialism*, a doctrine denying the existence of 'spirit' and maintaining instead that life, including human nature and identity, is completely reducible to physical and chemical properties.

D.H. Lawrence's novel *The Rainbow* (1915), another exploration of the human consequences of industrial modernity, gives voice to materialism through a female doctor of physics whose name, Frankstone, is a barely concealed allusion to Frankenstein, Mary Shelley's figure for the overweening arrogance of scientific knowledge:

> 'No really, ... I don't see why we should attribute some special mystery to life – do you? We don't understand it as we understand electricity, even, but that doesn't warrant our saying it is something special, something different in kind and distinct from everything else in the universe – do you think it does? May it not be that life consists in a complexity of physical and chemical activities, of the same order as the activities we already know in science? I don't see, really, why we should imagine there is a special order of life, and life alone –' (*TR* 408).

Ursula Brangwen is soon to discover, from her own work in the laboratory, that there is more to life than is to be found in Frankstone's philosophy, and on this basis she refuses to marry her lover, Anton Skrebensky, in whom she detects a fatal modern automatism. When the reductive principle of the sheer materiality of the living is internalised by such impressionable beings as children, they too become reduced: mechanical, ghostly and inhuman, like Dickens's Bitzer, whose skin was 'so unwholesomely deficient in the natural tinge, that he looked as though, if he were cut, he would bleed white' (*HT* 50).

Students of literature also know that the obverse of science is to be found, not just in a richer sense of the human, but in imaginative literature, as a repository of those riches. Coketown has a public library and, to the consternation of Thomas Gradgrind, patrons persist in reading literature instead of mathematics: Defoe instead of Euclid, Goldsmith instead of Cocker. This is because they like to wonder, and what they wonder about are 'human nature, human passions, human hopes and fears, the struggles, triumphs and defeats, the cares and joys and sorrows, the lives and deaths, of common men and women!' (*HT* 90). The latter could, in itself, though at a level of some generality, describe *The Rainbow*, within which Lawrence's choice of 'Frankstone', figuring in a cast of otherwise purely naturalistic names, seems to suggest that science is worthy only of caricature, undeserving of the dignity otherwise accorded to human beings by a complex novel of social and psychological realism.

Since its inception as an intellectual discipline in the early twentieth century, 'English' or literary studies has prospered on the back of the idea that it defends the 'human' against the reductive mechanisms of science.

The idea has taken various forms, with differing degrees of subtlety. Neil Belton maintains that, by the mid-century, literature had been elevated within British national culture to the position of 'moral arbiter', not just of the humanities, but of human values in general. Within this climate, 'science was, it almost went without saying, an insult to human values'.[2] For F.R. Leavis, who more than any critic helped to establish the humanistic reputation of D.H. Lawrence, this was because literature and its study connoted an extraordinary comprehensiveness: while scientists were restricted to 'technical knowledge and . . . specialised intellectual habits', meaning that they could not derive from their work 'all that a human being needs', the judgements of a literary critic were 'judgements about life'.[3] Nevertheless, this exaltation of the literary over the scientific did not necessarily exclude the idea that literature and science might be studied together. Leavis was always insistent that his students read some (carefully selected) history of science, and in his time a burgeoning of primers establishing the interdisciplinary credentials of literary studies helped to place science as part of a rich 'background' from which literature drew its ideas and inspiration.[4]

From the late 1960s, structuralist and post-stucturalist theories have offered a radical challenge to the assumptions of Leavisite humanist criticism, starting as they did from the scientific analysis of linguistic and semiotic systems. Whether the human subject is imprisoned within a linguistic system by which meaning is determined, or in which meaning is endlessly deferred, these theories seemed to bracket out of literature the question of human value as embodied, primarily, in the figure of the author as the source of creative intent. Yet, while humanist critics railed against the importation of 'scientific' influences, poststructuralism furnished a new version of the idea that literary scholars alone might be in a position to teach science what it did not know, either about itself or about the 'human' in general. Thus Roland Barthes, in 'From Science to Literature' (1967), attributed to science a naïve view of language as transparent and instrumental. Misrecognizing the fact that, like all human activity, it is *constituted* as discourse, science persisted, argues Barthes, in believing itself to be a 'superior code'. 'Writing', however, sought to be a 'total code'; it was the role of literature to '*represent* actively to the scientific institution just what it rejects, i.e., the sovereignty of language', and of structuralism in particular to provoke the scandal by making as its aim the 'very subversion of scientific language'.[5] Leavis, one might argue, had chosen the phrase 'the third realm' to designate a very similar, primary human world of 'collaborative creation' whose condition was language, without which 'the triumphant erection of the scientific edifice would not have been possible'.[6]

The guiding principle behind contemporary studies of the relations between science and culture – an exciting, burgeoning interdisciplinary field, to which I hope the present book will contribute – has been that culture is their shared domain, and that we stand to gain much from a recognition of the cultural, and specifically discursive, dimensions of science. The tendency thus to celebrate a radical dissolution of disciplinary boundaries has masked the perpetuation of an older hegemony within which literary scholars have been able, as it were, to have the relationship between science and literature on their own terms. If science *is* fundamentally a linguistic phenomenon, then literary studies can continue to hold a master key. What if this assumed relationship were inverted? What if we were to suggest, and from within literary studies, that science is the shared medium, and that we have much to gain from recognizing in culture a mode of scientific rationalism? What if science were to be seen as the guardian of a rich and complex sense of human value, and literature the repository of limited and reductive definitions? What if materialism were the domain of creative imagination, and literature the source of a mechanistic recitation of 'facts'?

These provocative questions are not meant to instal the superiority of science over literature. They seek, rather, to test out how far certain assumptions about the 'human' value of the literary might have become inscribed, at the expense of science, in the thinking, even of those of us who study the interrelation of science and literature and pride ourselves on our interdisciplinarity. We are delighted to learn that science is an imaginative activity; are we similarly moved by the prospect of imagination as a scientific activity? How deep is our investment in the humanistic project of literary studies, and to what extent does this investment rest upon a set of inherited assumptions about science? Intuitively, it feels like a good thing to continue to speak up for the 'humanistic'; but what is this position worth if it rests upon a caricature of science-as-Other? What, in fact, might the term 'humanist' mean in this context?

Michael Hardt and Antonio Negri have recently noted the surprising emergence, in the later work of Michel Foucault, of a revived mode of Renaissance humanism, whereby the postmodern idea of self-fashioning revisits the older, 'ethical care of the self'.[7] How, they ask, was this possible in the work of Foucault, renowned scourge of humanism and proclaimer of the death of Man? There is, however, they maintain, no disabling contradiction, once we link Foucault's entire project to Spinoza's refusal, three hundred years earlier, 'to accord any laws to human nature that were different from the laws of nature as a whole'. Hardt and Negri call Foucault's position an 'antihumanist (or posthuman) humanism', characterized by a refusal to think the human as a transcendent category. The death of the human occurs precisely *when* it is separated from materiality, rendered unique and different. Paradoxically, then, the humanist project is defined by a continuous exploration of our 'kinship', in Donna Haraway's terms, as matter, both with organic and with inorganic forms.[8] Since Darwin, we have had a century and a half to accommodate ourselves to the notion that we exist in a continuum with organic nature. The confrontation of our kinship with machines feels like a much more recent event, and it reminds us of how

deep, in literary humanism, is the taboo separating the human from
the mechanical. But what if we need to cross this line in order to extend
our understanding of the human, and what if we are dependent upon a
materialist science to take us where literary cultures refuse to go? What if
materialism itself is, in this light, both an imaginative and a humanizing
doctrine?

The second version of a horse, at the head of this Introduction, is from
the first of a series of six lectures, given by T.H. Huxley in 1863, explaining
the principles of scientific method to working men. As if to confirm the
worst fears engendered by Dickens's Bitzer, Huxley is quite explicit from the
outset that his aim is to 'reduce' a horse to 'its most simple expression'. After
verbally dissecting the horse's structure, from its skin to its skeleton and
organs, and representing this in simple diagrammatic form, Huxley proceeds
to 'reduce the whole of the microscopic structural elements to a form of
even greater simplicity', and finally shows how naturalists have come to the
conclusion that the 'hundreds of thousands of species of creatures' on earth
are 'all reducible to . . . five, or, at most, seven, plans of organization' (*MPN*
155–6,166). Yet, when we read Huxley's version closely, we find that it is
not, itself, reducible to the reductive. In support of the proposition that a
horse is 'not a mere dead structure', Huxley presents three slightly modified
juxtapositions of the terms 'life' and 'mechanism' within the short space of
two sentences: 'living . . . machine', 'living animal . . . active machine' (modified by 'beautifully-formed'), and 'working of that machine, which is what
we call its life'. These reiterations-with-modification alone suggest a level of
hesitancy or anxiety: there *is* a taboo to be negotiated, and it cannot be done
by the simple assertion that life and mechanism are synonymous. Given,
however, that the proposition *is*, after all, that the horse is a machine, the
rhetorical effort is to change our idea of what it means to say so. There are
two levels of discourse about the machine: one which draws attention to
the metaphorical status of the horse-as-steam engine, which somehow *is*
reductive and not quite good enough (note 'as it were'); and one which
asserts more directly that the horse is a machine because a machine *can be*
'living', not to mention beautiful.

What is really at stake in calling living creatures, living machines? In the
great upsurge of rationalism and scientific optimism that swept nineteenth-
century European cultures, it was often no reproach to be compared to a
state of mechanism. Something of this is felt in Walter Benjamin's observation on the 'phalansteries' of the French utopian social theorist Charles
Fourier, independent working and co-operative communities which seemed
to some orthodox commentators at the time to be the height of fantasy and
madness. If machinery can mean 'great complexity of structure', what might
this definition not embrace? Why shouldn't it refer to a human culture? If
Huxley calls the horse a beautiful living machine, what do we lose and what
do we gain? For Neil Belton, nothing is more representative of the extin-

guishing of a 'creative energy of rationalism' within British national culture, and of the 'fatal weakening of its imaginative capacities', than its neglect of Huxley's work.[9] In the latter half of the nineteenth century, Huxley became a pre-eminent cultural agent for science, but gradually fades from view within a culture which came to 'value the purely literary above all else' (only such a culture, argues Belton, locked into a 'Two Cultures' debate, could prefer the 'irrepressible triviality' of Huxley's grandson Aldous). Yet when, as I suggest above, we look closely at Huxley's materialism, there may be more there than a literary-humanistic culture predisposes us to find there.

The present book, at least in its proportions, is a modest response to all those who have pointed out to me, over the years, that a study of D.H. Lawrence and science could, surely, only ever be a very slim volume. Was not Lawrence deeply and volubly antagonistic to the scientific reduction of life to mechanism? The answer I propose is a complex 'yes and no'. Yes, in that Lawrence maintained a critical vigilance towards science as a mode of knowledge, and towards its political as well as epistemological implications. No, in that the alignment of life with mechanism through the concept of matter is not always and necessarily reductive, and in that there is a rich intellectual and cultural context surrounding the issue, both in Lawrence's time and in our own, that we need to explore in answering the question. It is already well established that Lawrence's writing drew from a tradition of materialist and evolutionary thought which emphasised human kinship with 'nature'.[10] It is less well established that this same tradition could emphasise kinship with inorganic matter, and therefore by possible extension with mechanism and technology, on the basis that, as T.H. Huxley put it, 'the MATTER constituting the living world is identical with that which forms the inorganic world' (*MPN* 167).

The main proposition of this book is that in recent thinking about the 'posthuman' condition, drawing from philosophy and cultural theory as well as from 'harder' science, we find a means of understanding more clearly and more fully the complexity of Lawrence's encounter with the science of his time. I would want, however, to guard against charges either of anachronism, or of congratulating Lawrence on having anticipated a later movement of thought. In part, I maintain that posthumanism is a theoretical construct, a way of *thinking* the human, whose emergence in the latter half of the twentieth and the beginning of the twenty-first centuries does not disallow its application to earlier periods. In part too, however, my case is that there are significant connections to be made between the moment of the posthuman, with its debates around the relationship between humans, creatures and machines, and the moment of post-Darwinian evolutionary materialism with which I associate Lawrence. A representative figure in this argument is Henri Bergson (1859–1941), a philosopher of enormous influence and celebrity around the time of Lawrence's intellectual formation, and whose work constituted a sustained critical interrogation of prevailing assumptions about science and scientific logic. Bergson's work fell dramatically out of favour soon after this period, but has recently been revived, in the form of a 'new Bergsonism', by those who are developing ideas about the posthuman condition.

What emerges will not, I hope, look simply like a new book on D.H. Lawrence, even though the reassessment of Lawrence's reputation as an irrationalist is central to the book's argument. Such a reassessment involves carefully uncoupling Lawrence from a literary-critical tradition which continues, even in postmodern times, to limit what we can say about him, and does so, as I have already suggested, because of certain embedded assumptions about science, the natural and physical sciences in particular. The book is, then, also a study of how we *construe* 'science' from the perpectives of literary studies and contemporary critical theory. In the wake of 'Sokal', this of course is a sensitive area for any literary critic. In 1996, the scientist Alan Sokal published a hoax article, 'Transgressing the Boundaries: Toward a Transformative Hermeneutics of Quantum Gravity', in the journal *Social Text*.[11] Sokal's concern could be said to relate back to the potentialities of Roland Barthes' 1967 essay, where Barthes enjoined writers and structuralist critics to disabuse science of its naïve realist view of itself and replace it with an understanding of the 'total code' of language. Taken to a certain logical conclusion, this view of language could turn into a fully-blown postmodernist relativism, undermining all claims to truth and objectivity in science, and licensing literary and cultural critics to deal confidently with science from their position of linguistic expertise. Were *Social Text* to publish the article, Sokal wagered, this would prove the postmodern position to be a front for careless thinking and complacent attitudes.

The hoax had mixed effects both for science and for those in the humanities, and certainly sounds a warning to any critic writing about science from the perspective of literary studies – especially one who claims, in the study of D.H. Lawrence, to give science more of its due. It is, however, worth noting an irony. A few years before the hoax, Bruce Robbins, one of its subsequent victims as editor of *Social Text*, sketched out a proposal to 'reject the science/literature opposition as such'.[12] He did this, however, from a position within literary studies not dissimilar to that of Sokal within science: that is, Robbins questioned the strategy by which a construction of realism as naïve is juxtaposed against the greater sophistication and knowingness of modernist and postmodernist forms. Robbins thus suggested that the interrelated study of science and literature need not always occur through the collapsing of the former into the latter. While we are fond of saying that sciences such as ethnography might take a literary form, we are, he argued, 'less fond of saying ... that the literary is among other things a vehicle of information'. The reprise of Facts, then, from a wholly unexpected source? However mediated, unreliable and multiple, literature for Robbins is a source of information – for example in supplying students with a sense of cultural history, which they might get from nowhere else – and, more precisely, has a 'cognitive' value: the discipline of literary studies has stressed a 'unique identity that differentiated it from science', and in so doing relinquishes to science its own cognitive claims. In making a case for literary studies, Robbins also makes a case for the value of the *cognitive* as such.

In its determination to restore a significance to the scientific, in and for itself, in Lawrence's work, this book no doubt lays itself open to a Sokalian gaze. Readers, moreover, might well look at my treatment of science and find it, in the final analysis, suspiciously textual. It is a central part of my argument that science, to use a phrase of Gillian Beer's, is precipitated as writing. In bringing its fieldwork and laborious experimentation into the domain of language, I claim, we see materialist science genuinely pursuing its cognitive goals and grappling with its most tenacious epistemological problems. This is also a way of saying that science-in-itself and science as a discursive and therefore ideological phenomenon are in no sense mutually exclusive. The reader will therefore, in the end, have to decide whether this is not simply yet another sleight-of-hand justification of a literary and culturalist approach. Part I is dedicated to revising our sense of what science might have meant in Lawrence's context: a field of dialogue and debate, intimately entwined with his personal as well as intellectual development; a heightened concern with epistemology, with how and what it is that we know; something, perhaps, rather less sure of itself than we might imagine. In Part II, through a series of clear focal points – animals, humans (including their cultures), and machines – I explore areas of interconnection between contemporary theories of posthumanism and Lawrence's sustained investigation of what T.H. Huxley called the 'question of questions' for his generation, that of 'man's place in nature'. I would not be unhappy for the reader to conclude that the book has been a kind of defence of humanism, provided that they are also able to conclude that in the process the concept of humanism has been submitted to a rigorous dialectical analysis, even to the extent of emerging somewhat unrecognizably as, in Hardt and Negri's terms, an 'antihumanist (or posthuman) humanism'. In this sense another of the book's aims is to allow, through the discussion of science, a critical dialogue to take place between humanism and posthumanism. I would, however, be more unambiguously happy if at least some aspects of the 'posthuman D.H. Lawrence' presented here seem, at least initially, unsettling and unrecognizable to the reader. Forty years ago, the American critic Eugene Goodheart had cause to observe that Lawrence had been made to serve causes not of his own choosing, the cause in this case being the moral tradition of the novel.[13] It is an intuition of mine, built up over a long period of study, that Lawrence himself, while ultimately reconciled to an association with the 'human' and 'humane', would have been dismayed to be associated with some of the critical positions which have done most to establish his literary reputation as a guardian of those values.

Part I
Science

1
Thinking Matter

1. Biological knowledge

'Evolution', wrote Henri Bergson in *Creative Evolution* (1907), 'reveals to us how the intellect has been formed, by an uninterrupted progress, along a line which ascends through the vertebrate series up to man'. The intellect had evolved as a tool with which to 'think matter'; that is, to secure the 'perfect fitting of our body to its environment' and to 'represent the relations of external things among themselves'. Yet, this fortunate sense of 'uninterrupted progress' must be tempered, Bergson insists, by a recognition that something in the very nature of intellect as an *evolved* (rather than, for example, divinely ordained) entity places a necessary limitation on it. From this evolved condition,

> (I)t must also follow that our thought, in its purely logical form, is incapable of presenting the true nature of life, the full meaning of the evolutionary movement. Created by life, in definite circumstances, to act on definite things, how can it embrace life, of which it is only an emanation or an aspect? Deposited by the evolutionary movement in the course of its way, how can it be applied to the evolutionary movement itself? As well contend that the part is equal to the whole, that the effect can reabsorb its cause, or that the pebble left on the beach displays the form of the wave that brought it there (*CE* ix–x).

If the human being is in or of the natural order, what can it know about that order? Without the distance separating subject and object, knower and known, what is the status of human knowledge? How can we 'think matter' if we are, at the same time, thinking matter?

In his intellectual formation, Bergson had been profoundly influenced by the earlier work of the British sociologist Herbert Spencer. In Spencer too, the theorisation of evolution combines with a sometimes painstakingly detailed preoccupation with the nature and limits of human intellectual activity. Here, for example, in his *First Principles* (1862), we find Spencer reflecting closely upon the 'mind of the botanist' at work. How, he asks, does the botanist classify what he sees?

> Each plant he examines yields him a certain complex impression. Now and then he picks up a plant like one before seen; and the recognition of it is the production in him of a like connected group of sensations, by a like connected group of attributes. That is to say, there is produced throughout the nerve-centres concerned, a combined set of changes, similar to a combined set of changes before produced. Considered analytically, each such combined set of changes is a combined set of molecular modifications wrought in the affected part of the organism. On every repetition of the impression, a like combined set of molecular modifications is superposed on the previous ones, and makes them greater; thus generating an internal plexus of modifications, with its answering idea, corresponding to these similar external objects. Meanwhile, another kind of plant produces in the brain of the botanist another set of molecular modifications – a set which does not agree with the one we have been considering, but disagrees with it; and by the repetition of such there is generated a different idea answering to a different species (*FP* 429).

Spencer, like Bergson after him, embraces what Gunter calls a '*biological theory of knowledge*'.[1] Thought is a movement of matter: classifications emerge from 'complex impressions', creating 'molecular modifications' which gather into 'plexuses' within certain nerve centres in the brain. The passage slides, perhaps questionably, between the terms 'mind' and 'brain'; what is unquestionable is that an 'organism' is under analysis.

There are, however, important distinctions to be drawn between the theories of Bergson and Spencer. For Spencer, the fact that we might be able to examine and understand the intellect as a natural phenomenon was only the latest triumphant step in that 'uninterrupted progress' of which Bergson was later to write. He seemed relatively untroubled, for example, that his image of the scientist, observing himself in the act of observing, and so on, suggests a potentially infinite regression fatal to the ability of science to take up an objective viewpoint from the outside of things. In this he partakes of an *epistemological* confidence which is characteristic of this moment in the history of evolutionary theory. Even Charles Darwin (whose prose could often appear to be in danger of collapsing beneath the weight of its own modesty) famously claimed that the theory of natural selection would be of particular importance for psychology, the study of the human mind, where 'open fields for far more important researches' would emerge. These researches would be based on a 'new foundation, that of the necessary acquirement of each mental power and capacity by gradation' (*OS* 367–8).

Such confidence belongs not so much to 'science' per se as to a broader formation of class and culture. Thus Terry Eagleton writes of the 'supreme confidence in reason' which a progressive middle class derived from the example of the Enlightenment, and according to which 'nature, society and even the human mind itself were now raw materials in its hands, to be analysed, mastered and reconstructed'.[2]

The Darwinian 'necessary acquirement of each mental power and capacity by gradation' is echoed in Bergson's 'uninterrupted progess'. Yet for Bergson, and in contrast to Spencer, the biological theory of knowledge only serves to inaugurate a whole epistemological problematic; it becomes the cue for innumerable new questions, rather than self-congratulation at the power of intellect. Bergson broke with Spencer through a critique whose subtlety and surprising paradoxical precision bespeaks the strength of a prior indebtedness. Spencer had dealt tidily with epistemological doubt in *First Principles* through an initial section on the 'Unknowable', leaving the ground clear for the considerably more exciting prospects of the Knowable. Some things, he argued, are simply not thinkable, and these attest to the inscrutability of the Unknown Cause of the Universe (I will return to the detail and nuance of Spencer's argument in Chapter 3). For Bergson, this represented a curious blend of excessive pride and excessive humility. If knowledge is defined by what the brain can do in representing consciously to itself the nature of things, then it is indeed trapped within an infinite regression. How *can* it represent itself? In *Matter and Memory* (1896), Bergson had consistently represented the brain as an 'image' in order to signify its inaccessibility. Because the brain is itself a part of the material world, an 'insignificant detail' in an 'immense picture', we can depend upon it in only a limited sense; however highly evolved, the thought-world of the human animal cannot hope to 'embrace' that process of which it is a product (*MaM* 4). But *Creative Evolution* moves to the emphasis that 'the line of evolution that ends in man is not the only one'. There are 'other forms of consciousness' which, though lacking the reflexivity of intellect, have nevertheless developed ways of knowing enabling them to function in the world, and which thus 'express something that is immanent and essential in the evolutionary movement' (*CE* xii). Perhaps we have placed too much stress on the conscious faculty of intellect as the measure of knowledge; perhaps there are in us certain other modes of knowledge to which the brain does not give conscious access – modes which we signify with terms such as intuition, instinct, habit, and the unconscious? In this light Spencer's stress on the intellect turns on its head and becomes a form of pessimism, surrenduring too easily to metaphysical explanation any form of knowledge of which we cannot become fully conscious. If we have grounds for more confidence, it is because we *are* material beings located *in* nature, with, therefore, direct, experiential forms of knowledge – somehow, somewhere other than in conscious intellection. Our definitions of knowledge, Bergson implies, have been too *human,* too fixated on the sovereignty of intellect, whereas evolutionary theory should surely encourage us to examine what it is to be creaturely. Paradoxically, of course, it would take the most strenuous efforts of thought, and a relatively new, ambitious, perhaps initially unreadable philosophical language, to get behind current models of consciousness and knowledge, legitimised as they increasingly were by the logics of science.

Bergson's work began to unpick the confident logic of evolutionary science using tools supplied by science itself. In highlighting a condition of irony or paradox at the heart of science, and thus of a crisis of scientificity itself, we tend to identify Bergson as a 'modernist' philosopher, his moment that of the early twentieth century rather than the mid- to late-nineteenth century. Friedrich Nietzsche, a modernist similarly preoccupied with the 'all too human', had already identified Kant and Schopenhauer as earlier 'courageous thinkers' of modernity who had 'used the arsenal of science to demonstrate the limitations of science and the cognitive faculty of science itself'.[3] Modernist thought thus comes to be characterized by a doubled or distinctly ambivalent stance towards science: a material definition of mind is drawn from evolutionary theory, and thenceforth becomes the means whereby the scientific knowledge which generated evolutionary theory is itself called into question. Popular narratives of Darwinian evolutionism, such as Winwood Reade's *The Martyrdom of Man* (1872), show how the moment of the emergence of mind out of matter could be construed as one of an amiable awakening or enlightenment: the bodies of animals develop in complexity through evolutionary time until 'certain grey lumps of matter' emerge, and 'out of these rises a spirit which introduces the animal to himself, which makes him conscious of his own existence'.[4] Nietzsche's version of this process is similarly dependent upon an evolutionary paradigm, highlighting the slow transition from sea creatures to land creatures, but with darker consequences, because the transition gradually obliges the evolving creature to rely on the consciousness, its 'weakest, most fallible organ'. Thereafter arises the malady of interiorization or 'bad conscience', a condition in which humans, because of the intervention of mind, are unable to act freely on their instincts: 'what a mad, unhappy animal is man!'[5]

In a similarly Nietzschean turn of phrase, D.H. Lawrence has his character Lovat Somers meditate upon the dilemma of being 'an animal saddled with a mental consciousness' in the novel *Kangaroo* (1923). In a memoir of Lawrence, Brewster Ghiselin has observed that 'the "uttermost mystery" for him, . . . was how man, in the state of an animal moving in instinctive consciousness, in dynamic relation with his environment, came to say "I am I"'.[6] Ghiselin gives some intimation here of how far, for a writer like Lawrence, an evolutionary materialist stance could be the starting point for thought and speculation rather than – as the denigration of the terms in popular polemics often implied – the end of all discussion. In 'religion versus science' debates (a misleadingly simplistic formula), adversaries tended to attribute to each other a finalism of argument. 'Materialism' would be vilified as 'mechanistic' and 'reductive', as if to predicate matter as the irreducible ground of being and consciousness was to imply a certainty of knowledge which rendered all further argument futile. Here, for example, in an article from 1911, A.J. Balfour generates a familiar characterization of a materialistic naturalism against which to set the complexities of Bergson's thought:

> To the naturalistic thinker there is, of course, no Absolute, and no soul. Psychic phenomena are a function of the nervous system. The nervous system is material, and obeys the laws of matter. Its behaviour is as rigidly determined as the planetary orbits, and might be accurately deduced by a being sufficiently endowed with powers of calculation, from the distribution of matter, motion, and force, when the solar system was still nebular.[7]

Balfour maintained that any such theory was incompatible with the reality of freedom; the claim that reason was 'mechanically determined' was 'essentially incoherent'. He therefore claimed to find an 'irrationality' at the heart of naturalism, in the sense that it conferred upon matter an originating status which precluded analysis and was therefore, paradoxically, occult.

However, in a critique of Balfour, the sociologist J.M. Robertson observed that '(M)aterialism is not a pretence of knowing all about what the universe is made of'. Rather, for Robertson, both naturalism and materialism are stances of sceptical negation (of 'Supernaturalism' and 'Spiritism' respectively), modes of enquiry that take as their starting point the untenability of theistic 'explanations' of the universe without seeking to replace these with final explanations of their own.[8] Thus materialism comes to resemble most closely what Balfour himself characterized, in the intellectual influences of Mill and Spencer in the second half of the nineteenth century, as a 'creed' of 'scientific agnosticism' – precisely that position of creative doubt or scepticism which Balfour sought to mobilize *against* materialism.

'I cannot be a materialist', wrote a young and impassioned D.H. Lawrence to his progessive local minister, the Rev. Robert Reid, in 1907, following a journey through the poverty-stricken Nottingham district of Sneinton; 'but . . .'. In equally emphatic vein, Lawrence goes on to indict the idea of a Christian God who might touch the human condition. The trip had prompted him to reflect on how remote was the modern idea of a 'Cosmic' God, grounded in the theory of the 'indestructability of matter', to the everyday suffering of some, who seem born to have bacteria 'created and nurtured' on them, to their eventual, ruthless destruction: a rejection, then, of a certain materialist theology (*LI* 40–1). However, the pleas that follow are equally thoroughly materialist in their acceptance of the human condition as largely determined by biological and environmental circumstance. Lawrence complains that Christian theism is *intellectually* inadequate to the task of responding to the dilemma of the human as a condition of thinking matter. In an earlier letter to Reid, it is clear that he had sought answers to such dilemmas from Christianity and found it wanting: of the 'tremendous issues' of the day, he writes, 'somehow we hear of them almost exclusively from writers against Christianity', leading to the reiteration in the second letter that 'these questions will not be answered' (*LI* 36–7). Even as he must have been aware of the cruder popular conception of the 'materialist' thinker, Lawrence knew that to ask such questions was also to be a materialist: materialism was a mode of intellectual enquiry, not a creed of certainties and fixed laws. Science is thus drawn more closely to epistemology, its quest for knowledge inseparable from the enigma of material consciousness, its status as a matter of *thinking* – which might embrace thinking about thinking – not to be underestimated.

2. D.H. Lawrence and science

> Surely the universe has arisen from some universal living self-conscious plasm, plasm which has no origin and no end, but is life eternal and identical, bringing forth the infinite creatures of being and existence, living creatures embodying inanimate substance. There is no utterly immaterial existence, no spirit (*SM* 180).

Lawrence had read the article by Balfour on Bergson, referred to in the section above, and enthusiastically circulated it among friends for discussion; he was also familiar with the writings of J.M. Robertson. He had read Bergson and Herbert Spencer, Schopenhauer and Nietzsche, as well as Winwood Reade's *The Martyrdom of Man*. As a young man, he scandalized his beloved Chambers family by acting as the apostle of evolutionary materialism and naturalism, introducing them to Darwin's *Origin of Species* and Zola's fiction, 'filling our heads with rubbish', as the women of the family apparently felt.[9] At this time, as his lover Jessie Chambers has famously recorded it, 'the materialist philosophy came in full blast', with his reading, alongside Darwin, of Spencer's *First Principles*, T.H. Huxley's *Man's Place in Nature*, Ernst Haeckel's *The Riddle of the Universe*, and William James's *Pragmatism* and *The Varieties of Religious Experience*.[10] He subscribed for a time to the journal *The New Age*, whose thrust towards a culture of radical socialism in Britain involved a continuous assessment of the impacts of science on contemporary life and thought. Throughout his working life, he kept up with key publications in a range of the new sciences which characterized this period of extraordinary intellectual ferment: anthropology (J.G. Frazer's *The Golden Bough*, E.B. Tylor's *Primitive Culture*, Jane Harrison's *Ancient Art and Ritual*, Leo Frobenius' *The Voice of Africa*), psychology and psychoanalysis (Freud, Jung and Trigant Burrow, as well as James), and relativity physics (Einstein, A.N. Whitehead).

In the early drafts of what was to become his *Studies in Classic American Literature*, Lawrence began to elaborate a combined theory of psychology and physiology which became known, notoriously, as his 'solar plexus philosophy', and which he himself described as an attempt to write 'pure science'. In the same drafts, he wrote that 'there is no immaterial existence, no spirit'. We recall that, according to Ghiselin, the 'uttermost mystery' for Lawrence was the question of how the human animal came to say 'I am I'. The emergence of human self-consciousness led to what T.H. Huxley designated as the 'question of questions' for mankind and therefore, by implication, for science as he saw it: 'the ascertainment of the place which Man occupies in nature and of his relations to the universe of things' (*MPN* 52). It would not be implausible to read the whole of Lawrence's creative project as sharing, with post-Darwinian science, this exploratory quest to delineate man's place in nature.

Where science is concerned, there is however another and more familiar Lawrence. 'I have tried', wrote this Lawrence, 'and even brought myself to believe in a clue to the outer universe. And in the process I have swallowed such a lot of jargon that I would rather listen now to a negro witch-doctor than to Science' (*FU* 151). On the grounds that 'there is nothing in the world that is true except empiric discoveries which work in actual appliances', he goes on to repudiate – 'I won't be told' – the theory that the sun is a ball of blazing gas. In similar vein, 'All right,' he writes to Earl and Aschah Brewster, 'let white include all colours, if you like. – Only, white does *not* include all colours. It is only pure colourless light which includes all colours. And of even that I am doubtful. I doubt the exact sciences more than anything else . . .' (*LIII* 718). Most notorious in this catalogue of apparently wilful denials of fundamental scientific theories, there is his rejection of evolution. Who better to attest to this than Aldous Huxley, both a friend of Lawrence's and a prominent, if self-appointed, mediator between the domains of science and literature in twentieth-century British culture?

> Lawrence's dislike of science was passionate and expressed itself in the most fantastically unreasonable terms. 'All scientists are liars', he would say, when I brought up some experimentally established fact which he happened to dislike. 'Liars, liars!' It was a most convenient theory. I remember in particular one long and violent argument on evolution, in the reality of which Lawrence always passionately disbelieved. 'But look at the evidence, Lawrence', I insisted, 'look at the evidence'. His answer was characteristic. 'But I don't care about evidence. Evidence doesn't mean anything to me. I don't feel it *here*'. And he pressed his hands on his solar plexus. I abandoned the argument and thereafter never, if I could avoid it, mentioned the hated name of science in his presence.[11]

In his final published work, *Literature and Science* (1963), Huxley could still declare that, 'for Lawrence, the scientific approach was, of course, completely out of the question'.[12]

What is the relationship between these two Lawrences? What might it mean to explore the significance of the first in the face of the familiarity of the second? How does science matter to Lawrence, and Lawrence matter to science? Aldous Huxley again suggests a point of departure. For it was not the case, Huxley argues, that Lawrence had an 'incapacity to understand' science: he had an 'extremely acute intelligence', was a 'clever' man as well as a genius. Instead, Huxley's claim is that Lawrence's rejection of the aims and methods of science was precisely dependent upon a very thorough understanding of them. I will return, in the next section, to Huxley's further rationalization of this position in terms of Lawrence's loyalty to an artistic 'gift' which was incompatible with scientific method. Instead let us pause at the suggestion that Lawrence had a profound engagement with science, and that his 'rejection' of it was a position of critical intelligence. This might be aligned with a revised conception of 'science' in the Lawrentian context: science, for example, as a set of debates around the enigma of 'thinking matter', the position and meaning of the human intellect within the natural order, and thus around the deep mutual implication of evolutionary science and questions of epistemology. What do we know and how do we know it? How has the evolution of 'intellect', whether across deep evolutionary time or in terms of the modern scientific revolution, shaped and modified knowledge? To pose the issue thus is to suggest that Lawrence was in tune with contemporary, post-Darwinian science in its critical interrogation of all aspects of the 'human'. Yet in the literary criticism within which Lawrence's reputation as a humanist was forged, neither this version of Lawrence nor this version of science is readily available.

3. Lawrence, science and humanist criticism

Huxley's terms 'passionate' and 'fantastically unreasonable' remind us that the orthodox view of Lawrence's 'dislike' of science is invariably entwined with a broader conception of his stance on reason or rationality. 'In his preferences', writes Linda Ruth Williams, 'Lawrence is an exemplary irrationalist.'[13] What, then, might it mean to describe Lawrence as an irrationalist? Let us define irrationalist thinking here as a critical philosophical position on certain modes or definitions of reason, and thus as an important and recurrent feature of nineteenth- and twentieth-century thought. Lawrence's irrationalism might be connected to two strands: existentialism, and Frankfurt School critical theory. If we map modern existentialism through Kierkegaard, Nietzsche, Heidegger and Sartre, then Nietzsche, with whose writing Lawrence was familiar, constitutes the clearest point of reference.[14] In Nietzsche the analysis of reason is conducted through a detailed attention to linguistic structure, or rather to the 'snare of language' within which the 'arch-fallacies of reason' are 'petrified'. Thus, in *The Genealogy of Morals* (1887), Nietzsche argues that the unexamined use of the linguistic subject presents all actions as 'conditioned by an agent', thus separating into 'doer' and 'deed' what, in a different language system, might be conceptualized as a single event. Nietzsche here prefigures the theories of linguistic relativity to be found in the work of early twentieth-century anthropologists such as Benjamin Lee Whorf and Edward Sapir: worlds are determined by languages, and the structures of common sense enshrined in language can, if we are not vigilant, be transferred into science:

> The common man actually doubles the doing by making the lightning flash; he states the same event once as cause and then again as effect. The natural scientists are no better when they say that 'energy *moves*', 'energy *causes*'. For all its detachment and freedom from emotion, our science is still the dupe of linguistic habits; it has never yet got rid of those changelings called 'subjects'.[15]

In *Dialectic of Enlightenment* (1944), a key text in Frankfurt School theory, Adorno and Horkheimer see the Enlightenment programme to 'disenchant the world' expressed in the emergence of a totalitarian 'instrumental' rationality. Thought, restricted to 'organisation and administration', becomes an image of the commodity form itself – 'ideation' is an instrument and the concept, similarly, an 'ideal tool' for the domination of nature by bourgeois society. As in Nietzsche's critique, ideological assumptions are located in the claims of science to neutrality and objectivity – in this case, 'self-preservation, the constitutive principle of science', is the means by which 'the social work of every individual in bourgeois society is mediated through the principle of self; for one, labour will bring an increase in capital; for others, the energy for extra labour'. Thought is thus locked into a self-fulfilling condition, 'always decided from the start', and in which 'everything . . . is converted into the repeatable, replaceable process, into a mere example for the conceptual models of the system'; the requirement to 'think about thought' is set aside.[16]

When Lawrence, in his own words, 'pause(d) to think about' thought, we find some awareness that rationality does not always coincide with its own image. Arguing for a '*complete* imaginative experience, which goes through the whole soul and body', he observes that it is not 'Reason herself' that has to be defied, but 'her myrmidons, our accepted ideas and thought-forms': once freed from eighteenth- and nineteenth-century definitions, reason is almost infinitely adjustable, 'slippery as a fish by nature', and as likely to sanction the truth of an absurdity as of a syllogism (*P* 297–8).

It is, nevertheless, uncommon to find Lawrence linked to intellectual traditions concerning the critical scrutiny of reason. We are more likely to see him, *pace* Huxley, pressing his hands on his solar plexus, or for that matter pointing to the fly of his trousers.[17] Such images reinforce T.S. Eliot's notorious and crucial assessment of Lawrence's *incapacity* for 'what we ordinarily called thinking'.[18] In these cases, it is not that Lawrence critically inter-rogated certain kinds of thought, but that he couldn't think; not that he questioned the status of ideas, but that he had none. Undoubtedly, one source of this particular version of an 'irrationalist' Lawrence is Lawrence himself. As we have seen and will continue to see, Lawrence could often be relied upon to reinforce the impression that he did not have a coherent idea in his head. Such instances are not negligible, and in due course I will have cause to reflect upon the strategic importance of Lawrence's often-feverish anti-rationalistic protestations. Another source, however, is a literary-critical tradition, informed by humanist and romanticist assumptions, which has done much to frame our paradigms of Lawrence, and within which it can be construed as positively advantageous to be dissociated from science and rationality.

Huxley's memoir again provides a touchstone. On 5 June 1914, Lawrence wrote a famous letter to his editor Edward Garnett, defending the psychol-ogy of his early draft versions of *The Rainbow* by applying to it a language of 'carbon' and 'allotropic states', suggesting thereby strong analogies between chemical analysis and human psychology (*LII* 182–4). Noting how strange it seemed that a 'hater of scientific knowing' should use such a lan-guage, Huxley reminds us that Lawrence analysed things 'not intellectually, but by an immediate process of intuition' – that he was able, 'as it were, to *feel* the carbon in diamonds and coal, and to *taste* the hydrogen and oxygen in a glass of water'.[19] The phrase 'as it were' designates the kind of hesitant leap of faith which finds an echo in the view of Eliseo Vivas that Lawrence '*seems* to have been able to look on the universe as primitive man *probably* did' (my italics).[20] In Michael Black's *D.H. Lawrence: The Early Fiction* (1986), even these hesitancies are discarded. Lawrence 'feels as direct intuitions those significances and relationships which in others had been literary bor-rowing, esotericism, nostalgia or playacting'; 'without needing to reflect', Black maintains, Lawrence '*knows* his kinship with the sun, the evening star, Orion, who are friends and protectors; and the moon, who is a threat. Other living creatures are in the world with him in a way that they are not for ordinary people.'[21]

Such modes of criticism are clearly indebted to Romanticism's extensive re-shaping of ideas about artistic value and poetic subjectivity. The artist or poet has a special, 'intuitive' knowledge which transcends that of the common intellect to which ordinary people and scientists are confined; the imagination appears to give the artist a more direct, less mediated knowl-edge, an ontological sense of dwelling *in* the material world, and thus able to feel or taste elements prior to the process of intellectualization. The artist is helpless in the face of the onrush of inspiration which is the embodiment of genius: 'to this strange force', writes Huxley of Lawrence, 'to this power that created his works of art, there was nothing to do but submit'. The artist is thus aligned at once with the perspectives of 'primitive man' and with the kind of authoritative role in civil society envisioned, for example, by Percy Shelley in *A Defense of Poetry* (1821). For Shelley, poetry gives access to an 'eternal truth' which transcends the time- and space-bound conceptions even of the individual, originating poet; yet secular modernity has proliferated discourses of knowledge, primarily through the growth of the sciences, which have worked to conceal the visionary truth of poetry:

> The cultivation of those sciences which have enlarged the limits of the empire of man over the external world has, for want of the poetical faculty, proportionally circumscribed those of the internal world; and man, having enslaved the elements, remains himself a slave. . . . Poetry is indeed something divine. It is at once the centre and circumference of all knowledge; it is that which comprehends all science, and that to which all science must be referred.[22]

In its context, as Raymond Williams has noted, we must grasp the historical, oppositional and 'defensive' function of this conception of the trans-historical poet. In the phrase 'empire of man' and its correlative, the 'enslavement' of the material world and of ourselves, Shelley sees science as the necessary instrument of the specific sociopolitical order of industrial capitalism, and locates art as the utopian space within which what is threatened might, through its designation as a more fully 'human' condition, be defended. Lawrence shares with Shelley this critique of science as an ideological phenomenon, and a connecting thread between their romanticisms and the later critiques of the Frankfurt School should, even through these brief illustrations, be evident. While, however, as Williams notes, it is 'wholly valuable to present a wider and more substantial account of human motive and energy than was contained in the philosophy of industrialism', the danger of such a specialized and mystificatory image of art or poetry is the reduction of art to an 'abstraction' or 'self-pleading ideology', thereby reproducing the very logic of commodification or instrumentalization at issue.[23] Art is isolated, the faculty of imagination 'specialised . . . to . . . one kind of activity', the faculty of science to another; poetry and science are hypostatized in opposition, the one representing the preservation of the 'human', the other everything that is antithetical to the human.

This account of Romanticism elides, for the time being, the complex thinking about artistic and scientific epistemologies, and about psychologies of perception, evident for example in the work of Coleridge – and Lawrence has often been associated with Coleridge's project.[24] My point is that the simplified dichotomies of art and science, human and anti-human, which were made available or could be deduced from romantic ideology, became particularly serviceable to a literary criticism which was basing its claim to disciplinary integrity on the uniqueness of literature as a form and on the defence of the 'human' as its moral justification. Eliseo Vivas takes it as read that science has 'sterilising and debilitating effects on our attitude to the universe'; Lawrence 'managed to a great extent to avoid' such effects.[25] A disdain for science is similarly ingrained in the distinction between the literary and the algebraic in Michael Black's reflections on the role of symbolism in Lawrence's early novels, where 'algebraic' stands for simple one-to-one correspondence between symbol and meaning. The moon, lilies and pollen, in the scene from *Sons and Lovers* in which Mrs. Morel is locked out in the garden, do not 'stand for' single referents, and the volatility in a system of signification in which Siegmund McNair's (*The Trespasser*) 'dreams' are also 'flowers', prevents the system from becoming 'logical and deducible', which would, Black asserts, be 'deathly'.[26]

The word 'deathly' is a rhetorical reminder of how far these critical approaches were initially grounded in the work of F.R. Leavis. Disagreement with T.S. Eliot's adverse judgement became the cornerstone of Leavis's sustained endorsement of Lawrence as the great 'creative genius' of twentieth-century English Literature. Leavis did insist that the terrain of debate was the nature of 'intelligence', arguing that Lawrence's work required of his readers a new assessment of the concept of thought itself: 'It is Lawrence's greatness that to appreciate him is to revise one's criteria of intelligence and one's notion of it. Eliot's finding him incapable of thinking is a failure of intelligence in himself.'[27] This process of revision was, however, notoriously obstructed by Leavis's manner of dealing with rational explication and, by extension, with science and the scientific. In anticipation of our interest, in the present book, in a science evolving towards the 'posthuman' replication of human intelligence, let us take as a brief example Leavis's discussion of the idea of the computer.

In a lecture from the early 1970s, Leavis alluded to recent encounters with the director of a city art gallery and a philosopher, both of whom had expressed excitement about the computer and, in particular, about the idea of computer-generated poetry. He starts from the assumption that the proposition, 'a computer can write a poem', is absurd, 'preposterous and ominous' in the first place – an assumption reinforced by the stigmatization even of the inclination to believe or take an interest in it: 'That any cultivated person should *want* to believe that a computer can write a poem!'[28] A further justification of his position – 'the difference is an essential one; the computerial force of "poem" eliminates the essentially human – eliminates human creativity' – confirms a circularity of logic: the most we can say about the meaning of 'computerial' is that it is not 'human', and vice versa. Language is denied an explanatory role except as the repository of self-evident 'essences'; yet, while terms such as 'human' and 'computer' are locked into a system of absolute, polarized difference, a theory of language as necessarily fluid and indeterminate works to ward off further enquiry. It was vital, claimed Leavis, to understand that key words are 'incapable of definition'; their life cannot be fixed and circumscribed, and 'there lies their importance for thought'.

In his second (1976) book on Lawrence, Leavis demonstrates how Lawrence might be woven into a critical position on a science whose threat was embodied in the computer:

> In 1930, the year in which Lawrence died, the computer was not there for him to have heard of it, but in a sense he foresaw it. For his intelligence told him that 'objectivity' . . . was a deadly fallacy, and that science, which in the course of recent centuries had invested the assumptions behind 'objectivity' with the authority of clear commonsense, was advancing to new conquests over life at an acceleration.[29]

It is not my intention here to elaborate detailed critiques of Leavis's resistance to critical theory and of the mystificatory elements in his own, post-romantic theorizing of literature. In fact, key elements of the critique of science he attributes to Lawrence will figure prominently in my own account of a posthuman Lawrence as this book proceeds: the undermining of 'objectivity', consonant with relativity physics and the placing of the observer within the field of enquiry; the status of science as ideological 'commonsense'; the 'deadly' threat, identified by current ecological critique, posed by an ideology of 'conquest' over life as matter to be subjugated. The issue here is to what extent the 'fixing', 'circumscribing' and 'defining' effects of objectivity are attributes of science itself, and to what extent they are an effect of Leavis's own critical discourse. Convinced that to embark on rational, objective analysis was to become part of the problem under analysis, Leavis had few alternatives in his discussion of science other than the application of rhetorical counters: science as 'Technologico-Benthamism', or as something which could be 'weighed or tripped over or brought into the laboratory or pointed to'.[30] Similarly, Lawrence's relation to science was amenable to no fuller articulation than the opposition of living creative genius to a deathly mechanism.

Leavis' influential and idiosyncratic formulations must, however, be seen as part of a broader critical and historical tradition of humanism. As Donald Benson has argued, Victorian humanist thinkers such as John Henry Newman and Matthew Arnold helped propagate an image of science which was alien to the actual work of scientists and scientific theorists such as John Tyndall, A.J. Balfour and John Theodore Merz.[31] For Newman and Arnold, the task of the humanist, affiliated to a Shelleyan aesthetic, was to transform the inert and limited knowledge of science into beauty and higher meaning. Paradoxically, this locked into place an unquestioned faith in the ability of science to discover facts about the physical world, and thus to arrive at a condition of certainty, which was not shared by scientists themselves. Post-Darwinian science was increasingly bound up in the enigma of thinking matter or, as Benson puts it, 'the active participation of mind in the construction – as opposed to the simple discovery – of scientific knowledge and the vital role of the imagination and its instruments, specifically analogies and models, and of language and other symbols in this process'.[32] It is thus 'more than a passing irony' that scientists should place human consciousness as an enigma at the heart of scientific knowledge, 'treating science as an essentially human and even humane activity', while the 'humanists' depended, for their claims about culture, upon the construction of a 'reductive popular conception' of science which had no room for such subtleties. 'It was Arnold', notes Benson, 'who defined the humanist's responsibility as the criticism of life, yet who was unable to extend that criticism to science in a serious way'. In invoking Lawrence's critical stance on science with the pronouncement that 'Life is unamenable to mathematical or quantificative finality of treatment, and every creative writer is a servant of life', Leavis similarly seemed oblivious to any possibility that the scientist might be in a better position than the creative writer to announce life's fugitive qualities.

In thus claiming a crucial link between art as 'creativity' and the defence of the 'human' from the deathly, reductive methods of science, humanists tended to elide the fact that what it meant to *be* human had become a renewed and central preoccupation of post-Darwinian science. Leavis could refer to the 'essentially human' in a way that science could not, the essentialism safely enclosed within a set of contradictions. Leavis for example consistently noted with approval Lawrence's wholeness and harmonious integrity, as a model of human subjectivity. Yet if this wholeness was to be truly organic and creative, it had to be mobile and unpredictable, its harmony also a condition of dissonance, and therefore not amenable to the fixities of science and rational logic. Critics looking to re-read Eliot's notion of Lawrence's 'incapacity' as the substance of imaginative genius have thus tended to alight gratefully upon a reminiscence of Earl. H. Brewster concerning a visit Lawrence made to Ceylon in 1922. 'When', Brewster recalls, 'I urged him to write at greater length on his philosophical and psychological conceptions, he would shake his head and say, "I would contradict myself on every page." '[33] This, for Vivas, was a 'cruel, because lucid' acknowledgement on Lawrence's part of his own "theoretical incompetence', while David Ellis uses the quotation to support a 'common sense' reading of Lawrence's philosophical writings, separating out the valuable 'intuitive insights' from the clear evidence of his weaknesses in the field of logic.[34]

Francis Mulhern has described Leavis's advocacy of Lawrence as a case of 'a criticism in communion with its ideal object'.[35] Perhaps then, it is within the general domain of humanist criticism that Lawrence was invented as an 'ideal object'. The requirement that Lawrence adhere to an image of himself which excludes science means that an inordinate weight has been carried by a version of his early intellectual development propagated by Jessie Chambers. According to Chambers, Lawrence's materialist reading came in 'full blast'; it was an attempt, she claims, to 'fill up a spiritual vacuum by swallowing materialism at a gulp', and in these terms, practically doomed to failure. While, Chambers admits, Lawrence was deeply impressed by this reading, 'it did not carry him far'; he 'seemed to feel compelled to take up a rationalist standpoint with regard to religion, although it made him miserable', and 'he would try to represent himself to me as a complete materialist, but he was too emphatic to be convincing'.[36] This account has remained generally unquestioned, the materialism seen as a temporary staging post in the trajectory, for example in the accounts of John Worthen and Daniel Schneider, towards Lawrence's true identity as '*homo religiosus*'.[37]

It may, however, be possible to unhinge the self-evidence of Chambers' reminiscences without questioning their essential integrity. First, the assumed model of materialist science is monolithic, something capable of being 'swallowed . . . at a gulp', and thus upholding the humanist ideology of science as both certain and inherently circumscribed. There seems no possibility here of an indeterminate and epistemologically self-questioning science, nor thereby a sense of how 'it' might seep into and be sustained within other areas of thought, whether culturally or in terms of Lawrence's own particular formation. Robert Alan Donovan's assessment of Matthew Arnold's conception of science in terms of a 'curious insensitivity to the claims of science as a mode of intellectual culture', springs to mind.[38] Also, there is Chambers' model of Lawrence himself, and in relation to science. In July 1930, Chambers wrote to her sister Mary: 'The greatest scientists of today admit that science can only go so far, and that the kind of truth that true inspiration teaches is beyond the reach of science. That is true of Einstein, and all the great figures in the scientific world today.'[39] As we have seen, Lawrence too could draw strict boundaries around science, and in a more intemperate vein than this serene Christian pietism. Yet it is questionable whether Lawrence's critique of science coincides in any meaningful sense with that of Chambers, with its faith in 'true inspiration' and its glib universalizing. A comparison of this, for example, from the essay 'Hymns in a Man's Life', sees an initial similarity turn into a significant contrast:

> Even the real scientist works in the sense of wonder. The pity is, when he comes out of his laboratory, he puts aside his wonder along with his apparatus, and tries to make it all didactic. Science in its true condition of wonder is as religious as any religion. But didactic science is as dead and boring as dogmatic religion. Both are wonderless and productive of boredom, endless boredom (*PII* 599).

Eschewing any simple dichotomy between science and religion, this is an affirmation of 'real science' and of the 'wonder' that can transfigure both science as well as religion: Gradgrind's science turned on its head. Elsewhere Lawrence was to reiterate the distinction, within science, between the 'real' or 'alert' and the 'didactic' or 'dogmatic'. Perhaps, then, there is a sense in which Chambers' account of Lawrence's encounter with science tells us more about Chambers than it does about Lawrence.

I have suggested that dominant paradigms of science and of the creative artist within humanist criticism inhibit an appreciation of the complexities of Lawrence's engagement with science. While humanists from Newman and Arnold, through Aldous Huxley and F.R. Leavis and his successors, presented themselves as the defenders of human values against the sterility of science, post-Darwinian scientists opened up the question of the human as 'thinking matter', submitting it and their own epistemologies to the kind of critical interrogation which was impossible within the metaphysics of transcendence that humanism had set for itself. Lawrence was immersed in these scientific debates, and the result is a complex combination in his work: on the one hand, a deep and sometimes seemingly evangelical commitment to the redemption or retrieval of the 'human' from the threats posed to it by modernity; on the other hand, a resolute refusal to entertain any fixed, orthodox, pious or sentimental views about the value of the 'human'. 'That which the word 'human' stood for was despicable and repugnant to her'; this we learn of Ursula Brangwen, who in *Women in Love* is associated at other times with passionately humane responses, and who has listened in bewildered fascination to Rupert Birkin's view that 'man is one of the mistakes of creation – like the icthyosauri' (*WL* 244, 128). How far might Hardt and Negri's conception of an 'antihumanist (or posthuman) humanism' be applicable to this complex combination in Lawrence? In the next section, I want to suggest how we might begin to use contemporary theories of the posthuman to re-read Lawrence's preoccupation with the human as an evolved condition of thinking matter.

4. Posthumanism

Let me begin with a broad characterization. 'Posthuman' tends to designate a perceived change in the nature of the human brought about by developments in the fields of cybernetics, neuroscience and genetics and their resultant technologies since the Second World War. Such technologies might include artificial intelligence (AI) and robotics, computer and communication technologies, micro-science and prosthetics (including in particular the treatment and rehabilitation of humans through, for example, drugs, micro-surgery, implantations, artificial limbs and replacement organs), and genetic science. In the sense that these are interventionist technologies, the 'posthuman' tends to combine connotations of evolutionary development with those of transgression and loss. A notion of some integrally 'human' condition is confronted with its demise in the form of the irretrievable splicing together of the cybernetic and the organic – the cyb-org, or cyborg.

The clear potential, suggested above, for a dystopian reading of the posthuman, has been recently exemplified in Francis Fukuyama's *Our Post-*

human Future: Consequences of the Biotechnology Revolution (2002). 'Human nature exists', claims Fukuyama, 'is a meaningful concept, and has provided a stable continuity to our experience as a species'; but, citing Aldous Huxley's novel *Brave New World* (1932), Fukuyama argues that Huxley was correct in his prediction that 'the most significant threat posed by contemporary biotechnology is the possibility that it will alter human nature and thereby move us into a "posthuman" stage of history'.[40] Fukuyama's macroeconomic diagnosis of the 'threat' of the posthuman pivots on the conviction that dire consequences for the continuity and stability of human life can only be avoided through strict surveillance and regulation, of genetic engineering in particular, exercized by governments with the support of scientific expertise.

Once we move beyond the level of generalized conception, however, posthumanism emerges as a field of active contestation and discrimination. Fukuyama's reading is antithetical to alternative conceptions of the posthuman which have circulated for some time in the discourses (to which his work does not attend) of philosophy and critical theory. Here, for example, we might find a utopian posthumanism of 'lived social and bodily realities in which people are not afraid of their joint kinship with animals and machines'.[41] Donna Haraway's *Cyborg Manifesto* is a plea for the renewal of radical left politics in the late 1980s, urging the left to throw off the shackles of dualistic thinking, the most prominent instance of which is the dichotomy between an aggressive, techno-scientific industrial culture and a resistant 'imagined organic body' – the figure of nature, perhaps. In Haraway's concept of 'joint kinship', while Darwinian evolutionary theory all but erases the boundary between humans and animals, late twentieth-century machines make 'thoroughly ambiguous' the distinction between nature and technology: 'our machines are disturbingly lively, and we ourselves frighteningly inert'. In Haraway's 'cyborg' then we find, not robotic depletions of the actual, bodily human, but a figure for an enhanced state of awareness of the material base which connects us to the organic and the inorganic, and which might constitute the ground of an emancipatory politics.

At the same time, Haraway is acutely conscious that at least one version of a cyborg future constitutes a paradoxical re-inscription of that dualistic thinking with which the subjugation of the world, natural or political, is associated. Referring to the rise of cybernetic science in post-1945 states, and principally in the US, Haraway sees the 'main trouble' with cyborgs as that they are 'the illegitimate offspring of militarism and patriarchal capitalism, not to mention state socialism', an instance of a dominant techno-culture seeking 'the final imposition of a grid of control on the planet, . . . the final abstraction embodied in a Star Wars apocalypse waged in the name of defence'.[42]

How might such contradictions be explained? It is helpful here to turn to N. Katherine Hayles' *How We Became Posthuman: Virtual Bodies in Cybernet-*

ics, Literature, and Informatics (1999), a consistently important reference point in the argument of the present book. Hayles offers a provisional outline of four grounding assumptions with which to think the posthuman:

> First, the posthuman view privileges informational pattern over material instantiation, so that embodiment in a material substrate is seen as an accident of history rather than as an inevitability of life. Second, the posthuman view considers consciousness, regarded as the seat of human identity in the Western tradition long before Descartes thought he was a mind thinking, as an epiphenomenon, as an evolutionary upstart trying to claim that it is the whole show when in actuality it is only a minor sideshow. Third, the posthuman view thinks of the body as the original prosthesis we all learn to manipulate, so that extending or replacing the body with other prostheses becomes a continuation of a process that began before we were born. Fourth, and most important, by these and other means, the posthuman view configures human being so that it can be seamlessly articulated with intelligent machines. In the posthuman, there are no essential differences or absolute demarcations between bodily existence and computer simulation, cybernetic mechanism and biological organism, robot teleology and human goals.[43]

It is noticeable that only the last of these points is necessarily tied to the development of late twentieth-century technologies. The first two points are interpretations of an evolutionary history driven by Darwinian natural selection. Posthumanism is a way of *thinking* the human, stimulated perhaps by contemporary science, but allowing us to re-read the 'accidental' emergence of forms of life and consciousnes within deep evolutionary time. Reverence for the power of intellect is somewhat modified by a view of consciousness as 'an evolutionary upstart trying to claim that it is the whole show when in actuality it is only a minor sideshow'.

Hayles' reference to Descartes is crucial. At the centre of a posthumanism informed by evolutionary theory is a critique of Cartesian dualism, that conception of mind and body as separate 'substances' hierarchically arranged, so that the body becomes the 'mechanism' subject to the will of the mind (and thus, by extension, the animal condition, lacking in mind according to Descartes, becomes subject to the will of the human intellect). In the more holistic developmental thinking of posthumanism, and in direct continuity with the materialism of late nineteenth-century science, mind is a product of material evolution, invested with no transcendental status or power: consciousness just happens to have evolved in human bodies, and human bodies just happen to be the 'instantiation' of intelligence, 'an accident of history' rather than 'an inevitability of life'.

It is here that a materialist anti-Cartesianism contains the seeds of its own undoing. If bodies are just as material as the prostheses with which, in posthumanism, we threaten to de-nature ourselves (bodies, in other words, can be thought *as* prostheses, and thus as continuous with the 'artificial'), and if consciousness is simply an (evolutionary) accident that has happened to those bodies, then mind can, in theory, be disentangled from bodies. In her critical polemic around the politics of posthumanism, Hayles maps the story of 'how information lost its body' in the scientific search for the technological or 'artificial' reproduction of intelligent life. By this means an originally *materialist* theory of mind, integral to the theory of the 'Knowledge Age', could transmigrate into the view, sponsored and endorsed by the US Republican statesman and former leader of the House of Representatives Newt Gingrich, that ' "The central event of the twentieth century is the overthrow of matter." '[44]

Hayles' title, *How We Became Posthuman*, conceals an irony. It is not, *pace* Fukuyama, that contemporary technologies are fashioning a sinister deviation from human nature. Rather, according to a certain conception, we have always been posthuman; 'human' is a much more recent invention. Posthuman thinking generates a *dual* sense of the relative lateness of the human condition, at once biological and conceptual. First, there is the speck of time occupied by the human on the evolutionary scale; second, there is the far more recent historical emergence of 'man', in the terms of Michel Foucault's genealogy of the human sciences, from within European cultures of the sixteenth century. Despite the elevation of human identity and consciousness from within the developing scientific humanism of this period, ' "man" ', Foucault insists, is 'neither the oldest nor the most constant problem that has been posed for human knowledge'.[45] Hayles' critique of Cartesian dualism is Foucauldian in as much as it emphasises the ideological context which links together the supremacy of the mind and the implicit subjugation of the material world through the force of intellect in Descartes' philosophy, with the historical rise of individualism and its corollary in the rise of capitalism. The posthuman, she argues, does not mean the end of humanity, but rather of 'a certain conception of the human, a conception that may have applied, at best, to that fraction of humanity who had the wealth, power and leisure to conceptualise themselves as autonomous beings exercising their will through individual agency and choice'.[46] The power of this liberal humanist individualism has, indeed, been such that it has been able to appropriate the very posthumanism which had seemed to threaten it: intelligence, separable from the bodies that carry it, becomes a new version of the sovereign Cartesian mind.

In posthumanism, there are ways of thinking the human which radically challenge our assumptions about individual personhood. Cognition, for example, may have been, for longer than we have imagined, 'distributed', in the terms of contemporary neuroscience, its faculties franchised out across the various tools, systems and environments (the latest, sophisticated instances of which are virtual computer environments) we have devised in order to perform complex functions of which the brain and nervous system alone would be incapable. Similarly, contemporary neuroscientists striving to give a materialist account of the faculty of memory have seized upon the concept of the 'dissipative structure'. Beneath the apparent continuity of the self is the physical fact that, over a lifetime, the whole tissue of the body changes and renews itself many times over. While Fritjof Capra sees memory in this way as a constantly changing assembly of cells which make for 'temporary structures of cognition', we can see the general idea of the dissipative structure anticipated in earlier evolutionary primers such as that of Winwood Reade, who maintains that 'a live form . . . is continually being injured by the wear and tear of its own activity; it is continually darning and stitching its own life'.[47]

'A coherent, continuous, essential self', concludes Hayles, 'is neither necessary nor sufficient to explain embodied experience.'[48] Here posthumanism emerges as a perhaps unforeseen convergence of evolutionary science and post-structuralist philosophy. Both are critiques of the Cartesian *cogito*, proposing instead a decentred subjectivity which offers a challenge to humanist essentialism. The 'new Bergsonism' occupies this conjunctural space, signalling a revival of interest in the work of Henri Bergson, with whose modernist interpretation of evolutionary thought this chapter began. Perhaps the founding document of this movement is Gilles Deleuze's short study *Bergsonism* (1966), first published as an English translation in 1991. This is the Deleuze who, with Felix Guattari in *Anti-Oedipus: Capitalism and Schizophrenia* (1972), consistently invokes D.H. Lawrence in the name of the human as a nexus of 'desiring machines', and as an alternative to the static and self-fulfilling character of Freudian ego psychology. Lawrence demonstrates, they claim, that men and women are not 'clearly defined personalities' but 'vibrations, flows, schizzes and "knots"', in the analysis of which 'the so-called human relations are not involved' (*A-O* 351, 362, 323).

In a lucid summary, Sean Watson reminds us that the first principle of Bergsonian philosophy is that there is no separation of mind and body, consciousness being 'entirely reducible' to the complex movement of matter.[49] Of a more precise significance, however, are the means by which Bergson sought to establish his second principle of absolute continuity between consciousness and the material world 'outside'. Bergson set out to deconstruct the inside/outside dichotomy itself, through an examination of representation and memory. In the first case he sought to dispense with the classical conception of representation as an intermediary process, as if there were a hidden agent in our heads, translating and representing the perceived world for the purposes of thought. Instead, consciousness is a temporary articulation of body, brain, nervous system and environment: as Deleuze puts it, 'we perceive things where they are, perception puts us at once into matter, is impersonal, and coincides with the perceived object'.[50] In the second case, memory for Bergson is not the storing of a bank of images or representations but the temporary co-ordination of matter into structures of cognition: 'we don't have memories', Sean Watson notes, 'we *are* memories'.[51]

The 'new Bergsonist' revival gives us a clue to the exploration of the associations between the materialism of D.H. Lawrence's time and the posthumanism of our own. This is the Lawrence who, as we shall see, declared himself more interested in 'that which is physic, non-human in humanity' than in the 'old-fashioned human element'; who asked whether the hand writing his essay should be any less 'himself' than his mind or his brain; and who speculated on the notion of 'physical thought' in non-human creatures, in terms of a condition in which 'all the tissue of the body is all the time aware'.[52] In literary criticism, the effort to connect Lawrence with the posthumanism of deconstructive philosophy, and thus to revise his 'irrationalism', is already well under way. Uniting the work of, for example, Bersani, Ragussis, Schneider, Doherty and Jewinski, is a recognition of Lawrence's concern with the error of logocentrism – that is, with the mistaking of a linguistic description of the world for that world itself. Bersani finds in Lawrence an awareness of a *mise en abîme*, the basis of the deconstructive turn, by which 'the very act of expressing a radical imagination in language and literature limits its realization, perhaps even erases what is radical in imagination'.[53] In Lawrence's fiction, Bersani argues, there is a rigorous exploration of the consequences of this for the idea and possibility of knowledge – not simply a self-defeating exercise, but a 'commitment to a constantly renewed struggle for rational utterance'. As Jewinski in his Lacanian reading puts it,

> If Lawrence is granted the view that *the human* does not exist, that *the human* is a perverse and monstrous extension of the *abstraction* called *humanity*, then Lawrence's fiction might no longer be considered either irrational or nonrational, but rather the legitimate extension of 'rationality' and 'objectivity'. Man has only language-bound devices of the intellect for articulating his world; however, his essential being is not language-bound, the 'self' is only 'like' a language, one that can be suggested but never elucidated in any but its own terms.[54]

The specifically North American context out of which these critics write is not insignificant. As I suggested earlier, the collective investment of a British humanist tradition in Romantic assumptions renders problematic the identification of Lawrence with a progressive tradition of rationalism. Even when Raymond Williams sought to challenge Leavisite high culturalism, warning against an image of Lawrence as the 'familiar romantic figure', his own version of Lawrence as fierce critic of industrial capitalism was not completely free of a moral mythology of sensuousness and spontaneity antithetical to 'mechanical abstraction'.[55] It thus remains arresting, to the ears of a British critic, to hear that 'Lawrence's mind worked easily and naturally (at) the highest levels of abstraction' (Daniel Schneider) or that Lawrence demonstrated an 'extraordinary and vigorous complexity in his deployment of dialectical terms' (Jonathan Arac).[56] The one notable exception in recent British criticism is Anne Fernihough's *D.H. Lawrence: Aesthetics and Ideology* (1993). In this work, Fernihough seeks to delicately disentangle Lawrence from conventional and, in particular, fascistic versions of irrationalism, delineating instead an 'anti-imperialist aesthetics' dedicated to a 'retrieval of the material world' and an acknowledgement, as Lawrence found it in Cézanne, that 'matter *actually* exists'.[57]

My sympathies with Fernihough's groundbreaking study will be evident at various points in the forthcoming chapters. My point of divergence is from Fernihough's contention that the logocentric model of language which Lawrence found and criticized in realist art was also the 'prerequisite of scientific discourse and, by extension, technology, a technology which, for Lawrence, is inseparable from Western expansion and imperialism'.[58] This threatens to reiterate (on Lawrence's behalf, as it were) the caricature of science embedded both in humanist and poststructuralist critical theory. We need instead, I suggest, more nuanced versions of science and of the machine, of the kind to be found within contemporary posthumanist discourse. Here, the sheer ambivalence of the machine and its curious material 'kinship' with the human takes us back to an earlier moment in Lawrence criticism, and to a text which I must also acknowledge as an important influence and precursor. Colin Clarke's *River of Dissolution: D.H. Lawrence and English Romanticism* (1969) boldly began the 'demolition' of the Leavisian humanist Lawrence. Lawrence's approach to the machine, Clarke demonstrated, was not simple, and it had been an extraordinary act of critical selectivity to claim that it was. In a characteristic strategy of 'double-talk', Lawrence groped his way towards a sense that mechanism was invested with a 'paradoxical but genuine vitality': how easy was it really, Clarke challenged the reader, to decide in Lawrence 'just how lethal the lethal-seeming mechanization of the miner's life' actually was?[59] For Clarke, the ambivalence was explained by the tradition of English decadent romanticism and its fascination with corruption and death as inherent in life; his study is curiously oblivious of all other cultural and historical contexts. But, I suggest, the insights of Clarke's reading of Lawrence and mechanism are waiting to be developed, both in terms of Lawrence's own science, and that of the contemporary posthuman.

There are, however, different kinds of posthumanism. The posthuman, observes N. Katherine Hayles, is with us to stay; the question is, what *kind* of posthumanism we want. Alternative versions of the posthuman construe the importance of *matter* in radically and politically different ways: it can, as we have seen, constitute the basis of Haraway's 'joint kinship', or the military-industrialist subjugation of a world treated as *raw* material. Lawrence came to realise that the most profound debates and decisions concerning the conscious shaping of a (post?)human future were made from *within* scientific discourses, and it is to the subtle discriminations to be made between different versions of science that this book turns its attention.

2
Science, Ideology and the 'New'

1. 'Born scientific'

> As they worked in the fields, from beyond the now familiar
> embankment came the rhythmic run of the winding engines,
> startling at first, but afterwards a narcotic to the brain. Then the
> shrill whistle of the trains re-echoed through the heart, with fear-
> some pleasure, announcing the far-off come near and imminent
> (*TR* 12–13).

In Lawrence's novel *The Rainbow* (1915), the Brangwens of the mid-nine-
teenth century experience industrial technology in the body: the winding
engines of the pit become 'a narcotic to the brain', the whistle of the trains
re-echoes 'through the heart'. The variations in Lawrence's fictional treatment of the relationship between humans, technology and the natural
world suggest a constant process of reappraisal. At the beginning of the story
'Odour of Chrysanthemums' (1911), for example, a nameless woman stands
'insignificantly trapped between the jolting black waggons and the hedge'
as a locomotive thumps past on its way to Brinsley Colliery. Despite the
engine's 'loud threats of speed', however, it is 'outdistanced at a canter' by
the colt which is startled from the 'flickering' gorse.[1] Revisiting this scenario
in *Women in Love* (1920), Gerald Crich holds his terrified Arab mare to the
level-crossing gate while the train goes past, in a display of power which
horrifies the watching Brangwen sisters. A one-legged signalman observes
the scene from the safety of his 'little signal-hut', 'like a crab from a snail-
shell' (*WL* 93), while further on, near a second level crossing, a disused and
rusting industrial boiler has been reclaimed by hens and wagtails.

The latter two scenes stage the relationship between technology and
nature as contestatory, with nature granted a subtle victory; humans occupy
a range of positions within this contest, from the insignificant to the dominant, from helpless submission to the control (in Gerald Crich's case,
through ownership) both of nature and of technology. The Brangwens of

The Rainbow, however, strike a different note, not of contest but of the erasure of boundaries. The collieries and trains, initially external and disruptive, 'startling' and 'shrill', become organically integrated through a sensual experience of sublimity, mixing 'fear' with 'pleasure', and thus becoming as 'familiar' as the canal-carrying embankment which initially, around 1840, made them 'strangers in their own place'. The incursions of technology into landscape and working practices become, in time, incursions into the body; a material, palpable and visible process becomes an equally material but invisible, internalized form of life. Technology and nature are not locked into pure, hypostatized difference: rather, the human seems to be the locus within which technology can *become* nature, through habituation.

'Never were as many men of a decidedly empiricist proclivity in existence as there are at the present day', wrote William James in *Pragmatism* (1907) a text which, according to Chambers, appealed strongly to Lawrence in his formative period. 'Our children', James adds, 'are almost born scientific' (*PR* 11). In what ways and with what consequences was science becoming as 'natural' to humans as the technology which subtly entered and modified the bodies of the Brangwen family? In this chapter I want to examine, in Lawrence's earlier work and thought, the appeal of the scientific as a discourse of the 'new', as it figures in three instances: the New Theology movement; the journal *The New Age*; and the concept of the New Woman. I want to suggest thus how far 'science' for Lawrence became mutually imbricated with religion, politics and gender in the intimate processes of identity-formation as much as in the more explicit articulation of ideas and positions. In this manner science is redefined as an *ideological* as well as intellectual resource, a separation which is nevertheless fraught with danger if we theorise 'ideology' too narrowly as an affective structure inculcating false consciousness instead of knowledge. Affective and intellectual are a complex fusion, but in the traditional treatment of science from the perspective of a history of *ideas*, it has been too easy to isolate, demonize and thereby limit the significance of science in Lawrence's development. A concept of scientific ideology leads to the proposition that Lawrence was both inside and outside science simultaneously – though a discourse of the posthuman might suggest, rather, that science was inside and outside Lawrence.

In the Brangwens of *The Rainbow*, Lawrence highlighted the power of science-as-technology to intervene in and transform everyday experience. From the 1830s in Britain, a parallel process could be said to have occurred in the domain of the meanings and images of science. According to Morrell and Thackray, organisations such as the British Association for the Advancement of Science (BAAS) mounted a sustained effort to construct an 'ideology' of science as a 'visible' and 'distinct' resource in British society, not just in the physical presentation of science as spectacle (science fairs, carnivals and public demonstrations), but also in the *discursive* clarification of science as a field of knowledge. William Whewell's *History of the Inductive Sciences* (1837) exemplified the efforts of the BAAS, by virtue of which science 'ceased to be a synonym for all knowledge and became the party label of a particular mode of understanding possessed – so it was said – of superior power'. Boundaries were drawn within which the 'scientist', newly coined by Whewell, presided over a domain which remains familiar today: 'science as value-free and objective knowledge; science as the key to economic and technological progress; science as the firm fruit of proper method; science as an available, visible and desirable cultural resource'.[2]

At the same time, however, the nascent ideology of science was held in place by a contradictory claim with which Lawrence, in his formative period, would have been equally familiar. 'What is Science?', asked Herbert Spencer in *First Principles*. 'To see the absurdity of the prejudice against it,' he continued, 'we need only remark that Science is simply a higher development of common knowledge; and that if science is repudiated, all knowledge must be repudiated along with it . . .'. 'Nowhere', he concluded, 'is it possible to draw a line and say – here science begins' (*FP* 14). T.H. Huxley echoed Spencer in claiming science to be 'nothing but *trained and organised common sense*':

> The method of scientific investigation is nothing but the expression of the necessary mode of working of the human mind. It is simply the mode at which all phenomena are reasoned about, rendered precise and exact. There is no more difference, but there is the same kind of difference, between the mental operations of a man of science and those of an ordinary person, as there is between the operations and methods of a baker or of a butcher weighing out his goods in common scales, and the operations of a chemist in performing a difficult and complex analysis by means of his balance and finely-graduated weights . . . . (*MPN* 189)

Science, then, as a new, distinct and powerful tool; science as the simple and 'necessary', common-sense working of the human mind. The strength of science as an ideology might be said to lie in the mutual sustaining of these strictly contradictory positions within the appearance of a coherent whole. In the following sections we will see something of the dialectical interplay between them in Lawrence's complex, developing engagement with science.

2. Religious crisis and the New Theology

> 'It's not religious to be religious.'
>
> Paul Morel, in *Sons and Lovers* (1913)

'Far more than in any dogma, Lawrence was interested in the question as to how the old religious ideas stood in relation to the scientific discoveries that were sweeping away the familiar landmarks.'[3] The religious crisis of Lawrence's early twenties is now well-documented, its main sources being Jessie Chambers' biographical account and two letters sent by Lawrence to the Rev. Robert Reid in 1907. Reid was a crucial figure in the intellectual circle formed by a network of local chapels. He had formed the Eastwood Congregational Literary Society in 1899, and gave lecture-like sermons, including a sequence of four in December 1907 on 'Religion and Science'. In the first letter, Lawrence explains that his religious beliefs had been 'seriously modified' by his materialist reading, and seeks an explanation of orthodox and non-conformist church views on evolution and how the theory would bear on concepts of sin, heaven and hell (*LI* 36–7). The second letter sees Lawrence opening out into a more impassioned revelation of his dilemma – 'I cannot be a materialist' – following a visit to the slums of Sneinton, and it contains a significant glimpse of how he saw his own religion, clearly humanistic in orientation, shaping itself out of diverse, undogmatic influences:

> A man has no religion who has not slowly and painfully gathered one together, adding to it, shaping it; and one's religion is never complete and final, it seems, but must always be undergoing modification. So I contend that true Socialism is religion; that honest, fervent politics is religion; that whatever a man may labour for earnestly and in some measure unselfishly is also religion (*LI* 40).

From the young-old Lawrence, with the weight of 22 years on his shoulders, this is a mobile, secular and rationalistic expression of spirituality. The strong religious impulse is sufficiently open and flexible to be channelled and defined in any number of ways. John Worthen argues that the years 1906–1908 were a period of frustration as well as of discovery and stimulation for Lawrence. At college, he quickly became dismayed at 'not finding himself the inhabitant of an advanced, intellectual community'; at home, and despite Reid and his circle, Christian religion was 'still an unassailable fact of life, its faith unquestioned and often unquestioning'.[4] While Jessie Chambers could disarm science with apparent ease, it is evident that the questions Lawrence insisted on posing, concerning Christianity's ability to reconcile itself with the materialism it seemed to want to embrace, would 'not be answered'. At the root of Lawrence's dilemma, it seems, was the need for an alert Christianity to prove itself worthy of critical dialogue with science.

In this light it is instructive to briefly examine the texts, now largely forgotten, to which Lawrence referred in his dialogue with Reid: Robert Blatchford's *God and My Neighbour* (1903), Philip Vivian's *The Churches and Modern Thought* (1906), and R.J. Campbell's *The New Theology* (1907). As Stuart MacIntyre has indicated, a 'keen working-class interest in mid-Victorian science' was sustained in the early twentieth century due to the continued printing of key evolutionary materialist texts, in cheap editions, by publishing houses such as Watts and the Rationalist Press Association.[5] The three texts in question all mobilise a 'religion versus science' framework, which to a strictly middle-class readership might have begun to seem dated. Each is a rationalist response to the perceived inadequacy of Christian theology to answer the challenges of science, with marked variations in tone and strategy. Blatchford proclaims a nationalistic Socialism in declamatory mode, defending his position from the charge of 'infidel' by outlining a history within which Christianity had consistently and often bloodily suppressed the progress of science or 'heresy' – for 'religion, being based on fixed authority, is naturally opposed to knowledge' – only for that '"infidelity"' to become in time the 'enlightened religion of today' (*GMN*, 197, 6). Vivian's is a calmer documentary overview of the current embattled position of Christian theology, relying heavily on the collation and quotation of other sources. The two are united, however, in their uncompromising critique of Christianity's consistent and often bloody suppression of the progress of knowledge (for which 'science' becomes a virtual synonym), and in their denial of the possibility of reconciliation between religion and science. Campbell, by contrast, writing as a Liberal Christian, claims to represent the 'religion of science', enlisting science, 'the only method which carries weight with the modern mind', in a paradoxical attempt to re-spiritualize Christianity and close the gap between traditional theology and everyday experience.

There is a concrete linguistic sense in which the polemics of Blatchford and Vivian were resourceful texts for Lawrence in this period of religious crisis. Explicitly, Lawrence disliked the 'violence' of Blatchford's militancy. Yet, as Worthen has astutely noted, Lawrence borrows from the style and tone of Blatchford in his letters to Reid. Reflecting on his Sneinton experience, the question 'how . . . shall I reconcile it to a belief in a *personal* God', echoes Blatchford's 'I cannot believe that God is a personal God, who intervenes in human affairs. I cannot see in science, nor in experience, nor in history any such signs of a God . . .' (*GMN* 10), while his anger at biological suffering, 'Men – some – seem to be born and ruthlessly destroyed; the bacteria are created and nurtured on man, to his horrible destruction', also finds its echo thus: 'What of the infinite goodness of God in teaching the cholera microbe to feed on man? What of the infinite goodness of God in teaching the grub of the icheumon-fly to eat up the cabbage caterpillar alive?' (*GMN* 80).

Such sentiments are reinforced in Vivian's text, and Vivian's dramatizing of positions also finds its way into Lawrence's voice: '"How can we believe in a *personal* God?" asks the Rationalist. "A person must have limitations, or he ceases to be a person"' (*CMT* 164). Vivian places a heavy emphasis on the Churches' growing recognition of the 'duty of thinking'. Its failure, however, to pass this on to congregations – 'How is it, then, that we hear so little about Evolution from the pulpit?' (*CMT* 127) – recalls Lawrence's complaint that 'we hear of them' (the key issues) 'almost exclusively from writers against Christianity'. Vivian's critique resolves itself into an optimistic declaration of a 'scientific humanitarianism working on rational principles for the peace and happiness of all mankind ' – a progressivism which we do not quite find in Lawrence's wary, troubled letters. Yet even here, in Vivian's third-person sketch of his own progress, discriminating between the known and the unknown, we may find echoes not only of Lawrence's demand, 'what comfort can I draw from an unknowable', but also of his own declaration of the way a secular religion is pieced together: 'A man', Vivian writes, 'may enter, and generally does enter, upon his enquiry biased in favour of religious belief of some kind . . . . But as his enquiry proceeds there comes a time when his religious bias disappears . . . he discovers that what he thought was known, and had actually been revealed, is unknown. How can he believe in and worship the Unknown?' (*CMT* viii).

These rhetorical echoes suggest that Blatchford and Vivian made available to Lawrence certain structures of interrogation. While maintaining a critical distance both from militancy and from implicit faith in Enlightenment, we sense in Lawrence the pull of a passionate, humanitarian rationalism which found in socialism the continuation of an *intellectual* Christian spirituality which the established church itself had consistently reneged upon. If this is a recognizable cultural pattern for the educated working class, making it 'natural' for the 'educated young of Eastwood' to turn away from religion and towards 'the familiar alternatives – rationalism, humanism, social responsibility and political belief', we should be wary of thereby delimiting it as a brief phase of Lawrence's early development.[6] As the Reid letters reveal, Lawrence was deeply impelled by a sense of human and social injustice; rationalism, in the closely entwined forms of science and socialism, was the context in which he became aware of questions that could not be answered in 'a nebulous atmosphere of religious yearning'. While he would not relinquish his religion – 'I do not wage war against Christianity – I do not hate it' – neither would he relinquish rationalism.

In this light R.J. Campbell's *The New Theology* might have seemed an attractive alternative in its fervent attempt to forge a reconciliation between the two. Yet this is a text that elicited from Lawrence a curiously ambiguous judgement: he found it, he confessed to Reid, 'untenable, indeed almost incomprehensible to an ordinary mind that cannot sustain a rationalist attitude in a nebulous atmosphere of religious yearning'. Writing in the paper *The New Age* on 4 April 1907, Wilkinson Sherren aligned New Theology with 'the Labour Movement' and 'the Woman Movement' as one of three prominent 'signs of the times', and Jessie Chambers confirms that Campbell's thesis prompted most debate at the time within Lawrence's circle. Jonathan Rose records that, when the independent working-class woman Ruth Slate embraced the modernist 'New Theology' of R.J. Campbell, she came close to ostracism by her family.[7]

Campbell presented the New Theology as a universal, empirically verifiable encoding of spiritual truth, which those within the Church should work to articulate through rationalist principles. His argument for an absolute definition of truth – 'all truth is really one and the same' – implied that, as long as a scientific discovery is *true*, it is by definition also a religious truth' (*NT* 153). 'Dissonance between science and religion' thus becomes, not the 'natural' state of affairs as in Blatchford and Vivian, nor even undesirable, but, on the contrary, theoretically impossible. Human self-presence is the basis of Campbell's critique of Haeckel's materialism: in positing a Godless universe, 'the outcome of the fortuitous interaction of material forces, without consciousness and definite purpose behind them', Haeckel fails to realise that 'to disbelieve in God is an impossibility; every one believes in God if he believes in his own existence' (*NT* 18, 15). The search for truth which leads Haeckel to reject God is, in itself, proof of his belief in God. This strategy is duly applied to specific tenets of faith such as the Trinity. 'To use the mind at all', Campbell claims, 'we have to use this doctrine'; we are thus all (including Haeckel) trinitarian thinkers without knowing it. This somewhat presumptious project, acquainting everyone with the fact what they are really thinking or doing is an instance of faith, depends upon invoking science to discredit the superstitions of that faith, and then reinscribing revelation in the findings of science. Thus the Fall, the Virgin Birth, the Atonement, and even the immortality of the soul could be rationalized and re-read in terms of the 'comparatively new science of psychology': 'the mass of evidence for the persistence of individual self-consciousness after death is increasing rapidly, and is being subjected to the strictest scientific investigation' (*NT* 192).

'"It's not religious to be religious"', remarks Paul Morel as he challenges Miriam's soulful religiosity. A crow is religious in flight, but only 'because it feels itself carried to where it's going, not because it thinks it is being eternal' (*SL* 291). '"God doesn't *know* things, he *is* things."' Bitterly, he later observes to Clara Dawes that, had he stayed with Miriam, they would now be '"jawing about the 'Christian Mystery', or some such tack"'; yet Paul's Agnosticism is itself 'such a religious Agnosticism that Miriam did not suffer badly' (*SL* 371, 267). Campbell's New Theology undoubtedly provided an example of how religion might be rescued from the 'religious' by a process of reinterpretation. In Lawrence's case, anything done with a passionate integrity, such as politics or work, became religious. But there remains his evident dissatisfaction and even bafflement with Campbell – not only 'untenable' and 'incomprehensible', but 'practically an agnostic' and a 'mystic' combined, and one who did not 'solve any problems'. The latter seems particularly ironic, given that the *raison d'être* of *The New Theology* was precisely to 'solve' the epistemological riddles thrown up by evolutionary materialism, and to heal the wound between religion and science, smoothing over the differences between them with a distinctive combination of metaphysics and homely common sense. Yet here, perhaps, is the clue to the incoherence of Lawrence's reaction. The positions of Blatchford and Vivian had the virtue of clarity: science and religion were forever distinct, irreconcilable, and only socialism could hope to achieve a reasonable accommodation between them. Campbell claimed his reconciliatory exercise to be relatively unideological, steering a safe course between 'practical materialism' and 'dogmatic anti-quated theology'. Yet Lawrence remained unhappy with it, and it is unlikely that he could have failed to see in Campbell a more manipulative strategy than was evident in either Blatchford or Vivian. Are there differences between science and Christian theology? Let us, then, re-write the one in terms of the other, and all will be well. Ironically, given the mystical con-ception that 'truth is one even under contradictory forms of statement', con-demning language to be forever 'approximate' to it – 'statements of truth are but conventional symbols at best' – Campbell's text helplessly foregrounds the transparently *rhetorical* nature of the exercise. Everything we know about Lawrence's early religious crisis points to his sense that the dominant epis-temological questions were too tenacious to be assuaged by rhetorical sleight of hand. What emerges in *The New Theology* is a kind of glib pragmatism, in which pressing questions, not only of epistemology but also of politics and social justice, could be met by linguistic ingenuity.

Campbell's mediatory liberalism finally, however, revealed its own sense of fragility, and its inability to step outside of ideology, in gesturing towards an alternative politics within which to fuse the humanitarianisms of science and Christian spirituality:

(A)ssuredly Christianity has, for the moment, lost its hold. Can it recover it? I am sure it can, if only because the moral movements of the age, such as the great Labour movement, are in reality the expression of the Chris-tian spirit, and only need to recognise themselves as such to be irre-sistible. The wagon of Socialism needs to be hitched to the star of religious faith (*NT* 7).

Here Campbell's humanitarianism rejoins those of Blatchford and Vivian, endorsing the 'social instincts' of brotherhood and community in explicit opposition to the fragmentary impulses of individualism. What role might science have played in the contexts of Lawrence's early socialism?

3. Science and socialism: *The New Age*

It is clear that Lawrence and his early Eastwood circle saw themselves as hitched to 'the wagon of socialism' in some form or other. Introducing his paper 'Art and the Individual' to the circle in spring 1909, Lawrence spoke with playful irony of the collective aspiration to become 'perfect citizens – communists – what not'. In a second, written-up version of the paper, he began with a quotation from 'a Socialist member of Parliament' stressing that the current priority of socialists was to assuage the purely material needs of the poor and unemployed, and only after that to 'make the conquest of the intellectual and artistic world'. Satirizing this viewpoint from the rather arch, tongue-in-cheek aesthetic perspective of those who are 'not hungry and thirsty for material things', Lawrence writes this time not in the name of communists, but of 'we who are readers of "The New Age"'.[8]

Something of the intellectual texture of Lawrence's early socialism can be gleaned from a consideration of the weekly paper *The New Age*. Chambers notes that a member of the circle, a 'Socialist and a Suffragette' (possibly Alice Dax), had introduced them to it, and we know that Lawrence subscribed for a period between 1908 and 1909, suggesting a possible acquaintance stretching back to 1907, a landmark year for the paper when ownership and editorship changed hands. 'He liked it', observes Chambers, 'far more for its literature than its politics. He was never really interested in politics, and was quickly irritated and bored by the subject. We used to enjoy particularly the 'Literary Causerie' by Jacob Tonson'.[9] The paper attained a certain iconic importance for Lawrence: in the play *A Collier's Friday Night*, written around 1909, and in the unfinished novel *Mr. Noon*, drafted in the early 1920s, the paper figures in the opening scenes. What kind of writing and debates did Lawrence encounter in *The New Age*? If its function was, as Chambers has it, to inform Lawrence's developing aesthetic and cultural agenda, what role if any did science play in this agenda?

On 2 May 1907, A.R. Orage and Holbrook Jackson became owners and editors of the paper. Orage's subsequent reputation is as an influential advocate of Nietzsche, turning *The New Age* into one of the principal vehicles of Nietzschean philosophy in British culture of the period. Yet *The New Age* was primarily a political paper, and remained so throughout the years of Orage's editorship. Founded in 1894, with clear leanings towards socialism, the paper's shifting affiliations are registered in a sequence of subtitles, from 'A Journal for Thinkers and Workers' and 'A Democratic Review' through to Orage and Jackson's transformative gesture in 1907: 'An Independent Socialist Review of Politics, Literature, and Art'. From this point the paper is firmly dedicated to the establishment of a socialist politics in Britain, adopting an interested yet vigilant and critical position *vis-à-vis* the emergent Parliamentary Labour Party and its intellectual foundation, the Fabian Society. From within the latter, Orage had inaugurated the Fabian Arts Group, to 'interpret the relationship of art and philosophy to Socialism'.

The New Age became a means of disseminating ideas 'concerning the relationship between culture and the political and economic objectives of Socialism'.[10] Orage slowly began to build on the paper's openness to ideas and a trenchant mode of critique; its prior 'enthusiastic advocacy of the ideals of life' becomes a commitment to 'the new Social ideal' as embodied in the work of Plato, Ibsen, Goethe, Schopenhauer, Morris, Ruskin,

Whitman and Carpenter. The emergent socialism is non-doctrinal, 'disavowing any formula', and marked by the insistence that, despite the political strides made by the Labour movement, a Socialist transformation of society cannot occur until imaginative and intellectual stimulation have created the general will for revolution. No previous socialist review, it is argued, has attempted to co-ordinate the 'ideal and the reforming efforts of men' and to bend them thus to a single purpose.

This deployment of a Nietzschean vocabulary of 'will' in the service of socialist ideals signals a gradual increase in references to Nietzsche over the early months of Orage's regime; yet *The New Age* remains primarily a political paper, dealing prominently with the issues of the day in domestic and international affairs. The new culturalist influence emerges slowly in the character of its feature writing: A.J. Penty on 'The Restoration of Beauty to Life'; an animated debate around H.G. Wells' proposals for a Socialist Party; articles on 'Ibsen's Women' and 'Charles Dickens as a Socialist'. The paper develops a more cosmopolitan and internationalist ambience, explicitly dissociating itself from the parochial nationalism of Robert Blatchford's *Clarion*: Orage's first editorial insists that 'for us the barren negation of the old radical little-Englandism is impossible'. A distinctive interdisciplinarity was allied to this anti-parochialism: Orage, Wallace Martin argues, 'deliberately attempted to make *The New Age* a presentative periodical which would mediate between specialized fields of knowledge and public understanding', in the face of an increasing professionalization of disciplines.[11]

The recognition of this rich interdisciplinarity is, I think, very significant for our understanding of Lawrence and of the varied and hybrid modes of writing he was to develop. The 'Literary Causerie' to which Jessie Chambers referred was a short, anecdotal literary gossip column written in satirical style by Arnold Bennett. Chambers' brisk dismissal of the political content of the paper compares with her similar bracketing of science in Lawrence's development. It would, however, have been an act of extraordinary selectivity to concentrate on the 'Causerie' at the expense of the paper's broader interests. Granting that Chambers hints at a certain vanity and aspiration towards an involvement with the literary world, it remains implausible that a writer of Lawrence's intellectual appetite could have singled out this feature, or filtered out the literary elements of the paper at the expense of the rest. The function of the paper under Orage was, on the contrary, precisely to articulate the aesthetic in its relationship to the political, as part of a social totality, and thus to subvert that intellectual division of labour by which a politics of the Left could be suspected, in its liaison with Marxism, of being overly economistic and deterministic. To the contrary charge that *The New Age* was becoming too aesthetic in orientation, Orage responded on 28 January 1909: 'But the fact is that Socialism in *The New Age* is losing its bony statistical aspect and putting on the colours of vivid life'. Unashamedly, for Orage the socialist utopia would coincide with a new civilization of high culture based on the centrality of imagination as a primary creative power, counterbalancing the current overemphasis on the scholastic: 'much modern culture really incapacitates the sympathetic imagination'. At times, this high-culturalist emphasis became explicitly provocative. Orage wrote that he was 'appalled . . . at the poverty of imagination of Socialists who conceive of Socialism as no more than a redistribution of the wages of shameful toil'; and a refusal to entertain the sentimentalized idea of uncultured masses awaiting enlightenment produces an astonishing emphasis in the introduction to a series of articles entitled 'Towards Socialism' (3 October–28 December 1907). 'Nothing', Orage declaims, 'can exceed the hatred with which the Socialist hates the poor'; they 'get in the way of our plans', 'obstruct our sunlight' and make of themselves 'an intolerable and disgusting spectacle'. If there is provocative irony here, displacing a hatred of poverty onto those who suffer it, it is deeply buried, though Orage does argue that only when poverty is abolished can a great civilization be built.

It is intriguing to speculate upon the impact such an emphasis on the politics of imagination might have had on the Lawrence who wrote to Robert Reid about Sneinton. But if, in *The New Age*, utopia was tied to a culturalist agenda, then it was equally inseparable from a scientific vision. In Orage's observations on the poor we hear echoes of a scientific discourse on modernity shared by many across the political spectrum and rooted in the idea of social and technological progress. Orage knew that imagination alone could not produce the socialist utopia; rather, he subscribed to an enlightenment vision equally crucial to industrial capitalism, though distinctively fusing technological progress with a return to Eden:

> The most daring enterprises are opening before the eyes of men – the conquest of the irrational forces of nature, the subjection and transformation of all the devils and titans of earth and water, air and sky, the re-creation of Eden, and the return of man to the primaeval garden. That, at least, is the aim that Socialists have. And we are intolerant of anything less (3 October 1907).

Along with this vision of conquest and control went the necessary manipulation of human population itself. If poverty was to be addressed in part by economic transformation, it was partly also to be addressed by successful 'breeding': 'If we breed more paleoliths than civilized men we shall inevitably resume a paleolithic culture . . . . (T)he question is not of changing human nature, but the much more practical problem of providing conditions for the multiplication of the desirable and the extinction of the undesirable' (10 October 1907).

Propositions based on eugenics, the science of social and racial engineering founded by Francis Galton's work on hereditary genius, were a key element in *The New Age*'s utopianism. In the paper, Lawrence could access detailed debates around post-Darwinian evolutionary theory, but almost invariably with regard to the possibility of moulding the future development of the human species. If anything claiming scientific legitimacy had attained the 'common sense' status of ideology in Lawrence's early development, it may have been the idea of 'good breeding'. In their first editorial, the new editors proclaimed that 'the darling object and purpose of the universal will of life is the creation of a race of supremely and progressively intelligent beings', guaranteeing their co-operation with this 'purpose of life'. An anonymous article of 15 August 1907, 'Breeding a Race', presented eugenicist propositions as truistic: 'everybody without exception is prepared to admit that we ought to encourage the healthy and discourage the unhealthy from breeding'. A proposal by the novelist Eden Philpotts for a 'State Department of the Unborn' in March 1908 attracted support from other prominent eugenicists, leading to the advocation of policies on the state subsidy of mothering and on 'care in the cause of conception'. The latter reveals the biological or hereditary essentialism at the core of eugenicist thinking: 'it matters comparatively little', argued Havelock Ellis, 'what sort of education we give children; the primary matter is what sort of children we have got to educate'. Socialism, no less than 'Individualism', is seen to depend upon 'the breeding of individuals who count'; Caleb Saleeby called for 'immediate legislative action' to prevent reproduction in those deemed to be unfit. Such arguments seemed to modify the apparent amoralism of Orage's attitude to the poor by displacing sympathy and compassion from suffering individuals – the poor, the mentally or physically weak, or disabled – onto the general welfare of the human species (or British race) pursued via methods of 'social hygiene'.

Yet, at the same time, a series of articles by M.D. Eder, 'Good Breeding or Eugenics', published between 2 May and 25 July 1908, shows how far, and with what degree of subtlety, the paper was able to open up its scientific agenda to self-conscious critique. Eder begins by tempering confidence about the ongoing development of an understanding of heredity crucial to the cultivation of 'good human stock'. First, invoking the mathematician Poincaré, he insists that the laws of nature are 'simply convenient expressions': wherever we look in science, we find muliplicity – 'there are as many mathematics as there are mathematicians'. Second, he cites the question of class in the professional development of science, and particularly in the formation of eugenic principles. 'The scientific gentlemen who have been carrying on these valuable researches belong to the English middle class'; hardly surprising, then, that this should be the class whose fertility is encouraged by eugenics. Both factors emphasise the *situated* and ideological nature of scientific knowledge: the word evolution itself, Eder argues, has become a 'foundling hospital where we imprison, without further ado, all ideas of doubtful parentage', and we should be suspicious of any value-laden suggestions of what is 'higher' or 'lower' in nature or of what constitutes, for example, 'progress' or 'criminality' or 'insanity'.

From this sceptical opening, Eder's articles stage a nuanced debate around the impact of the emergent Mendelian genetics on evolutionary theory. Eder's preference is for the 'fluctuating variation' theory of the Dutch botanist De Vries, according to which a periodical tendency for sudden mutation is seen to be programmed into a species of plants or animals. De Vries thus attempted to revive a theory which Darwin had discredited, that of 'saltation' or sudden leaps in nature, while accepting that natural selection resumes once the rupture of mutation had occurred. The importance of this theory for Eder, as a scientist and socialist combined, lies in a potential for creative change based on the plasticity and unpredictability of nature – 'living things are extraordinarily capable of modification'. It is augmented by the work of Hans Driesch, on the growth of the fertilized egg, positing the 'infinite educability of animal tissues'. Driesch had concluded, contrary to the germ-plasm theory of August Weismann, that each division of the egg involves, not a division of separate materials which subsequently correspond to different parts of the mature organism, but a division of identical materials. For differentiation and growth to occur, the egg must behave in a way comparable to a conscious being, with actions which are 'not accounted for by any chemico-physical laws'.

The blend of evolutionary theory which gradually emerges from Eder's articles is a nuanced social Lamarckianism, in which the boundary between the biological and the social is consistently undermined: 'tissue' is 'educable'. Without arguing for deep patterns of genetic modification over generations, Eder sees it as undeniable that profound modifications to parents can affect offspring. Such transmission may not be direct, so much as the communication of a disposition or susceptibility which subsequent environmental conditions either encourage or discourage. Disease might be one manifestation, but in the human animal the influence of that part of the organism we call 'mind' would be another: 'Does anyone now believe that mind does not affect mind and body? Surely in such closely related organisms as mother and child we should expect a rapport to exist.' Eder borrows the words of J. Arthur Thomson, a translator of Weismann, to argue the point that, when these mental influences are embodied in broader cultural experience, they can be so powerful as to constitute, in effect, 'the same thing as if acquired characters were transmitted'; they are 're-impressed on the bodies and minds of successive generations, though never ingrained in the germ-plasm'.

Eder's politics are thus grounded in a theory of tentative balance, biologistic without being deterministic, stressing the interrelatedness, complexity and unpredictable creativity of life. Education and environment are integral to an evolution which, in a recurrent refrain in the series, teaches us 'the oneness of all things in the universe – the relationship, more or less intimate, that exists between what are called inorganic and organic things'. From this basis, Eder builds a sustained polemic against what is seen as the crude and politically coercive science of the work of Karl Pearson, early eugenicist and founder of biometrics. Subjected to satire are the sources from which Pearson compiles his statistical evidence for the inheritance of intelligence – the degree results of fathers and sons from Oxford, or questionnaires to middle-class families or schoolmasters. Eder excoriates a study of tuberculosis, out of which Pearson had recommended the discouragement of marriage in 'artisans', on the grounds that 'in a very large proportion of cases it does not lie in the power of the individual to maintain in the stress of urban life a wholly safe environment' (20 June 1908). For Eder this exemplified the discrepancy between Pearson's often hesitant presentation of his mathematics and 'the utmost vehemence and cocksureness' of his biological and economic deductions (9 September 1908). Science and class politics are equally at issue: given that it is the tendency to the disease that is inherited rather than the disease itself, the choice for Eder is clear: do you remove the human beings with the tendency, or the social conditions which encourage the spread of the bacillus? Tuberculosis is a 'poor man's disease', and the socialist answer is 'plain': 'the whole superstructure of modern civilisation must be swept away. We must learn to put another value on human lives than that of their commercial potentialities. "The stress of urban life" is making us into machines and machine-tenders' (20 June 1908).

In this defence of human value from the structures of urban and industrial capitalism, and from the perils of mechanism, Eder condemns the quantificatory methods of the biometricians not because of their scientificity, but because they are not scientific *enough* to comprehend the complexity of determining factors in human development:

> It is not strange that those who pretend to measure inherited traits to a decimal point, who are dissatisfied with any statement about living things that cannot be expressed in some mathematical formula, entirely ignore that which most impresses us. It is not strange because laboratory workers deal only with inanimate objects, and living things astonish us by their diversity, their extreme plasticity, their ready response to alteration in their circumstances or ways of living (27 June 1908).

Readers of Lawrence, and of traditional humanist criticism, will recognise a familiar note here: science deals only with dead things, and cannot account for the elusive subtlety of the living. Eder's articles demonstrate how far removed from Arnoldian and Leavisite caricatures of science were the debates and contexts in which Lawrence might have encountered this idea. From Eder, we derive a sense that science is always ideological and interested; that debates around evolutionary theory and its implications must be conducted at a high level of detail and discrimination; and that a science able to deal with the diversity and plasticity of life could only be a highly differentiated version of materialism rather than an alternative to it. Science in *The New Age* was thus an ideological battleground, the idea of the disinterested pursuit of knowledge all but disappearing from view. It was central to a vision of radical and intelligent social change, and equally instrumental in the hegemony of bourgeois capitalism, with the latter sometimes given a quite unequivocal emphasis. In the words of J.L. Redgrave Cripps, 'science has – especially during the last century – simply been the toady of Capitalism, under whose gracious patronage it has thrived and grown so self-conceited that it now thinks itself to be the most important activity in the world'. Eder explicitly foregrounds the symbiotic relationship between socialism and science in his own thought. Hence, in the last two articles in the series, the emphasis shifts towards a critique of marriage as the agent and cornerstone of bourgeois eugenics. Soon after, *The New Age* publishes a translation of Auguste Forel's essay 'Free Marriage', arguing for a new concept of marriage within which the sexual relationship is liberalized while the parental commitment to the raising of children is legally strengthened. Here, as in Eder, a commitment to positive eugenics – the reproduction of healthy human beings – coincides with an excoriation of capitalism: 'The reign of Capital – that is to say, of money – must cease, and economic reform must be affected in the direction of the complete reward of all labour; for the power of money corrupts sex relationships, and prevents them from being sane and natural.'

Within the space of a few years after Lawrence had encountered *The New Age*, 'M.D.' or David Eder, after collaboration with Sigmund Freud and Ernest Jones, became a principal advocate and practitioner of the 'subjective science' of psychoanalysis in Britain. He also became a good friend and confidante of Lawrence himself. Marriage, and the adjustment of relations between the sexes, becomes the explicit critical focus of Lawrence's fictional work, as if to confirm, not only the importance of translating scientific debate into fictional and cultural practice, but also the necessity of attending closely to the question of gender in the many-sided debate over 'man's place in nature'.

4. Science and gender: the New Woman

A woman is mystically, passionately absorbed in the contemplation of nature, polarizing a man into hard, ironical detachment. In Lawrence's earlier fiction, this scene is consistently reworked and revised. In *The White Peacock*, the narrator Cyril picks guelder rose berries for Emily, who is traumatized after having had to kill a stray dog which had been worrying the sheep. 'She stroked them softly against her lips and cheek, caressing them. Then she murmured to herself: "I have always wanted to put red berries in my hair".' Presenting Emily next with a crown of golden-leaved convolvulus, Cyril likens her to a Pre-Raphaelite image of an 'earnest, troublesome soul', caring only for the 'eternal pips' of the apple without being able to enjoy the flesh. 'She looked at me sadly, not understanding, believing that I in my wisdom spoke truth, as she always believed when I lost her in a maze of words.' When the gathering of fallen beechnuts prompts another sorrowful outpouring, this time about lost childhood, Cyril concludes that 'Emily had the gift of sorrow. It fascinated me, but it drove me to rebellion' (*WP* 69–70).

In *Sons and Lovers*, the scene becomes a recurrent motif of the failing relationship between Paul and Miriam. Miriam is to be found 'quivering' in 'communion' with the flowers, with Paul 'hating' her for it. In the culminating scene, Miriam persuades Paul, 'hard' and 'ironical', 'dissatisfied with himself and with everything', to look at the daffodils in her garden: 'Miriam went on her knees before one cluster, took a wild looking daffodil between her hands, turned up its face of gold to her, and bowed down, caressing it with her mouth and cheeks and brow' (*SL* 257). Paul 'stood aside with his hands in his pockets, watching her'; he observes her 'fondling' the flowers 'lavishly', 'bowing' and 'crouching' to them, 'sipping' them with 'fervid kisses'. A stream of accusations is released by Paul, 'mechanical' and almost involuntary, his body like 'one weapon, hard and firm against her': ' "Why must you always be fondling things! . . . Can you never like things without clutching them as if you wanted to pull the heart out of them? . . . You wheedle the soul out of things . . .".' Miriam is 'stunned by his cruelty'.

Early in *Women in Love*, the scene takes place in Ursula Brangwen's classroom, placing a more overt emphasis on the epistemological question which underpins them all – how to know flowers. Birkin, as school inspector, displaces Ursula's authority by interrupting the class on catkins in order to demonstrate how it should be done. He switches on the lights, making the room 'distinct and hard' after the previous 'soft dim magic' of the afternoon; Ursula's eyes are 'round and wondering, bewildered', her mouth 'quivered slightly'. The children should, Birkin insists, have crayons so that – in a distant echo of Gradgrind – they can record the 'facts' of difference between gynaecious and androgynous flowers, and it is these facts, rather than the 'subjective impression', of which a 'pictorial record' should be made (*WL* 36).

In a kind of reversal, it is Birkin who becomes 'absorbed' and 'intent', Ursula seeming 'to be standing aside in arrested silence'. But a familiar scenario is reasserted with the entrance of Hermione Roddice, who transforms Birkin's factual interpretation of the plants into her own 'strange' and rhapsodic discourse: ' "Little red flames, little red flames", murmured Hermione to herself.' Both Birkin and Ursula now stand apart, 'suspended', as they witness the 'strange, almost mystic-passionate attraction' the flowers hold for her.

What are the sexual politics of these scenes? In the essay 'A Propos of *Lady Chatterley's Lover*', Lawrence makes the schematic assertion that there are 'two ways of knowing': 'knowing in terms of apartness, which is mental, rational, scientific, and knowing in terms of togetherness, which is religious and poetic' (*PII* 512). It is tempting to map this onto the equally schematic impression of gender relations left by the scenes. Men, possessed of knowledge which tends towards the scientific, stand apart, 'an intellect like a knife' in Paul Morel's case, exposing the distorting emotional subjectivity of the woman's 'mystic' communion with the flowers. Yet each scene also hints at complexities beyond this simple external structure. Science is culturally associated with masculinity, and religious knowledge with femininity, but neither masculinity nor femininity, as cultural constructions, necessarily coincide with men and women. Cyril alludes to Emily's gullibility, yet he has little confidence in his own 'wisdom', which he associates with the power of language to convince and deceive. The uncertainty is echoed in the ambiguity of Cyril's own sexual identity. Similarly, just as Cyril can only ironically use the biblical symbol of the apple within a 'maze of words', Birkin refers at one point to 'the eternal apple', but in exasperation, 'hating his own metaphors'. Birkin too constantly pursues the enigmatic possibility of combining heterosexual love with a form of male companionship equally based on love.

In *Sons and Lovers*, the protracted struggle between Paul and Miriam is simultaneously a struggle within Paul's developing identity as a man and as an artist. The development of their love is filtered through a shared love of nature, though with crucial differences about how nature should be known. These are reflected in the adoption of roles, which in turn imply relations of power – teacher to pupil, as Birkin is school inspector to Ursula's teacher. Paul, 'beginning to question the orthodox creed', cuts analytically apart the religion in which Miriam 'lived and moved and had her being'. The violence of the scientific-analytic mode is expressed when Paul, trying to teach Miriam algebra, throws a pencil in her face; he is 'cruelly ashamed', the conflict in him combining exasperation with her misplaced attitude of religious devotion and intense pain at her suffering. Yet the conflict also arises because Paul is not entirely convinced by the scientific mode. He is becoming a committed artist, and the language of art and metaphor is always available to express empathetically the love of nature within which the relationship with Miriam develops. Thus, of their attraction to celandines:

'I like them', he said, 'when their petals go flat back with the sunshine. They seem to be pressing themselves at the sun'. And then the celandines ever after drew her with a little spell. Anthropomorphic as she was, she stimulated him into appreciating things thus, and then they lived for her. She seemed to need things kindling in her imagination or in her soul, before she felt she had them. And she was cut off from ordinary life, by her religious intensity, which made the world for her either a nunnery or a garden, or a Paradise where sin and knowledge were not, or else an ugly, cruel thing.

So it was in this atmosphere of subtle intimacy, this meeting in their common feeling for some thing in nature, that their love started (*SL* 179).

'Subtle intimacy' and 'common feeling' are forged, though in a context of tensions: Paul's personification of the celandines is an artistic anthropomorphism stimulated *by* Miriam, and is at odds with the masculine role of teacher-scientist.

There is, then, a sense in which the playing out of these tensions suggests an element of the performative rather than the essentialistic in Lawrence's theory of gendered identity.[12] It is true that, in a number of letters written to women friends between 1906 and 1908, we find Lawrence acting out the role of literary consultant, flexing his muscle with a scientific aesthetic which he applies with some manly though, it seems, un-selfconscious pride. Blanche Jennings is accused of 'foolish, feminine insinuations', and advised: 'To scorn emotions is to be a tottering emotionalist. Sentiment should be examined, analysed, known just as judgements – facts, if you like – are analysed.' Louie Burrows is warned that her essays contain too many adjectives and phrases which 'make the whole piece loose, and sap its vigour', while similarly in her short stories she should 'select the few salient details . . . , make some parts swifter, . . . avoid bits of romantic sentimentality . . .' (*LI* 45, 28–9). Jessie Chambers recalls the kind of tensions Lawrence's assumption of authority as a *botanist* (there are other reminiscences of this aspect of Lawrence) could create. In so doing Chambers effectively reworks the scenes we have been examining, writing for herself a much more resistant role than the fictionalized Miriam suggested:

There seemed no flower nor even weed whose name and qualities Lawrence did not know. At first I was sceptical of his knowledge.

'How do you know what it is?' I asked him.

'I *do* know', he replied.

'But *how* do you know? You may be wrong', I persisted.

'I know *because* I know. How dare you ask me how I know', he answered with heat.

I led him to where the foxgloves stood, like Indian braves, I said. He gave them that intense glance I was now so accustomed to I scarcely noticed it, and said nothing, and I thought he disliked my simile.[13]

The languages of art and scientific realism were not simply, as Graham Holderness suggests, alternatives from which Lawrence chose, the embrace of the former effectively consigning science to a brief if intense phase of his formation.[14] Lawrence's editorial recommendations are in fact easily assimilable with an Imagist aesthetic which was soon to emerge in, for example, the masculinist manifestos of Ezra Pound, recommending in poetic form something 'harder, saner, nearer the bone' and 'free from emotional slither'. This, for Pound, would be for the poet to embrace the 'way of the scientist'.[15] Science subtly informed aesthetics, just as aesthetics could modify the certainty of the masculine scientific pose. The assumed authority of Cyril, Paul and Rupert Birkin is undermined by their awareness of an entrapment in language, particularly metaphor, and this condition is summarized as an 'anthropomorphism', attributed to Miriam but transmitted to Paul. Yet, as Eder's articles in *The New Age* had suggested, science too was situated, human-centred knowledge, sharing the anthropomorphic condition as, it seemed, all discourses of knowledge must. The language of fiction provided a space for Lawrence to dramatize the many-sidedness of the epistemological problematic; yet art itself does not simply displace science in this dispensation, as the domain of an openness which science lacks. In certain respects Lawrence's art could be said to reinscribe dominant gender ideologies in less obvious ways. It is, after all, Lawrence's men, rather than his women, who become conscious of crisis in gender and epistemology, attesting perhaps to the continuing identification of men with knowledge and the 'adventure' of consciousness. The comparative one-dimensionality of women is particularly evident in *Sons and Lovers*, where the novel conspires against Miriam in its blending of Paul's observations with third-person narration, so that Miriam is interpreted through and for Paul.

Women are also caught in a peculiarly Lawrentian double-bind regarding the pursuit and acquisition of knowledge. The early narratives indict women for producing, in their male companions, feelings of violent antagonism or equivocation. Male rebellion from the intense emotive religiosity of the women takes the form of an entry into a rationalism which might, actually, be untrue to their characters, thus compounding the grievance: women are responsible both for the mystic-passionate communion with nature which repels men and for the rationality they take up in response. When the Brangwen women of the nineteenth century look out beyond the 'heated, blind intercourse of farm-life' towards the 'spoken world', where power is 'a question of knowledge', they do so on behalf of their menfolk, who are reluctantly dragged into that world. This prefigures a move, in the later fiction, into a more explicit sense of woman as the source of a mistaken 'idealism'.[16]

The complexities surrounding science and gender in Lawrence's earlier fiction are most vividly concentrated in *The Rainbow*'s treatment of the historical phenomenon of the New Woman. The 'New Woman' was essentially a *fin-de-siècle* conception personifying the development of female emancipation in the 1880s and 1890s through the rise of political feminism and educational and sexual independence for women. Sally Ledger has argued that the primary importance of the New Woman was as a 'discursive construct', a conceptual space within which women's aspirations could be articulated as well as contested.[17] In Lawrence's case this should not obscure the fact that, following an adolescence of 'having to define himself against a background of women', some of the most important influences in his circle would have been women, such as Alice Dax and Blanche Jennings, whose intellectual energies were inseparable from their socialist-feminism.[18]

The Clara Dawes of *Sons and Lovers* is Lawrence's first serious fictionalization of the New Woman. Instrumental in the 'defeat' of Miriam, Clara nevertheless features in a cowslip-picking scene in which her resistance to the activity – 'I don't want the corpses of flowers about me' (*SL* 291) – condemns her to the margin. Paul dismisses her approach with 'that's a stiff, artificial notion', the scene revealing how a love of flowers still constitutes the basis of what intimacy remains between himself and Miriam; though at the same time, Miriam's mystificatory justification of the picking – 'if you treat them with reverence you don't do them any harm. It is the spirit you pluck them in that matters' – attracts a more ambivalent rebuff; '"Yes . . . But no, you get 'em because you want 'em and that's all".' When such a *ménage* reappears in *Women in Love*, as we have noted earlier, there is a more decisive aspect of resolution: mystic-passionate womanhood is concentrated, and effectively exorcised from the novel, in the figure of Hermione Roddice, with Ursula, now an educator, juxtaposed with the watching Birkin. This role must, we might say, be connected to Ursula's prehistory in *The Rainbow*, where Lawrence mounts his most sustained representation of New Womanhood. In a discussion of representations of the New Woman and motherhood, Ledger rightly points out that Lawrence allows the personality of Anna Brangwen, Ursula's mother, to 'collapse into bovine, contented maternity'.[19] Yet Ledger neglects the more obvious point that *Ursula* is the novel's focus of enquiry into the 'New Woman'. The rise of Anna's daughter, whose painful and determined entry into the world of education and teaching achieves the breaking of a historical pattern, highlights the *questionability* of Anna's collapse into an unreconstructed motherhood.

Lawrence's placing of Ursula in the laboratory confirms Ledger's point about the discursive construction of the New Woman, in the sense that the scene refers intertextually to a closely contemporaneous novel, *Ann Veronica* (1909) by H.G. Wells. A brief comparison is revealing. For Ursula, the study of biology for her degree has a transformative effect. She decides to take Honours in Botany, 'the only study that lived for her', thereby escaping from the 'second-hand' realm of languages and literature. Ursula's disillusionment with university stems in part from a clear political critique of materialism in the *economic* sense: behind the pretence of the 'religious virtue' of knowledge and enlightenment she detects nothing more than a preparation for the industrial-capitalist market place, the college a 'little, slovenly laboratory for the factory' or 'inner commercial shrine', the professors offering 'commercial commodity that could be turned to good account in the examination room' (*TR* 403–4). At this time too, as she approaches her finals year, Ursula is increasingly beset by an awareness of an alternative existence, the nature of which she struggles to define, but which is mediated through the narrative voice as an apprehension of a 'glimmering' darkness, haunted by wild shadowy shapes, whose existence is denied by the culture of progress and enlightenment. She is conscious now of having a history behind her – the affair with her schoolmistress, Winifred Inger; her love for Anton Skrebensky and their engagement, interrupted by his military service; Anthony Schofield's proposal of marriage; friendship with enlightened New Women such as Maggie Schofield and Dorothy Russell; her experience as a teacher at Brinsley Street school – but of having emerged still directionless. On the afternoon of this key scene in the laboratory, she is excited in anticipation of Skrebensky's imminent return, and works with 'feverish activity' at 'some special stuff' under her microscope, a single-celled 'plant-animal' lying 'shadowy in a boundless light'. At the same time she is still 'fretting' over the earlier conversation with Dr. Frankstone, who had put to her a purely *scientifically* materialist view of life. The absence of 'purpose' or teleology prompts Ursula to consider the 'intention' or 'will' of the 'incalculable physical and chemical activities', 'nodalized' under her microscope: did the creature 'intend' simply to be itself, and in that sense is it 'mechanical' and 'limited'?

> Suddenly in her mind the world gleamed strangely, with an intense light, like the nucleus of the creature under the microscope. Suddenly she had passed away into an intensely-gleaming light of knowledge. She could not understand what it all was. She only knew that it was not limited mechanical energy, nor mere purpose of self-preservation and self-assertion. It was a consummation, a being infinite. Self was a oneness with the infinite. To be oneself was a supreme, gleaming triumph of infinity (*TR* 408–9).

In Wells' novel, Ann Veronica Stanley gains entrance to Central Imperial College as a student of comparative anatomy, thereby escaping from the clutches of her middle-class home and parents, and from the mounting pressures of courtship and offers of marriage. Like Ursula, Ann Veronica has encountered the ideas of the New Woman, becoming in her case actively involved in the Suffrage and Socialist movements. In the biology lab, Ann Veronica discovers the 'surpassing relevance' of science, concentrated in one aim: 'to illustrate, to elaborate, to criticise and illuminate, and make ever plainer and plainer the significance of animal and vegetable structure' (*AV* 130). A turning point in her scientific career is, however, the discovery of Capes, the demonstrator working under the scientist Russell. As her work with Capes takes its course, Ann Veronica becomes possessed with a craving, 'like a new-born appetite', for beauty, and discovers in Capes a similar preoccupation, leading him in discussion to display a 'quite unprofessional vein of mysticism in the matter'. Then, in the scene of revelatory significance which Lawrence could be said to have borrowed, Ann Veronica is working on 'microtome sections of the developing salamander' under a microscope. The scene shifts from Ann Veronica at the microscope, to Capes helping her at the microscope, to Ann Veronica scutinising Capes at the microscope, with 'something' then leaping inside her:

> She became aware of the modelling of his ear, of the muscles of his neck and the textures of the hair that came off his brow, the soft minute curve of the eyelid that she could just see beyond his brow; she perceived these familiar objects as if they were acutely beautiful things. They *were*, she realised, acutely beautiful things. Her senses followed the shoulders under his coat, down to where his flexible, sensitive-looking hand rested lightly upon the table. She felt him as something solid and strong and trust- worthy beyond measure. The perception of him flooded her being (*AV* 147–8).

As Ann Oakley notes, Wells presents Capes as the 'romantic solution' to the dilemmas of the New Woman.[20] Ann Veronica 'began by being interested in his demonstrations and in his biological theory, then she was attracted by his character, and then, in a manner, she fell in love with his mind' (*AV* 140). The final chapter of the novel presents the tableau of Mr. and Mrs. Capes standing by their hearth, some four years later.

How do these versions of women and science compare? For each woman, biology is a radical and inspirational science because its concern with 'life', the 'one study that lived' for Ursula, takes it beyond disciplinary boundaries: for Ann Veronica, its theoretical generalizations 'radiated out' into 'a world of interest that lay altogether outside their legitimite bounds'. In each case its stress on material connectedness relieves the (New) woman of the burdens of selfhood and social identity, Ann Veronica identifying with an 'eternal Bios' driven by natural selection and Ursula glimpsing something entirely separate from the known human world. So biology in each case becomes, first, a medium for something which seems to transcend it (beauty for Ann Veronica, religious epiphany for Ursula) and, second, a means of resolving issues in their personal and sexual lives. Following a discussion with Capes of the role of beauty in sexual selection, charged with personal significance, Ann Veronica seems to accept the functional rather than mys- tical definition: beauty, as Capes puts it, is not a 'specially inserted' quality, but 'pure life, life nascent, running clear and strong'. The romantic irre- sistibility of this particular embodiment of Bios means that Capes provides biological justification for the aesthetics of sexual selection and for the per- petuation of a heterosexual division of labour. Science in *Ann Veronica* matters only as a function in the marriage plot; once Ann Veronica has her man, it has completed its task and disappears.

The parallel scene in *The Rainbow* leads, by contrast, directly to Ursula's rejection of Skrebensky and of the marriage plot. Her enhanced apprehension of life initially leads to a more passionate acceptance of Skrebensky; her love for him grows in this second phase of their relationship. But the strength of her love is also inseparable from a sense of liberation from social convention, to which the rejection of marriage is crucial. Skrebensky is broken by this rejection, and Ursula thereby comes to realize in him a utilitarian and instrumentalist version of reason which her own, alternative experience of science enables her to analyse and dismiss. He 'seemed made up of a set of habitual actions and decisions', and is destined to go to India and take up his place as a member of the ruling class. Skrebensky himself realizes the 'cold, stark, ashen sterility' of this conventional world but, unlike Ursula, is unable to revoke it and the idea of marriage which is its embodiment in the sphere of personal relations. Ursula's sense of material connectedness with the single-celled organism under her microscope leads to the rejection of love and marriage in favour of 'something impersonal', though this can only be interpreted and ventriloquised by Ursula in terms of conventional sexual morality – 'was she just promiscuous'? (*TR* 440).

Lawrence's deployment of the New Woman in the laboratory appears, on this reading, less ideologically manipulative than that of Wells. He allows Ursula to retain science as a vital resource in her intellectual and sexual development and independence, where science appears in *Ann Veronica* as a pretext in a boy-meets-girl scenario. *Is* it science, however, that Ursula retains? As I have suggested, Ursula's experience with the microscope is one of religious epiphany, a recognition of the self's 'oneness with the infinite'. Is this just a reprise of woman in mystic-passionate communion with nature? There is an immediate plausibility to this reading, and to the broader suspicion that neither Wells nor Lawrence are prepared to allow the New Woman an authentic engagement with science *in itself*. Where Ursula's laboratory moment differs is in being as much Bergsonian as mystic-passionate. Through the intent scientific gaze itself, observing the 'bright mist of . . . ciliary activity' and the 'gleam of its nucleus', she arrives at a sense of 'creative', material identification, questioning the rigour of the logic by which identical reproduction or 'self-preservation' are, somewhat paradoxically, seen as the only goal of evolution. This logic, as Bergson had noted in *Creative Evolution*, cannot account for genuine change, the emergence of difference or of the unforeseen; it leaves science, in a recurrent phrase of Lawrence's, as a 'post-mortem activity', always able retrospectively to interpret change that has occurred in terms of a modified continuation of the same, but never able to predict the change itself. 'Laboratory workers', Eder had noted, encounter only inanimate objects. Only through her laboratory work, however, can Ursula study biological science with sufficient rigour to begin to understand what Eder called the 'astonishing diversity' and 'extreme plasticity' of living things.

If to articulate this critical version of science through Ursula is, in a sense, to feminize it, the novel thereby reveals the limitations of the dominant masculine ideology of science as represented by Skrebensky. Moreover, in the extraordinary episode of Winifred Inger in the chapter 'Shame', the novel reveals how highly discriminative this critique could be. In a sudden narrative about-turn, breathtaking in one who claimed that the novelist should always keep his 'finger out of the scale', Ursula's delicately handled, sensual affair with Winifred fails as the elder woman's life is redefined as 'perverted'. (*TR* 319). In an unlikely and unholy alliance, Winifred is married off to Ursula's industrialist Uncle Tom with unseemly haste; their consummation lies in a 'worship' of the machine, of 'impure abstraction, the mechanisms of matter', freeing them from 'the clog and degradation of human feeling'. Educated, socialist-feminist lesbianism is married to the mechanised, utilitarian horrors of Wiggiston, Lawrence's Coketown; Ursula needs to be separated from an extreme and sexually decadent version of science, and is rewarded with Lawrence's preferred version, in which 'the true scientist works in the sense of wonder'. Yet, in comparison to *Ann Veronica*, we see how far *The Rainbow*'s construal of science was able to challenge sexual stereotypes, at the same time as it enacts a subtler and more distant intertextual rewriting of a science antithetical to 'wonder' in *Hard Times*. Ursula's version of a wondering science is not that of Jessie Chambers' 'religious inspiration', but emerges out of the complex epistemological preoccupations of contemporary science itself. To this unpicking of stereotypes in gender and science we might add Peter Middleton's intriguing suggestion that, in the depiction of Ursula's grandfather, Tom, we find 'a portrait of a subject capable of a rationality largely confined to the senses, instincts and emotions'.[21] I want to return to this suggestion in Chapter 6. In the next chapter, however, I will suggest how the term 'wonder' might be rewritten as a mode of active uncertainty, agnosticism, intense critical inquiry, to be found in precisely those scientific texts which are held to constitute for Lawrence an impoverished and unsatisfactory materialism.

3
Writing Matter: Science, Language and Materialism

1. 'Alert' and 'didactic' science

> The actual fact is that in Cézanne modern French art made its first tiny step back to real substance, to objective substance, if we may call it so. . . . It seems a small thing to do: yet it is the first real sign that man has made for several thousands of years that he is willing to admit that matter *actually* exists.
>
> 'Introduction to These Paintings'

What did it mean for Lawrence to connect the art of Paul Cézanne with the 'actual existence' of matter? The judgement was in no sense purely art-historical. Early in 1929, Lawrence completed 'Introduction to These Paintings', the essay in which the claim was made, and as the year progressed two further, sustained discursive essays, 'A Propos of *Lady Chatterley's Lover*' and *Apocalypse*, emerged. Despite their differing focuses, all three essays show Lawrence, at this late stage in his life, returning to the subject of science with renewed, if still highly critical, interest. Science, he wrote in a draft fragment of *Apocalypse*, had become a 'nothingness' of the same order as the atom which now, according to modern physics, was unimaginable; and therefore, 'I give it up' (*A* 164). Yet Lawrence had spent most of his creative life claiming to give science up, and the essays suggest that he still had not quite succeeded.

Since the 1914 *Study of Thomas Hardy*, Lawrence had been building ambitious historical and theoretical frameworks around his aesthetic judgements, and the evaluation of Cézanne in 'Introduction' is no exception. Towards the end of the sixteenth century, the argument goes, the spread of syphilis inculcated a fear of the body and its sexuality which came to exercise a devastating effect on the imaginative capacities of a 'northern consciousness' soon also to be influenced by Protestantism and Puritanism. The plastic arts, Lawrence insists, are founded upon 'the intuitional perception of the *reality* of substantial bodies', and the creative act itself is dependent upon the interpersonal flows of sexuality and procreation (*P* 559, 556). However, with the rare exception of William Blake, European and American art takes flight from the body, trying out a variety of escape routes: for English art, into landscape painting; for Impressionism, into light; for Post-Impressionism, into the geometrical abstractions of Cubism. Nor is aesthetic discourse immune to this process: in a famous passage, Lawrence indicts the aestheticism of Clive Bell and the concept of 'Significant Form', as a mode of apology for or collusion with the flight from matter into idealism. Art and its discourses are in this sense only the nodal expressions of a more pervasive condition characterized as the 'modern bourgeois consciousness'. 'Vision', argues Lawrence, becomes merely 'optical', the fear of the body encoded in an ideal of scientific objectivity which establishes an ever greater distance between subject and object. The implicit subjugation and domination of matter is also expressed in the formation of a bourgeois sexual morality which keeps the body safely at a distance.

This, nevertheless, is a relatively recent history, and cannot account for the 'several thousands of years' in which matter was apparently denied existence. Readers of Lawrence know that it needs to be inserted into a broader history of *idealism*, traced back in his earlier writings to the philosophy of Plato and then in the love ethic of Christian theology. In *Twilight in Italy* (1916), for example, Lawrence sees the old Mosaic law of the Father increasingly challenged throughout the Middle Ages by a Christian emphasis on the 'God which is Not-Me'. As if in anticipation of a dystopian posthumanism, the movement of the Christian religion of love was 'towards the elimination of the flesh' (*TI* 116). In the religion of the Old Testament, flesh is 'supreme and god-like', knowing no other than its own sensuality: an old spinner woman he encounters on the terrace of the church of San Tomasso, and representative of the survival of this mode of being in modern Italy, 'was not aware that there was anything in the universe except *her* universe' (*TI* 107). Christianity, however, emerges as the expression of an evolving intellect capable of self-consciousness, where the latter consists in a separation of self from the world which it is not. The love ethic, orientated towards the recognition of others, is mirrored in the emergence of the scientific subject–object relation – albeit a relation complicated by the fact that in it the nature of *subjectivity itself* changes, so that the subject now objectifies itself *as* a subject. Momentarily, Lawrence argues, in the art of Renaissance Italy, the principles of Law and Love met in balance. Soon, however, the 'Northern races' pressed on ahead in their Christian pursuit of scientific enlightenment – self-consciousness, abstraction, 'purposive industry' – while Italy was impelled to 'go back' to the dark, sensual religion of the Father.

'Idealism' is thus located within a complex network of mutual associations between the domains of religion, politics, art and science. While Lawrence's prose can on occasions give the impression of pinpointing clear causal relations, the overall effect is less certain. For example, of post-

Renaissance Christianity as encapsulated in the English Puritan revolution of the seventeenth century, he writes that '(I)t was this religious belief which expressed itself in science', and in 'the empirical and ideal systems of philosophy' (*TI* 120). This shows how far Lawrence had travelled from the 'religion *versus* science' formulae of his early formation; it also guards against the simple demonisation of science as the cause of all our woes. A certain theology gives rise to a certain science, but that science, historically delimited, might not exhaust the meanings of 'science'. Crucially, while Lawrence was attracted to a science with the emancipatory potential to draw us closer to an understanding of matter and its complex movements, he comes to the conclusion that modern science, in its actual account of matter, threatens the opposite: it *idealizes* matter.

To underline this analysis, the 'Introduction' makes a sustained attempt to discriminate between different kinds of science, and thus to encourage the reader to consider science within the framework of epistemology – that is, of the theory of what we know and how we know it. The starting point of this enquiry is the notion that true creativity can apply as much to scientific as to artistic 'discovery'. In each case, Lawrence argues, the 'whole consciousness' must be involved, with 'mind' and 'intuition' working together in varying degree. There is, perhaps, a preponderance of intuitive or *'physical'* awareness in the creation of the art-work, and of the intellect in the scientific discovery; yet, he claims, modern scientists tend to work with the mind alone, forcing the instincts and intuitions into 'a prostituted acquiescence' (*P* 574). The same kind of balance is held to apply to our ability to understand or appreciate scientific phenomena. Three examples are given to illustrate the point. First,

The very statement that water is H_2O is a mental *tour de force*. With our bodies we know that water is *not* H_2O, our intuitions and instincts both know it is not so. But they are bullied by the impudent mind. Whereas if we said that water, under certain circumstances, produces two volumes of hydrogen and one of oxygen, then the intuitions and instincts would agree entirely. But that water is *composed of* two volumes of hydrogen to one of oxygen we cannot physically believe. It needs something else. Something is missing. Of course, alert science does not ask us to believe the commonplace assertion of: *water* is H_2O, but school children have to believe it (*P* 574).

In the second example, Lawrence rails against the linguistic and statistical hyperbole of modern astronomy. In such discourse, the mind is 'revelling' in words and figures, achieving an 'ecstasy' which is 'occult'. The body, however, constitutes an epistemological limit, a point beyond which the 'instinct and intuition can grasp no more', for 'the mind can assert anything, and pretend it has proved it'. This same sense of bodily limit is invoked in the final example, where Lawrence shifts to confessional mode to discuss the 'laws of evolution'. Tacitly, he refers to the hold that evolutionary theory has had over his thought, acknowledging 'years' of 'rather desultory or "humble" acceptance'. Now, however, he realizes that his 'vital imagination makes great reservations'; he cannot, 'with the best will in the world', believe that all of life has evolved from one original form, and has to violate his 'intuitive and instinctive awareness of something else' in order to do so. Seeking for anyone who might make him feel the truth of the laws, he finds only 'egoistic', 'cocksure' and 'ranting' scientists who cannot convince him that their knowledge is intuitively, instinctively sound.

This extended treatment of science raises a number of further questions. How do we read the deployment of terms such as 'instinct' and 'intuition' and their antithetical relationship to mind and intellect? Are these binaries anything more than the jaded and superficial by-products of a vague romanticism? What does it mean to grasp a scientific law, even if only in part, with the body? What might a science produced by 'the mind alone' actually look like? In this chapter, I want to suggest that Lawrence's model of an 'alert' science can be situated within a body of writing about the nature of matter. 'Alertness' here becomes an alertness to the complexities of materialist debate, and in particular to the role of language or writing itself in the configuration of knowledge. Lawrence saw in Cézanne a bold step towards the representation of an intensely problematic 'objective substance'; yet art history can equally see this as a movement towards abstraction, within which it is the substance of paint itself that is foregrounded – a reflexive turn towards the means of representation, rather than an embrace of a materiality beyond representation. Similarly, science comes increasingly to a realization of its textual condition, even as it knows it cannot be collapsed into that condition. In the texts he read, Lawrence found science transforming itself into, or becoming entrammelled within, the problems of epistemology.

Lawrence's writing about matter can be read in the interrelated context of three bodies of work: the amelioristic pragmatism of William James; Henri Bergson's philosophical enquiries into the thinking of matter; and John Burnet's seminal work *Early Greek Philosophy* (1892/1908). 'Is the world one or many? – fated or free? – material or spiritual? . . .', asked James in *Pragmatism* (PR 25). Lawrence had long been acquainted with James's proposal of the *'pragmatic method'* as the means of settling 'interminable' metaphysical disputes, and James's manner of posing the disputes would have reminded him that post-Darwinian evolutionary science had revitalized the central problems of a deeply embedded Western philosophical tradition: what is the world made of, and how do we know it? John Burnet's account of the early Greeks was a crucial contribution to Lawrence's awareness of the longevity of this tradition and yet also of the historical variability it embraced. His first encounter with the text, in July 1915, was a key moment in that gradual disentangling from Christian thought whose earlier stages we examined in the previous chapter. Lawrence confessed to Bertrand Russell that he had been 'wrong, much too Christian', in his philosophy, and to Ottoline Morel the determination to 'write all my philosophy again. Last time I came out of the Christian Camp. This time I must come out of these early Greek philosophers' (*L* II 364, 367). Burnet argued that 'the thing we call science' came into being with the early Ionians: it was 'an adequate description of science to say that it is "thinking about the world in the Greek way"' (*EGP* v). Yet, as Robert Montgomery puts it, such a science emerged 'before the abstract concept had even been evolved as a tool of thought', providing Lawrence with 'a way of thinking that was at once scientific and religious and that existed long before Christianity'.[1]

It seems likely that Lawrence had revisited Burnet for the 1929 essays. His analysis of the Book of Revelation in *Apocalypse* places a heavy emphasis on the influence of the early Greeks. Moreover, returning to 'Fragment 2', in which Lawrence had declared his final disavowal of modern science, an extended comparison of 'religious' and 'scientific' ways of knowing the universe takes as its starting point a recognition of the radical cultural difference of early Greek science:

> Besides, if we take the very earliest scientists, we do not jeer at them for saying the very things the old religions say. 'Water is the cause of all things', says Thales, and modern scientists refrain from jeering. But it needs a close study of the pagan conception of the universe in the sixth century B.C. to know what was really meant by water. And at the same time the scientists hate it when Thales is supposed to have said: All things are full of gods. – They consider he never would have said it. Yet it seems exactly the thing a 'scientific' mind might have said at the end of the seventh century, and leads us in to a profoundly interesting and revealing study of what Thales can have meant by 'gods' (*A* 160).

To ask what 'water' or 'the gods' might have meant, historically (and in a tone of scholarly curiosity which Lawrence for the most part strove to exclude from his prose – hence perhaps his suppression of this fragment), demonstrates a strong sense of cultural and conceptual relativity. 'What do we *mean* by matter?' James had similarly enquired, in a chapter pragmatically considering key metaphysical problems. Just as Nietzsche had claimed to identify the 'arch fallacies of reason' petrified in the conditioning activity of the linguistic subject – lightning *flashes*, energy *moves* – so James had turned his attention to 'the odd distinction between substance and attribute, enshrined as it is in the very structure of human language, in the difference between grammatical subject and predicate' (*PR* 43). We only know the 'substance' of chalk through the attributes which, it is said, it displays and which inhere in it – whiteness, friability, solubility in water, and so on. But the distinction implies that the substance, chalk, is an essence which is deeper than or interior to its attributes and therefore strictly inaccessible. So, argues James, with words like 'climate' and 'weather'; 'climate' organizes a number of thermometer readings as if to imply some causal entity which lies *behind* a day or a number of days, while meteorologists' use of the term *'episodic'* to describe the chaotic and unpredictable atmospheric conditions of Boston shows the organizing capacity of the term 'weather', intellectualizing the discontinuous in terms of a fragment of a continuous narrative (*PR* 43–4, 80).

James's summary of what the Washington weather bureau does with each 'bit' of Boston weather – 'It refers to its place and moment in a continental cyclone, on the history of which the local changes everywhere are strung as beads are strung upon a cord' (*PR* 80) – recalls precisely the manner of Henri Bergson's recurrent analysis of the Eleatic School. The existing textual fragments of Parmenides and Zeno, central figures in the School, were available in Burnet's anthology. Zeno had sought to support the materialism of Parmenides, defined as an indivisible oneness or *'it is'*, by pointing to the logical absurdities of the contrary view of the Pythagorean atomists that matter was a condition of multiplicity, the 'many'. If matter consists of units, Zeno maintained, then there can be no point at which those units become indivisible: the very idea of a unit of quantity contains the ability to divide it. Moreover, if units are separable one from another, they must occupy something called space; but by the same token, if space exists, it too must be 'in' something – 'So space will be in space, and this goes on *ad infinitum*, therefore there is no space' (*EGP* 317). In what philosophy came to know as Zeno's fallacy or paradox, the atomistic theory of divisible units of matter leads strictly to the theoretical impossibility of movement. 'You cannot cross a race-course', because 'You cannot traverse an infinite number of points in a finite time. You must traverse the half of any given distance before you traverse the whole, and the half of that again before you traverse it'; similarly, 'The arrow in flight is at rest', for 'if everything is at rest when it occupies a space equal to itself, and what is in flight at any given moment always occupies a space equal to itself, it cannot move' (*EGP* 318–19).

Bergson's critique of this position is instrumental to his own theories of *élan* and duration, although, as Marie Cariou has recently argued, he misreads Zeno's intention as literal instead of as a parodic exposé of the Pythagorean position.[2] According to Bergson, Zeno's argument misleadingly intellectualizes any movement from A to B by conceiving of it as the traversal of an imaginary line made up of endlessly divisible points. The concept of a series of intermediate points allows the possibility that the line *might* halt at each one, and even if it does not actually do so, 'I incline to consider its passage as an arrest, though infinitely short, because I must have at least the time to think of it':

As every point of space necessarily appears to me fixed, I find it extremely difficult not to attribute to the moving body itself the immobility of the point with which, for a moment, I make it coincide; it seems to me, then, that the moving body has stayed an infinitely short time at every point of its trajectory (*MaM* 247).

However, Bergson maintains, 'we must not confound the data of the senses, which perceive the movement, with the artifice of the mind, which recomposes it': when I am conscious of my hand travelling from A to B, I know that the movement is an indivisible whole, and if my sight allows my imagination to divide anything it is 'the line supposed to have been traversed' rather than the movement itself. There *is*, Bergson concludes, such a thing as real movement, which is indivisible; we need to relinquish the attempt to 'think the movable by way of the immovable' (*CE* 299); that is, by way of discrete units of quantity. If, therefore, by the same token there is real matter, then this too needs to be reconceptualized as the continuity of states or actions: '*All division of matter into independent bodies with absolutely determined outlines is an artificial division*' (*MaM* 259).

For thinkers of the early twentieth century, the early Greeks highlighted the terms of contemporary debate around materialism and idealism, and also the paradoxes informing that debate. In the preface to his third edition (1920), Burnet acknowledged the still-controversial nature of his decision to make Parmenides the 'father of materialism'. Existing orthodoxy emphasised that for Parmenides the 'being' or 'it is' was ultimately inaccessible to the world of sense, turning primary substance into 'a sort of "thing in itself"', a definition which in subsequent science it had 'never quite lost' (*EGP* 182). A radical idea of substance thus *becomes idealism* in its insistence that what we apprehend is not the reality of matter in-itself; it is reasonable to assume that when Lawrence refers to a 'several thousand years' tradition of denying matter he is looking back to this. Updating both the tradition and the paradox, William James observes in *Pragmatism* that Berkeley's 'idealism' is actually a pragmatistic corroboration of matter as something known through the senses, our sensations constituting effectively 'its sole meaning'. What was, on the other hand, 'the most effective of all reducers of the external world to unreality' for Berkeley was the 'scholastic notion of a material substance unapproachable by us, *behind* the external world, deeper and more real than it, and needed to support it' (*PR* 44). Cézanne's return to matter thus flew in the face of what was itself known as a *materialist* tradition; as Montgomery again notes, Lawrence's key assertion in at least one key work of philosophy, *Psychoanalysis and the Unconscious*, to which I will return in a later chapter, is that '"pure idealism is identical with pure materialism"'.[3]

How then might this network of sources – James, Bergson, Burnet and the Eleatics – enable us to reassess Lawrence's focus on science and the question of matter in 1929? Set against the bluff and impatient Johnsonian stone-kicking which is often the impression left by his rhetoric – Cézanne reacquaints us with matter, while science, revelling in words, facts and figures, denies it – there is evidence of a tradition of the closest dialectical scrutiny around the question of 'things' and how we might know them. As James wrote,

> Permanent 'things' again; the 'same' thing and its various 'appearances' and 'alterations'; the different 'kinds' of thing; with the kind used finally as a 'predicate', of which the thing remains the 'subject' – what a straightening of the tangle of our experience's immediate flux and sensible variety does this list of terms suggest! And it is only the smallest part of his experience's flux that any one actually does straighten out by applying to it these conceptual instruments (*PR* 82).

What James highlights here is the crucially ambivalent role of language or the 'conceptual instrument' in these debates. First, there is a palpable distrust of language, embodied in the anxiety that knowledge about the world might be reduced or 'straightened' into 'verbal solutions'; the phrase is James's but, as we shall see, it is echoed in many similar formulations in scientific and philosophical discourse of the period. 'Philosophy lives in words', he wrote, 'but truth and fact well up into our lives in ways which exceed verbal formulation.'[4] Yet, at the same time, James could alert his readers to a growing recognition (corroborated in Eder's writing for *The New Age*) that scientific theories are, likewise, 'a man-made language, a conceptual shorthand, ... in which we write our reports of nature' (*PR* 30). Similarly, for Bergson, science, whether modern or ancient, is 'tied down to the general condition of the sign'. It is the 'essence' of science to handle signs which, although of 'greater precision' and 'higher efficacy' in science than in normal language, nevertheless partake of the essential linguistic quality of immobility: 'to denote a fixed aspect of the reality under an arrested form' (*CE* 329). In this sense language for Bergson coincides with or is the expression of that 'cinematographical method' which prevents us from conceptualizing true movement; it can articulate only the imaginary line of infinitely divisible points between A and B rather than the movement itself, condemning us to the perpetual disappointment of 'the child who tries by clapping his hands together to crush the smoke' (*CE* 308).

'Alert' thinking about science was thus an *epistemological* alertness, entwined with and dependent upon linguistic analysis. In order to 'think movement' at all, declares Bergson, and whether in the framework of space or of time, 'a constantly renewed effort of the mind is necessary' (*CE* 329): to re-examine, for example, habitual notions of human development and its discernible stages – infancy, adolescence, maturity, old age – it is necessary to replace the formula '"the child becomes the man"' with '"there is becoming from the child to the man"'. In this light it is unsurprising that Lawrence should question the conceptualization of 'water' through a close attention to linguistic detail: water, 'under certain circumstances, produces', replaces water 'is *composed of*', with the qualifications 'very statement that' and 'if we said that' highlighting a crucial, self-conscious linguistic hesitancy. What is the 'something else' or 'something missing' that Lawrence seeks? The temptation to read this as an attempt to admit into the analysis a rogue irrationalism of the bodily 'instincts and intuitions' is offset by the sense that 'alert science' is a condition of semantic scrutiny which does not ask us to accept unthinkingly the proposition '*water* is H_2O'. The 'something else' required is an alternative language of knowledge denoted by the terms 'instincts and intuitions', and for which Lawrence had found substantial intellectual precedents. As Deleuze notes, 'intuition' in Bergson was a mode of philosophical 'precision': 'neither a feeling, an inspiration, nor a disorderly sympathy, but a fully developed method'.[5] It was in this sense that Bergson believed the philosopher should 'go further than the scientist' (*CE* 369), into a realm of unfamiliarity exceeding 'the human state'.[6] Alternatively, evolutionary discourse, not only in Bergson's contestatory mode but also from Darwin to Samuel Butler's *Life as Habit* (1910), made available a way of conceptualizing 'instinct' as a mode of 'inherited memory' or unconscious, bodily knowledge.

In the rest of this chapter I want to examine the necessary entwining of language and science in texts which formed the basis of Lawrence's early materialism. This need be seen neither as the dilemma of science's imprisonment within language, nor as a collapsing of scientific epistemology into linguistic relativity. Rather, language plays a full part in the quest for scientific knowledge, even as that quest is problematized by science's growing awareness of its modern(ist), epistemological limits. If, as I have begun to suggest, William James's pragmatic interventions come to typify this situation, it is worth noting Cornel West's astute assessment of the Jamesian position. The pragmatic theory of truth, West argues, shifted 'talk about truth to talk about knowledge, and talk about knowledge to talk about the achievements of human powers and practices'. In so doing, James 'rejects all forms of epistemological foundationalism yet preserves a realist ontology'; while we can afford no complacency in thinking matter, such scepticism forms the very basis of a conviction that things exist and can be known.[7] In the writing of late nineteenth-century evolutionary science, we see what it might mean to realize the significance of this delicate balance.

2. Darwin, origins and the arbitrary

> In the beginning – there never was any beginning, but let it pass. We've got to make a start somehow. In the very beginning of all

things, time and space and cosmos and being, in the beginning of these was a little living creature. But I don't even know if it was little . . .

Where you got the living creature from, that first one, don't ask me. He was just there. (*FU* 21–2)

The usual abbreviated title of Charles Darwin's seminal text, *The Origin of Species* (1859), is misleading in at least one important sense.[8] 'Origin' was an emotive word for Darwin's Victorian readership, for where lay the source of distinct species but in individual acts of divine Creation? This orthodoxy remained firm, despite a tradition of evolutionary or 'transformist' thinking stretching back well before 1859, and was bolstered in fact by the 'natural theology' established by William Paley's 1802 text of that name, whose theories of design were, as Cosslett argues, highly influential in the formation of Darwin's science.[9] Darwin's *Origin*, however, famously sidestepped acts of creation. As its full title (*The Origin of Species by Means of Natural Selection or, the Preservation of Favoured Races in the Struggle for Life*) indicates, the aim of the text was to explain a theory, natural selection, whereby the origin of any species was merged into a continuum of change covering the now-unthinkably vast timespan of the earth's history. Nor, Darwin did his best to insist, did the *Origin* have anything to do with the origin of life itself. If the 'origin' of species means anything at all, then, it is as an act of classification, by which we decide at which point a creature has attained to a sufficient degree of distinctiveness to be called a species rather than, say, a variety. Origins lie in language: they have nothing to do with essential material identities. It would, noted Darwin, with an ironic twinkle, come as 'no slight relief' to naturalists to be freed from 'the endless disputes whether or not some fifty species of British brambles are true species' – freed, in other words, from 'the vain search for the undiscovered and undiscoverable essence of the term species' (*OS* 365). Origins instead partake of the arbitrariness of human decision-making in language:

(I)t will be seen that I look at the term species, as one arbitrarily given for the sake of convenience to a set of individuals closely resembling each other, and that it does not essentially differ from the term variety, which is given to less distinct and more fluctuating forms. The term variety, again, in comparison with mere individual differences, is also applied arbitrarily, and for mere convenience sake (*OS* 108).

However, as commentators were quick to point out, Darwin could not completely have his way with the word 'origin'. The theory of natural selection could not be advanced without some negotiation of the origin out of which evolution unfolded, for evolution implies, in theory, the ability to trace descent. Darwin sought to preserve some vestige of design – perhaps as much for his own needs as for the sake of public opinion – in referring to 'the laws impressed on matter by the Creator'; but what could be known about the original form of this matter? Unable to circumvent the need for something to kick-start natural selection, Darwin was drawn in the concluding chapter of the *Origin*, with an unconvincing hesitancy, to speculate upon 'some four or five progenitors' from which all animals have derived, plants from an 'equal or lesser number', and then by a process of analogy to infer that 'all the organic beings which have ever lived on this earth have descended from one primordial form, into which life was first breathed' (*OS* 364). But, as the scientist and contemporary reviewer Thomas Wollaston wryly observed, if we can admit that life was first 'breathed' into one form, why should the Breather stop at one?[10] In his Belfast Address of 1874 to the BAAS, John Tyndall noted with scepticism the element of vagueness surrounding the 'one primordial form', observing that an anthropomorphic notion of creation, 'which it seemed the object of Mr. Darwin to set aside, is as firmly associated with the creation of a few forms as with the creation of a multitude'.[11]

Origins, then, matter, both to our knowledge of the universe and natural order, and to the logics of scientific explanation. 'We've got to make a start somehow', though who knows the dimensions of that first creature: 'he was just there'. Lawrence's knockabout treatment in *Fantasia of the Unconscious* (1922) gently parodies what he knew to be an issue that bedevilled materialist science. 'When we postulate a beginning', he had written in more sober vein, 'we only do so to fix a starting point for our thought'; 'science', he continues, 'supposes that once the first forces were in existence, and the first motion set up, the universe produced itself automatically, throwing off life as a by-product, at a certain stage' (*SM* 176, 178). Jacques Barzun underlines the point, confirming that Darwin was not the only one of Lawrence's materialist thinkers to have to confront the question of the 'origin':

> Huxley and Spencer scouted the idea of a Creator making a live creature: that was incredible and superstitious; everything must be explained by the 'more rational' system of small increments; but almost in the same breath they requested their hearer to grant them, for scientific purposes, the creation of life in a single small piece of matter. Only grant it and they would explain the rest.[12]

Strictly and paradoxically, the evolutionary materialism of Darwin, Huxley and Spencer required an emanation of something from nothing to make it thinkable: its naturalism is dependent upon a moment of supernatural intervention. Aware of this logical contradiction, and thus periodically fond of teasing science by referring to its 'occult' conditions – 'It is marvellous how science proceeds like witchcraft and alchemy, by means of an abracadabra which has no earthly sense' (*FU* 156) – Lawrence drew an alternative logic or sense from Parmenides, whose 'It is' dispensed with origins and endings; in Lawrence's words, 'There never was a beginning, and there never will be an end to the universe. The creative mystery, which is life itself, always was and always will be. It unfolds itself in pure living creatures' (*SM* 176).

At stake in the issue of the origin was thus the precision and rationality with which we think matter. In dwelling on the issue at length in his famous Belfast Address, John Tyndall was unequivocal about the need for clarity and rigour: the only alternative, he maintained, to 'open(ing) our doors freely to the conception of creative acts' was to 'radically change our notions of matters'.[13] His far-reaching address did not stop at the origin of matter, but confronted further questions of origin which were also questions of boundary and change: how does the inorganic become the organic, and how does matter become consciousness? Existing notions of matter, deriving from the physics of Democritus, and 'as defined for generations in our scientific textbooks' (we think of Lawrence's observation on schoolchildren and H_2O), rendered such transitions logically impossible, because they implied a process of physical mechanism whose animation lay elsewhere. Descartes' absolute division of the material and mental into utterly heterogeneous entities extends and reinforces this impossibility.[14] However if, argues Tyndall, we trace 'the line of life' back to the minutest organisms, and continue on into inorganic nature, where (in the manner of Zeno and Bergson) the ceaseless division of the fragments of a magnet cannot erase the polarity of the whole, we arrive at the necessity for a new definition of matter: not as an empty physical capacity waiting to be animated by 'life', but as *life* in itself, containing the 'promise and potency' of all forms. Such materialism, Tyndall concedes, may be 'different from what you suppose'.[15] Lawrence's version of this new-old materialist logic – life simply unfolding itself in creatures – can at times make him sound like the most recalcitrant of empiricists: 'There is nothing in the world that is true except empiric discoveries which work in actual appliances' (*FU* 151). By contrast, evolutionary science appears as a mode of abstraction, both in its requirement of a supernatural origin and in the teleology which begins to accrete around the notion of natural forms unravelling in ever-greater fitness and sophistication. As Anne Fernihough has argued, Lawrence detected, in evolutionary theory and its assumption of a linear, progressive model of time, a deferral and devaluation of bodily, creaturely identity: presence is rendered abstract, subordinated to the narrative of which it is seen to be a part.[16]

Yet in certain respects, the Darwin of the *Origin* could hardly have disagreed with Lawrence's position. Lawrence's passion for living, empirical proof echoes Darwin's insistence that his theory is based, more than ever before, on looking at what is really there in nature: if only biologists would do so, the artifice of their taxonomy and the species/variety distinction which sustains it would be immediately revealed. '(T)here are not many men', he boasted, 'who will laboriously examine internal and important organs, and compare them in many specimens of the same species'. To do so is to realise that nature consistently eludes or exceeds our categories: 'systematists', he noted pointedly, 'are far from pleased at finding variability in important characters' (*OS* 37).

In this sense the *Origin* is a text which wrestles consistently and explicitly with the paradoxes of its own making. We must look at what is there; yet to do so is to find that nothing is 'there' in the accepted sense except a condition of process – things so radically in a state of becoming something else as to invite Bergson's dissolution of the linguistic category of the subject itself: 'there are no things, there are only actions' (*CE* 248). 'Science', argues Lawrence's narrative voice in one of the many discursive interludes in the novel *Kangaroo* (1923), 'must start from definition, or from precise description'. Again, Darwin would hardly have disagreed. 'It is so easy to hide our ignorance under such expressions as "the plan of creation", "unity of design", &c., and to think that we give an explanation when we only restate a fact'; in moving towards explanation based on natural selection, 'the terms used by naturalists . . . will cease to be metaphorical, and will have a plain signification' (*OS* 363, 365). But is there any compatibility between a language of precision and a condition of evolutionary process? Lawrence continued:

> And you can never define or precisely describe any living creature. Iron must continue iron, or cease to exist. But a rabbit might evolve into something which is still rabbit, and yet different from that which a rabbit now is. So how can you define or precisely describe a rabbit? There is always the unstable *creative* element present in life, and this science can never tackle. Science is cause-and-effect (*K* 294–5).

Darwin's attempt at common-sense negotiation – 'species come to be tolerably well-defined objects, and do not at any period present an inextricable chaos of varying and intermediate links' (*OS* 137) – can never be so entirely convincing as to expunge the fundamental arbitrariness of the species/variety distinction elaborated elsewhere in the text.

Lawrence's 'alert' science might thus be located within the contradictory spaces of the *Origin of Species*. 'However we may differ from him,' wrote Samuel Butler, 'it is he himself who shows us how to do so, and whose pupils we all are.'[17] Despite its passages of assertiveness, at which Darwin dares to realize the momentous significance and future potentialities of his theory, the *Origin* is a tentative and provisional abstract of an enormous body of research: constantly apologising for its inability (due to the urgency of the need for publication) to include the necessary weight of evidence; continually alluding, in a model of Popperian falsifiability, to the ways from which it might be differed, whether in the form of the 'imperfection' of the geological record, the absence of a theory of genetics to help account for heritability or variation, or of the many other 'difficulties on theory'. The aim of the *Origin* was to persuade the reader that the material evidence of evolution through natural selection could be *seen*: in geological strata; in the findings of comparative anatomy; in the analogous breeding of domestic animals and cultivation of plants. Because this meant seeing *change*, the text becomes preoccupied with the question of intermediacy and related issues: linkage, gradation, limit, transgression, the transition from quantitative to qualititative difference. As Darwin saw it, 'the chief cause of our unwillingness to admit that one species has given birth to other and distinct species, is that we are always slow in admitting any great change of which we do not see the intermediate steps', yet the living world does not present evidence everywhere of 'innumerable transitional forms' (*OS* 362, 132). Faced then, as it were, with a blinding lack of evidence, and with the necessity of having to conceive of change occurring though the vastness of evolutionary time rather than through the Biblical span, we return to the idea of a science which of necessity renders the immediate present illusory, and the unobservable, real. For this reason, perhaps, evolutionary science was regularly drawn to the rhetoric of extremes:

> The difficulty is the same as that felt by so many geologists, when Lyell first insisted that long lines of inland cliffs had been formed, and great valleys excavated, by the slow action of the coast-waves. The mind cannot possibly grasp the full meaning of the term of a hundred million years; it cannot add up and perceive the full effects of many slight variations, accumulated during an almost infinite number of generations (*OS* 362).

This may of course be an example of what Lawrence called 'occult ecstasy' in science, an implicit 'revelling' in the mind's inability to 'grasp' words and figures. The illogical phrase 'almost infinite' – for where does the finite become the infinite? – reveals the blind spot in the thinking of origins which Lawrence, with the help of the early Greeks, had detected in evolutionary science. But also implicit is a degree of speculation on the nature of knowledge and the knowing faculty itself. What is it for the mind to 'grasp'? Does Darwin assume that, beyond a certain magnitude in the phenomenon to be thought, the mind cannot go? If so, how are such limits set? The epistemological anxieties of the *Origin* are periodically registered in a dialectic between the faculties of reason and imagination. In another famous passage concerning the difficulties of intellectual 'grasp', Darwin asks how it might be possible to think the evolution of the eye by natural selection, given that we do not know of any of the 'transitional grades' of the organ's development. An evolved eye initially seems, he confesses, 'absurd', and 'insuperable to the imagination'; but 'reason' ought to conquer the imagination, in allowing us to build, from the first elementary nerves becoming sensitive to light, up to the extreme sophistication of the eye of the eagle. Thus 'reason' is presented as a faculty superior to imagination in the creative effort to think the otherwise unthinkable. 'Imagination' is the means by which we 'unavoidably' compare the creation of the eye to the construction of a telescope, but this, Darwin maintains, confirms its merely anthropomorphic character, presumptuously comparing the works of the Creator (through natural selection) to those of the human intellect. Reason goes further, incorporating and developing imagination (as in Bergson's estimation of philosophy's relation to science), so that the realm of the thinkable can move beyond a recognizably 'human' state.

It is likely that Lawrence could still find in Darwin evidence of that dogmatic, egotistical science of which he was so suspicious: 'as natural selection works solely by and for the good of each being', the *Origin* proclaimed, 'all corporeal and mental endowments will tend to progress towards perfection' (*OS* 368). But the fascination of the text lies in the uneasy, often contradictory co-existence of this ideological vision of progress and perfection, with an alertness to the vulnerability of his theory and to the precarious conditions of the possibility of scientific knowledge itself. I have elsewhere described this as a version of Keatsian 'negative capability' in the *Origin*, a creative problematizing of the thinking of matter and change.[18] In the terms of Cornel West's definition of Jamesian pragmatism, Darwin clung fervently to a realist account of creaturely being, whilst rejecting the essentialist foundations which had previously made such being explicable. In the next section, I will suggest that an even more unlikely source of this productive dialectic for Lawrence was Herbert Spencer's *First Principles*.

3. Herbert Spencer: thinkability[19]

Herbert Spencer's influence as a popular theorist of evolution may have surpassed that of Darwin in late nineteenth-century British and European culture. In the fifth and sixth editions of the *Origin*, Darwin modified his comments on psychology in order to concede a certain priority to Spencer's version of evolution, more Lamarckian than natural-selective. Modern commentators seem, however, unable to dispense with a note of satire in sketching connections between the Spencerean 'synthetic philosophy', ground out in a prose style of somewhat relentless turgidity, and a life which, as George Eliot put it, offered 'little material' for the biographer.[20] In contrast to the elements of apologetic provisionality in Darwin's writing, Spencer's rigid independence (the myth is that he did not read books, and certainly not those of thinkers with whom he sensed disagreement) was expressed in a single-minded theoretical determination and confidence. Again, there is a surprisingly firm critical consensus that what Spencer sought was a scientific theory which would explain and justify a prior *ideological* position. Malthusian demographics had indicated that a ceaseless struggle for the means of existence – Spencer's 'survival of the fittest' – was nature's mechanism for dealing with the catastrophic implications of sustained, unhindered population growth. This combined, for Spencer, with a belief that the economic individualism of *laissez faire* led eventually to social and moral perfection. As Adrian Desmond puts it, 'Spencer needed to establish a directional change in history – a forward-moving, *progressive*, ceaseless change; and it was this social imagery that was largely back-projected into nature.'[21] A Lamarckian developmentalism first served this purpose, giving way in his later work to an all-encompassing law of matter or 'persistence of force' by which all aspects of life are evolving inexorably from the homogeneous to the heterogeneous, the simple to the complex, the chaotic to the harmonious. Evolutionary biology in Spencer was thus the foundation of sociology: the relentless, wave-like progress of evolution was as discernible in the development of human society and culture as it was in the matter of the cosmos and of all organic life. Spencer's faith in this idea of evolution was, as Burrow puts it, so strong that 'it did not wait on scientific proof'.[22]

Lawrence had read Spencer's *First Principles* (1862); in *Sons and Lovers*, a young Paul Morel gently derides his mother's out-of-touchness with '*You* don't care about Herbert Spencer' ('And *you* won't, at my age', she replies) (*SL* 251). Roger Ebbatson detects ideas which are 'pure Spencerean doctrine', a 'naked doctrinal indebtedness' in the *Study of Thomas Hardy* and then in the rhythmic and generational patterns of *The Rainbow*.[23] Sure enough, in the *Study*, Lawrence seems to rehearse Spencer's idea of progressive differentiation, albeit hedged by a certain hesitancy in the recurrent phrase 'as if':

> It seems as though one of the conditions of life is, that life shall continually and progressively differentiate itself, almost as if this differentiation were a Purpose. Life starts out crude and unspecified, a great Mass. And it proceeds to evolve out of that mass ever more distinct and definite particular forms, an ever-multiplying number of separate species and orders, as if it were working always to the production of the infinite number of perfect individuals, the individual so thorough that he should have nothing in common with any other individual. It is as if all coagulation must be loosened, as if the elements must work themselves pure and free from the compound (*STH* 42).

Is this, perhaps, the early, 'desultory' and 'humble' acceptance of the laws of evolution that the Lawrence of 1929 reflected back upon? For at least one other critic, however, Spencer's 'inadequacies' could not have been lost on Lawrence; Spencer, like Haeckel, represents the 'positivist temper at its most superficial' and, while a valuable source of 'scientific ideas and formulations', could have been 'of little use to Lawrence *philosophically*'.[24]

How then might we reconstruct the significance for Lawrence of a thinker like Spencer? A clue lies, perhaps, in paying attention to *First Principles* in terms of its manner of enquiry as much as in its 'ideas' or doctrine. I have already suggested, in Chapter 1, that Spencer's writing showed a highly self-conscious concern with the nature of thought processes. Accordingly, the evolutionary theory in *First Principles*, which, for Roger Ebbatson, impressed Lawrence so deeply, begins to unfold only in the second half of the text. Prior to this, and especially in Part One, 'The Unknowable', the reader encounters a strenuous attempt to establish clearly what it is and is not possible to know. If we compare, here, Spencer's detailed treatment of 'origins' with that of Darwin, he appears to go directly to the centre of the *epistemological* territory that Darwin had declined to enter. We may, Spencer maintains, speculate upon how life began, but is it possible to conceive of origins *per se*? Three theories of the origin of the universe – self-existence, self-creation, and creation by external agency – and four fundamental concepts – Space, Time, Matter and Motion – are examined. Taking, for example, the theory of the creation of the universe by external agency, Spencer immediately problematizes the ubiquitous assumption, whether of the 'rudest creeds' or of modern society, that this creation is analogous to human manufacture:

> Now not only is *this conception one which cannot by any cumulative process of thought, or the fulfilment of predictions based on it, be shown to answer to anything actual*; but it *cannot be mentally realized*, even when all its assumptions are granted. Though the proceedings of a human artificer may *vaguely symbolize* a method after which the Universe might be shaped, yet *imagination of this method* does not help us to solve the ultimate problem; namely, the origin of the materials of which the Universe consists. The artizan does not make the iron, wood, or stone, he uses, but merely fashions and combines them. If we suppose suns, and planets, and satellites, and all they contain to have been similarly formed by a 'Great Artificer', we suppose merely that certain pre-existing elements were thus put into their present arrangement. But whence the pre-existing elements? The production of matter is the real mystery, which *neither this simile nor any other enables us to conceive*; and *a simile which does not enable us to conceive this may as well be dispensed with* (FP 26–7; my italics).

Here Spencer, like Darwin, is convinced of the habitually anthropomorphic nature of our thinking about the universe, embodied as it is in 'analogy', 'symbolization', 'imagination', 'simile'. He aligns himself more closely with the Eleatics and with Bergson, however, in the persistent effort to identify the difficulty surrounding the thinking of the origin of matter. We can form a 'conception' of the universe as created by a divine artificer, but this conception differs from something that can be 'mentally realized'; it might 'vaguely symbolize' the origin, but it does not precisely 'answer to anything actual'.

Spencer's theory of thought is a kind of conceptual literalism or reflectionism, assuming a clear distinction between conceptions which are 'symbolic' and those which are 'real'. Scale or magnitude plays a crucial role: some things are too big to think, some too small. We can no more think the reduction of the tiniest unit of matter to nothing than we can think the Earth or the universe as a whole. Language, Spencer concedes, does represent a kind of 'verbally intelligible' thinking: the word Earth does indeed call up in us a state of consciousness, while we can join 'the word *self* to the word *existence*' and thus 'form a conception of existence without a beginning', in the manner of Parmenides, perhaps. But such conceptions, effectively constituting a 'large proportion' of our consciousness, are 'indirect' rather than 'actual' conceptions; they are not even conceptions 'properly so-called', but are 'only' symbolic (*FP* 20). Spencer figures the remoteness of 'real' or pictorial conceptual plenitude in a series of reworked phrases: 'by no mental effort can we do this', 'a thing of which no idea is possible', 'now it is impossible to think this'. It is equally impossible, Spencer maintains, to 'say at what point in the series our conceptions . . . become inadequate' (*FP* 22); yet, the very distinction between 'real' and 'symbolic' commits him to the theoretical possibility of gradation between the two, and to a critical vigilance surrounding the moment of transition, which is always a moment of loss: 'When our symbolic conceptions are such that no cumulative or indirect processes of thought can enable us to ascertain that there are corresponding actualities, nor any fulfilled predictions be assigned in justification of them, then they are altogether vicious and illusive, and in no way distinguishable from pure fictions' (*FP* 22–3).

'"You don't walk upon flowers in fact; you cannot be allowed to walk upon flowers in carpets"' (*HT* 52). In Dickens's *Hard Times*, Thomas Gradgrind's version of factual perception issues in an aesthetic warning to Sissy Jupe. From the perpective of a humanistic literary studies, it is tempting to compare Spencer's prohibition of symbolic conceptions and the vicious and illusory fictions they engender with Gradgrind's prohibition of flowery carpets. Since the linguistic turn in literary studies and philosophy, Spencer's theory appears severely reductive and simplificatory of the complex relationship between language and thought, and we glimpse something of how easy it was for Spencer's work to become discredited in the twentieth century. It is, then, worth pausing upon the similarities in the epistemological concerns of Spencer and Lawrence. Both found the origin of matter from nothing to be unthinkable (a 'mystery' for Spencer, 'occult' for Lawrence), driving Spencer in *First Principles* to the supernatural haven of a divine 'unknowable', while Lawrence came to the pragmatic position that the creative mystery simply 'always was'. Both were deeply distrustful of the *conceptual* faculty of human consciousness, and Lawrence's critique of idealism could be said to be latent in Spencer's theory of symbolic conception and its perils. Compare, for example, Lawrence's objections to 'all this modern stuff about astronomy', the mind revelling in a 'sort of ecstasy' of words and 'absurd figures', with Spencer on our knowledge of the Solar System:

And even in the case of such an utterly inconceivable object as the Solar System, we yet, through the fulfilment of predictions founded on our symbolic conception of it, gain the conviction that this stands for an actual existence, and, in a sense, truly expresses certain of its constituent relations. So that having learnt by long experience that our symbolic conceptions can, if needful, be verified, we are led to accept them without verification. Thus we open the door to some which profess to stand for known things, but which really stand for things which cannot be known in any way (*FP* 22).

We must assume that 'known' in the final sentence means a 'real' rather than 'symbolic' conception. What emerges is a significant reminder of Lawrence's argument that an abstract or linguistic proposition is *not identical with* a verifiable, experiential knowledge of something. Like Lawrence, Spencer teases apart the common-sense, logocentric assumption that, for example, 'water *is* H$_2$O', opening out the possibility – which was central to Bergson's philosophy – that matter might be thought otherwise. The mind, as Lawrence had it, can assert anything, and pretend it has proved it.

This rethinking of the relationship between Spencer and Lawrence suggests that Spencer's determined, utilitarian rationalism is a possible *source* of Lawrence's critique of science, not simply as one of its objects. To do so is to set aside Spencer's 'ideas' as a homogeneous body and to focus instead on *First Principles* as a discursive space within which a number of contradictory positions might be played out, even in the face of their author's attempts at maintaining coherence. Such contradictions emerge fully in the distinctly Lawrentian aim of ensuring against 'the dangers of falling into the insanities of idealism' (*FP* 137); a brief look at this aspect of *First Principles* also reveals how we must again disengage Lawrence and Spencer. If 'symbolic' conception was a danger, it was also, for Spencer, an inevitable characteristic of the human, condemning us to a relativistic knowledge: external, material reality certainly does exist, but our intellect is confined to its own systems: 'no thought can ever express more than relations'. The most certain fact of all, Spencer maintained, was that the power of the universe was 'inscrutable'.

Spencer's reconciliation of science and religion was thus carefully paradoxical, in a way reminiscent of Campbell's *New Theology*: the 'essentially irreligious' position becomes the 'essentially religious' one, in that only the man of science is truly in a position to know that 'in its ultimate nature nothing can be known' (*FP* 89, 54). The challenge remained for Spencer to integrate this position into a philosophy which insisted on a *materialist* conception of knowledge, articulating together intellect and external world in a material continuum. Bergson maintained that, in Spencer, all eyes had for a moment been turned towards a philosopher whose idea of evolution claimed to trace 'the progress of matter toward perceptibility' along with 'the advance of the mind toward rationality', and in which 'the complication of correspondences between the external and the internal would be followed step by step' (*CE* 363).

When, in *First Principles*, Spencer makes efforts to square this idealist-materialist circle, and to dissociate his work from the dangers of idealism, his focus turns increasingly to the role of language, and in particular to the uses of language which distinguish an advanced civilization from the 'vulgar' and 'uncultured'. The prevalence of idealism can, he argues, be traced to the misinterpretation and contamination of the Kantian terms 'phenomenon' and 'appearance' in ordinary discourse. These terms have mistakenly come to embody the inherent *deceptiveness* of visual perception, as if we lived in 'a world of phantasms'. If, however, 'when discussing the nature of our knowledge', we were to regard the process of perception as 'tactual' rather than 'visual', the 'idea of unreality' would disappear; we would no longer conflate the undoubted fact that we can have 'no knowledge of the nature' of the object touched with doubts about whether or not the material world existed at all. Any slight residual danger of idealism could then be eradicated by a 'further verbal correction':

> We increase the seeming unreality of that phenomenal existence which we alone can know, by contrasting it with a noumenal existence which we imagine would, if we could know it, be more truly real to us. But we delude ourselves with a verbal fiction. What is the meaning of the word *real*? (*FP* 137).

Again, Spencer argues, the philosophical meaning of 'real' has been infected by the vulgar: the 'peasant' deludedly sees reality and appearance as the same thing, existing outside of himself, although the 'metaphysician' repeats this error in assuming that consciousness can only embrace the *appearance* of reality, thus ascribing to the real a quality of being 'left outside', as if known 'apart from all acts of consciousness'. What each seems to forget is that the 'idea of reality can be nothing more than some mode of consciousness' – that 'by reality we mean *persistence* in consciousness' (*FP* 138).

In this redefinition of perception as 'tactual', Spencer strives to think beyond the Cartesian distinction between matter and consciousness, even gesturing towards a critique of the representationalism implicit in his own notion of symbolic conception. The body is in and of the material world, its knowledge defined by touch as well as vision. In later chapters I will indicate the importance of this mode of materialism for Lawrence and for contemporary posthumanism. For the moment, however, we must note how far such materialist claims are co-extensive with scrupulous linguistic analysis and the practice of reformulation. 'Misinterpretation' is at issue; 'verbal corrections' are pitted against 'verbal fictions'; the 'meaning of the word *real*' becomes an 'idea of reality' and then a 'mode of consciousness'. As John Tyndall noted in his Belfast Address, there was 'no very rank materialism' in Spencer's position on the origin of life. As *First Principles* proceeds, it becomes ever more rooted in a theory of consciously linguistic 'correction'; in attempting to eradicate one version of idealism, the text effectively instals another, this time founded on language as the *semiotic* material of our knowledge. The progress of science is seen to lie in an increasing abstraction, the grouping of relations of phenomena into laws, and those laws into groups of more general laws, leading to causes more and more abstract, in a process Spencer theorizes as 'the dropping of all concrete elements of thought' (*FP* 85–6). On the other hand, his theory of the evolutionary development of language posits an inexorable advance towards the concrete and specific. Borrowing Coleridge's term 'desynonymisation', Spencer contends that social usage gradually modifies and differentiates terms which were by derivation equivalent, showing that 'between two words which are originally of like force, an equilibrium cannot be maintained' (*FP* 381). A key passage spells out this process of linguistic advance:

> Strike out from our sentences everything but nouns and verbs, and there stands displayed the vagueness characterizing undeveloped tongues. Each inflection of a verb, or addition by which the case of a noun is marked, by limiting the conditions of action or of existence, enables men to express their thoughts more precisely. That the application of an adjective to a noun, or an adverb to a verb, narrows the class of things or changes indicated, implies that the additional word serves to make the proposition more distinct. . . .
>
> Again, in the course of its evolution, each tongue acquires a further accuracy through processes which fix the meaning of each word. Intellectual intercourse slowly diminishes laxity of expression. By-and-by dictionaries give definitions. And eventually, among the most cultivated, indefiniteness is not tolerated, either in the terms used or in their grammatical combinations (*FP* 337–8).

First Principles crucially elides or misrecognizes the potential conflict between these two modes of scientific advance – towards 'the dropping of all concrete elements of thought', and towards precision in language. Instead, Spencer's theory of language grounds a whole narrative of cultural superiority over the 'undeveloped tongues' of 'aboriginal races' and 'peasants'. Dictionary and grammatical definition inform the supremacy of modern realist art forms over the naïve and limited products of ancient and 'primitive' cultures, the latter homogenized together as 'tales of primitive times, like those with which the story tellers of the East still amuse their listeners', the 'romantic legends of feudal Europe' and 'the mystery plays and those immediately succeeding them' (*FP* 291, 342). Unlike these 'mostly unnatural forms', exhibiting 'no natural connexions', a 'good modern work of the imagination' evinces an 'approach to truth of representation': improbabilities and impossibilities are 'disallowed', we see 'fewer of those elaborate plots which life rarely furnishes'; 'realities are more definitely pictured' (*FP* 342).

The reader might be forgiven for wondering what modern works of art Spencer had in mind here, or for regretting his straying into aesthetic territories of which he knew little. Certainly, he appears ill-equipped to anticipate the anxieties or innovations of the modernists. Yet, from another perspective, the unresolved tensions and contradictions of *First Principles* are those of scientific modernity, and Lawrence could have found, as in Darwin, an intriguing combination of the alert and the didactic – 'alert', in its highly reflexive and detailed discussion of the limits of the knowable and of the relationship between matter and consciousness; 'didactic', in the blithe progressivism which concludes that 'science may be described as definite knowledge, in contradistinction to that indefinite knowledge possessed by the uncultured' (*FP* 341). The 'alert' parts of *First Principles* themselves give the lie to their 'didactic' alternatives. Meanwhile Lawrence, as I will demonstrate more fully in Chapter 6, increasingly sought out the cultures and experiences of those whom Spencerean science disdained, seeking to expose the inability of that science to think the human other than in the terms of a linear, timebound logic of evolutionary 'advance'. Even in the early Spencereanism of the *Study of Thomas Hardy*, we can locate an intimation of its limitations; of Spencer, as well as Huxley and Darwin, Lawrence wrote,

> (T)hese last conceived of evolution, of one spirit or principle starting at the far end of time, and lonelily traversing Time. But there is not one principle, there are two, travelling always to meet, each step of one lessening the distance between the two of them. And Space, which so frightened Herbert Spencer, is as a Bride to us (*STH* 98).

Spencer's 'fear' of Space is a curious reprise or echo of the critique which Bergson had only recently made of his old mentor, the accusation being that '*the usual device of the Spencerean method consists in reconstructing evolution with fragments of the evolved*' (*CE* 364). Just as Spencer sought refuge in a safely walled distinction between the knowable and the unknowable, so he cuts up the material world into fragments retrospectively deduced from the evolutionary process, without being able to account for the creative act of becoming, which Bergson sought to elaborate with the concept of duration. The basis of this critique in Lawrence and Bergson is not that Spencer's thought is idealist because over-intellectualized, but that it is not rigorous enough to recognize its idealism – 'imprisoned', as Birkin retorts to Hermione with a typical dialectical twist, regarding the idea of over-educated schoolchildren, 'within a limited, false set of concepts' (*WL* 41). Nevertheless, if Lawrence detected a certain evasiveness in Spencer's approach to the dilemmas of thinking matter, still more might he have found it in an evolutionary primer of enormous popularity, Ernst Haeckel's *The Riddle of the Universe* (1899).

4. Ernst Haeckel: the language of substance

Revising his early poem 'The Wild Common' for a new edition of *Collected Poems* in 1928, Lawrence observed: 'It has taken me twenty years to say what I started to say, incoherently, when I was nineteen, in this poem' (*P* 252). Of the various changes made to the poem, a key element is the introduction of the word 'substance'; along with the gorse bushes, 'leaping/Little jets of sunlight texture', and the rabbits, 'handfuls of brown earth', there is 'I on the bank all substance':

> But how splendid it is to be substance, here!
> My shadow is neither here nor there; but I, I am royally here!
> I am here! I am here! screams the peewit; the may-blobs burst out in a
>   laugh as they hear!
> Here! flick the rabbits. Here! pants the gorse. Here! say the insects far
>   and near
>
> (*CP* 33)

In the more wistful and elaborate second half of the earlier version, a love-inspired soul sickness is contrasted with the vigorous physical world upon which the soul depends:

> What if the gorse flowers shrivelled and kissing were lost?
> Without the pulsing waters, where were the marigolds and the songs of
>   the brook?
> If my veins and my breasts with love embossed
> Withered, my insolent soul would be gone like flowers that the hot
>   wind took
>
> (*CP* 894)

While each version of the poem is a celebration of the Lawrence-persona's physical continuity with the natural world, the revised version dispenses both with the word 'soul' and with the sense of its physical fragility, substituting the self as 'substance', 'marvellous stuff', and a conceit on its 'quivering' shadow, trailed around like a white dog on a lead. This more robust and exclamatory version presents substance as ineradicable and not to be confused with ideas of an immaterial soul – 'all that is God takes substance!'

A reading of 'The Wild Common' suggests that Lawrence characterized his twenty-year writing life as a project embodying the search for a language of nature which might embody the complex position of the human within it. The word 'substance' inevitably invites comparisons with the work of the German biologist Ernst Haeckel, whose *The Riddle of the Universe* (1899) was a part of Lawrence's formative materialist reading. By 1903, Joseph McCabe's translation for the Rationalist Press Association had sold 75,000 copies in Britain, having sold 100,000 in its first year of publication in Germany. For Roger Ebbatson, the influence of Haeckel's monism or pantheism 'went deep' in Lawrence's early and middle fiction,'radically extending' his concept of nature.[25]

The *Riddle* elaborates a 'law of substance', representing the 'inseparable connection in reality' of two laws independently arrived at in the history of science: Lavoisier's law of the persistence or indestructibility of matter (1789; invoked by Lawrence in the letters to the Rev. Reid), and the law of persistence of force or conservation of energy attributed both to Mayer and to Helmholtz in the 1840s. Haeckel's monism recognizes 'one sole substance in the universe, which is at once "God and Nature"; body and spirit (or matter and energy) it holds to be inseparable' (*RU* 16). Thus, 'we adhere firmly to the pure, unequivocal monism of Spinoza', in whose pantheistic system 'the notion of the *world* is identical with the all-pervading notion of god', united in the 'universal substance' which is the 'all-embracing divine essence of the world'.

Such heightened rhetoric highlights the distinction between Haeckel's writing of science and that of Darwin or Spencer. The *Riddle* is a populist and interventionist work, stridently rejecting both a theoretical materialism (which would 'dissolve the world into a heap of dead atoms') and a theoretical spiritualism (which would 'reject the notion of mattter'). Such disabling binary oppositions are instead merged into a re-writing of the concept of the soul, thus linking Haeckel with Darwin in the identification of psychology, the 'scientific study of the soul', as the key science of the future, the 'foundation and postulate of all other sciences' (*RU* 72). This reconciliatory effort was not, however, the only typical element of materialist debate in Haeckel; the text was also preoccupied with the enigma of thinking matter and the infinite regress it entailed:

> The only source of our knowledge of consciousness is that consciousness itself; that is the chief cause of the extraordinary difficulty of subjecting it to scientific research. Subject and object are one and the same in it: the perceptive subject mirrors itself in its own inner nature, which is to be the object of our enquiry (*RU* 140–1).

Nevertheless, with an insouciant brio lacking in Darwin and Spencer, Haeckel negotiated this 'extraordinary difficulty' with a linguistic strategy of equally extraordinary directness. The dualism of matter and spirit or consciousness disappears in a discourse which fuses the two via the concepts of 'psychoplasm', 'soul-substance' and the 'soul-cell'. These signify the 'albuminoid carbon-combinations' which are the 'definite material substratum' of psychic activity. Even the atom, Haeckel observes, 'is not without a rudimentary form of sensation and will – that is, a universal "soul" of the simplest character' (*RU* 184).

It is difficult to deny what Montgomery calls the 'almost comic' quality of such negotiations.[26] Haeckel's treatment of ether, a concept which enjoyed a particularly ambivalent status in contemporary scientific epistemology, invites a similar response. As Spencer had put it in *First Principles*, available theories on the exercise of force, on matter, through space, 'cannot be represented in thought' (his familiar refrain) except through the mediation of a 'hypothetical fluid': 'Mentally to represent this exercise, we are hence obliged to fill the apparent vacuity with a species of matter – an ethereal medium' (*FP* 202). 'Ether' was thus a point at which science became peculiarly conscious of itself as a *signifying* practice, requiring the predication of this absent term in order to make the fundamental concepts of science thinkable; the existence of ether was not so much known as necessarily inferred. Spencer noted that this did not solve but simply shifted the problem, for if we enquire into the constitution of this medium, are we not, then, subject to the same, infinitely regressive difficulties of conceivability as the concept of ether was originally designed to eliminate? Haeckel too confronted the problem; if we suppose that ether consists of 'minute homogeneous atoms (for instance, indivisible etheric particles of a uniform size)',

> (I)t must further be supposed that there is something else between these atoms, either 'empty space' or a third, completely unknown medium, a purely hypothetical 'inter-ether'; the question as to the nature of this brings us back to the original difficulty, and so on *ad infinitum* (*RU* 186).

As in the *Origin* and *First Principles*, however, the scientist, armed with an ideology of science as definite and progressive knowledge, cannot afford to be detained in the epistemological difficulties he appears, himself, to have unearthed. In diagrammatic form, Haeckel shows the world to be cleanly divided into Mass and Ether, with their qualitative distinctions denoted as follows: Ether is 'etheric', that is, 'neither gaseous, nor fluid, nor solid', and 'not atomistic' but 'continuous', while Mass, perhaps unsurprisingly, is 'not etheric', but 'gaseous, fluid or solid' and 'atomistic', 'discontinuous' (*RU* 188).

The very gesture by which Haeckel claims to denote the constitution of matter is that which reveals the issue to be locked into a system of pure linguistic difference, one element explicable only as the pure negation of its other. 'Ether' becomes distinctly ponderable, as it were, as soon as it is defined by negation as imponderable. Yet this performance in logic can still be augmented by the claim that the existence of ether is a 'positive fact' acknowledged by physicists for the past twelve years; while 'no expert in this department', Haeckel hypothesizes that it is best likened to 'an extremely attenuated, elastic and light jelly' (*RU* 186). This throws into ironic relief the *Riddle*'s famous jibe at the expense of theism, whose logical conclusion, Haeckel claimed, was a conception of God as a 'gaseous vertebrate'.

How far should we dwell satirically on the apparent absurdities of *The Riddle of the Universe*? In the essay 'The Two Principles', Lawrence reflects on the creation of the world. 'If we try to conceive of God, in this instance', he writes, 'we must conceive some homogeneous rare *living* plasm, a *living* self-conscious ether, which filled the universe (*SM* 178–9).'

It is not just in the vocabulary of 'plasm' and 'ether', mediating between matter and spirit, that this writing declares its debt to Haeckel; it continues to share with the *Riddle* a distinctive foregrounding of the struggle to find a *language* of nature. Lawrence's concern with the Spencerean challenge of the 'unthinkable' origin of the cosmos here translates into the question of what happens when we 'try to conceive of' God. The italicized 'living' shows Lawrence striving for a distinctive, Parmenidean sense: life here means always-already created rather than an entity supernaturally added to inert matter. In the phrase 'must conceive', the argument seeks a new linguistic resolution which involves mediating between certain available languages: esotericism, Christianity, science. 'We need to find some terms', Lawrence notes elsewhere in the essay, to express the connections between the elements and the soul. Haeckel is similarly far from un-selfconscious about his terms. Enlarging upon the decision to give to the material basis of psychic activity, 'without which it is inconceivable', the 'provisional name of "psychoplasm"', he writes:

> We have given to that part of the protoplasm which seems to be the indispensable substratum of psychic life the name of *psychoplasm* (the 'soul-substance', in the monistic sense); in other words, we do not attribute any particular 'essence' to it, but we consider the *psyche* to be merely *a collective idea of all the psychic functions of protoplasm*. In this sense the 'soul' is merely a physiological abstraction like 'assimilation' or 'generation' (*RU* 89).

In 'provisional', 'given the name of', 'merely' a '*collective idea*' and an 'abstraction', along with the elaborate combination of italics, parentheses and quotation marks given (presumably with some faithfulness) in McCabe's quotation, there is a strong sense of Haeckel's struggle to steer a course of the newly-thinkable through the unacceptable alternative rhetorics of scientific orthodoxy and supernatural figuration. Moreover, this is a recognizably Darwinian effort in its strict anti-essentialism, connecting with Haeckel's recognition that, in the evolutionary chain of being which connects 'all conceivable gradations' of psychic life from unicellular organisms to the cortex of the human brain, it is nevertheless impossible to 'draw a hard-and-fast line' or 'determine mathematically' the emergence of consciousness as such: 'some zoologists draw the line very high in the scale, others very low' (RU 143).

The sense of the arbitrary and of the provisional in scientific language and taxonomy thus emerges throughout Haeckel's Riddle. As in Darwin and Spencer, while it was hardly Haeckel's aim to hurl his theories into an abyss of linguistic relativity, his writing seems constantly to bring him to the brink of that position. The alertness of a science to its epistemological vulnerabilities comes into conflict with the 'didactic' need to assert the inevitable progress of scientific rationality: evolutionary theory calls up both positions. Haeckel thus constituted another model of this integral conflict within modernist science. But what distinctions need to be made between Lawrence's particular writerly search for a language of nature and that of Haeckel, whose un-Christian, monistic and pantheistic materialism clearly held attractions for Lawrence? We might return here to the status of the word 'soul', which for Haeckel was 'merely a collective title for the sum-total of man's cerebral functions'. This constitutes a curious prefiguring of Lawrence's treatment of the term in Psychoanalysis and the Unconscious, where he gives some indication of why 'soul' might have proved inadequate or inappropriate for the revised version of 'The Wild Common'. In conscious opposition to Freudian discourse, Lawrence posits his own definition of the 'unconscious', as the first, fused foetal cell in which is embodied each unique human individuality. 'Soul', he admits, would be a better word: 'by the unconscious we do mean the soul':

> But the word soul has been vitiated by the idealistic use, until nowadays it means only that which a man conceives himself to be. And that which a man conceives himself to be is far different from his true unconscious. So we must relinquish the idea word soul (FU 215).

No less than Haeckel, Lawrence seems entrapped in language, even in the moment at which what he wishes to denote is the domain of the pre-linguistic or non-semiotic – the origin of the human as pure substance. Both writers see 'soul' as a word that has been reinvented: for Haeckel, in scientific discourse, as synonymous with the brain; for Lawrence, in idealism, as a term equivalent to what he also called 'personality', the conscious idea or image of the self. Haeckel's pragmatic decision is to run with this change, because the fused language of the 'psychoplasm' or 'soul-cell' solved neatly for him the problem of reconciling materialism and idealism. For Lawrence, more deeply immersed in the problems of linguistic choice and their epistemological consequences, no such reconciliations were possible.

For this reason, perhaps, the term 'riddle' resonates differently across the two writers in their search for a language of nature. Like Darwin's *Origin*, the title of Haeckel's text is in a key sense misleading. When, in the 'Conclusion', Haeckel's definition of the 'riddle' is pursued, we find that it is not strictly a riddle at all, but rather a single remaining question or unsolved problem for science – that of 'substance'. What, asks Haeckel, is the 'real character' of substance? Immediately it is asked, the question is dismissed as a kind of category error fruitlessly generated by pure metaphysics: 'We do not know the "thing in itself" that lies behind these knowable phenomena. But why trouble about this enigmatic "thing in itself" when we have no means of investigating it, when we do not even clearly know whether it exists or not?' (*RU* 310). The 'gloomy' *problem* of substance is one thing, the 'clear' *law* of substance another. Underpinning this blithe uncoupling of the scientific from the philosophical is a common-sense epistemology based on the physiological and nervous systems common to 'all rational men': this produces a consensus of 'presentations' which we know, on this shared basis, to be '*true*', 'knowable' and 'real'.

By contrast, Lawrence's encounter with the problem of substance and its knowability, particularly in the context of evolutionary theory, is frequently presented in the form of a riddle: When is a rabbit not a rabbit? When is a glow worm a glow worm? When is a man a man? When is water not water? In 'The Two Principles', we find Lawrence's first attempt at unpicking the scientific formula for water, setting it within and against the language of alchemy. It can, he argues, be proved that water is a chemical compound of two gases, but is it, he asks, not more true that thoses gases are 'the first naked products of the two parent-elements, water and fire'? What if the prior truth is that water '*produces*' (the italics are Lawrence's) hydrogen and oxygen when 'fire' is introduced, that is, when heated (*SM* 182)?

This is neither an unscientific or irrational Lawrence, nor a Lawrence who sought to collapse issues of scientific epistemology into issues of language. It was however a Lawrence who had seen, in the writing of Haeckel and others, how far questions of materialist knowledge *were* questions of language, such that they could not be sidestepped by earnest appeals to the scientific common sense embedded in the cerebral and nervous systems of 'all rational men'. Reading and writing science, Lawrence could not fail to be aware of the growing self-consciousness of science itself. Hence the significance of two figures now to be considered, T.H. Huxley and William James, for whom the representation of ideas of the scientist and scientific activity became co-extensive with their own scientific work.

5. T.H. Huxley: honeyed words

Earlier, in the Introduction, I suggested that the writing of T.H. Huxley works to problematize images of 'materialism' generated by a humanistic literary tradition. As Belton has argued, the neglect of Huxley within a British culture fixated on the association of the literary with the human or humane indicates a diminishing of that culture's 'imaginative capacities', even an eradication of a certain 'creative energy of rationalism'. Even as Belton seeks to restore what is distinctively *scientific* to Huxley's intelligence, he also challenges the restrictions of that 'Two Cultures' framework whose emergence, ironically enough, was closely related to the caricatures of science produced by nineteenth-century humanists.

Such ambivalence around 'science' and the 'scientist' was certainly crucial in Huxley's own ceaseless 'publicizing' of science. In part, he sought to assert science's own cultural adequacy; in part too, science was to join literature and the arts as an equal partner in a fully rounded cultural education. The existing hegemony against which he saw himself striving is outlined in the 1880 essay 'Science and Culture':

> How often have we not been told that the study of physical science is incompetent to confer culture; that it touches none of the higher problems of life; and, what is worse, that the continual devotion to scientific studies tends to generate a narrow and bigoted belief in the applicability of scientific methods to the search after truth of all kinds? How frequently one has reason to observe that no reply to a troublesome argument tells so well as calling its author a 'mere scientific specialist'.[27]

While William Whewell is credited with the invention of the modern concept of scientist in the 1830s, Huxley was undoubtedly the first to make a reality of the scientist as a major public intellectual. Some recent commentators, largely culturalist in their approach to science, go so far as to see this work of promotion as Huxley's main achievement. James Paradis describes Huxley's construction of the scientist-as-'unique cultural agent' as a major 'literary' creation, while Adrian Desmond, more bluntly, refers to Huxley's 'real work' as that of 'a publicist – a one-man lobbying machine'.[28] In reading the collection of essays and lectures entitled *Man's Place in Nature*, Lawrence would certainly have found a vigorous and articulate multi-dimensionality in Huxley's promotion of the work of science: first, his considerable palaeontological fieldwork and its famous conclusion that 'no absolute structural line of demarcation, wider than that between the animals which immediately succeed us in the scale, can be drawn between the animal world and ourselves'; second, his explication of the theoretical and methodological foundations of science *per se*, in terms of induction and deduction, hypothesis, probability and causality; and third, his endorsement of the educational, and hence socio-political, value of the sciences.

It is generally agreed, however, that the distinctive character of Huxley's interdisciplinarity is intimately associated with his talents as a writer. In the Belfast Address of 1874, Tyndall had included Huxley among a select group of scientists whose clear and vigorous literary style disdained scientific isolationism. More recently, Paradis too attributes 'literary sensitivity and talent' to Huxley. Neil Belton, however, highlights the potential limitations of this image of the 'literary' Huxley, with his acerbic comments on Aldous Huxley's essay on his grandfather, 'T.H. Huxley as a Literary Man' (1935). Belton accuses the younger Huxley of applying to scientific discourse an emptily formalistic model of the literary, praising his grandfather's prose for its use of alliteration, allusion and caesura sentences in a literary criticism of 'quite stunning banality', and thus reducing Huxley's early defences of Darwinian theory to an analogy with the 'candied porkers' he would make out of orange-peel for his grandchildren at Christmas time.[29] Implicitly, therefore, Belton questions a humanistic model of the literary aesthetic, 'contentless' in the sense that it deprives literary language of any cognitive value: the 'sombre' and 'gifted' polemicism of Huxley is, by contrast, valued by Belton for its 'wrestling with difficulty' (a phrase of Burke's).

A further irony here is that, in line with Darwin, Spencer and Haeckel, Huxley's conception of the language required by science necessitated a conscious disavowal of the very skills which were essential to his communicative mission. He could, for example, dismiss vitalist arguments about the origin of living beings by associating them with verbal sophistry: the response of Diogenes to such arguments, Huxley maintained, was simply to get up and walk around his tub; 'the man of science', likewise, 'says nothing to objectors of this sort', but gets up and walks onward, 'showing what science has done and is doing' (*MPN* 187). Science is legitimized by disdaining the merely verbal or dialogic in favour of a more direct and practical mode of knowledge. Similarly, in his influential lectures to working men, Huxley's egalitarian appeal was based upon a model of scientific knowledge as praxis, an orientation towards making and doing, hands before heads, which forged a natural alliance between the scientist and the craftsman and manual labourer. Just as *doing* science was more important than mere scientific book-learning or 'paper philosophy', so, he declaimed in 'Technical Education' (1877), 'clever talk touching joinery will not make a chair . . .'; 'Mother Nature is serenely obdurate to honeyed words.'[30] If the humanists could caricature science, Huxley would play them at their own game: 'he emasculated the liberal arts', observes Paradis, 'through stereotype'.

The faculty of language was also crucial to Huxley's evolutionary science, in particular to its famously tenuous distinction between the human and the simian. With his own, hypothetical interlocutor's insistence that ' "we are men and women, not a mere better sort of apes . . ." ', Huxley agrees:

'whether "*from*" the brutes or not, we are assuredly not "*of*" them' (*MPN* 102). The considerable semantic weight borne by these two italicized terms is eased somewhat by his view of language and the difference it exemplifies between structure and function. Language is that which 'constitutes and makes man what he is', distinguishing the human from 'the whole of the brute world':

> I say that this functional difference is vast, unfathomable, and truly infi-
> nite in its consequences; and I say at the same time, that it may depend
> upon structural differences which may be absolutely unappreciable to us
> with our present means of investigation. What is this very speech that
> we are talking about? I am speaking to you at this moment, but if you
> were to alter, in the minutest degree, the proportion of the nerve forces
> now active in the two nerves which supply the muscles of my glottis, I
> should suddenly become dumb. The voice is produced only so long as
> the vocal chords are parallel; and these are parallel only so long as certain
> muscles contract with exact equality; and that again depends on the
> equality of action of those two nerves I spoke of. So that a change in the
> minutest kind in the structure of one of these nerves, or in the structure
> of the part in which it originates, or of the supply of blood to that part,
> or of one of the muscles to which it is distributed, might render us all
> dumb. But a race of dumb men, deprived of all communication with
> those who could speak, would be little indeed removed from brutes. And
> the moral and intellectual difference between them and ourselves would
> be practically infinite, though the naturalist should not be able to find a
> single shadow of even specific structural difference (*MPN* 262).

Just as the physical mechanisms of speech are precariously balanced, so this passage counterbalances the meticulous detail of those mechanisms with the language of metaphysical hyperbole: 'wondrous universe', 'vast, unfath-omable and truly infinite', 'practically infinite'. Huxley's own performance, with its persuasive rhetorical questions, balanced structures, extended sentences and vivid imagery, is a precise example of the wondrous poise of speech. While a materialist account of the vocal chords, their nerves and blood supply emphasizes the fortuitous or accidental nature of evolutionary development, the passage at the same time strives to preserve a teleology of absolute and inevitable human progress.

Only 'shallow rhetoricians', Huxley observes, would argue that the idea of a common material origin for all living things was degrading and brutalizing to humans. Huxley was, of course, a supreme rhetorician, the delicate balance between physical and metaphysical being entirely characteristic of his prose: so that the essay 'On the Relation of Man to the Lower Animals', setting out to display the 'chief facts' in a 'form intelligible to those who possess no special acquaintance with anatomical science', ends in celebrating 'that great Alps and Andes of the living world – Man', in the umistake-able artifice of Wordsworthian Romantic sublime. What then is really at stake in the question of Huxley's rhetoric? In the recent critical accounts of Paradis and Desmond, we are encouraged to read what Paradis calls Huxley's 'fine dramatic art' as a mode of manipulation, a more or less conscious form of subterfuge of the same order as is implied in the revelation that Huxley's 'science' was really a front for his cultural agency. Belton, sceptical of such accounts because of the way in which they instal a contemporary cultural-ism ahead of an understanding of the complexity of what science itself meant in Huxley's context, insists that Huxley's 'wrestling with difficulty' is a scientific as well as linguistic activity. When Huxley operates a distinction between language that signifies and language that does not – to look at a series of stratified rocks, with its constant succession of natural forms, and offer the explanation that ' "They were so created" ', is 'only a paltering with words', whereas with an evolutionary explanation 'the facts receive a meaning' (*MPN* 252–3) – he is engaging closely with a cognitive problem which can only be worked through in language.

Man's Place in Nature is therefore another text in which Lawrence would have found evolutionary materialism characterized by linguistic alertness. More distinctively Huxleyan was the link between alertness and the 'wonder' of the material world as revealed by science. As I suggested earlier, beneath the surface of Huxley-as-Gradgrind's explicitly 'reductive' approach to the horse is a level of linguistic manoeuvring and hesitancy which keeps epistemological questions open. The reductive and the complex are not mutually exclusive: the reductive is, rather, a way of gaining some local or strategic rational purchase within the broader context of the 'utterly condi-tional nature of all our knowledge' (*MPN* 275). Paradoxically, the confidence of Huxley's science can only be legitimized by an awareness of the com-pletely provisional nature of its knowledge, and by a condition of constant openness to falsification and self-scrutiny. In this sense Huxley's vaunted agnosticism is expressed in the careful discriminations he makes concern-ing biology as a 'branch of knowledge':

> Now, so far as we know, there is no natural limit to the existence of the Euglena, or of any other living germ. A living species once launched into existence tends to live for ever.
>
> Consider how widely different this living particle is from the dead atoms with which the physicist and the chemist have to do! (*MPN* 267).

Despite holding to the conviction that 'the MATTER constituting the living world is identical with that which forms the inorganic world' (*MPN* 159), Huxley could be surprisingly forceful about the contrast between the dynamic material dealt with by the biologist and the 'dead atoms' of the physicist or chemist. ' "May it not be," ' we remember Lawrence's Dr.

Frankstone asking, ' "that life consists in a complexity of physical and chemical activities, of the same order as the activities we already know in science?" ' This question of whether or not we should attribute 'some special mystery' to life was still locked into the enigma of the qualitative transition from dead atoms to consciousness. 'What', continued Huxley in the lecture on 'The Educational Value of the Natural History Sciences', 'is the cause of *this wonderful difference* between the dead particle and the living particle of matter . . . ? that difference to which we give the name of Life?' (my italics):

> I, for one, cannot tell you. It may be that, by and bye, philosophers will discover some higher laws of which the facts of life are particular cases – very possibly they will find out some bond between physico-chemical phenomena on the one hand, and vital phenomena on the other. At present, however, we assuredly know of none; and I think we shall exercise a wise humility in confessing that, for us at least, this successive assumption of different states – (external conditions remaining the same) – this *spontaneity of action* – if I may use a term which implies more than I would be answerable for – which constitutes so vast and plain a practical distinction between living bodies and those which do not live, is an ultimate fact . . . (*MPN* 267–8).

If Frankstone then is a Huxleyan materialist, it may be in the revised sense that her propositions are put to Ursula in *The Rainbow* in the form of tentative questions, the conversation ending 'on a note of uncertainty, indefinite, wistful'. F.R. Leavis's characterization of 'life' as a 'necessary' word incapable of definition might be re-read in this context, not as a philosophical smokescreen but, in Huxley's terms, as a 'wonderful difference', a point left open for further enquiry. Biology both had and did not have a clear object of enquiry: it was, to be sure, the 'Science of Individual Life' (as Lawrence similarly emphasised that life was to be found nowhere but in individual creatures), but as such its object was constantly in transition: 'living things have no inertia and tend to no equilibrium', so that 'the actual wanderings of matter are as remarkable as the transmigrations of the soul fabled by Indian tradition' (*MPN* 160).

Huxley, Paradis argues, provided Victorians with a new concept of self as a 'physical entity', bringing them 'face to face with their biological selves'.[31] If the human became thus strange to itself, it was because the fugitive 'wanderings of matter' called for an open epistemology, in which biology was in no simple sense destiny. 'Living bodies' are 'nothing but extremely complex bundles of forces held in a mass of matter, as the complex forces of a magnet are held in the steel by its coercive force'; the integrity of the humanistic self is deconstructed from within, by the plurality of these forces, and from without, by the distribution of forces in a network extending beyond individuality: 'The energy localised in certain human bodies, directed by similarly localised intellects, has produced a collocation of other material bodies which could not be brought about in the state of nature' (*MPN* 305).

The function of the intellect in the latter helps to explain a profound shift in Huxley's later work, where he strove to dissociate himself from crudely deterministic social Darwinisms, and from a perceived role as apologist for individualistic, *laissez faire* economics. 'Society', Huxley now argues in *Evolution and Ethics*, 'is usefully to be considered as distinct from nature', it being merely a piece of sophistical wordplay to claim that, because humans are part of the natural or cosmic process, so too are their societies and cultures. An analogy is found in the garden, and the art or 'artifice' of gardening, whose precise aim is to eliminate the struggle for existence and the process of natural selection. The fact of nature's ceaseless struggle to undo man's garden proves the point that 'ethical nature, while born of cosmic nature, is necessarily at enmity with its parent'.[32] For the sake of 'the great work of helping one another', there is no doubt which side Huxley is finally on; politically, a connection between a 'distributed' version of the posthuman self as a bundle of energies, and a radical vision of co-operation, suggests itself. Appropriately, then, his greatest scorn is reserved for those who would extend the principle of artificial cultivation to human stock. Huxley does not refer to 'eugenics', preferring terms which ranged from 'pigeon-fanciers polity' to 'reasoned savagery', but it is clear that he saw it as an illegitimate move to extend the metaphor of artificial selection to the manipulation of human societies. It is much harder to identify 'weak' humans than to identify 'weak' plants, and 'there is no hope that mere human beings will ever possess enough intelligence to select the fittest'; 'surely', he mused, 'one must be very "fit" indeed, not to know of an occasion, or perhaps two, in one's life, when it would have been only too easy to qualify for a place amongst the "unfit"'.[33]

Huxley's writing thus demonstrates the potential complexity of a relationship between the alert and the didactic (or ideological) in science. As in Eder's writing for *The New Age*, the critical target is a politics based on the scientific evidence of a nature that is *fixed*. If a politics is to be truly emancipatory, they argue, it could only be based on the scientific evidence that nature is unfixed. '(A)ny one who is practically acquainted with scientific work', argued Huxley in 'The Progress of Science' (1887) 'is aware that those who refuse to go beyond fact, rarely get as far as fact'.[34] Ostensibly a reminder of the role of hypothesis in scientific methodology, this also suggests the paradox that a science of rigour can only proceed from the fundamental *instability* of the concept of fact. Lawrence was surrounded by a science of deep epistemological scepticism. In the work of William James, this became a dedication to 'overhauling the very idea of truth'.

6. William James: reality in the making

William James stands as a transatlantic counterpart to T.H. Huxley in Lawrence's early materialist reading, the two connected by a seemingly effortless rhetoric and the persona of the conciliatory public agent, at the service of a modernist project of cultural agency, synthesis and progress. For Cornel West, James sought 'to mediate between the old and the new – religion and science, *Gemeinschaft* and *Gessellschaft*, country and city, vocation and profession – in order to lessen the shock of the new for the educated middle class'.[35] Jessie Chambers suggests that *Pragmatism* 'especially appealed' to Lawrence when he read it in the year of its publication, 1907, and that he liked and recommended James's earlier work, *The Varieties of Religious Experience* (1902).[36] A reference in *Psychoanalysis and the Unconscious* to 'the mysterious stream of consciousness', 'immortal phrase of the immortal James!', which 'stream of hell . . . undermined my adolescence', playfully registers some level of knowledge of the earlier still and widely influential *Principles of Psychology* (1890), if not a more general debt to James.

In the first part of this chapter, I presented James as a key figure for Lawrence in the critical scrutiny of ideas about matter. In his attentiveness to thinking matter, James inevitably confronted the deeply embedded influence of linguistic structures. Such an encounter, I have argued, is equally relevant, though with varying degrees of conscious engagement, in the writings of Darwin, Spencer, Haeckel and Huxley, and forms the basis of what we might understand as an 'alert' science for Lawrence. If we can regard this as something like a linguistic turn in science (though my hesitancies around this interpretation should by now also be evident), then it is very sharply exemplified in James' first major work, *Principles of Psychology* (1890).

In the Preface to *Principles*, James defines and delimits psychology as a natural science of 'finite individual minds'. As such, he later explains, psychology is, like physics, a 'naïve' science which assumes that knowledge is irrefutably based on the fourfold 'irreducible data' of (1) The Psychologist, (2) The Thought Studied, (3) The Thought's Object and (4) The Psychologist's Reality. This science could have no concern with 'metaphysics', being purely empirical and physical: the reader will find in the book mainly a 'mass of descriptive details', with brain and nerve physiology as its foundations. By the fourth chapter, however James is apologizing for an increasingly 'metaphysical' direction, 'metaphysics' in the process being redefined as 'nothing but an unusually obstinate effort to think clearly'. The effort of thinking is directed towards what Tyndall had described as the 'unthinkable' passage from matter to consciousness. As evolutionists, James notes, we must assume that all living forms are simply the results of the redistribution of original materials; yet, with the emergence of mind, an 'entirely new nature seems to slip in, something whereof the potency was *not* given in the mere outward atoms of the original chaos' (*PP* 146).

How, then, do evolutionists deal with this? When the 'evolutionary afflatus' is upon them (James now chooses to speak as if apart from this group), writers such as Tyndall and Herbert Spencer will 'leap over the breach whose flagrancy they are the foremost to announce, and talk as if mind grew out of body in a continuous way' (*PP* 147). The choice of 'writers' rather than 'scientists' is significant, for attention is drawn to the way in which each postulates this continuity. Here James devotes a long and detailed footnote to Spencer's 'great word', 'nascent', used as a 'sort of bridge' between inert matter and consciousness, but allowing Spencer to outdo himself in 'vagueness'. In a careful analysis of passages from Spencer's *Principles of Psychology*, James's concern is with the way certain words carry the burden of work. When Spencer, writes, for example, about the stimulation and co-ordination of ganglia in order to give rise to consciousness, he is held to make the words 'raw material' and 'implication' 'do the *evolving*'; when he accounts for consciousness in terms of a certain variety and rapidity of ceaseless stimuli, he is accused of drawing in a weakly metaphorical sense upon the idea of people entering a theatre through a turnstile.

James's critique, then, is hardly that of a philosopher who has eshewed 'verbal solutions'. Attacking Spencer for his lack of 'rigor' means denouncing the bridging word 'nascent' as a 'verbal quibble'. What therefore characterizes this chapter of *Principles* is precisely James's own recognition that issues of the 'thinkable' are necessarily performed in language; we cannot think the emergence of consciousness outside of the domain of signification. We are, as it were, back in the (semiotic) realm of ether. 'We ought', struggles James, 'sincerely to try every possible mode of conceiving the dawn of consciousness so that it may *not* appear equivalent to the irruption into the universe of a new nature, non-existent until then'; more firmly, '*If evolution is to work smoothly, consciousness in some shape must have been present at the very origin of things*'; finally, as the title of the section indicates, 'Evolutionary Psychology *Demands* a Mind-Dust' (my italics) – that is, the concept of a 'Mind-Dust' is required in order to make evolution 'work'.

Principles, then, becomes increasingly preoccupied with the 'Methods and Snares' the psychologist must confront before 'science' can proceed; sections are entitled 'A Question of Nomenclature' and 'The Misleading Influence of Speech'. In this seemingly helpless drift into issues of language, the seeds of a later philosophy of pragmatism are sown. Within the phrase 'if evolution is to work smoothly', for example, lies the necessity for 'evolution' as a system of explanation to make sense in the terms of formal logic: James arrives at a theory of the soul or 'mind-stuff', 'that well-known spiritual agent in which scholastic psychology and common sense have always believed', because it constitutes 'the line of least logical resistance, so far as we have yet attained' (*PP* 181). The evidence of nature and the relatively autonomous demands of human systems of language and logic are finely counterbalanced: the emergent philosophy denies absolute and *a priori* truths in favour of a relativism based on what meanings 'work' most successfully for us: 'The truth of an idea is not a stagnant property inherent in it. Truth *happens* to an idea' (*PP* 92).

James thus arrives at pragmatism some years before its 'official' codification in his Boston lectures of 1906. While appearing to emerge seamlessly out of empirical science, its particular mode of reasoning or 'common sense' establishes a distance both from science and from existing philosophy: it had 'no prejudices whatever, no obstructive dogmas, no rigid canons of what shall count as proof'; it would 'entertain any hypothesis' and 'consider any evidence' (*PR* 38).

> Pragmatism represents a perfectly familiar attitude in philosophy, the empiricist attitude, but it represents it, as it seems to me, both in a more radical and in a less objectionable form than it has ever yet assumed. A pragmatist turns his back resolutely and once and for all upon a lot of inveterate habits dear to professional philosophers. He turns away from abstraction and insufficiency, from verbal solutions, from bad *a priori* reasons, from fixed principles, closed systems, and pretended absolutes and origins. He turns towards concreteness and adequacy, towards facts, towards action and towards power. That means the empiricist temper regnant and the rationalist temper sincerely given up. It means the open air and possibilities of nature, as against dogma, artificiality, and the pretence of finality in truth (*PR* 28).

Even though pragmatism is a reconciliatory philosophy, James identifies himself clearly with the empiricist temper, as a 'lover of facts in all their crude variety', as against the rationalist temper, which seeks abstract and monistic modes of final explanation. Paradoxically then, the recommended mode of the empirical scientist coincides with a scepticism about scientific knowledge. Science 'bursts the bounds of common sense', dislodging the authenticity of sense-experience in favour of the 'ultimate reality' of primary things – atoms, ether, magnetic fields – which are invisible and impalpable. This, James concedes, gives us an unprecedented technological and practical 'control of nature', and in a moment of anticipation he sees a posthuman dystopia: science may lead to the annihilation of human *being* by its own powers, man's 'fixed nature as an organism' proving inadequate to the transitions demanded by the intellect (*PR* 84–5). But every science must finally confess 'that the subtlety of nature flies beyond it, and that its formulas are but approximations'; new, modernistic kinds of scientific 'thing' create more disputes than ever within the scientific community, warning us that it is only '*as if* reality were made of ether, atoms and electrons. . . . The term "energy" doesn't even pretend to stand for anything "objective"' (*PR* 98).

The 'as if' formula, and the principle of metaphoricity it represents, is precisely that which Lawrence uses to unsettle the self-evidence of 'water *is* H_2O', comparing its discourse to the alternative alchemistic vocabulary of fire and water. And in this sense, Lawrence's theoretical approach to the relation between language and science is pragmatistic: regardless of the supposed advance of scientific knowledge, we have two alternative vocabularies available to explain a material phenomenon: which works best? In James, therefore, epistemological doubt, and a pragmatist theory of language, derive from the same source. James is convinced of the anthropomorphism inherent in language: 'all human thinking gets discursified'; 'our nouns and adjectives are all humanized heirlooms, and in the theories we build them into, the inner order and arrangement is wholly dictated by human considerations . . .' (*PR* 97, 114). Unlike Bergson, however, James works beyond a model of language as inherently *arresting* the flow of phenomena and experience. In rationalist and 'professional' philosophy, he notes, words such as 'God', 'Matter' and 'Reason' are held to contain essential or universal principles: 'You can rest when you have them.' The viability of the pragmatistic method in philosophy, by contrast, can only be guaranteed by a model of language in which meaning is constantly subject to social change and renegotiation:

> (I)f you follow the pragmatic method, you cannot look on any such word as closing your quest. You must bring out of each word its practical cash-value, set it at work within the stream of your experience. It appears less as a solution, then, than as a program for more work, and more particularly as an indication of the ways in which existing realities may be *changed* (PR 28).

'There was always confusion in speech', reflects Birkin in *Women in Love*. 'Yet it must be spoken. Whichever way one moved, if one were to move forwards, one must break a way through. And to know, to give utterance, was to break a way through the walls of the prison, as the infant in labour strives through the walls of the womb' (*WL* 186). Lawrence's embrace of modern science is often defined in terms of his declared gratitude to the new physics of Albert Einstein, whose theories of relativity 'knocked the external axis out of the universe' (*FU* 25). In the same work, however, he observes that *humans* are in greater need of a theory of relativity than the universe. It may be that this need, and the modes of linguistic and cultural relativism which might inform it, were first impressed upon Lawrence by James's *Pragmatism*. Relativity here signified a repudiation of any fixed or absolute principles, a complete openness to evidence and experience, a complex theory of language which saw humans as enmeshed within it, yet also able thereby to constantly remake reality, and a refusal to grant superiority to modern over ancient or primitive consciousness. James's sympathetic reading of mystical states in *Varieties of Religious Experience* ('I am', Lawrence had written to the Rev. Reid, 'by nature emotional, perhaps mystical') is particularly relevant to the latter case, in that they are held to 'break down the authority' of ratio-nalistic consciousness, showing the latter to be only one among many pos-sible 'orders of truth'.[37]

However, in the political commentary which formed the Epilogue to his school history textbook, Lawrence revealed the limits of his acceptance of pragmatism. Uncontentiously enough, he explains that pragmatism means 'that a thing is only good if it is common sense, if it works'. He then, however, proceeds to correlate pragmatism with the redistribution of wealth inscribed in the programme of revolutionary socialism: redistribution could only mean rationing, which is something, as the war had proved, that we all hate. 'It may be lovely common sense', Lawrence concludes, 'but what's the good, when we detest it? There must be something inside us which plumps for *uncommon* sense'.[38]

It had been consistent, since the *Study of Thomas Hardy*, for Lawrence to align radical labour politics with capitalism, in the manner of Jean Bau-drillard's *Mirror of Production* (1973) argument: capitalism dictated to labour the terms of its struggle, and these were the money-orientated, greed-driven terms of bourgeois political economy itself.[39] The alignment of pragmatism shows his recognition of what is plain to any careful reader of James's text; namely, that pragmatism was a philosophy ideally suited to market princi-ples, within which truth is established in terms of its cash value. James's human relativism was a theory of the free-market circulation of languages and ideas, the principle of agreement or consensus to be decided by the laws of market demand. However attractive to Lawrence was the creative human element in Jamesian pragmatism, with reality always 'in the making', he could not ultimately accept the smooth reduction of questions of truth to the all-too-human relativism of local and strategic functionality. James appears to rescue reason from all dogmas and foundations, only to tie it finally, in a pervasive rhetoric, to the emptily differential exchange value system of capitalism; Lawrence's endorsement of an irrationalism, 'uncom-mon sense', is at once a political and philosophical gesture, recognising how far James reneges on the idea of an open and alert epistemology even in the process of affirming it.

7. Coda

In a recent interview, Christopher Norris reflects back upon the affair of the Sokal 'hoax'. The contemporary culture war of which it is a part, Norris argues, often seems sharply polarized between, on the one hand, scientists who dismiss any sociological or cultural-historical angle as 'so much igno-rant or scientifically illiterate twaddle' and, on the other hand, postmodernists who regard any talk about truth as 'some kind of oppressive "total-itarian" discourse'. This situation, Norris maintains, is 'just a travesty of what really goes on when scientists reflect on the way they work and think'; science 'doesn't and shouldn't claim to possess the absolute, definitive truth about anything', but instead is based on conjecture and the rigorously applied principles of verifiability and falsifiability.[40] In this chapter I have tried to indicate how, in the texts of Darwin, Spencer, Haeckel, Huxley and James, Lawrence would have encountered what really goes on when scientists reflect on the way they work and think by *writing*. The drift in the work of William James, from empirical science to metaphysics and linguistics, and finally to a theory which relativizes the whole idea of truth, is discernible in and applicable to all of these writers. In part this is a historical argument, concerned with the way modern science dealt with the epistemological challenge of evolutionary theory; in part too, however, it is a more general argument about the necessary precipitation of science in language. A prototype for the latter might be found in J.M. Coetzee's 1982 article, 'Newton and the Ideal of a Transparent Scientific Language', where Coetzee locates in Newton's *Principia* a 'real struggle' to 'bridge the gap between the non-referential symbolism of mathematics and a language too protean to be tied down to single, pure meanings'. Coetzee's close analysis of Newton's language is framed by a question deriving from the Von Humboldt–Sapir–Whorf hypothesis on linguistic relativity: if Newton had worked in a radically different medium from Latin and English, might he have been better able to do justice to his thought?[41] This 'real struggle' in language – a struggle, in effect, to think matter – provided Lawrence, I argue, with a model of an 'alert' science in which a reverential approach to nature and materiality is inseparable from a sense of the fragile provisionality of knowledge. In Part II of this book, Lawrence's irrationalist insistence on knowing how 'not to know' is read as a product of this model of science, and as the basis of his exploration of a complex posthuman condition.

Part II
The Posthuman

4
Posthuman D.H. Lawrence?

In 'Why the Novel Matters' (1925), an essay on the special kind of 'knowledge' possessed by the novelist, Lawrence chips irreverently away at the foundational status of the Cartesian mind–body dualism. Why should he look at his hand, as it writes, and conclude that it is 'a mere nothing compared to the mind that directs it'? The hand 'flickers' with a life of its own, and comes to learn and know things through touch. It slips along, jumps to dot an *i*, gets cold or bored – in fact, has its own 'rudiments' of thought. 'Why should I imagine that there is a *me* which is more *me* than my hand is?' (*P* 533)

How, Lawrence asks, with the impression of a wry common sense, do we actually experience our aliveness, our consciousness? Without the idea of a controlling mind to divert our attention, we might well conclude that our hands are alive, get bored, and have their own knowledge. The account hovers between a holistic model of the human, in which the hand is as much '*me*' as anything else, and a decentred, composite model, in which the human organism is an ensemble of innumerable living parts each with their own relative autonomy. There is room for both of these models in contemporary thinking about the posthuman, as well as an implicit agreement with Lawrence that any rigorous thinking about human consciousness and its place within the material totality of 'nature' must go beyond Descartes' theory of the separation of mind and body.

In Part I, I suggested that we reconfigure what science meant for Lawrence as a set of complex and open-ended debates revolving around the enigma of thinking matter. Within such debates, the evolutionary theory of natural selection unsettles the self-evidence of Descartes' dualism: if matter is the shared and continuous substrate of the organic and the inorganic, of humans, animals and machines, then it is difficult to adhere to the view that the mind is a different *kind* of substance from the contrastingly inert, mechanical body. Yet the same evolutionary theory demonstrates that mind *has* evolved, as a distinct phenomenon which changes things irrevocably in the natural order. A substance in common is one thing; the crucial qualitative transition from the insentient to the sentient, from inert to conscious matter, quite another.

What then is it, as Lawrence enquired of the *cogito*, to be 'living', that 'vague and almost uninterpretable word' (*P* 423)? The materialist tradition for Lawrence did not *resolve* the definition of 'life' so much as intensify and diversify debates around it. As I have tried to show, Lawrence was attuned to a set of intricate arguments, going back to the early Greeks, concerning the nature of materialism. He was aware that one prominent version of materialism required the predication of a supernatural or 'occult' appearance of a first speck of matter, a something from nothing, in order for the machine of evolution to then kick into gear. He found this disingenuous and intellectually unsatisfactory, and saw in it the justifiable popular condemnation of materialism as reductively simplistic. In the same way, the popular conception of materialism's antithesis, vitalism, asserted 'life' as a mysterious, autonomous entity rendering the enigma of material origins superfluous. Yet this too was to trivialize and distort the project of Bergson's philosophy. In *Creative Evolution*, as Keith Ansell-Pearson has observed, Bergson strove to dissociate his work from mysticism: the explanatory power of a 'vital principle' and its apparently tangential relationship to matter might still be tenuous, but it did 'at least serve to remind us of our ignorance, when mechanism simply invites us to ignore the ignorance'.[1]

For Lawrence, then, 'science' lay in the complex field of negotiation between these caricatures of materialism and vitalism. It constitutes the neglected source of an aesthetic preoccupied with questions of epistemology, of what we know and how we know it. Positing science thus, as a mode of radical scepticism, means challenging that caricature of a 'deathly' and mechanical, monolithic other, constructed by a discourse claiming for itself the antithetical values of 'humanism'. In its literary-critical manifestations, this was the discourse which did most to enhance Lawrence's reputation as a writer, at the same time sequestering him in a Romantic image of spontaneous irrationality. Moving beyond the confines of this humanism makes it possible to begin to see modern science as a *source* of Lawrentian reverence and wonder for 'life' rather than as an obstacle to it. Distrusting its own claims to objectivity, increasingly sceptical of its own boundaries and categories, science becomes richly humanistic in its indefinite extension of the debate around the human. We arrive again at the paradox of Hardt and Negri's 'antihumanist (or posthumanist) humanism', according to which it is only when the human is decisively *uncoupled* from the animal and the machine that we cease to be truly interested in it.

In Part II, I want to explore more fully the possibility of a 'posthuman', or posthuman humanist, D.H. Lawrence, along the lines of what Haraway has called a 'kinship' between humans, animals and machines. Immediately, it is necessary to point out that 'kinship' implies a somewhat cosier relationship than either Lawrence or, I think, Haraway herself envisages. We may feel ourselves to be familiar with Lawrence's sense of kinship with the animal, though in the next chapter I seek to indicate how thoroughly Lawrence wanted us to re-think our assumptions about the relationship. Far less familiar, however, is likely to be the sense of kinship with the machine. In part, this is due to the success of humanist criticism in fixing in place an image of Lawrence as Manichean advocate of the sacredness of nature and scourge of science and technology. In part also, it is because, where science and technology are concerned, Lawrence seems always to be at his most voluble when denouncing them. The traditional humanist position is, in other words, hardly unfounded, and if the present book runs against the grain of received opinion on Lawrence and science, still more conspicuously does it run against the grain on Lawrence and the machine. Thus far, I have tried to explain Lawrence's position in terms of the distinction he insisted upon between 'didactic' or 'dogmatic' science and 'alert' science; there was science that was blithely sure of its epistemological mastery, and science that was subtly uncertain of its foundations. In the rest of the book, I want to suggest that 'alert science' involves the appeal to a new kind of epistemology which might confirm the insistent questioning of realism and objectivity in the sciences of the later nineteenth century, and which prepares the ground for a radical rethinking of the machine. Bergson's work, with its radically unfamiliar philosophical language, emerged to address this need, but it is, arguably, in its readoption, a century later, for a science of the posthuman, that the work finds a context more conducive to its reception. Here I refer to the unforeseen conjunction between 'hard' neurological and biotechnological science on the one hand and, on the other, poststructuralist philosophies of the self. Bergson's work has been rediscovered as a means of articulating the connections between these fields under the broad rubric of the 'posthuman', even though many of those thinkers and scientists implicated might not subscribe to such a term.

In Part II, then, with the present chapter as a bridge between the two Parts of the book, I want to explore the possibility that Lawrence's crucial ambivalence around science might best be seen when filtered through the concerns of contemporary posthumanism. In such a context, the question of 'life' as a qualitative distinction remains central, though the angle of approach to it can seem rather more technological than semantic, as for example in contemporary debates around the meaning and status of Artifical Life. Hayles details, for example, how the 'Tierra programme', developed by Thomas S. Ray in the 1990s, aims to confer upon silicon software systems the biodiversity of natural evolution: 'organisms' and 'species' are encouraged to mutate and thus evolve in spontaneous and unpredictable ways by reversing the polarity of a bit once in every 10,000 instructions. Are hesitant scare-quotes around *organism* and *species* appropriate or justified here? Does the humanist literary critic, such as Leavis, have any greater claim to pronounce upon the difficulty and indeterminability of 'life' than the scientist of the posthuman? Or, is it possible that posthumanism has reopened the question with greater vigour and precision than we find in humanism?

As Hayles notes, when Humberto Maturana's work on the frog's visual cortex issued in the theory of autopoiesis – 'living systems operate within the boundaries of an organisation that closes in on itself and leaves the world on the outside' – Maturana realized that a radically new language was needed to embody this challenge to realist epistemology. This was not, however, a need to replace the traditional *objectivity* of science with a polarized *subjectivity*, as if to imply that knowledge could *only* ever be entirely 'situated'. Despite the reflexivity of autopoesis, the organism is not on this theory a closed system; the materialist grounding of Maturana's work meant that the organism remained always physically *related* to its environment, and the concept of 'structural coupling' emerged to account for this. Rather the need, manifest in a whole range of posthuman thinking, was as Haraway has put it, to find an alternative to the established discourse of binaries *per se* – a way of thinking which does not rest upon the hypostatized differences of inside and outside, subject and object, organic and inorganic, nature and culture, but which bodies forth the *simultaneous* involvement and separation of the knowing subject and the material world. The concept of the cyborg is, now, our most familiar way of signalling this new, both/and epistemology in the domain of the human. In the terms of Cornel West's assessment of Jamesian pragmatism, a realist ontology is preserved while simultaneously rejecting 'all forms of epistemological foundationalism'.

It is from the perspective of this epistemology of the posthuman that I hope to reassess what looks, at first glance, like one of Lawrence's most wilfully obtuse, irrationalistic gestures – the insistence, reiterated in the postwar works of philosophy, that we must 'know how not to know'. In what remains of the present chapter, I want to highlight certain key passages from Lawrence's writing, and suggest how we might begin to see a posthuman Lawrence emerging from them. I began with Lawrence on Descartes, because of the axiomatic status within posthumanism of the idea that there is no dualism of kind between mind and body, that mind is a relatively late product of a material evolutionary process and therefore that, in the words of Sean Watson, 'consciousness is entirely reducible to the complex movement of matter'.[2] Reducible or not, it is, as I have already indicated, nevertheless true that the intellect, however late, can proceed to generate the idea of the dualism from which – as it were – it benefits, and that this too is an integral part of the materialist position. Charles Darwin's guilty self-accusation in the pre-*Origin* notebooks – 'oh you Materialist!' – followed precisely from the recognition that, once evolved, the human intellect could proceed to invent its own hegemony.[3] Where, for Descartes, the sovereign ego was proof of God's existence, Darwin's growing conviction was that both the

sovereign ego and the divine reality might be artefacts of the
conception, including that of the inferiority of the body, could b
by this 'evolutionary upstart'; alternatively, as Hayles puts it wit
to the work of the neuroscientist Francisco Varela and others, consciousness
'is an epiphenomenon whose role it is to tell a coherent story about what
is happening, even though this story may have little to do with what is happening processurally'.[4] Lawrence, too, was conscious of this 'upstart' quality,
as the *Study of Thomas Hardy* demonstrates:

> The mind itself is one of life's later developed habits. *To know* is a force,
> like any other force. Knowledge is only one of the conditions of this force,
> as combustion is one of the conditions of heat. *To will* is only a mani-
> festation of the same force, as expansion may be a manifestation of
> heat. And this *knowing* is now an inevitable habit of life's developed late,
> it is a force active in the immediate rear of life, and the greater its
> activity, the greater the forward, unknown movement ahead of it (*STH*
> 41–2).

As the similes make clear, knowing and willing are the same kinds of force
as combustion and expansion. 'Habit' is a phylogenetic application of a
word used in Samuel Butler's *Life and Habit* to denote the ontogenetic internalization of behaviour as unconscious 'memory'; such memory attains the
status of an *instinct* which is then, via Butler's Lamarckianism, passed on in
heredity. For Lawrence, 'life' too develops habits over deep time, the mind
being one of these late habits. The fact that this shows Lawrence apparently
adopting a Spencerean model of seamless progressive differentiation, from
the 'great Mass' to the distinctiveness of individual intellect, should not
blind us to the idiosyncratic take on temporality which the passage also
displays. Mind, for Lawrence, is not a case of simple advance: knowledge,
including the activities of work, goes back, 'retracing some proved experience'. While man is a 'palpitating leading-shoot of life', the mind does not
easily coincide with this: it acts 'in the immediate rear of life', but then the
greater *its* activity, the greater the 'unknown' movement ahead. Clearly
then, while adhering to a model of the evolution of mind, Lawrence wishes
to problematize any resultant teleology: we are alerted by the distancing
strategy of 'as if' in the *Study*'s characterizations of evolutionary differentiation – 'almost as though this differentiation were a Purpose', '(I)t is as if all
coagulation must be loosened' (*STH* 42). Sure enough, the *Study* is from the
beginning a deft exposure of the ideological colouring of evolutionary logic
as embodied in the concept of 'self-preservation' – a critique to which I will
return in due course.

For the moment, let us emphasize the connection between an anti-
Cartesian, material evolution of the mind, and a sense, closely related to
contemporary posthumanist thinking, that the fact of consciousness should

not override our understanding of the materiality which (historically and physiologically) precedes it. We return here to a familiar element in Lawrence studies, the letter of 5 June 1914 to Edward Garnett. Disappointed with Garnett's criticisms of the 'psychology' of characters in a draft of what was to become *The Rainbow*, Lawrence tries to justify his approach via his recent interest in Italian Futurist art. 'Tries' is an operative word: the letter's solecisms bespeak the struggle to articulate something which lies on the taboo-haunted borderline between the human and its constitutive substance. Centrally, the effort is to discriminate exactly what he takes and rejects from Marinetti's manifestos:

> (W)hen I read Marinetti – 'the profound intuitions of life added one to the other, word by word, according to their illogical conception, will give us the general lines of an intuitive physiology of matter' I see something of what I am after. I translate him clumsily, and his Italian is obfuscated – and I don't care about physiology of matter – but somehow – that which is physic – non-human, in humanity, is more interesting to me than the old-fashioned human element – which causes one to conceive a character in a certain moral scheme and make him consistent (*LII* 182).

While, Lawrence asserts, the characters of Turgenev, Tolstoy and Dostoevsky might themselves be extraordinary, the 'moral scheme' within which they become defined and knowable *as* characters, with a certain consistency, is 'dull, old, dead'. He confesses to know what Marinetti means when he claims to be more interested in the 'incomprehending, inhuman alliance' of molecules in a piece of steel, or the heat of a piece of wood or iron, than 'the laughter or tears of a woman', though Marinetti is at the same time 'stupid' to *compare* a woman with inorganic matter, for example in the assertion that the aforesaid heat is 'more passionate' than the woman. The sense that Lawrence might want to dissociate himself from an anti-humanism or a subtler anti-feminism on Marinetti's part seems, however, to be immediately withdrawn in that what interests *him* in the woman's laugh is '*the same* as the binding of the molecules of steel or their actions in heat' (my italics); it is 'the inhuman will, call it physiology, or like Marinetti – physiology of matter, that fascinates me'. Thus the initial repudiation of 'physiology of matter' turns out to be a fascination with it, and the woman – somewhat transgressively, perhaps, from any 'old-fashioned human' perspective – is objectified anew:

> I don't so much care about what the woman *feels* – in the ordinary usage of the word. That presumes an *ego* to feel with. I only care about what the woman is – what she *is* – inhumanly, physiologically, materially – according to the use of the word: but for me, what she *is* as a phenomenon (or as representing some greater, inhuman will), instead of what she feels according to the human conception (*LII* 183).

The evident strains in this passage, with its italics, ungrammaticality, and reminder of the constraints of contemporary usage, suggest the wish to break free of a language of the human. The critique of Futurism's stupidity suggest that epistemology, and a precise understanding of what science means, are what is really at stake. The Futurists, Lawrence implies, have the right kind of gut reaction about the way humanistic pieties need to be rethought, but they are too obedient to an inverted logic, looking for 'the phenomena of physics to be found in human beings' instead of a 'new human phenomenon'. Thinking matter was a new *kind* of matter, its knowledge of itself locked into paradox, and therefore, as Bergson had warned, not amenable to the application of science's subject–object relation: the science of physics could not explain the emergence of such sentient life, only rather provide a retrospective interpretation on its own terms. Lawrence concludes with an outline of the revised epistemology to which Garnett should address himself:

> You mustn't look in my novel for the old stable ego of the character. There is another ego, according to whose action the individual is unrecognisable, and passes through, as it were, allotropic states which it needs a deeper sense than we've been used to exercise, to discover are states of the same single radically-unchanged element. (Like as diamond and coal are the same pure single element of carbon. The ordinary novel would trace the history of the diamond – but I say 'diamond, what! This is carbon'. And my diamond might be coal or soot, and my theme is carbon.). . . . Again I say, don't look for the development of the novel to follow the lines of certain characters: the characters fall into the form of some other rhythmic form, like when one draws a fiddle-bow across a fine tray delicately sanded, the sand takes lines unknown (*LII* 183–4).

If, as I propose, these famous epistolary passages can be re-read as the basis of a posthuman D.H. Lawrence, then we need to be clear about how this differs from and yet relates to a merely *materialist* Lawrence. Materialism there certainly is: the 'greater, inhuman will' of which the woman is an instance or phenomenon is no divine will but, it seems, a shared, 'physic' and 'non-human' base or 'single radically unchanged element' uniting the human species. Individuality and character are redefined as changing 'allotropic states' of this element. The individual, for which Lawrence borrows the Freudian term 'ego' to designate an *idea* of the self, becomes 'unrecognizable', its impulses subsumed within a collectivity which is subject to material forces in the same way as sand in a tray obeys the fiddle-bow drawn across it. The sand, however, takes 'lines unknown'. We cannot, as Bergson insisted, know the living phenomenon before it has emerged. The passages become posthuman, then, in their intense wariness about the perils of reductiveness within materialism. We cannot accept the disappearance of the human into matter, looking for the 'phenomena' of physics in human beings, yet neither can we refute the science which is surely the basis of a physiology of matter. How can we know how *not* to know scientifically, when science is so important to our materialism? What are the alternatives?

These questions are implicit in Lawrence's constant scrutiny of the science of the Futurists – a science which, he seems to decide, is simply not alert enough to the questionability of its own assumptions. Clarification is provided in a slightly earlier letter, to A.W. McLeod, in which Lawrence had again tried to explain his interest in Futurism (LII, 180–2). He applauds the purging of the emotions of 'the old forms and sentimentalities', and even 'loves it' when Marinetti presents Italy as a 'great mechanism', his own interpretation being that Italy is faced with a 'mechanical' and 'dead' stage through which it must pass, appraising everything according to its 'mechanic value' and subjecting everything to the 'laws of physics'. There is no simple, reflex reaction against mechanism here. Yet the futurists are 'ultra-ultra intellectual', producing the most 'self conscious, intentional, pseudo scientific stuff on the face of the earth'. Where, in the second letter, he glimpsed something important in Marinetti's scientific attention to 'intuitions' and 'illogicality', here he accuses the Futurists of using their intuition 'for intellectual and scientific purpose'. There is, it seems, a fine epistemological line separating a new Bergsonian science from the recurrence of the old masquerading as the new. Lawrence hardly knows what the former might look like, as the travails of these letters make clear, but the pursuit or unravelling of it becomes the project of his work. Most revealingly, perhaps, he writes to Macleod that the Futurists 'will progress down the purely male or intellectual or scientific line'. In reminding us of this ideological critique, of the gendering and historicizing of scientific epistemology, Lawrence also calls to mind the utopian ungendering to be found in Donna Haraway's posthuman dispensation. To 're-source' and 'revivify' art through the joint work of 'man-life and woman-life, man-knowledge and woman-knowledge, man-being and woman-being', may not quite be the kind of de-essentializing that Haraway has in mind; yet we recall, too, that men in Lawrence do not always coincide with men-knowledge, nor women with women-knowledge.

What we call mind or intellect is, then, perfectly continuous with, if a relatively recent product of, those evolutionary movements of matter which have made up what Lawrence calls the 'non-human' or 'physic' in humanity. If we are to concede priority to this materiality, dethroning the Cartesian ego or *cogito*, we need to understand how such continuity works – in other words, what it means to say that our posthuman selves are immersed in the material world. Contemporary posthumanism develops various ways of thinking the nature of such involvement, but I want to continue with Lawrence's contribution, in a text which represented his first sustained attempt to set out a philosophy of 'pure science'. In the early drafts of *Studies in Classic American Literature*, begun in 1917, Lawrence addresses the tricky coexistence of holistic and dualistic conceptions of subjectivity and consciousness from within materialism. Apparently unequivocally, he claims that we have two 'distinct fields of consciouness' or 'living minds'. One is the physical or 'primary' mind, located in 'the great plexuses and ganglia of the nervous system and in the hind brain', and the other is the 'ideal' or mental consciousness (or, 'which we recognise as mental'), located in the brain.

We are, however, he insists, wrong to think of the nerves and blood simply as the vehicles of mental consciousness; the kind of consciousness Lawrence attributes to these bodily phenomena seems to confirm a direct continuity with the consciousness of non-human creatures, in the passage which follows:

> What we call 'instinct' in creatures such as bees, or ants, or whales, or foxes, or larks, is the sure and perfect working of the primary mind in these creatures. All the tissue of the body is all the time aware. The blood is awake: the whole blood-system of the body is a great field of primal consciousness. But in the nervous system the primary consciousness is localised and specialised. Each great nerve-centre has its own peculiar consciousness, its own peculiar mind, its own primary percepts and concepts, its own spontaneous desires and ideas. The singing of a lark is direct expression from the whole primary or dynamic mind. When a bee leaves its hive and circles round to sense the locality, it is attending with the primary mind to the surrounding objects, establishing a primary *rapport* between its own very tissue and the tissue of the adjacent objects. A process of rapid *physical* thought takes place, an act of the primary, not the cerebral mind: the sensational, not the ideal consciousness. That is, there is a rapid sensual association within the body of the bee, equivalent to the process of reasoning; sensation develops sensation and sums up to a conclusion, a completed sum of sensations which we may call a sensual concept (*SM* 135).

This remarkable piece of writing finds Lawrence thinking hard (he cannot even begin to study Nathaniel Hawthorne until he has considered 'the bases of human consciousness'), and with all the resources available to him from materialist science, about knowing how not to know. An epistemology somehow, perhaps, appropriate to the human as thinking matter is figured in locutions – physical thought, sensual concept – which assert that an entire bodily experience is 'equivalent to the process of reasoning'. In this sense the passage bears the closest relation to Bergson's bold reappraisal of the faculty of memory (bearing in mind that, for Samuel Butler, memory as a bodily process was the basis of 'instinct') and to the implications of this reappraisal for traditional theories of perception and representation.

Rather in the way that the 'tissue' of Lawrence's bee establishes a rapport with the tissue of adjacent objects, 'pure perception' for Bergson is 'the act ... whereby we place ourselves in the very heart of things' (*MaM* 73); or, in Deleuze's summary of this proposition, 'we perceive things where they are, perception puts us at once into matter, is impersonal, and coincides with the perceived object'.[5] Perception and consciousness do not *re-present* sense data to them-/our-selves, but instead constitute an entire physical state of continuity between self and other: they are not states *of* something, but states *per se*. The challenge this poses is to our deep-seated assumption that perception is 'a kind of photographic view of things' (*MaM* 31), necessitating the concept of representation as an intermediary process which assumes, as Sean Watson puts it, 'a homunculus hidden inside our heads looking at images projected onto a screen and listening to sounds from hidden internal speakers'.[6] Echoing Lawrence's satire on the 'funny sort of superstition' which is the apparently common-sensical Cartesian view, Bergson attributes the strength of this assumption to the 'magician's wand' of customary philosophy, which constantly requires us to set apart matter and representation as different, discontinuous things. This philosophy commits us to the habit of spatialized thinking; we are 'strongly obsessed by images drawn from space', a tendency which appears even more pronounced when we turn to the apparent accumulation of perceptions and consciousness into the faculty of memory. As Ansell-Pearson notes, Bergson understood memory 'neither as a drawer for storing things away nor as a faculty'; to ask *where* memories repose when we are not using them is to ask the wrong kind of question, dictated again by our habits of spatialization (Deleuze, in *Bergsonism*, discusses the philosophical necessity in Bergson of discriminating between true and false problems, and to contest the 'social prejudice' whereby problems are set for us, to which the discovery of solutions becomes the *raison d'être* of life).[7]

Perhaps the most difficult aspect of Bergson's effort here is his call for that paradigm shift by which we might begin to think of memory in terms of real time or duration rather than in terms of space. Memory is not called up, so much as it happens: it is not *of* something, but *is* something; we don't have memories, but are them. The sense that memory is an actual physical event is inscribed in Bergson's deployment of 'actualize' through which to indicate that memories occur not as the calling-up of previous images but as whole, if temporary, cognitive structures which we experience, or rather become, in the duration or real time of lived experience. If, then, 'to *picture* is not to remember', and if 'there is not, there cannot be a region in the brain in which memories congeal and accumulate', does this imply some mystical access to or emergence of the 'real past' in memory? Bergson certainly seems to indicate that the past is real and continuously available: 'is it not obvious that the photograph, if photograph there be, is already taken, already developed in the very heart of things and at all the points of space?'

(*MaM* 31). However, such a past cannot be static or consistent, because it is dependent upon a self which is, in Bergsonian terms, never the same, always in process. Bergson thus questions a materialist logic by which the flow of force travels in one direction only, as if 'consciousness, with all its functions, is born of the mere interplay of material elements', in the same way that Lawrence was to question Futurist science. Contrastingly, because perception is part of matter, matter cannot exert any powers other than those we can perceive; or, perceptions are not in the brain, the brain is in them. Memory is neither 'out there' nor 'in here', but both conjoined, so that the body is 'a section of the universal becoming':

> It is then the *place of passage* of the movements received and thrown back, a hyphen, a connecting link between the things which act upon me and the things upon which I act, – the seat, in a word, of the sensory-motor phenomena (*MaM* 196).

It may help to step back here from paraphrase in order to note the similarity of the *linguistic* effort in Bergson and Lawrence. Each writes – if I can briefly sound more postmodern than I might wish – in order to shatter the transparent surface of received scientific common sense. As Lawrence's bee circles in its locality, its relation is one of 'rapid sensual association', the experience of consciousness as a bodily totality – blood, tissue, nervous system – embedded in or connected to its physical environment. For Bergson, human perception, consciousness, even memory, are similarly modes of physical *action*, though it is stressed that the connection with environment is brought into being by the organism's interests or choices within it. Is it more absurd to see consciousness staged or re-presented in a small cinema in the brain, or to see it as a total physical state hitched to the environment? To cite the humanistic touchstone from Lawrence's poem 'Thought',

> Thought is a man in his wholeness wholly attending.
> (*CP* 673)

This 'wholeness', however, might signify more, or less, than humanism would be prepared to answer for. Contemporary neuroscience and evolutionary psychology seem increasingly to corroborate the theory that the mind does not produce representations. Yet if the Bergsonian act of memory means, in effect, that 'a new entity comes into existence in the world', then the 'wholeness' of this identity is a complex *composite* condition – a 'temporary articulation of the body, brain, nervous system and environment' – in which the *integrity* of the self on traditional humanist lines is radically undermined.[8]

As well as constituting a state of environmental conjuncture, the body may not even be present to itself in ways previously understood. I have already mentioned the idea of 'dissipative structure', traceable from the evolutionary through to the posthuman moment. This idea, as elaborated for example in Fritjof Capra's *The Web of Life*, provides the sense of self as a dynamic biological structure which enables Bergson's theory of memory. 'The skin of the human body replaces cells at the rate of 100,000 per minute, the human pancreas replaces its whole physical structure every twenty-four hours'.[9] As Norbert Wiener had much earlier observed, identity is located not so much in 'stuff that abides' as in patterns of organisation 'that perpetuate themselves'.[10] In Varela and Maturana's 'autopoiesis', this sense of a perpetually reconstitutive self implies creativity and invention, the production of genuinely unforeseeable innovation or, in a term crucial to Bergson and Deleuze, 'becoming'. While, according to Hayles' account, an earlier moment in the history of cybernetics construed the self in terms of *homeostasis*, the ability of the organism to self-regulate in changing and possibly dangerous environments in order to maintain the stable internal state necessary for the continuity of life, *autopoiesis* introduces a more active emphasis: the living system not only repairs itself but reflexively constructs the 'out there' from within the limits of its own organization or patterning. The system may be closed in on itself, but this does not prevent it setting the terms of its own necessary interaction with the environment, thus selecting and in a sense dictating what that environment *is*. The dynamic state which is memory can thus be defined, in Sean Watson's words, as a 'dissipative-structure, built through the rapid coordination of millions of dissipative processes taking place throughout the body – co-ordinated into a 'temporary cell assembly' – a real entity that *is* a piece of duration.[11]

In *Matter and Memory*, Bergson had hesitantly outlined the implications of his theories for the integrity of the self. It was indisputable, he maintained, that 'there are, in a sense, multiple objects, that one man is distinct from another man'. However,

> (T)he separation between a thing and its environment cannot be absolutely definite and clear cut; there is a passage by sensible gradations from the one to the other: the close solidarity which binds all the objects of the material universe, the perpetuity of their reciprocal actions and reactions, is sufficient to prove that they have not the precise limits which we attribute to them (*MaM* 278).

We must remember that the import of this 'close solidarity' lies in reciprocity: if environment impinges upon the self, the self also determines the environment. In the letters on Futurism, and in the passage on 'physical', creaturely thought, Lawrence similarly sought to blur the 'precise limits' of subject/object, inner/outer relations, subverting a *narrowly* materialist rendering of cause (matter) and effect (self). We partake of species-wide 'allotropic states', yet we should not thereby seek for the phenomena of physics in human beings; like bees, our 'tissue' connects us to the locality, but this is through an act of attention or *'rapport'* actualized by the creature itself.

'The humanist consciousness', observes Amit Chaudhuri, in an important new reading of Lawrence to which I will return, 'in order to operate, has to inhabit a fixed vantage point, from which it comprehends the world, and even tries accomodatingly to "understand" objects and cultures different from itself'.[12] The breaching of the conceptual limits of the human-ist, and of the one-way, spatialized theory of consciousness that accompanies it, opens out onto a number of ways of thinking 'wholeness' as a paradoxically dispersed or decentred condition. If the self is, as we have seen, dissipative, then it is also 'distributed'. As Hayles puts it, 'every day we participate in systems whose total cognitive capacity exceeds our individual knowledge'. Summarizing the work of Edwin Hutchings on the navigational systems of seagoing vessels, Hayles identifies virtual computer technologies as only the latest highly sophisticated instances of an ancient posthumanist tendency to franchise out the functions of consciousness in order to perform complex actions of which the brain and nervous system alone would be incapable. The development of 'wideware', as the neuroscientist Andy Clark calls it, can thus be read into the origins of toolmaking and agriculture; modern humans, Hutchins maintains, are not necessarily 'smarter' than cavemen, but have simply 'constructed smarter environments in which to work'.[13]

The fundamental ambivalences of posthuman thinking about the autonomous self are thus perhaps crystallized in the key concept of 'embodiment'. There is always an anti-Cartesian thrust to the term, an implication of wholeness working to subvert the mind–body dualism. Hayles' discussion revolves around the necessary distinction between embodiment as an explanation of the contexts through which actual bodies memorize, learn and behave, and 'the body', an abstract or universalized term grounded in Michel Foucault's analyses of the ways in which a disciplinary society controls its subjects. Concepts such as the 'incorporating practices' of Paul Connerton in *How Societies Remember*, by which 'habit is a knowledge and a remembering in the hands and in the body; and in the cultivation of habit it is our body which "understands"', reveal just how continuous are such posthumanisms with the evolutionary thinking of memory and habit in Lawrence's time. Such practices are, Hayles insists, always forms of enculturation without at the same time ceasing to be physical and 'natural'. They can challenge, therefore, a structuralism whose idealist affinities with Cartesianism are embedded in the notion that discourse shapes and delimits matter. Embodied experience, argues Mark Johnson in *The Body in the Mind*, 'bubbles up' into language; if we had exoskeletons instead of endoskeletons, Hayles concludes, our main systems of metaphor would be very different from what they are now. 'To look at thought this way', she reminds us, 'is to turn Descartes upside down.'[14]

Yet, at the same time, it is not difficult to extrapolate from the notion of distributed cognition a sense of estrangement from the body, of the kind indicated in Hayles' proposition that, for the posthuman, the body itself might be 'the original prosthesis we all learn to manipulate'. If the body is part of our 'wideware', where then are 'we'? The answer for a neuroscientist such as Andy Clark is that we are no more, or less, than 'a complex causal web spanning brains, bodies and world'.[15] In Hayles' critique, it is a short step from this position to the return of Cartesian instrumentalism with a vengeance – subtle embodiment overridden by a technoscientific conception of 'bodiless information', and the human standing aside to make way for the rise of intelligent machines at the service of a military-capitalist ideology of domination.

Keith Ansell-Pearson has traced a different path to the erasure of embodiment, in a 'non-organismic mapping of evolution' from Bergson through to Deleuze and Guattari and to the popular and influential genetic theories of Richard Dawkins.[16] Bergson distanced himself from a Spencerean notion of evolution as 'a story of perfection and progress' because he saw in this story the false assumption that the *raison d'être* or teleology of evolution lay in the increasingly sophisticated elaboration of *organisms*. Arguing against this assumption, Bergsonian vitalism risked accusations of superstition and mysticism in its positing of a life-force which only contingently avails itself of the organism in order to develop: '*like a current passing from germ to germ through the medium of a developed organism*'. It was, for Bergson, an accident of evolution that life and consciousness became concentrated in the forms we call 'organisms', just as Jean-François Lyotard asserts that the lesson of contemporary techno-science is that 'complexification' is not a destiny of matter but a possible event which has taken place, 'at random, but intelligibly, well before' the evolution of the human.[17] While Lyotard sees in this a debunking of human narcissism, it is surely, rather, the whole tendency of matter to coalesce into the organic that is at stake. Bergson strove to think of movement 'without the support of an invariable substance underlying all becoming', and similarly of human existence as a flow or succession of states without an 'impassive' – or 'old stable'? – ego to unite them. For Ansell-Pearson, however, it is Dawkins – ironically enough, from within orthodox Darwinian theory – who provides a contemporary scientific rationale for Bergson's gestures towards the non-organismic. For Dawkins, 'evolution cannot be restricted to individual organisms, since at the molecular level one is dealing with populations of genetic material whose communication is not governed by fixed or deterministic organismic boundaries'. Here is the significance of Dawkins' 'extended phenotype'; we should think of the basic replicating unit of evolution as the famously 'selfish' gene or gene-fragment or network, whose effects extend far beyond the host or individual organic body:

An animal's behaviour tends to maximize the survival of the genes 'for' that behaviour, whether or not those genes happen to be in the body of the particular animal performing it.[18]

Such a logic, argues Ansell-Pearson, also informs Deleuze and Guattari's deconstruction of the models of hierarchy and development which govern our thinking about human and animal life. There is, they argue, no reason why 'animal becomings' should be conceptualized as the desirable attainment of a finished condition, as if to fulfil a state ideally perfected elsewhere. The dominant teleological metaphor of evolutionary 'descent' – the genealogical tree, for example – is unsettled in Deleuze and Guattari by an alternative of transversal communication: the rhizome, which operates via variation, symbiosis, offshoots and contagion. Such an alternative to conventional organicism or organismic thinking demands a vocabulary of the '*machinic*'; and Lawrence's work is found, by Deleuze and Guattari, to exemplify this alternative, as I discuss in more detail in Chapter 7.

Where then might Lawrence be placed in relation to these unrecognizable metamorphoses of the organic and of embodiment? Is the Lawrence of the blood and the solar plexus really to be aligned with a posthumanism which, in certain manifestations, recognizes no essential differences between cybernetic mechanism and biological organism? Before addressing these questions in a more detailed study of animals, humans and machines in Lawrence, let us briefly return to the subject of evolutionary theory. What Lawrence undoubtedly shares with much posthuman thinking is a critical scepticism towards evolution as the master narrative of life. Despite the much-quoted declaration, in *Mornings in Mexico* (1927), that he disbelieved in evolution 'like a long string hooked on to a First Cause', and 'preferred' instead to believe in 'what the Aztecs called Suns: that is, Worlds successively created and destroyed' (*MM* 12), we know that this impression of irrational impulsiveness is deceptive. While the late 'Introduction to these Paintings' had referred to a struggle into disbelief after years of 'desultory acceptance', the early *Study of Thomas Hardy* already shows an astute unpicking of a certain evolutionary logic. The *Study* begins with the fable of an ancient paleolithic old man, who feels obliged to warn the children around him to be more careful than the 'reckless' poppy and to save their energy in the name of self-preservation. Secretly, however, the old man believes that the 'red outburst' of the poppy's flower is the primary fact or culmination of the poppy's existence, with the accompanying mechanisms of reproduction strictly secondary. When his 'educated grandson' presents him with the modern evolutionary interpretation – reinvigorated in Dawkins' 'selfish gene' theories – that the flower is the 'excess that always accompanies reproduction', and exists to bring the bees and flies, the old man dies. But his shade returns, muttering 'inaudibly', "If there is always excess accompanying reproduction, how can you call it excess?" Lawrence later satirically summarizes his point:

> There is always excess, the biologists say, a brimming over. For they have made the measure, and the supply must be made to fit. They have charted the course, and if at the end of it there is a jump beyond the bounds into nothingness: well, there is always excess, for they have charted the journey aright (*STH* 31).

'Whatever remains excessive to an isolable system', writes Ansell-Pearson of Bergson, 'is untouched by science, since it regards the existence of this excess as negligible to its own monitoring of a system's activities. But it is this excess which is important to Bergson...'.[19] It is clear that Lawrence's thinking shared with Bergson's *creative* evolution a sense of an anthropocentric or all-too-human interpretation structuring orthodox evolutionary theory. According to what logic is the flowering of the poppy placed as a secondary mechanism serving the primary aim of self-preservation? If, Lawrence asked, the primary aim of life is to preserve the means of continuity through reproduction, does this not mean the endless deferral of individual, actual being? Lawrence's account shows how intention or teleology can be smuggled into evolutionary theory and how, in the broader context of the *Study*, the interests served by this smuggling are those of bourgeois political economy.

Critiques of evolutionary logic carry over into the posthuman. As Hayles explains, Maturana and Varela consistently argue that 'evolution and reproduction are logically and practically subordinate to autopoiesis'.[20] The current emphasis on genetics had, they claimed, exaggerated the 'master' role of DNA in cellular composition and radically underestimated the 'holistic nature of living systems'. Underpinning this challenge, as in Lawrence and Bergson, is scepticism about an organismic and progressive narrative which effectively shelters or guarantees the status of the human being as the achieved, culminating point of the natural order. Yet there are, perhaps, unforeseen complications in this challenge to evolutionary logic, which might effectively commit Lawrence to a more radically posthuman position than he could have bargained for. For example, Lawrence's explicit critique of the advance of science and technology is modelled upon evolutionary 'progress', and in this respect could be said to resemble Francis Fukuyama's posthuman dystopia, in which human nature is imperilled by a rampant but increasingly sophisticated biotechnology. Lawrence wrote in *Apocalypse* of the 'long slow death of the human being' (*A* 26), which began with an objective approach to the cosmos and continued with the emergence of science and machinery, both (reminding us of the Lawrence of Leavis) 'death products'.

These views figure evolutionary history, via mind, as an inexorable progress towards the condition of the machine. However, the implication of some alternative posthumanisms is a *reversal* of this chronology. 'You know', the male, dialogic voice in Jean-François Lyotard's essay 'Can Thought Go On without a Body?' argues, 'technology wasn't invented by us humans. Rather, the other way around . . . (E)ven the simplest life forms, infusoria (algae, several million years ago), are already technical devices'.[21] Or, as Daniel Dennett gleefully concludes from his discussion of the self-replicating macromolecules, DNA and its ancestor RNA,

> To put it vividly, your great-great- . . . grandmother *was* a robot! Not only are you descended from such macromolecular robots but you are com-posed of them: your haemoglobin molecules, your antibodies, your neurons, your vestibular-ocular reflex machinery – at every level of analy-sis from the molecular on up, your body (including your brain, of course) is found to be composed of elegant machinery that dumbly does a won-derful, elegantly designed job.[22]

Do we in fact get closer to the condition of technology as we go further 'back' down the evolutionary ladder? What if any movement 'back to nature' is actually a movement back to technology? In Lyotard, evolutionary advance looks increasingly like a movement towards Bergsonian creative becoming, and less and less like what we take to be the condition of the machine:

> The further one climbs the ladder of organized beings, the more one observes that the immediate reaction is delayed, 'prevented', and that this inhibition explains the indeterminacy, unpredictability and growing freedom of the actions these beings can perform.[23]

Nevertheless, Donna Haraway maintains of the late-twentieth century world, 'our machines are disturbingly lively, and we ourselves frighteningly inert'. We have seen that the liveliness of machines is not necessarily anti-thetical to 'life', either in the materialisms of Lawrence's time or of our own. Equally, the inertia of the human, the sense that evolutionary temporality might be upside-down, and the human the cul-de-sac of creation, is strongly evident in Lawrence's thinking. In one of his earliest reflections on cultural otherness, Lawrence recalls sitting on the roof of a lemon-house overlook-ing Lake Garda. His friend, the aged padrone, aspires after the wealth of England's industrial revolution, 'machines, machine-production, money, and human power'; he wanted to go

> (W)here the English have gone, beyond the Self, into the great inhuman Not Self, to create the great unliving creators, the machines, out of the active forces of nature that existed before flesh (*TI* 60).

Momentarily, Lawrence is entranced by the stillness, historical and physical, of the scene before him, connecting it with a past so lovely that 'one must look towards it, backwards, only backwards, where there is peace and beauty and no more dissonance'. He thinks of 'horrible' England', 'the great mass of London, and the black, fuming, laborious Midlands and north-country'; and yet, he concludes, it was 'better' than the padrone's 'monkey-like cunning of fatality': 'It is better to go forward into error than to stay fixed inextricably in the past.' How might we read this but as another 'surprising' example of the idea, which Raymond Williams found in *Women in Love*, that 'perhaps we shall have to evolve beyond being human'?[24] What could it be but a human commitment to some kind of posthuman condition?

5
Animals

1. Anthropomorphism and the meaning of animals: Coetzee and Lawrence

> 'Just think of St. Mawr! I've thought so much about him. We call him an animal, but we never know what it means'.
>
> *St. Mawr*

White peacock, fox, ladybird, kangaroo, flying fish, plumed serpent, escaped cock. Looking afresh at the titles of some of Lawrence's fictions reminds us of a certain preoccupation with the creaturely; as it stands the list excludes *St. Mawr*, the novella whose title names a horse, and *Women in Love*, which constitutes perhaps Lawrence's most sustained fictional treatment of animals. To draw attention thus to the fiction is to divert it from the poetry as the most obvious locus of Lawrence's fascination with creatures: tortoises, elephants, dogs, bats, fish, goats, mosquitos, snakes, lions and wolves. In a very recent study, Amit Chaudhuri offers a challenging reassessment of this poetry of the creaturely. Dissenting from the established view of the success of these poems in evoking the peculiar integrity and difference of the non-human, Chaudhuri's Lawrence embodies an 'alternative aesthetic'. According to this, the artifice of the poems lies in a condition of intertextuality which requires a collective and participatory approach to the construction of the meaning of animals. Creatures emerge, not in the integrity of their otherness, but as unfinished and provisional elements in a process of *bricolage*; Lawrence's necessary recourse to a pre-existent symbolic system produces an 'exhibition of stuffed beasts and birds, his collection of textual mannequins, his pantomime of nature'.[1]

This is not simply to imply, however, that Lawrence's poetry is locked into its linguistic or textual condition. Thinking of nature in terms of wholeness and integrity belongs, as we have seen, to a certain powerful ideology of romantic humanism. Donna Haraway argues that to reconceive humans as cyborgs is to bypass the customary 'seduction to organic wholeness'; for

Chaudhuri, 'the organically whole image is exactly what Lawrence wishes to undermine', because it represents the destruction, by a 'colonizing culture' predicated upon life as individual consciousness, of a way of seeing organic life in terms of relationship, 'touch' and 'contact'.[2] Chaudhuri thus connects with Fernihough's conception of Lawrence's 'anti-imperialist aesthetic' as a precise intervention in the theorization of organicism.

My purpose in this chapter is to supplement the readings of Chaudhuri and Fernihough by examining how Lawrence's *narrative prose* similarly calls the organic, and the animal, into question. Lou Witt – twenty-five, rich, and frustrated in marriage – buys St. Mawr, but, despite his beauty, the troublesome stallion offers no easy alternative to the dissatisfaction with men and human relationships Lou shares with her mother. On the basis that such wholeness might more probably be found in non-human creatures than in Nietzsche's 'poor, unhappy' human animals, Lou is certainly seduced by the possibilities of St. Mawr. Something, however, has 'gone wrong' with the horse, and no one quite knows what. Nor is the difficulty a case of one-way traffic: if, from its position of apparent superiority in the natural order, the human intellect asks a question of St. Mawr, St. Mawr is, equally, forever 'gleaming a question' at Lou. We surmise that the questions animals ask of us are fundamentally other than the questions we ask of them; Lou could not discern 'what was his non-human question, and his uncanny threat' (*StM* 31). The horse thus becomes a perpetual matter of thought to Lou, a process in which the term 'animal' is itself rendered problematic: 'we call him an animal, but we never know what it means'.

This question of the *meaning* of the organic but non-human world is recurrently posed in Lawrence's writing, as if to lead us back to the question itself: what does it mean, to ask what the non-human means? Is it, for example, to attempt to discriminate between different human interpretations of the non-human, or is it an altogether different kind of question? Sometimes, what is at stake is the displacement by modern science of a mode of knowledge of 'nature', as when Cyril, Lettie and Leslie in *The White Peacock* come across some ' "sad and mysterious" ' snowdrops in the woods. ' "What do they mean, do you think?" ', asks Lettie, concluding that they 'belong' to 'some knowledge' from 'an old religion, that we have lost' (*WP* 129). More often, however, the question seems to address a fundamental alterity or ontological gap. *Anthropomorphism* is the concept that emerges in Lawrence's work to confirm the circumscribed or tautological condition of human knowledge. We can debate the meaning of 'animal' within different systems of knowledge, but what if these meanings are by definition human and thus bear no relation to that which the animal is or experiences? When we ask the question, what does the animal mean?, what *kind* of answer might we expect?

In his recent interlinked fictions, *The Lives of Animals* (1999) and *Elizabeth Costello* (2003), J.M. Coetzee proposes Lawrence as a reference point in his exploration of the complexities of anthropomorphism. Elizabeth Costello, a novelist, vegetarian, ecological thinker and animal rights campaigner, has been invited to speak about and debate her theories at the university where her son, John, is a science lecturer. While the novella somewhat transparently uses Costello's sessions at Appleton College as a device with which to stage its intellectual debates, it insistently reminds us that thought goes on within human bodies. Costello is ageing, tired and frail, and her presence in John's household generates tension and conflict; her vulnerability is highlighted in an unexpected conclusion, in which her son pulls the car over to the side of the road and, embracing her 'old flesh', reassures his mother that ' "It will soon be over" ' (*LA* 69).[3]

The shock of this quasi-spontaneous gesture prompts the reader to look back for an interpretation. In the immediate context, Elizabeth has been tearfully berating herself for applying her high-principled critique to John's family, when what she actually sees in them is ' "Only kindness, human-kindness" '. ' "I no longer know where I am" ', she laments, a situation of disorientation and suffering which can be read back into the punishing contradictions of her intellectual and ideological stance. Elizabeth's disavowal of Enlightenment rationality is based on equating its instrumentality with the limits of anthropomorphism: reason, she argues, is 'the being of a certain spectrum of human thinking' (*LA* 23). Thus, if the questions we ask of the non-human are anthropomorphic, so too will be the answers we elicit. Behavioural psychology becomes the focal point of Elizabeth's critique, illustrated by the investigation of the mental capacities of apes by Wolfgang Köhler, a scientist stationed on the island of Tenerife between 1912 and 1920. When Sultan the ape is subjected to an experiment which requires him to build constructions in order to get food, he begins thereby to see ' "how the man's mind works" '; the experiment, argues Costello, draws the ape away from a certain ' "purity of speculation" ' and towards the 'lower' mode of practical or instrumental reason which is what the experimenter seeks to attribute to him (*LA* 28). As N. Katherine Hayles similarly puts it, summarising the conclusions of Heinz von Foerster, an early pioneer of cybernetics, 'Behaviorism does not demonstrate that animals are black boxes that give predictable outputs for given inputs. . . . Rather, behaviorism shows the cleverness and power of the experimenter in getting animals to behave as such.'[4]

The problem Elizabeth faces is that her own theory of the limits of reason confirms the possibility of using anthropomorphism as a *reductio ad absurdum* which can effectively undermine the cognitive claims of any human position whatsoever – including, that is, those which appear, as Elizabeth does, to offer an alternative to rationality. Challenging Thomas Nagel's argument, in the essay 'What Is It Like to Be a Bat?', that anthropomorphism makes it impossible for us to know what it is like for a *bat* to be a bat, Costello retorts that if, in moments of extremity ('before my whole structure of knowledge collapses in panic'), we can imagine what it is like to be dead, then we can imagine what it is to be a bat; what we can share with bats as 'embodied souls' is the experience of fullness of being or 'joy', a fact recognised but suppressed by Descartes, who insisted instead that the animal is 'no more than the machine that constitutes it' (*LA* 33). Something of this 'joy', albeit attached to a creaturely wholeness that transcends the human state, is evident in Gethin Day's rapt observation of a school of porpoises in the unfinished Lawrence story 'The Flying Fish',

> (T)he strong-bodied fish heading in perfect balance of speed underneath, mingling among themselves in some strange single laughter of multiple consciousness, giving off the joy of life, sheer joy of life, togetherness in pure complete motion, many lusty-bodied fish enjoying one laugh of life, sheer togetherness, perfect as passion.[5]

The criticism to which Costello remains open is, as her irritated philosopher daughter-in-law Norma puts it, that ' "there is no position outside of reason where you can stand and lecture about reason and pass judgement on reason" ' (*LA* 48). Any proposition can be adjudged to be self-defeating, in the sense that it is structured by human interests, even if it is about the non-human. Coetzee has Elizabeth suffer the practical consequences of such a contradiction when she offends the Jewish poet Abraham Stern with an analogy between the Holocaust and the everyday slaughter of cattle for meat – as he sees it, an anthropomorphic 'trick with words' which exploits the reality of the Holocaust for the purposes of an argument which does not carry the same moral weight. Elizabeth cannot, it is implied, keep her own interests out of the argument, and in an effort to declare a sensitivity to the preciousness of life, whether human or creaturely, she ends up creating precisely the opposite effect.

On her own terms, the frustrations Elizabeth experiences relate to her use of a discursive rather than literary mode – a situation of multiple irony when we consider Coetzee's recent tendency in intellectual production to write discursively in fiction and to fictionalize when required to be discursive. To think ourselves out of anthropomorphism and into the experience of another creature or being requires a condition of the 'heart' which she calls the 'sympathetic imagination'. It is, she maintains, a condition absent in the Nazi soldiers administering the exterminations in the death camps, but integral to the poet. Here Elizabeth cites Lawrence, alongside Blake and Ted Hughes, Hemingway, Gary Snyder and Robinson Jeffers, in a line of poets who ' "celebrate the primitive and repudiate the Western bias toward abstract thought" '. Something about the framing of this view in Elizabeth's narrative makes it sound uneasily like cliché. When she turns to elaborate further upon what such primitivism might mean, it emerges subtly modified – no longer that imaginative leap which enables us to know what it is for a bat to be a bat, but rather, poetry that '"does not try to find an idea in the animal, that is not about the animal, but is instead the record of an engagement with him"' (*LA* 51).

Lawrence shares with Coetzee an acute consciousness that arguments about animality, and especially the kinds of endorsement of animality with which he became associated, were susceptible to the threat of the anthropomorphic *reductio*. Birkin's transgressively violent verbal attack on Hermione in Ursula's classroom – '"What is it but the worst and last form of intellectualism, this love of yours for passion and the animal instincts?"' (*WL* 41) – testifies to this, as does Kangaroo's furious response to Lovat Somers' Nietzschean analysis of the '"all-too human"' and subsequent enthusiasm for the '"magic of the dark world"': '"What does that nonsense mean? Are you traitor to your own human intelligence?"' (*K* 206). From what kind of position, then, does this allow Lawrence's own narratives to address the question of the animal? How is anthropomorphism to be negotiated? In the rest of the chapter, I want to explore Lawrence's narrativization of animals in the light of Costello's definition of primitivism as 'the record of an engagement'.

2. *The White Peacock*

> 'Be a good animal, true to your animal instinct', was his motto.
> With all this, he was fundamentally very unhappy – and he made
> me also wretched (*WP* 147).

Nowhere in Lawrence's fiction is there such an intensity of human contact with the organic and the creaturely than in his first novel. Perhaps fittingly, then, the nature of its beauty is elegiac; the people of Nethermere are seen in relation to a world which, in a complex combination of ways, they will inevitably lose. With the marriage of Lettie and Leslie, and the forthcoming marriage of George and Meg, Part Three signals the beginning of a 'painful' exile: the 'children' of Nethermere had been a 'small nation with language and blood of our own', the waters and woods 'distilled in the essence of our veins'; but 'it was time for us all to go' (*WP* 237). Gravitation to London occurs, bringing previously inconceivable scenarios such as the Hampstead dinner party at which Cyril and George are reunited with Lettie and Leslie. Nor is exile simply the prerogative of a generation who have just crossed the 'bright sea' of their youth. The Saxton parents, the father a 'pure romanticist, forever seeking the colour of the past in the present's monotony' (*WP* 185), are prevented from settling into middle-age contentment: they emigrate to Canada, evicted from Strelley Mill Farm because of the perpetual dispute with the squire over the rabbits.

The novel's elegiac richness is therefore a doubled condition: it is not just that they must leave their world of natural beauty, but also that it never existed in the first place. The very real temptation to find aspects of the idyll or paean in *The White Peacock* is crucially dependent upon its obverse, the unavailability of a romantic, pantheistic sense of indistinguishable oneness with nature. Only when we realise our profound human *mis*placement in nature can the acute, painfully restorative potential of natural beauty be felt as a desideratum. The sheer ambiguity of 'man's place in nature' is translated into two central studies of misfit or dysfunction. First, in a benign sense, there is Cyril Beardsall, the curiously disembodied experiment in first-person narration that Lawrence was never to repeat. Cyril's life history, ideas and interests are, if not absent, then perpetually subordinated to others in his role of companion or chaperone. While in some respects his close romantic friendship with Emily Saxton prefigures the exhaustively treated struggle for sexual equilibrium in the Paul Morel and Miriam Leivers of *Sons and Lovers*, Cyril remains always an observer of heterosexuality, his ambiguity expressed in a physical attraction towards the significant men in his life – George, Annable, even Leslie Tempest. 'I myself', he observes, on a windswept day that signifies ceaseless, purposeless organic instability, 'seem to have lost my substance, to have become detached from concrete things and the firm trodden pavement of everyday life' (*WP* 83).

The central problem of the novel, however, is posed in the figure of George Saxton. George is doomed to unfulfilment, unable to decide what to do or how to be. Initial impressions suggest the opposite: in the stark scenario in which Lettie must choose between him or Leslie, George is the easygoing, 'natural' working man, 'indifferent to all claims', whose physical allure is provocatively invoked by Lettie – '"Ruddy, dark, and really thrilling eyes"' – in response to Leslie's accusation that she has been '"flirting with a common fellow"' (*WP* 19). But, to the extent that this will become a common Lawrentian scenario – the presentation of physical and mental, sensual and intellectual, labouring and non-labouring types as alternatives – its simple polarity is, equally characteristically, quickly problematized. Cyril talks endlessly to George of chemistry, botany and psychology, of 'life, of sex and its origins; of Schopenhauer and William James', but Lawrence confers upon George an intelligence of open and assimilative power: he 'had hardly a single dogma', 'understood the drift of things very rapidly, and quickly made these ideas part of himself' (*WP* 59). Like his father, who is 'quickened' into 'advanced radical, almost socialist' activity, the indignities of eviction and dispossession force upon George a realization of the limited parochialism of a life on the land, and in Nethermere: '"We known such a lot, an' we known nowt"' (*WP* 201). His father's alternative vision of a new agricultural start in Canada promises only to perpetuate an all-too-animal life – '"I might as well be Flower, the mare"' – and he determines instead to throw himself into the cultural and intellectual maelstrom of the city, where he reads socialist theory and takes this back to the midlands to deliver open-air lectures on the feminist-eugenicist topic of the state endowment of mothers (*WP* 296).

George's realisation, in keeping with this emergent intelligence, is that '"you and Lettie have made me conscious, and now I'm at a dead loss"'; he was '"born a generation too soon – I wasn't ripe enough when I came. I wanted something I hadn't got. I'm something short. I'm like corn in a wet harvest – full, but pappy, no good. Is'll rot"' (*WP* 238, 288). George draws for his analysis on analogy with the lower orders of nature, while recognising that it is precisely the dilemma of the human as thinking matter to be able to disrupt and apparently transcend that analogy. As Lawrence was to write in the *Study of Thomas Hardy*, wild creatures are 'like the fountains whose sources gather their waters until spring-time', but man's rhythm is 'not so simple' (*STH* 31). It is by now securely established that *The White Peacock* is Lawrence's 'red in tooth and claw' novel of Darwinian struggle for existence. 'Cruel' is its key word, and the system of human morality informing the concept of cruelty is constantly at issue. What is our 'place' in nature? Are we like or unlike animals and, if our intellect truly differentiates us, does it also exempt us from the imperatives of the struggle? Who, for example, is best equipped to win Lettie? The narrowing of sexual selection to a brutal choice between two alternatives shows how clearly Lawrence wanted to highlight this issue. In the highly-charged sequence which is the chapter 'The Fascination of the Forbidden Apple', Lettie tortures George with analogies between his own competition with Leslie and those played out in the creaturely world: '"I think a wood-pigeon must enjoy being fought for – and being won; especially if the right one won"' (*WP* 210).

The *right* one? The question raised here recalls the debates surrounding the definition of 'fitness' in Herbert Spencer's controversial interpretation of natural selection as a 'survival of the fittest'. As Raymond Williams notes, T.H. Huxley distanced himself from Social Darwinist appropriations of this formula by insisting that 'fittest' meant, not strongest or best, but 'that which in its situation was best adapted to survive'.[6] Lettie's discourse is charged with an awareness of such debates – she is 'too swift' for George when she invokes Schopenhauer, with the implication of mating as a sacrificial act on the part of the individual for the good of the species – and her cruelty seems designed to raise George's awareness of the complexities of natural selection when transferred to the human domain. Natural analogies are floated in order to be undermined: it would be good to be free like larks, but we can't, because we '"have to consider things"'; trees '"know how to die"', humans don't. '"Don't you think life is very cruel, George – and love the cruellest of all?"', she asks (*WP* 210). The irony here is that we would expect cruelty to take the form of natural force asserting itself, blind to issues of moral value or sentiment, yet in Lettie's case the necessity is to choose the 'weaker' option. Whatever are the factors that have made Lettie's choice of Leslie inevitable and a question of 'fitness' – '"the chord of my life is being twisted, and I cannot wrench it free and untwine it again . . . I am not strong enough"' – they must belong to the human realms of culture and class. We intuit this because Lawrence, in a scene which shows him far from oblivious to the strategies of romantic fiction, has George and Lettie part with a 'long, passionate embrace, mouth to mouth'; in some non-human realm, we sense, it is they who are the true or natural mates.

Little wonder, then, that the necessity of being a 'good animal' is declared by the unhappy and tragic figure of Annable. However briefly sketched, the character carries a powerful significance for the rest of Lawrence's writing as it unravels. It is certainly worth noting that, in the motto 'be a good animal', the novel explores and even satirizes a position which could, subsequently, all too easily attach itself to the popular irrationalist mythology surrounding Lawrence himself. Annable is a sketch or prototype to which Lawrence returns in the form of Oliver Mellors in his last novel, *Lady Chatterley's Lover*; in *The White Peacock*, Annable provides a variant on the problem of George. What the prototype investigates is the paradoxical entwining of animality and culture in humans. It *may* be our animal natures to produce culture and intellect; or, animality might itself be a certain condition of thought. As Lou Witt will put it, ' "men always do leave off really thinking, when the last bit of wild animal dies in them" ' (*SM* 61). Distinguishing Annable and Mellors as gamekeepers in what Worthen calls a '*déclassé*' role is their special combination of intellectuality with an inside experience of genteel upper- or upper-middle-class life, the intelligence enabling them to use or *perform* their different class identities as the occasion demands.[7] Annable studied at Cambridge before his education was terminated by his father's bankruptcy; he entered the church, met Lady Chrystabel and during a marriage of over three years was, according to his interpretation, exploited by her as a sexual and aesthetic object – a 'Poor Young Man' deriving from French romantic fiction, a Greek statue, and ' "her animal – *son animal – son boeuf*" ' (*WP* 151). Cyril finds him a 'thorough materialist', a hater of culture and 'a man of one idea: – that all civilization was the painted fungus of rottenness'; his physique and vitality are nevertheless a 'great attraction' to Cyril, and in a rather unconvincing narrative turn, begins to cultivates the acquaintance of this 'fine fellow'.

What is clear, however, is that Annable's animality is an *idea*, or a certain version of materialism, that he has derived from culture and applied singlemindedly, in a spirit combining self-mocking satire with a desire for indirect revenge, against a ruling class which has exploited him as its *own* aestheticized idea of animality. The victims of this policy turn out, though, not to be the ruling class, but his wife and 'lovely little litter' of eight children:

> '– aren't they a pretty bag o' ferrets? – natural as weasels – that's what I said they should be – bred up like a bunch o' young foxes, to run as they would . . .'.
> 'They're natural – they can fend for themselves like wild beasts do,' he replied, grinning (*WP* 131–2).

As the reader has seen the Kennels, and the exploits of the unfortunate Sam, Annable's boasts here are rent by contradiction, with the word 'natural' held up, via repetition, for ironic scrutiny. His children are *not* ferrets, weasels or foxes; they have, on the contrary, been artificially 'bred up' to be what he said they 'should be' – that is, unbred. 'Natural' in Annable's lexicon is erroneously limited to 'animal'; the neglect of the natural human propensity to be cultural ends in cruelty and impoverishment. The condemnation of his policy is felt most keenly, not so much in the refined disgust of the young people of Nethermere, as in the mournful words of his wife: ' "I canna manage 'em, I canna . . ." ' (*WP* 134).

The novel thus reveals the fault of Annable's concept of the 'good animal' to lie in an anthropomorphism which, paradoxically, fails to be anthropomorphic *enough* to treat humans as human. While we are certainly 'in' nature, as T.H. Huxley had put it, we are less securely 'of' it; the analogy must be constantly reassessed if it is to be of any analytic value. As if to question Annable's paradoxical idealization of the animal condition, the novel presents the people of Nethermere in constant contact with real creatures. This is to experience the amorality of the animal, understood by those who regularly engage with it: a chick wanders into the fire and roasts itself, with barely a murmur of protest from the Saxton family; a sow consumes three of her own young, but remains for George a 'fine sow', not an 'offence to creation' as Cyril would have it; a bee's wing is accidentally broken by George and so with an ' "Oh, dear – pity!" ' he crushes the creature between his fingers. George's 'mercy' killing of Mrs. Nickie Ben has a pitilessness about it – he smiles as he fastens the noose – which recalls the famously casual hanging of a litter of puppies by the young Hareton Earnshaw in Emily Brontë's *Wuthering Heights*, suggesting an inevitable comparison with that novel's transgressive notation of an order of natural or material compulsion, animal and human intertwined, which is oblivious to systems of morality and social conscience. For Lettie, the full cruelty of the natural order is brought home by the discovery in the woods of their exiled father, who momentarily wakes to hear 'the scream of a rabbit caught by a weasel', and eventually dies like a wild animal (*WP* 22).

Even here, however, the animal condition can be represented neither as pristine otherness nor as organic wholeness. Rabbits, the most pervasive of *The White Peacock*'s creatures, are hunted both by weasels and humans; one of the novel's moments of great blood-lust is when it falls to Leslie to practically decapitate a wounded rabbit 'in his excitement to kill it' (*WP* 50). But rabbits are also always focal points of political and economic dispute between the squire and the Saxtons as his tenant farmers. While the squire 'loved his rabbits' for the profit they could bring him in Nottingham, their freedom has the obverse effect on the Strelley Mill economy. As George puts it, ' "the valley is running all wild and unprofitable" ', the rabbits robbing him of the last vestiges of that productive interaction with the non-human which is 'farming': ' "As it is, we depend on the milk-round, and on the carting which I do for the council. You can't call it farming. We're a miserable mixture of farmer, milkman, greengrocer, and carting contractor. It's a shabby business" ' (*WP* 61). The Saxtons lay their rabbit traps for reasons of economy, not blood-lust; similarly Annable, the 'good animal', occupies the less-than-creaturely role of gamekeeper within this contested economy.

Nature in *The White Peacock* is thus an always-already 'managed' condition, informed by human interests and priorities. Human and non-human are locked into systems of conflict, dependency, but of necessary engagement and relationship. In the *Study of Thomas Hardy* (1915), Lawrence was to indicate the logical extension of this in the *idea* of Nature itself, always an instance of human colonization. Questioning the logic by which the *raison d'être* of flowering or blossoming is seen to lie in reproduction rather than in a fullness of being-in-itself, Lawrence notes that for biologists there is always the concept of 'excess', because 'they have made the measure, and the supply must be made to fit' (*STH* 31). Cyril Beardsall's regular scrutiny of his own and others' transformation of nature through the use of poetic figure highlights the seeming impossibility of ever eluding this anthropomorphism. As a result, Cyril's desires, like those of his friend George, are unplaceable. Looking into a lark's nest, Cyril momentarily envies the serenity, warmth and 'unison' of the 'two little specks of birds', but he is drawn out again towards the cold wind and the image of a 'cold swan', 'trailing its black feet' and 'clacking its great hollow wings': 'What did I want that I turned thus from one thing to the other'? When he later briefly returns to Nethermere to register the decline of George, *it* has forgotten *him*: 'I wanted to be recognised by something'. The fact that he can find no place, no guaranteed distinction of meaning between the animal and the human, further confirms Cyril's gravitation towards the city. While there, however, his observational stance both perpetuates the pastoral, and hints at a vision of human kinship with impersonal material forces, a 'complex mesh' of weaving and intermingling bodies:

> I like to sit a long time by the hollyhocks watching the throng of varied bees which poise and hesitate outside the wild flowers, then swing in with a hum which sets everything aquiver. But still more fascinating it is to watch the come and go of people weaving and intermingling in the complex mesh of their intentions, with all the subtle grace and mystery of their moving, shapely bodies (*WP* 285–6).

3. *Women in Love* and *St. Mawr*

Gerald's Arab mare, Mrs. Salmon's canaries, the cat Mino and his wild female companion, a herd of Highland cattle, Winifred Crich's Pekinese, Looloo, her rabbit Bismarck and the kitten Leo, a robin, and some yellowhammers.

If creatures are, literally, recurrent figures in *Women in Love*, still more is the creaturely recurrent as figurative expression. Gudrun cries 'like a seagull', Gerald is an 'amphibious beast', his head 'blunt and blind like a seal's', Christiana Crich is 'like a bird of prey, with the fascinating beauty and abstraction of a hawk', Birkin is a 'chameleon', Hermione has a 'horse-face', Loerke is 'some strange creature, a rabbit or a bat, or a brown seal'. There is 'the Pussum', though also, for Loerke, 'the Gerald'.

As in *The White Peacock*, the metaphorical likeness between humans and animals calls up the question of analogy, suggesting a kinship of unbroken continuity along the lines of a Darwinian evolutionary order. While such creatureliness does not always appear flattering to the human, *Women in Love* also regularly highlights the view that to be an animal is far *preferable* to being human, and in this sense the novel continually gestures towards a post-human condition in the most literal sense. Lawrence's horror and dismay at the war, unstated but implicit, are transposed into a searching examination of the most fundamental aspects of our claim to be human: love and marriage, freedom and equality, individual identity, the integrity of language. If the war is symptomatic of the nature of our evolution, then it can only be a matter of time before the processes of self-destruction are complete. For Birkin, this is a condition devoutly to be wished: humanity is a 'defilement' of the world, one of the mistakes of what he calls 'creation', and in that sense, as he reminds Ursula, neither inevitable nor permanent. Like the dinosaurs, we can become extinct, leaving the world both to those creatures who preceded us – ' "don't you find it a beautiful clean thought, a world empty of people, just uninterrupted grass, and a hare sitting up? . . . I much prefer to think of the lark rising up in the morning upon a human-less world" ' (*WL* 127–8) – and open for the evolution of 'marvellous', 'new', 'non-human' forms: we could, Birkin maintains, be ' "dispensed with" ', should we fail ' "creatively to change and develop" ' (*WL* 478).

Given that Ursula is profoundly sceptical of Birkin's melodramatic pessimism-optimism, it is significant that in her quieter moments she too develops a 'profound grudge against the human being', and expresses a belief in the need to fulfil an alternative to love which is ' "something inhuman" ' or which ' "isn't so merely *human*" ' (*WL* 438). The corollary is a love of children and animals, but 'best of all the animals, that were single and unsocial as she herself was':

> She loved the horses and cows in the field. Each was single and to itself, magical. It was not referred away to some detestable social principle. It was incapable of soulfulness and tragedy, which she detested so profoundly (*WL* 244).

We know, however, from the precedents in Lawrence (the espoused animalities of Annable and Hermione, say), and from the dilemma of Elizabeth

Costello, that this is immediately problematic. When Ursula looks at horses and cows, does she not see a principle of asociality which is her own desideratum? *Are* animals magically single? How appropriate, similarly, is Birkin's sense of the *pristine* to the condition of the hare or the lark? Lawrence's alertness to the perils of anthropomorphism translates, in the fiction, into a dialogizing of every stated position, and an insinuation that the ideas claiming to escape anthropomorphism might be the most anthropomorphic of all. The issue is raised with some explicitness in *Women in Love*. Walking along a lane, the sisters see a robin singing on a bush: Gudrun's ' "doesn't he feel important?" ' is matched by Ursula's image of a ' "little Lloyd George of the air" ' (*WL* 263–4). For days afterwards, Ursula sees robins as stout, short and obtrusive politicians, until a glimpse of some yellowhammers, 'uncanny and inhuman, like flaring yellow barbs shooting through the air on some weird, living errand', provokes a reaction of revulsion: it is 'impudence' to look at robins as if they were human beings, because they are, rather, the 'unknown forces' of 'another world'. ' "How stupid anthropomorphism is!" ', she concludes, craftily exonerating herself from the coining of the phrase by attributing it to the influence of Gudrun.

It would, nevertheless, be unwise to see in Ursula's exclamation a simple credo for the novel's treatment of the animal. *Women in Love*, on the contrary, amply demonstrates an often overlooked feature of Lawrence's writing: namely, its unhesitating willingness to anthropomorphize the animal. Mino the cat sits 'considering for a moment' before accosting the wild queen who enters the garden; he walks up to her with 'manly nonchalance', looks 'casually' down on her, and then, after cuffing her 'for pure excess', he 'pretended to take no notice of her' (*WL* 148–9). Winifred Crich is a pastiche of sentimental, gushing anthropomorphism towards her pet Pekinese, Looloo; yet it is the narrative voice that sees in the dog a 'grievous resignation', and attributes to him fretfulness, chagrin, mortification and reproach: he is, in conclusion, 'vanquished in his extreme agedness of being' (*WL* 236). The tendency has been established in *The White Peacock*: on a windy, sunny Sunday in June, fowls peck with 'sabbath decorum', pigs sleep in the sun, grunting 'from sheer luxury', and a squirrel lies on a tree 'listening', and then suddenly departs 'chuckling to himself' (*WP* 205). *Sons and Lovers* memorably contains a scene in which Bill, the bull terrier, is 'grinning all over' and 'panting with happiness' while playing with Paul, whom he 'adores' (*SL* 259). In *St. Mawr*, Lou reflects, in a passage of great beauty, on the 'sadness' of the horse, who 'had waited in vain for some one noble to serve' (*StM* 83–4).

Such anthropomorphisms might be placed within the broader problematic of how we treat animals *aesthetically*, a major and explicit concern of *Women in Love*. In the sense that we are bound to represent, or re-present, animality, art relates to the wider question of what we *do* with animals: how and how far we appropriate, dispose of, care for, frame and tame them. Such questions, then, bear significantly upon the problem of determining our 'place' in nature. Here, in contrast to *The White Peacock*, the emphasis is on the ownership of animals through domestication, in keeping with a focus no longer on rural community but on middle-class intellectuals sharing a mobility of class, location and circumstance. As representatives of a once-farming family whose history as such is surveyed in *The Rainbow*, Ursula and Gudrun Brangwen are now artists and teachers; Rupert Birkin is a schools inspector, about whose history very little is known, and Gerald Crich is a rich industrialist who inherits his father's mining company and, as such, bears a heavy responsibility for the 'resources' – human, animal, material – that are at his disposal.

Let us briefly survey the intricate, overlapping relationship in the novel between the organic, including the creaturely, and art, beginning with the art of sketching. First, there is Ursula's class, sketching catkins, and Birkin's intervention as inspector, advising the use of coloured crayons to emphasize the 'facts' (not the 'subjective impression') of difference between the male and female organs of the plant. Hermione Roddice's interruption of the scene prefigures two later moments: first, at Breadalby, when she comes across Birkin engaged in copying from a Chinese drawing of geese ("I know", he maintains, "what centres they live from – what they perceive and feel – the hot, stinging centrality of a goose in the flux of cold water and mud ..."[WL 89]), and then in the chapter 'Sketchbook', when Hermione encounters the Brangwen sisters sketching by the side of Willey Water and, with Gerald's hapless complicity, inadvertently drops Gudrun's book into the water.

Sketching is direct and spontaneous, tentative and provisional, yet aims to capture the essential features of the object. While in the latter sense it can be revelatory – Birkin claims, under the pressure of Hermione's interrogation, that he learns more of China from the drawing than 'reading all the books' – it at the same time expresses the fragility of knowledge as embodied in the fleeting relationship between subject and object. Hermione's clumsy interruptions, culminating in the ruining of Gudrun's sketchbook, betray her helpless distance from the sensitivity to animality she claims to espouse. Gudrun is, of course, central to this debate within the novel, both as an established artist who in the words of Thomas Crich to his daughter '"makes animals and birds in wood and clay, that the people in London write about in the papers, praising them to the skies"', and as a tutor to Winifred in drawing and modelling. Gudrun helps Winifred to sketch and capture the 'Looliness' of her Looloo, a 'grotesque little diagram of a grotesque little animal' (*WL* 236). Tutor and pupil are well-matched, in that while Winifred is a 'detached, ironic child', detachment and irony are characteristic of Gudrun's aestheticized attitude to the world: she is a perpetual onlooker and outsider, watching the Crich wedding guests with an 'objective curiosity' which enables her to 'stamp' and 'finish' them as if they were marionettes. Ursula notes that Gudrun always does nature in miniature, '"birds and tiny animals"' that '"one can put between one's hands"': she sees the world '"through the wrong end of the opera glasses"' (*WL* 39).

In apparent contrast to this aesthetic, though again in close engagement with the tendencies of modernism, the novel also stages a debate around so-called primitive art, focused around two key passages of response to the West African wooden fetishes kept by Halliday in his flat. First there is Gerald's shocked questioning of Birkin's estimation as 'high art' of the statuette of the African woman in labour, her face 'abstracted in utter physical stress' (*WL* 79). Second, there are Birkin's later, extended musings on another of the female figures, 'tall, slim and elegant', with a tiny, beetle-like face, short legs and 'protruberant buttocks'. Birkin's interpretation of the beetle-like face is that it represents 'thousands of years' of a process of dissolution into sensuality, directly antithetical to the Spencerean evolution of the white European races towards intellectual sophistication, yet at the same time also 'progressive': the woman embodies millennia of 'mindless progressive knowledge through the senses' (*WL* 253).

These diverse enquiries into current discourses on art, from the education of children, through to Gudrun's professionalism and Birkin's critical analysis, could be said to culminate in the extended discussion of modernism which is the centrepiece of the 'Snow' chapter.[8] In focusing on the photogravure of Loerke's bronze statuette of a girl on a horse, the scene is a reprise, in the aesthetic domain, of the first major instance of the human–animal encounter in the novel – that is, of Gerald Crich's taming of his Arab mare at the railway level-crossing in 'Coaldust'. What highlights the unity of the scenes is the reaction of Ursula to the treatment of the horse. In the first instance, Gerald holds the terrified animal at the level-crossing while his own colliery train rumbles past (Gerald, then, owns both horse and train). As if to emphasize the perversity of the act, the train, 'as if wanting to see what could be done', inexplicably brakes and reverses in front of the mare. The horse recoils 'like a spring let go', rebounds 'like a drop of water from hot iron', but Gerald, 'half-smiling', holds her 'with an almost mechanical relentlessness' (*WL*, 111). Gudrun sees Gerald initially as 'very picturesque' and the whole scene, transposed through the disinterested perspective of the guard in his van as 'spectacular' (that is, pertaining to spectacle), 'isolated and momentary' – both reactions in keeping with her aesthetic of distance. Gudrun is relatively static and 'spellbound'; she turns white at the sight of the horse's blood, and her only explicit protest is to cry at Gerald, like a 'gull' or a 'witch', '"I should think you're proud"', once the event is over. It is left to Ursula to react, throughout, hotly and passionately to the man's abuse of the horse. '"Let her go!"', she cries repeatedly, 'completely outside herself', and calling Gerald a fool – '"she's bleeding!"'. Gudrun 'hates' Ursula bitterly for this reaction; her powerful and naked voice is 'unendurable' (*WL* 111–12).

Ursula's determination to speak up for the 'sensitivity' of the animal – ' "Does he think he's grand, when he's bullied a sensitive creature, ten times as sensitive as himself?" ' – carries over directly into the argument over Loerke's statuette. Why, she asks, has Loerke made the horse stiff, stock, stupid and brutal? ' "Horses are sensitive, quite delicate and sensitive, really" ' (*WL* 430). For her, the human exploitation of a horse is identical, but transposed into the domain of art; the offence is doubled, however, by her intuition – correct, as it turns out – that Loerke has also physically abused the teenage girl who posed for the statuette. The difference in this scene is that Ursula can only make her argument on the basis of a realist aesthetic – the statuette should present a 'picture of a horse', but instead falsifies the horse, as an image of Loerke's own 'stock, stupid brutality' – which her companions, as modernists, have critically interrogated and rejected. Ursula's fury is matched by Gudrun's with her: ' "What do you mean by 'it is a picture of a horse'? . . . What do you mean by a horse?" ' What Ursula means, for Gudrun, is her own idea of a horse, in line with the hidden anthropomorphic tendencies of so-called realist verisimilitude; whereas, ' "there is another idea" ' (of art) ' "altogether" '. It is left to Loerke to articulate this idea in terms of a fully-blown modernist aesthetic of impersonality, involving the complete separation of the work of art and its manipulation of abstract '*form*' from the question of the representation of, or even relationship with, an anterior living world: ' "Do you see, you *must not* confuse the relative world of action, with the absolute world of art. That you *must not do*" ' (*WL* 431).

The reader might well connect Lawrence's complex manipulation of sympathies across these two scenes with the difficulties of anthropomorphism. Ursula's fervent defence of the integrity and sensitivity of the animal prompts affection; her outspokenness is the measure of a humane or humanistic response to the cynical or instrumentalist use of living matter as raw material. But its uncontrolled emotionalism is also, and particularly in the second scene, a source of unease: as she sits after the tirade, twisting her handkerchief, 'throbbing violently', and disliked by Gudrun, Loerke and Gerald, her lack of containment seems regrettable and embarrassing. In straying into aesthetic theory, Ursula is led into error: it is easy to deduce that her theory of art as representation is naïve and limited. Similarly, when Ursula is given the opportunity to question Gerald about his treatment of the mare at the level-crossing, her argument for the rights of the horse as a living creature – ' "She has as much right to her own being, as you have to yours" ' – is immediately exposed as sentimental and anthropomorphic, not only by Gerald, but also by Hermione, who has certainly voiced her own sympathy for the creaturely, and Birkin, her intellectual as well as emotional ally: ' "Nothing is so detestable" ', the latter notes sharply, ' "as the maudlin attributing of human feelings and consciousness to animals" ' (*WL* 139).

Lawrence therefore tends to insinuate that along with Ursula's appealing humanistic warmth goes an intellectual vulnerability, a lack of precision or tenacity in the thinking of matter. The chapter 'Mino' stages, as if for the benefit of a tentatively courting Birkin and Ursula, an analogy between the animal and the human, in the domain of sexual selection, which is reminiscent of *The White Peacock*. Mino's haughty behaviour is, as I have already indicated, heavily anthropomorphized by the narrative voice. However, when Ursula does likewise along the lines of a feminist politics, linking his 'bullying' to that of Gerald with the horse and interpeting both as the ' "assumption of male superiority" ', she begins again to sound shrill and impulsive. Lawrence has Ursula translate Birkin's notion of 'superfine stability' between the cats, with the female as a 'star' in the male orbit, into the word 'satellite' – ' "There – there – you've given yourself away!" '. In part, she is right to suspect as 'sophistries' Birkin's attempt to dress up traditional power relations in a new language of metaphysics; in part too, hers is a hasty misreading – Birkin has not said 'satellite'. Each is by turns frustrated and enamoured by the other's persistence: the playful sparring mimics, of course, the courtship rituals of the cats. Lawrence cannot resist closing with the fact that, when the landlady interrupts them to announce tea, they both look at her 'very much as the cats had looked at them' (*WL* 150–1).

I have focused here on the portrayal of Ursula because of the readiness with which we might conclude that she is, in Elizabeth Costello's sense, the 'heart' of *Women in Love*, a voice speaking for the sensitivity of the creaturely, and against the cynical detachment from and exploitation of matter *as if it were* inert raw material. Like Costello, Ursula misrecognizes her own anthropomorphism: she proclaims its 'stupidity', yet on several occasions is revealed to be more guilty of it than any of those around her. Differing from Winifred Crich, whose diabolic 'almost inhuman' chuckle connects anthropomorphism with monstrous transfigurations, hers is an anthropomorphism which attaches itself to its seeming obverse, the 'rights' of creatures to be free of appropriation by humans, to maintain their integrity and singleness.

The novel thus makes available a number of alternative positions on animals, the distinctions between these positions often seeming fluid and indefinite. Creatures are pristine and separate dwellers in 'another world', and therefore never to be anthropomorphized; yet creatures are, as Lawrence's own prose demonstrates, always ripe for anthropomorphic transformation. Creatures are far more sensitive and intelligent than humans; yet we cannot forget either the recurrent recognition of the *stupidity* of creatures. ' "Isn't it a *fool*? . . . Isn't it a sickening *fool*?" ', cries Gudrun with 'vindictive mockery' as she nurses an arm lacerated by the rabbit Bismarck (*WL* 242). Such mockery of the animal condition has already been dramatically demonstrated in Gudrun's eurythmic dancing before Gerald's Highland cattle; fear is present on both sides of the encounter, but Gudrun is driven to perist in her 'sardonic' and 'ironic' display (she shares the faint smile that Gerald wore when taming the mare) until she triumphs by running at the herd and chasing the terrified animals away. No more is Ursula exempt from this position. ' "How can one have any respect for a creature that is so easily taken in?" ', she proclaims, on seeing Mrs. Salmon's canaries tricked into sleep. This assumed stupidity of creatures is precisely what underpins Gerald's Cartesian-industrialist logic that the Arab mare is there for his use and that it is the function of a 'natural order' for man to subdue a horse rather than ' "go down on his knees to it" ' (*WL* 139).

The multiple response of Lawrence's fiction to the question of the meaning of animals has something to do with the fact that, as in Haraway's concept of posthuman kinship, distinctions between the human and the non-human might 'leak' in more than one direction. If what we share with animals is a bodily materiality, then analogy can work both ways: if we are like them, they are like us; to the extent that we are animal, they are human. Anthropomorphism in this light is less a ' "mistake" ' than an expanded acknowledgement of material kinship – expanded, that is, beyond the Darwinian emphasis on the creaturely in the human. We are reminded of Elizabeth Costello's insistence on the shared 'joy' of the 'embodied soul'. Lawrence's scandalous anthropomorphizing might thus be viewed as a self-conscious, Bergsonian provocation to think against the evolutionary grain.

At the same time, if to be animal is also to be human, then to be human is also to share the stupidity of the creaturely. Mrs. Salmon's canaries go to sleep because the cover over their cage reproduces the effect of night; their stupidity is a condition of automatic response or mechanism. While an Elizabeth Costello might contest this logic, attributing to the creatures a more speculative response, it is incontestable that the existence of reflex action (and with it the behaviourist attempt to turn learned response into reflex action) constitutes a crucial perspective on a shared bodily condition. In evolutionary discourse from Darwin through Samuel Butler to Bergson, *instinct* emerges as a concept which insistently calls into question the boundary between organic and mechanical. 'We cannot walk nor read nor write perfectly till we can do so automatically', wrote Butler, redefining life as 'that property of matter whereby it can remember'.[9] The material internalization of memory as unconscious habit is thus the ontogenetic model for heredity at a phylogenetic level: we do things instinctively and 'automatically' from birth because our bodies 'remember' what our predecessors – human or animal – did. Early education and 'the theological systems of the last eighteen hundred years' have, Butler claims, led us to 'under-estimate' the 'great powers' of animals, for example to communicate ideas to each other. The 'stupidity' of automatism becomes the intelligence of instinctive knowledge, a phenomenon which Lawrence echoes, in *Kangaroo*, in a beguiling phrase, as 'the stupendous wits of brainless intelligence' (*K* 299). Yet this instinctive intelligence is precisely what – foreshadowing Freud – we least understand in ourselves: 'all the main business of life is done', Butler maintains, 'unconsciously or semi-consciously'. In this transgressive territory, Butler is anxious and divided: he baulks, for example, at Ribot's contention that '"Instinct advances with a mechanical certainty"', proposing to replace the word 'mechanical' with the phrase '"with apparent certainty"', in order to uphold the theory that what distinguishes life from machinery is the disposition to slight variation; yet he is equally committed, and drawn, to the description of unconscious reaction and habit as automatism.[10] Butler's most acute anticipation of the contemporary cyborg emerges in the evolutionary view that 'machines are the manner in which man is varying at this moment'. The process, he stresses, is a natural one ('for all growth is only somebody making something'): machines become 'additions to our limbs', and in this sense become part of a conscious destiny. Drawing precisely on the roots of the term 'cybernetic', 'we are', Butler maintains, 'no longer without a helm, but can steer each creature . . . into *some* – and into a very distant – harbour'.[11]

In Lawrence, as the humanist critic knows, mechanism and automatism mean death to the living creature. Yet Lawrence consistently portays humans and animals in a shared condition of mechanism or automatism. Gerald's mare, we remember, not only spins and swerves 'like a wind' but rebounds 'like a drop of water from hot iron' and recoils 'like a spring let go'; Bismarck's body similarly flies 'like a spring coiled and released' (*WL* 110–11, 240). Paul Morel, in attacking Miriam, says things 'mechanically', his sayings 'jetted off' like 'sparks from electricity' (*SL* 258). Faced with Gudrun's performance in front of the cattle, Gerald can only 'automatically' repeat a question at her, while she similarly becomes aware of a question asking itself automatically and 'on the edge of her consciousness': '"Why *are* you behaving in this *impossible* and ridiculous fashion?"' (*WL* 168, 171). It is a commonplace observation on Lawrence's fiction that characters can be found consciously thinking or doing one thing while unconsciously thinking or doing another. When the thought 'enters' Henry Grenfell that he should marry March, he is 'arrested' for some moments in the middle of a field, a dead rabbit hanging in his hand; his mind 'waits' in amazement, calculates, and then acquiesces to the idea (*TN* 23).

Butler's ideas help us to frame the paradoxes of Lawrence's treatment of the engagement with animals. Ideas of evolution and instinct make it possible to think together the overt humanizing of animals on the one hand, and on the other the subjugation of animals on the basis of an intellect which cannot be wished away. Each of these positions avoids the predication of an idealized, animal otherness, because such a moral discourse of intense solicitude for the rights or politics of the animal condition *reproduces* or colludes with – as Lawrence might have deduced from Nietzsche – the objectifying distance of industrial-scientific ideology. Yet, again paradoxically, we acknowledge in Lawrence's writing the strong appeal both to the otherness and the sensitivity of the creaturely; his insistence is that these can only exist within an ensemble of positions which also emphasise material kinship.

Perhaps the strongest paradox, and the most forthright challenge to the taboos surrounding the mechanical and the organic, would be to suggest that our sensitivity and *loveliness* as creatures partake of the condition of the machine. *St. Mawr* explores these questions with a peculiar intensity of focus on the animal itself. On the point of buying St. Mawr, Lou Witt 'realizes' that the horse inhabits a world which was also, perhaps, that of the 'old Greek horses':

> With their strangely equine heads, and something of a snake in their way of looking round, and lifting their sensitive, dangerous muzzles, they moved in a prehistoric twilight where all things loomed phantasmagoric, all on one plane, sudden presences suddenly jutting out of the matrix. It was another world, an older, heavily potent world. And in this world the horse was swift and fierce and supreme, undominated and unsurpassed (*StM* 35).

This is a complex act of imagining, combining cultural and physiological perspectives. The historical framework combines human and evolutionary time: while all horses belong to a 'prehistoric' time before the evolution of humans, their post-human history varies according to their status in and treatment by different cultures. But Lou also speculates upon the perceptual apparatus of the horse, the 'phantasmagoric' single plane of things periodically interrupted by objects 'suddenly jutting out of the matrix'. This bears a striking resemblance to the conclusions drawn by a group of neuroscientists, including the young Chilean Humberto Maturana, in a paper entitled 'What the Frog's Eye Tells the Frog's Brain' (1959). Having planted microelectrodes in the frog's brain, the researchers effectively hitched the brain to a cybernetic circuit. Through this experiment, they were able to deduce that, for the frog, 'small objects in fast, erratic motion' (such as flies) 'elicited maximum response, whereas large, slow-moving objects evoked little or no response'. This showed that that the frog's perception actively constructs and organizes reality according to its own survival instincts instead of presenting an accurate picture. All knowledge, Maturana concluded, is situated; the scientist's knowledge of the frog's brain is no less selective than the frog's knowledge of its surroundings, because the frog's brain had become connected to a circuit which included the researchers, whose perceptions were 'at least as transformative as the frog's'.[12]

Maturana was to realise, as Hayles puts it, that while the conclusions about the frog 'blew a hole in realist epistemology', the methodology of the researchers themselves was still firmly rooted in the same realism, and that an appropriately 'new epistemology' was needed. Lewis, St. Mawr's groom, indicates that the troublesome horse needs to be met 'half-way', and thus symbolizes the tale's struggle towards a new epistemology which might bridge the gap from the human world to 'that terrific equine twilight'. When the crucial accident occurs, St. Mawr rearing and Rico pulling him back over onto himself, Lawrence's description wavers markedly between the animal, the mechanical, the mythical and the supernatural. St. Mawr is embedded by metaphor in the animal order: in struggling to his feet he 'gave a great curve like a fish' and rests in mid-position 'almost like some terrible lizard'. At the same time he 'shrank like a steel spring, away – not to be touched', and then 'seemed to be seeing legions of ghosts, down the dark avenues of all the centuries that have lapsed since the horse became subject to man' (*StM* 76–7).

This restless discourse embodies the difficulty of finding a perspective from which to know St. Mawr, and points to the irony of the phrase 'subject to'. St. Mawr is indeed subject to the various, speculative projections of the human imagination, whether in terms of myth or of machine, but it does not follow that he is either contained or containable. The explicit preoccupation of the story is subjection through domestication: do St. Mawr's various misdemeanours arise from the 'natural wild thing' in him or from the 'slavish malevolence of a domesticated creature'? Through the guise of Lou's thoughts, the narrative does not shrink from sketching out what a natural wild state would be:

> The wild animal is at every moment intensely self-disciplined, poised in the tension of self-defence, self-preservation, and self-assertion. The moments of relaxation are rare and most carefully chosen. Even sleep is watchful, guarded, unrelaxing, the wild courage pitched one degree higher than the wild fear. Courage, the wild thing's courage to maintain itself alone and living in the midst of a diverse universe (*StM* 82).

The beauty of this passage in its celebration of animal 'courage' lies in its quality of 'poise'. Just as the animal is poised in its individuality, and between sleep and waking, so the description, like the concept of instinct, is poised between the organic and the mechanical, the animal's unrelaxed 'self-discipline' and self-defence connoting an automatic readiness within a 'diverse universe' of harsh, Darwinian struggle. When such discipline is located by Lawrence in the instinct to hunt, for example in *The Fox*, the result is a version of 'fate' which might remind the contemporary reader of the smart precision killing of posthuman computerised warfare: once the hunter-as-machine has locked onto its prey, personal 'cleverness' is overridden – bullets fly home as 'a sheer projection of your own fate into the fate of the deer' (*TN* 24), and sexual rivals can be felled by the deft cutting of a tree. This 'psychic attraction' or 'hunter's telepathy' is also for Lawrence, significantly, a mode of 'abstraction', whether the hunter possesses a gun (for abstraction and the machine are generally synonymous in Lawrence) or not (*P* 28).

Speculation in *St. Mawr* on the nature and availability of the wild and pristine therefore involves a return to the debate which began with Annable, concerning the relationship between mind and animality and how these might be thought together. Here Lewis the Welsh groom is the focal point of Lou and her mother's discussion of 'real men' (*StM* 58–62). Mrs. Witt, impressed by Lewis's 'extraordinary' hair, attributes it to his stupidity, animality and absence of mind, lamenting the fact that life will give body or mind but never both together, even though she also recognizes in the groom's eyes – ' "the eyes of a human cat" ' – a 'strange sort of intelligence'. Lou exposes her mother's theories as conventional and modish: in Bergsonian manner she dismisses the faculty of mind as an overrated adumbration of the already known – ' "stringing the same beads over and over again" ' – and tries to raise the level of debate onto the subject of ' "real mind" '. Lou realizes that, for her, mind is not antithetical to but rather coincides with animality, once the latter is carefully interrogated (' "we never know what it means ..." '); paradoxically, the integrity she finds in animals rather than men – ' "Why can't one say in the same way, of a man: *He's a man?*" ' – is a function of their 'mystery' rather than of definition or intelligence. Real mind, she decides, is mysterious in its coincidence with the scientific understanding of instinct or, in Lawrence's vocabulary here, of intuition, as possessed by Lewis. Again the question is posed: do we conceptualize the automatism of instinct as stupidity (Mrs. Witt's verdict on Lewis), or does Lewis possess, as Lou puts it, ' "a good intuitive mind, he knows things without thinking them" ' – a mode of ' "thinking quick" '. Her mother persists in accusing Lou of wanting a 'cave man' to knock her over the head, but Lou, equally, insists on subtler discriminations: the cave man is 'a brute, a degenerate', and not a 'real human animal'; the latter would – if it were anywhere realized – combine the animal's ability to 'get life straight from the source' with 'real' thinking:

> A pure animal man would be as lovely as a deer or a leopard, burning like a flame fed straight from underneath. And he'd be part of the unseen, like a mouse is, even. And he'd never cease to wonder, he'd breathe silence and unseen wonder, as the partridges do, running in the stubble. He'd be all the animals in turn, instead of one, fixed, automatic thing, which he is now, grinding on the nerves (*StM* 62).

Mrs. Witt's blunt response – ' "There are no such men" ' – underlines the purely utopian nature of this projection. But in Lou's thinking we cannot translate utopian as 'idealized'. In the tale's major discursive interlude, the sight of St. Mawr struggling to his feet after the accident prompts in Lou a 'vision' of evil sweeping away the whole of mankind, a 'soft, subtle thing, soft as water', yet expressing itself in the iconoclasms of German fascism and Russian bolshevism. Idealism is the source of evil, requiring 'outward acts of loyalty, piety, self-sacrifice' to a sense of modernity based on inexorable progress, enlightened knowledge and equality. The repression required to sustain such ideals undermines and 'poisons' the real and the living, ultimately issuing in the determination to 'abolish death'. Lou's critical target here is an indiscriminately benevolent humanitarianism, a 'ghastly salvation army of ideal mankind', which would go on saving life, 'every parasite alive' and thus await the attendant chaos. The alternative is a 'survival of the fittest' with a fiercely Malthusian tone: 'The accumulation of life and things means rottenness. Life must destroy life, in the unfolding of creation' (*StM* 80).

Lou's vision of the wondering and 'lovely' human animal must then be distinguished from the insidious modern idealism of democratic-Christian preservation and benign mutuality between living things. As the story presents it, the contemporary encounter between human and animal reveals the absence of pristine states, and a shared, uncompromisingly mixed or impure condition in which the concept of mechanism plays a significant role. Lou senses from the beginning that St. Mawr is 'not quite happy', mirroring Mr. Saintsbury's view that '"if he was a human being, you'd say that something had gone wrong in his life"'. Yet the human being who appears least like St. Mawr is actually most like him. Rico, rich, rootless and impotent, playing at being an artist and gazing at St. Mawr 'with the artist's eye', a 'talking head', 'perfectly prepared for social purposes', glances at Lou, who has tamed him, 'just like a horse that is edging away from its master'. He is a dog that 'daren't quite bite', yet 'really more like a horse than a dog, a horse that might go nasty any moment' (*StM* 26–7). Rico's repressed, domesticated, all-too-human existence creates a state, identical to that of St. Mawr, in which he might 'erupt' at any moment. The containment of this involuntary condition also typifies the triangulated forces of his relationship with Lou and her mother. In their sexless marriage, Rico and Lou have 'a curious exhausting effect on one another', a 'strange vibration of the nerves, rather than of the blood'; while Rico is subliminally angry, Mrs. Witt is 'organically angry', the two together 'like a couple of bombs, timed to explode one day, but ticking on like two ordinary timepieces, in the meanwhile' (*StM* 24, 40).

St. Mawr provides sufficient evidence for the conventional humanistic reading that the state of mechanism is one of debasement and therefore the object of critique: Lou looks aghast at all of her friends, 'their wills fixed like machines on happiness, or fun, or the-best-ever', and despairs of 'rattling her bit in the great machine of human life' (*StM* 41, 94). Yet this reading does not cancel the parallel sense that to live might in large part *be* mechanical, that life and mechanism are not mutually exclusive. St. Mawr does not provide the redemptive organicism or animality the story seems to promise, and remains instead, like his human counterparts, stranded between personhood and mechanism. The story further challenges any idealized resolution through the organic alone, in its motif of a retreat from sexuality, shared by animals and humans alike: St. Mawr's refusal to perform in stud; Lou and Rico's marriage; Lewis's solitariness. Organic nature makes its own Malthusian and eugenic decision, as if generated unconsciously and automatically as a response to the equally mechanical principle of idealized preservation it sees around it. In this realm, then, we do elude the trap of anthropomorphism; we 'know' our animality, because it lives us, in a bodily sense. To have reverence or wonder for this condition in ourselves is to maintain an alert intelligence, trying to steer a course between the anthropomorphic dangers of instrumentalism on the one hand and mysticism on the other. Lawrence has Rachel Witt momentarily falter before this task. Lewis, she reflects, seems to occupy 'another world', like St. Mawr for Lou – a world 'dark and still, where language never ruffled the growing leaves'. Is this, however, an illusion – 'just bunkum', in fact, which she 'had faked up, in order to have something to mystify about'? She is reassured when she sees Lewis holding a bird that had stunned itself against a wire, reviving the apprehension of a world in which 'each creature is alone in its own aura of silence, the mystery of power: as Lewis had power with St. Mawr, and even with Phoenix' (*StM* 104). Is this, perhaps, because even Rachel Witt – brashly human, materialistic – knows what it is to possess 'non-human human being'?

4. *The Fox* and *Kangaroo*: 'non-human human being'

> Whether it was the thrusting forward of the head, or the glisten of fine whitish hairs on the ruddy cheek-bones, or the bright, keen eyes, that can never be said: but the boy was to her the fox, and she could not see him otherwise.
>
> *The Fox*

> Mr. Cooley came at once; and he *was* a kangaroo. His face was long and lean and pendulous, with eyes set close together behind his pince-nez; and his body was stout but firm. He was a man of forty or so, hard to tell, swarthy, with short-cropped dark hair and a smallish head carried rather forward on his large but sensitive, almost shy body. He leaned forward in his walk, and seemed as if his hands didn't quite belong to him.
>
> *Kangaroo*

In the novella *The Fox* and the novel *Kangaroo*, both published in 1923, the human being *is* an animal. What does this equivalence mean? Differences of narrative form suggest differences in the resolution of the question. *The Fox* takes the form of an animal fable. Two women friends in their late twenties take on the running of a smallholding in the lean years after the Great War, but cannot make it prosper. The fox that terrorizes their poultry and, once, casts a spell over Nellie March, emerges in the human form of Henry Grenfel, back from military service. Grenfel, as both hunter and bringer of deliverance to March, sustains the spell and persuades March to marry him, in the process hunting down both the fox itself and March's companion, Jill Banford, who is killed by the uncannily accurate felling of a tree.

Kangaroo is the rapidly written novel of Lawrence's Australian experience, and imagines a new political scenario for the country against a backdrop of fascism and bolshevism in Europe. Beginning in overtly realist mode, the novel details the dramatic experiences of the writer Richard Lovat Somers and his wife Harriet during a brief period of residence near Sydney. Sceptical about democracy in the manner of Lawrence's long essay 'Democracy', Somers attracts the interest of a group of radical nationalists called the Diggers, whose aim is to allow organised socialism to gain control of the country and then to displace it, by force, with an aristocratic politics under the leadership of the charismatic Benjamin Cooley or 'Kangaroo'. Cooley is killed and the Somers leave Australia. Meanwhile, in keeping with Somers' recognition of his own need for individual isolation and 'indifference' to the human world around him, the novel loses all semblance of narrative momentum and collapses into a series of metafictional reflections, including one of Lawrence's most sustained fictional excurses on scientific knowledge.

It is clear that the animality of the main protagonists is at least potentially redemptive: each has mysterious qualities to which others are impelled. Grenfel's sensual, hypnotic power over March is multiple: she lapses into his 'odour', 'indefinable, but something like a wild creature'; he penetrates her with the same gaze with which the fox itself had first 'entered her brain'; he 'produces' his voice 'in her blood' (*TN* 18, 25). March is rendered passive, relieved of the necessity of acting or thinking or of being 'divided in herself'; she subsides into a corner 'like a passive creature in its cave' (*TN* 18). As in *The Ladybird* and *The Captain's Doll* (companion novellae to *The Fox*), this sensual appeal forms the basis of an alternative mode of relationship within which the conventions of romantic love are entirely subverted. Love is never mentioned between Grenfel and March – he 'did not make love to her' – and March manages to be persuaded into marriage without ever explicitly agreeing to it. Somers, having met Kangaroo for the first time, declares himself ' "beyond thinking" '; the 'steady loveliness' of Kangaroo's 'warm, wise heart' overwhelms him. The curious appeal of Kangaroo's half-beauty, half-ugliness resolves itself into a concentration on his belly, neither very fat nor, as Jack Calcott puts it, ' "flat just there, like you and me" '. In the scene in which Kangaroo robustly declares his love for Somers, a 'sort of magnetic effusion' comes from his body: Somers, 'curled narrow in his chair like a snake', had 'deliberately to refrain from laying his hand on the near, generous stomach of the Kangaroo, because automatically his hand would have lifted and sought that rest' (*K* 136).

Following Nietzsche, Lawrence's writing consistently presents love in a tragically riven light: whilst it can, potentially, represent the human faculty of warmth, touch, and the spark of relationship, it has, in the long cultural formations of Christianity and capitalism, turned into an idealized commodity, actively obstructing or falsifying the actual human relations which constitute it. Grenfel's capture of March delivers her from the nervous, highly strung, over-conscious Banford, the unnaturalness of their relationship figured in the satire on their failure with the few creatures they have on the farm (March sometimes expected to see the fowls leaning 'against the pillars of the shed, in their languid processes of digestion'; '"Don't talk to me about Nature"', exclaims Banford [*TN* 8, 18]). However, Banford's death hardly heralds an optimistically-charged future. Released from the 'awful mistake of happiness', March is 'not glad' to have her spirit veiled 'as the Orientals veil the woman's face', and Grenfel is thus still 'foiled'. The story ends with the profoundly troubled and uncertain prospect of the emigration to Canada.

By contrast, Kangaroo represents a complete embrace and logical conclusion of the love ethic, seeking to extend its reach into a new national settlement which would '"let folks be happy again unconsciously, instead of unhappy consciously"'. So strong is the power of Kangaroo's animality that Somers must struggle, analytically, before finally identifying his 'love' as only another, if extreme, variant of the established malaise of abstract Christian caring: he must ask Kangaroo not to love him, if the love is of the 'awfully *general*' kind that seeks to save humanity. '"Let's be hard, separate men"', he concludes (*K* 209). But 'men' here is strictly paradoxical, for Kangaroo's fault is precisely that he is '"too human"', an accusation that enrages Kangaroo and leads to the counter-claim that Somers betrays his intellect. Somers' manliness is, however, only a different kind of creatureliness, as he is constantly drawn throughout the novel to the 'cold', isolated condition of the fishes and sea creatures, connected only by 'vertebral telegraphy'. Yet, in a curious and moving oscillation of sympathy, as Kangaroo lies dying and Somers prepares his papers in order to leave Australia, Somers visits Sydney Zoo. In a context of nature tamed and domesticated, and feeling a reflux of 'tenderness' in the warm sunshine, Somers feeds peppermints to an 'old-man kangaroo', whose gratitude is an image of anthropomorphized gentleness: 'with his great earth-cleaving tail and his little hanging hands', the kangaroo approaches Somers and 'lifted his sensitive nose quivering, and gently nibbled the sweet between Richard's fingers. So gently, so determinedly nibbled the sweet, but never hurting the fingers that held it' (*K* 339).

Somers feels for the kangaroo and his mate not love but a 'dark, animal tenderness, and another sort of consciousness, deeper than human'; the true alterity of this consciousness emerges later that evening, when Somers again goes to seek solace by the sea but encounters instead there a group of wild ponies 'waiting for him to come near'. When he 'talks' to them they are 'reassured', and 'glad a man was there' (*K* 340–1). Even as the ponies are anthropomorphized by the narrative, they confirm for Somers the gap in meaning or absence of mediation between the human and non-human worlds. Again, the enigma is posed by a question, and the question of what the question might mean: the elements – waves and full moon together on a night of 'liquid radium' – 'call' to Somers, but there is no 'living answerer'; the ponies might well have 'fluffy legs', but they are also something other, providing no 'animate answer'. The night is rather call and answer combined, leaving Richard aware of an impersonal God 'without feet or knees or face' – his own sense that of a 'bit of human wispiness' which is also a condition of 'non-human human being' (*K* 341).

The twisting and turning of logic in *Kangaroo* is necessitated by the problem of what 'non-human human being' might mean. Consistent with *Women in Love* and *St. Mawr*, *The Fox* and *Kangaroo* display a dialectical shifting between concepts, keeping open and varied the understanding of the engagement between the creaturely and the human. In a key scene in *The Fox*, the dead body of the fox is viewed from three prespectives. The narrative voice presents a 'lovely' golden-red dog-fox with a 'handsome' coat and a 'great full brush' with a 'delicate' tip. Banford's reaction – ' "Poor brute! If it wasn't such a thieving wretch, you'd feel sorry for it" ' – reveals itself as misplaced in more than one sense: the moralism implicit in invoking property ownership (theft) and in the extension of sympathy is an anthropomorphism at odds with the fixing of the fox as a 'brute' and 'wretch' lower in the natural order. March's contrasting response throws into relief the illogicality of sympathy for a beast that is already dead; for her and for Grenfel, death is a part of life, not to be lamented – the body is still beautiful and (repeatedly) 'wonderful', strange and incomprehensible, 'out of her range', and the relation to it through 'touch' makes her 'quiver' (*TN* 41–2). Repeatedly, the story draws attention to different modes of vision: Banford, in a reprise of Gudrun, looks at Grenfel 'as if he were some creature in a museum', 'objectively' and 'remotely' (*TN* 35–6); only when March is at a distance from him can she 'see' what a fool she has been and that he 'blinds' her, as her letter explains, to things as they actually are. The direct gaze of the fox into March's eyes, reproduced by Henry when he looks 'unthinking' at her (a look which 'startles' them both) establishes a connection or knowledge: to look objectively is not to know, whereas to look directly and unthinkingly is to establish relationship. In Coetzee's *The Lives of Animals*, a footnote briefly alludes to the historical dimensions of the gaze and its power relations between humans and animals: John Berger observes that 'nowhere in a zoo can a stranger encounter the look of an animal'; the animal will 'look sideways', 'scan mechanically', but a certain look with which 'all humans had lived until less than a century ago' was now 'extinguished'.[13]

In *The Fox*, however, the framing of this issue in the appropriately non-realist epistemology of the fable also limits its grasp and flexibility. Henry

Grenfel seems too narrowly foxy for March to relinquish very much of her humanness to him; hence, perhaps, the unease of the story's ending. What separates us from the animal condition might well problematize and unsettle our whole relation to it, but it has its pleasures too: it is March's conviction that in a full commitment to farming you ' "might as well be a beast yourself" ', and she too who might wish 'to paint curvilinear swans on porcelain, with green background' (*TN* 17, 8–9). If the meaning of a 'non-human human being' can only be sustained through the alertness of intellect – even if an alertness seeking to establish its own limits – then Grenfel is an unpropitious character; neither does Lawrence's satirical handling of the fable (Banford's complaint to March that her death would be just what Grenfel was ' "aiming at" ' is a somewhat heavy-handed anticipation of his later marksmanship) inspire confidence in this respect. Again, the posthuman 'leakiness' of the categories of human and animal needs to occur in more than one direction. If 'non-human human being' accommodates the human to the animal, then it should equally accommodate the animal to the human. Grenfel is simply too animal.

Lawrence returned to the question of this dialectic in *Kangaroo*, where as we have seen, kangaroos and ponies can be blithely humanized and, most memorably, Australian birds are not afraid of humans, 'listen', communicate, and seem to understand the human psyche. The kookaburra, 'a bird like a bunch of old rag', expresses this lack of fear and the 'unutterable apathy' and 'great indifference' of the continent in its organic life (*K* 178). Cooley's kangarooness, or indeed Somers' identity as a venomous snake, seem to be conditions of humanness as much as of animality; Cooley declares *himself* a kangaroo, yet is enraged by Somers' ' "traitorous" ' endorsement of the ' "magic of the dark world" ' (*K* 206). It may be, however, that the difficulty of sustaining this posthuman debate within the framework of a realist novel dealing with political structures led Lawrence, in the second half of the novel, to non-fictional, discursive strategies. ' "What was the good of trying to be an alert conscious man here?" ', reflects Somers, as he gazes down at a cliff-slope of ancient tree-ferns redolent of a prehistoric world (*K* 178). If *Kangaroo* is a novel about the creaturely, then its true location is not in its title but in Somers' beloved ocean, to which he regularly repairs in order to partake of its sheer indifference to the merely human.

In communicating itself to Lawrence's narrative mode, this Australian indifference settles into a restatement of the enigma of thinking matter, and then an extended meditation on its implications. Familiar positions are played out: Kangaroo defines love as a condition of equilibrium with things, which it is profoundly difficult for humans to achieve, because their consciousness is 'at once so complicated and so cruelly limited', having made the mistake of knowing so much *about* things that 'we think we know the actuality, and contain it' (*K* 134). Yet this, the burden of being an animal saddled with a mental consciousness, implies that 'man *must* have an idea of himself, . . . and those that deny it have got a more fixed idea than anybody' (*K* 263). Restlessly, as the novel fragments into 'bits', Lawrence seems unable to decide whether the recognition and articulation of some posthuman, 'non-human' vision of the human is best served by fiction or by discursive argument. Again this epistemological dilemma is registered in an ambivalence around the meaning of science. Some of his most trenchant challenges to science are laid down: anatomy (paraphrasing D'Annunzio) presupposes a corpse; science requires a precision of description which is antithetical to life; science can 'wriggle as hard as it likes', but 'the change from caterpillar to butterfly is utterly unscientific, illogical, and *unnatural*, if we take science's definition of nature' (*K* 295). Yet such Bergsonianisms are also a call for greater rigour in the definition of nature, which cannot help but draw on science. Condemning the study of 'collective psychology today' as 'absurd in its inadequacy', he makes his own detailed discriminations between different kinds of herd instinct, and in particular between the degenerate 'mob-instinct' and higher forms of 'vertebral' communicative telepathy. Reflecting on the bogus 'selling' of democratic-capitalist ideals, he notes that, when a man realizes he has been 'sold', 'something goes wrong with his whole mechanism'; '(S)omething breaks, in his tissue, and the black poison is emitted into his blood', leading to the condition of automatism – 'Most people are dead, and scurrying and talking in the death of sleep' (*K* 264, 266). As in *St. Mawr*, we find here a wavering between 'mechanism' as a normative description of bodily materiality, and as a condition of loss. Life, Lawrence can only conclude, 'makes no absolute statement'; it is 'so wonderful and complex, and *always* relative' (*K* 267). *Kangaroo* seems to find Lawrence on the verge of deciding that textual forms themselves are inadequate to account for this complexity; like Coetzee's Elizabeth Costello, he loses faith in fiction, but is equally unsure about rational discourse. From this perpective, as I wish to show in the final section of this chapter, it is significant that what is possibly Lawrence's most luminous piece of writing on the human engagement with the animal proceeds, as far as is possible, from the factual description of an actual encounter.

5. Real encounters: porcupines and frogs

Neither Elizabeth Costello, nor any of the other characters in Coetzee's *The Lives of Animals*, makes any reference to actual relationships of their own with animals. The point is made by Barbara Smuts, an animal psychologist and anthropologist, as one of four writers contributing short academic 'reflections' to Coetzee's text. Smuts in turn is the only one of these four to refer her observations beyond the realm of textuality. Drawing on extensive fieldwork experience of living in communities of baboons and gorillas, and on her relationship with her pet dog Safi, Smuts argues that to speak, as Costello puts it, 'from the heart', and to 'think ourselves into the being of another', requires not so much the poetic imagination as sustained immersion in the lives of animals – the heart must be 'embodied', and 'prepared to encounter directly the embodied heart of another' (*LA* 108). 'Doing good science' in this respect meant for Smuts observing and documenting with rigorous objectivity the behaviour of the animals she lived with; it also involved, as a paradigm of modernist, situated knowledge, meeting the subjective and intensely physical challenge of living and travelling with apes in remote African terrain without the accompanying presence of any other humans.

Smuts illustrates two sides of a very practically posthuman situation. She became – 'or rather, regained my ancestral right to be' – an animal, moving 'instinctively' in a shadowily familiar world; she also came to conceptualize animals as persons who happen to be nonhuman. Personhood is, she argues, not an essential quality of the human, but a definition of creatures as social subjects who are capable of entering into a relationship. Placing herself within the intricate system of baboon society, she became obliged to enter into *personal* and intimate relationships with baboons as individuals. In doing so, she confirms the analysis Costello shares with some posthuman theory, that behaviourist science can uncover in the animal only the purely functionalist or instrumentalist logics it expects to find there. To immerse onself in baboon society is, by contrast, to discover the condition and motivations of pleasure: while baboons, 'like the rest of us', feel dread, hunger and pain, their 'default state', writes Smuts, 'seemed to be a light-hearted appreciation of being a baboon body in baboon-land' (*LA* 110). Such insights, we are reminded, only follow from being *in relation* to the baboons, the relationship itself *constituting* personhood. Accordingly, for the human to relate to a creature 'as an anonymous object, rather than as a being with its own subjectivity' primarily entails a loss of personhood in the human.

I summarise Smuts' reflections in some detail because of the light they shed on Lawrence's posthuman rendering of the animal. We have seen what I have characterized as a bold and consistently 'anthropomorphic' treatment of animals as persons across Lawrence's writing. We have seen Lawrence's account of the loss incurred in the visual and artistic objectification of the living, especially in *Women in Love* and *The Fox*. Both aspects of Lawrence's critical challenge to realist epistemology seem here to be endorsed by the empirical work of a contemporary scientist, the result of whose empiricism is to offer a similar challenge. In addition, I want to argue, Smuts' insistence on the real encounter with the animal is complemented by the fact that Lawrence's most vivid writing about animals emerges out of just such encounters.

I focus here on *Reflections on the Death of a Porcupine and other essays* (1925), mostly written between July and August 1925 at Kiowa Ranch, New Mexico. The Lawrences had been living at the ranch, owned by Frieda, intermittently for over a year, and it became the setting for Lou Witt's paradisal retreat in the final section of *St. Mawr*. More curiously reminiscent of Banford and

March, however, was the fact that since early 1925 the Lawrences had been trying to set up the ranch as a self-sufficient farm, becoming, as the biographer David Ellis puts it, the 'anxious owners of Susan, a black and unruly cow', along with some hens.[14] Lawrence introduces Susan in the essay '... Love Was Once a Little Boy', posing the question of how he might 'equilibrate' himself with her as an instance of the more general dilemma of reconciling individuality with the relationship of love. Perhaps unsurprisingly, Susan will not be equilibrated. He may call her each day for milking, but sometimes she does not come, the calling 'a mere nothing against the black stillness of her cowy passivity' (*RDP* 333). The difficulties are focused in Susan's faculty of simultaneous knowing and not-knowing: she knows his voice, but not 'the advancing me, in a blue shirt and cord trousers'; she knows 'perfectly well' his grey horse, and yet does not, waiting until he advances towards her and then sheering off in apparent panic. Lawrence leaves open the possibility that this is either a mode of game-playing on Susan's part, or a genuine state of contradiction. Similarly, for him she can be a 'suspended ghost', 'standing like some spider suspended motionless by a thread, from the web of the eternal silence', but also still, peaceful and warm when she is being milked and knows his touch.

'Equilibrium? Harmony? with that black blossom! Try it!' – but it is, nevertheless, Lawrence asserts, a 'relationship', and part of a 'mystery of love: the individuality on each side, mine and Susan's, suspended in the relationship' (*RDP* 334). The convergence of this account of relationship with that of Barbara Smuts and her baboons is striking. Lawrence does not idealize away the reality of difference – to him she remains 'fractious, tiresome, and a faggot' – but neither does he deny the palpability of what he can only know through relationship, that is, Susan's quality of 'desirability', so subtle as to 'have nothing to do with function'.

If this is relationship, however, so too is the encounter with a porcupine in the title essay of the collection, where Lawrence relates the tale of his first-ever killing of an animal. He knows that porcupines ought to be killed because of the damage they do to pine trees, gnawing the bark away from the top. On a first encounter, he does not hide his repugnance at the sight of the creature, its 'squalid', 'lumbering', 'unpleasant' beetle's motion, 'bestial' and 'stupid', but he cannot bring himself to kill it, allowing the porcupine to slither back down a tree and escape, the animal having apparently 'decided' either that the watching man was harmless or that it was risky to go any further (*RDP* 349). However, the need is brought home to him when he discovers and tries to treat two strange dogs with quills puncturing their snouts. So, on the next encounter, the porcupine is killed, a cedar pole finishing the job that is begun with a single, wounding gunshot.

The killing prompts what begins as Lawrence's most uncompromising account of the struggle for existence. 'One must kill', because 'all creatures devour, and *must* devour the lower forms of life.' Skinning a rabbit reveals 'what an enormous part of the animal, comparatively, is intestinal, what a big part of him is just for food-apparatus' (*RDP* 354). A parade of examples – horses ceaselessly cropping the grass, Susan chewing the cud, chickens devouring flying beetles, and Timsy the cat butchering a chipmunk – contribute to the conclusion that the 'power' of the higher forms of life over the lower must inevitably, materially, perhaps mechanically ('food-apparatus') express itself in the subjugation of the lower: 'If the lower cycles of life are not *mastered*, there can be no higher cycle' (*RDP* 356).

This scenario, Lawrence insists, is 'not something to lament over, nor something to try to reform'. He cautions not just against the sentimentalization of our relationship with animals, but also against those principled philosophical and ideological positions which would serve to protect life from the exigencies of predation: the 'ridiculous' Buddhist, for example, who eats only two grains of rice a day; by extension, we might suggest, Elizabeth Costello's stance on animal rights and vegetarianism. Even the most 'idyllic' of farmers must fight for food as the basis of existence. In this wise Lawrence also implicitly acknowledges that humans, alone in the natural order, are capable of resisting or modifying the struggle – of transforming, that is, the imperative 'one must kill' into 'one must *not* kill'. 'How strangely', he notes, does food 'relate' humans with the 'animal and vegetable world'. We are *thinking* matter, idea-making animals, and the 'strange' consequence of this might be that we can actively prevent ourselves from living as much as enhance our living.

Lawrence knows that the question of man's place in nature is also the question of a whole political programme: 'There is no such thing as equality' (*RDP* 362). The human faculty for abstract thought gives rise to the conception of a democratic equality which denies the workings of power and its expression in hierachized cycles of existence. Yet here, his essay confronts a crucial paradox. Modern capitalist democracy, sustained by the ideology of a progressive, enlightened science, asserts free and equal, if competitive, market-based access to the exploitation of resources through the objectification and subjugation of nature. How does Lawrence's conception of 'mastery' differ from this? How is the devouring of the lower forms of life to be distinguished from the violent conceptual appropriation of those forms as raw material? How might the instrumentalist capitalism of Gerald Crich or Clifford Chatterley *not* imply the mastery of lower forms of life by the higher?

As we know, from his early formation, Lawrence was apprised of the appropriation of science and scientific ideas of nature by capitalism. To think beyond a collusion with this in the 'Porcupine' essay, he introduces the concept of the 'fourth dimension', and an accompanying distinction between existence and being. The guts of the rabbit prove to Lawrence that the struggle for *existence* is a material fact, defining us in time and space whether we like it or not. The ability to master and devour other forms of life is evidence of greater 'vividness' or vitality in the superior 'species, race or type': we exist 'relatively to all other existence', and 'there is no escaping this law'. But there is another and simultaneous conceptual framework within which each individual life-form has its own fullness of *being*, and in that sense is a 'nonpareil', incomparable and beyond hierarchy. This may be the 'fourth dimension', but it is dependent upon material existence, and is 'as material as existence'; 'only', Lawrence insists, 'the matter suddenly enters the fourth dimension' (*RDP* 359). Adhering strictly to materialist explanation, Lawrence nevertheless seeks a way of thinking life which neither reduces it to raw material nor idealizes it as possessing an abstract 'equality'. Rather, it seems, the reality of power is precisely what enables relationship; individual being can only truly be acknowledged when the sheer *differences* which make individuals what they are, including differences of power or 'vitality', are taken into account. To posit abstract equality, whether between humans or between humans and animals, is to blind oneself to material inequalities, and to pave the way for the violent appropriation of the other through idealization.

The fact that these conclusions are presented as 'the inexorable law of life' suggests the landmark quality of this essay, and confirms something of Elizabeth Costello's recollection, from her student days, that Lawrence 'gripped' them because he promised a 'form of salvation' if the 'dark gods' were worshipped and their observances carried out. Nevertheless, there is a sense in which the pairing of Lawrence with Coetzee's Costello, the prophet of mastery with the animal rights campaigner, is an unlikely one; Lawrence, Costello adds, turns out to be a false prophet. In expanding *The Lives of Animals* into *Elizabeth Costello*, Coetzee has Lawrence reappear in the context of a debate Elizabeth is having with her sister Blanche about the value of the humanities. What does humanism, and with it the central role of the literary, really stand for? Blanche, a nun devoted to humanitarian work in an impoverished African community, has no time for the scholarly humanism of writing and research: Elizabeth 'went for the wrong Greeks', and should have chosen Orpheus over Apollo, the sensual and protean over the rational, 'a phoenix', or, in her own version of a material Christ, someone whom people can touch – ' "put their hand into the side of, feel the wound, smell the blood" ' (*EC* 145).

In the light of Blanche's '*I do not need to consult novels*', it is ironic that the kind of sensual humanism she endorses is precisely that which Elizabeth hopes for from a literature of 'heart' or 'sympathetic imagination'. The phoenix, after all, is the Lawrentian icon for the flaming or blossoming of creative life from nothingness. Increasingly frustrated by the dilemma of anthropomorphism, fully aware that the literature of otherness might still be no more than human-centred, Elizabeth seems to lose faith in fiction and turn instead to the discourse on it, even though, as James Wood notes, 'the only means of arguing for the literary – for feeling over reason, imagination over thought – is via the literary'.[15] In her letter of response to Blanche, she observes that the humanities 'teach us humanity' and restore 'our human beauty' after (provocatively) the 'centuries-long Christian night'; as the terms hover between the normative and the evaluative, what the human is and what it might aspire to be, Elizabeth tries to pin it down to acts of which animals are incapable, such as the moment she uncovered her breasts for the pleasure of the elderly bed-ridden patient, Mr Philips. However, Coetzee is to have the novel press Elizabeth even further on her definition of humanity. In a hallucinatory final chapter, in which Elizabeth is at the gate or border patrol of what might be heaven, she is challenged to state what she believes in order to gain entry. After a first abortive attempt, and the rehearsal to herself of the kind of universalistic clichés (*'I believe in the irrepressible human spirit . . . I believe that all human kind is one'*) which might have attracted D.H. Lawrence's withering scorn, Elizabeth finally decides on a belief as far from the anthropomorphic as she can imagine. She believes, she says, in the tiny frogs that live in the mudflats of the Dulgannon river, remembered from childhood. In the dry season the frogs 'die', their bodily functions barely sustained in the depths of the mud; but when the rains come, 'the dead awake', and the frogs emerge to sing again 'in joyous exultation beneath the vault of the heavens' (*EC* 216). She believes, simply, that the frogs exist. Some things are not ideas, and are not called into existence by discourse: the frog's life-cycle might sound like allegory, but to the frog it is not – merely, 'the thing itself, the only thing'. The frogs embody, then, the animal 'indifference' of Lawrence's Australia; ' "I believe" ', says Elizabeth, ' "in what does not bother to believe in me" ' (*EC* 217–18).

We should not however conclude that the frogs exist entirely, for Elizabeth, in a state of alterity. If they are real, so too is the animal *in* the human. Elizabeth measures humanity by the attempt to take account of our own material otherness – *'I am an other'* – even as we know the attempt is framed by language and culture. Lawrence held similarly to 'non-human human being', even as he knew it could not, by definition, be grounded philosphically. For Costello, the continuity of the effort is what seems to count: Lawrence typifies the humanities in responding to the 'energies' and 'hunger' of readers for guidance in perplexity, and some false prophecy is an inevitable result. What authorized Lawrence, for example, to claim that, just as life is more vivid in a cat than in an ostrich, so life is more vivid in 'me, than in the Mexican who drives the wagon for me'? Or that, just as the great cat can destroy the greatest bird, so 'one race of man can subjugate and rule another race' (*RDP* 357–8)? In critically interrogating the taboos of humanism, what was Lawrence prepared to concede to the condition of thinking matter? In the next chapter, I examine more closely what humans and humanity meant to Lawrence.

6
Humans

> How curious it was that this was a human being! What Brangwen
> thought himself to be, how meaningless it was, confronted with
> the reality of him. Birkin could see only a strange, inexplicable,
> almost patternless collection of passions and desires and suppres-
> sions and traditions and mechanical ideas, all cast unfused and dis-
> united into this slender, bright-faced man of nearly fifty, who was
> as unresolved now as he was at twenty, and as uncreated.
>
> *Women in Love*

1. Eugenics past and present

In December 1916, Lawrence returned to Dollie Radford a copy of *Instincts
of the Herd in Peace and War* (1915) by Wilfred Trotter.

> I send you back Trotter also. I didn't like him very much. Oh, I *cannot*
> stand this scientific talk of instincts and bee communities and wolf packs
> and such like, as if everything worked from a mechanical basis. It is a
> great lie. They think a living being is a thing that can be wound up in
> the head, and made to go through the proper motions. It is just like
> anatomy: it examines every bit of the dog, but the dog is all *dead* dog. So
> they do with the human being: it is all dead humanity, that which is
> material to life, never that which is life itself. It irritates me exceedingly.
> I think all science, but particularly the sciences of psychology and soci-
> ology, are loud-mouthed impertinence; impertinent, that is what they are
> (*LIII* 59).

Trotter placed his work of 'biological psychology' (1915) at the services of
Britain's wartime effort towards the 'destruction of the German empire',
an effort seen as inseparable from 'the making of civilisation tolerable to
rational beings' (*IH* 156). Given this overtly political cast, it is intriguing to
note that Trotter's argument also belongs to the materialist debates with

which we have become familiar. His subject is the enigmatic condition of thinking matter and the implications of this condition for 'Man's place in Nature and Nature's place in Man'. Humans, Trotter argues, are no less instinctive than other animals, but the mind provides more diverse and complex ways of embodying those instincts. Nevertheless, human conduct is far less variable than has been supposed, and a systematic study of the general movement of instincts will help establish a 'true science of politics which would be of direct service to the statesman' (*IH* 99).

The question of gregariousness is the crux of Trotter's argument. Humans are seen to share with other advanced species, such as the bee and the wolf, the evolutionary tendency towards aggregation, the movement from unicellular to multicellular, reaping the rewards of this collective security in an escape route from the 'rigour of natural selection'. However, this state is complicated in humans by the simultaneous tendency towards complex individuation. As 'social animals', humans are thus *inferior* to bees or wolves, our 'capacity for varied reaction' obstructing the kind of *collective* intelligence enjoyed by those lower in the natural order. Our elaborate modes of rational explanation may not only blur and conceal true instincts, but more actively prevent them from reaching their goal, enabling man to 'obey the voice of instinct after the fashion of his own heart' (*IH* 213).

If then it is human *nature*, the 'fatal inheritance which it is ... impossible to repudiate', to distort our instincts, the idea of human nature as a settled or essential condition appears to be under severe strain. Trotter could not, however, allow the urgent political motivation of *Instincts* to be detained in such ontological difficulties. The War, a 'nodal point' of evolution and 'one of Nature's august experiments', plainly pointed up Nature's lesson that humans should undertake the conscious direction of their own destinies, as 'the only mechanism by which the social life of so complex an animal can be guaranteed against disaster and brought to yield its full possibilities' (*IH* 162). While German herd-identity constituted a regression back to the 'aggressive gregariousness' of the wolf-society, England presented the most 'complete' and fully evolved example of a 'socialized herd', characterized in Burkean terms by slowness of development and a laboriously won 'instinct' for national life. While Germany had 'left the path of natural evolution, or rather, perhaps, has never found it', England stood ripe to continue along the path, but only if it could cultivate its advantages by drawing on 'progressive' scientific theory for the 'natural' manipulation of national life. The way forward lay in a strategy combining eugenics with propaganda. Faced with what was seen as the steady increase of social degeneracy through mental instability, 'it remains', Trotter argued, 'for us to estimate in some rough way the characteristics of the unstable, in order that we may be able to judge of their value or otherwise to the State and the species' (*IH* 56). Similarly, in the name of national solidarity, material inequalities should not be allowed to obstruct the formation of a general moral equality. 'The best way to get our work done is to get the worker to want to do it'; their souls must be kept 'full of a burning passion of service'; the difficulty of this, when a man with 30 shillings a week sees others with £30,000 a year, points up the necessity of a system of persuasion which dissociates morality from material wealth without 'disturbing' those material inequalities.

Lawrence's irritation with Trotter's book might well be read as a reaction to the insanity of the war itself. Nevertheless, it is science and its 'loud-mouthed impertinence' that is the overt target, exemplified by a behaviourist eugenics peddling an impoverished conception of the human being-as-mechanism, a 'thing that can be wound up in the head, and made to go through its proper motions'. If this is the human as machine, it is also the Cartesian *animal* as machine, responding predictably to behaviouristic discipline. Trotter's proposals were nothing radically new; as we have seen in Chapter 2, eugenics was a pervasive discourse, and David Eder's writings for *The New Age* suggest the availability to Lawrence of advanced critical perspectives on it. It is, then, important to stress the *affinities* between Trotter's arguments and those of Lawrence and his intellectual socialist circle – arguments which we might otherwise view as critical of scientific orthodoxy. The notion of the evolution of intellect as a mixed blessing, encroaching upon, falsifiying or interfering with the instincts is, as we have seen, a position variously Spencerean, Nietzschean, Bergsonian and Lawrentian. In this sense Trotter broadly shares an analysis of thinking matter predicated upon a working distinction or dualism between instinct and intellect. More precisely, as we shall see further in this chapter, Trotter's claim that the intellect might achieve actual bodily effects, 'preventing' impulses from reaching their destinations, is mirrored in Lawrence's definition of idealism as 'the motivizing of the great affective sources by means of ideas mentally derived' (*FU* 210). Finally, Trotter's own version of knowing how not to know consists in the familiar rectification of an imbalance. Our momentous 'step in evolution', the mark of advanced intelligence, will be to recognize the advantages for Britain, and ultimately for the human species, of a prior stage of development in which strength through gregariousness is achieved at the expense of individual mental sophistication. Science thus maintains its authority by appearing to argue for its opposite; humans are 'too anxious to feel certain to have time to know', and the comforts of collective belief or 'herd-suggestion' must take precedence over the intrusive, 'alien and hostile' power of reason.

Such connections remind us of the dangers of assuming a separation between an unashamedly 'popular' and polemical text such as *Instincts* and the discourses of a 'higher' philosophical modernism. As Anne Fernihough has shown, in an argument in which she finds eugenics to be the 'dark underbelly of modernist theory', the complex social and political overtones of key modernist concepts have often been 'bleached out' by the time modernism reaches the textbooks as a mode of aesthetic formalism.[1] Trotter's was

undoubtedly, in its transparent and crudely manipulative eugenic motivations, a prime instance for Lawrence of a didactic or dogmatic science, and
he implicitly condemns it as such in the letter to Dollie Radford. In its reflections upon thinking matter, however, Trotter's work is of a piece with the
post-Darwinian, Bergsonian analyses of the evolution of intellect from which
Lawrence drew. Lawrence's protestations to Radford sound, in this sense,
somewhat shrill; a matter of months later, when he starts in on the essays
which will form *Studies in Classic American Literature*, he does not fight shy
of that 'scientific talk' of instincts and bee communities and wolf-packs
which he had earlier claimed to despise. The accompanying theories of
human physiology – the 'solar plexus' philosophy – find expression in at
least two works, *Education of the People* and *Fantasia of the Unconscious*, which
can without difficulty be assimilated to the discourse of eugenics. As re-
positories of advice on state educational practice and policy, and on the
parenting of children, each is clearly underpinned by the principle of the
conscious direction of collective destiny. The counter-enlightenment colouring of much of this advice would almost certainly see Lawrence accused in
some quarters, then or now, of 'loud-mouthed impertinence'.

What, then, do we claim in associating Lawrence with eugenics, in a
way that sees him explicitly refuting Trotter while, less knowingly perhaps,
adopting positions which were themselves enabled by or contained within
eugenic discourse? My proposal in this chapter is that a broad eugenic dispensation gave Lawrence the conviction that the 'human' comprises no
discrete, inviolable state or essence, but is subject to change. In the grievous political history of eugenics in the twentieth century, this assumption
of human *alterability* translates into manipulation, 'engineering', and the
potential for a totalitarianism whose extreme logical conclusion is the policy
of genocide. Lawrence's criticisms of Trotter, in the name of the sanctity
and integrity of the 'living being', show his fear and anticipation of this
dystopian possibility. In the assumption of *alterability* as such, however, the
human in eugenics is always-already *posthuman*, in so far as no *humanistic*
sense of unique essence or integrity can be assumed. If human nature never
was fixed, the theories and technologies of the contemporary posthuman
only confirm, as Hayles has it, that we always were posthuman.

Francis Fukuyama's *Our Posthuman Future* (2002) is a vivid demonstration
of how current advances in genetics and biotechnology, notably the anticipated completion of the genetic mapping of the human body via the
Human Genome Project, can produce the coupling of a dystopian posthumanism with a newly invigorated eugenics. With the unprecedented
possibilities of intervention in the reproduction of human life in his sights,
Fukuyama plays on liberal humanist fears of imminent threat to a human
nature which for him, as I have already indicated, 'exists, is a meaningful
concept, and has provided a stable continuity to our experience as a species'.
Fukuyama has reason to be ingenious, however, when it comes to defining

more closely what human nature is, namely, 'the sum of the behaviour and characteristics that are typical of the human species, arising from genetic rather than environmental factors'. The suspicion of a circularity in this argument – what defines the human is what is typical to the human – is confirmed in Fukuyama's careful delineation of the 'nature' in human nature as a condition of 'typicality' rather than 'essence'. Thus, while exploiting and appearing to speak on behalf of a human essence that we generally 'believe' to exist, Fukuyama actually avoids elaborating human nature in any terms other than the typicality of a 'statistical artefact', 'something close to the median of a distribution of behaviour or character-istics'. Humans are, in other words, what they have tended, on average, to be and do.

The ingenuity is politically motivated. In comparing the two moments of eugenics, broadly separated by a century, Fukuyama characterizes the earlier moment, 'the deliberate breeding of people for certain selected heritable traits', originating with Galton and pervading the political spectrum in the US and Europe, as hanging like a 'spectre' over 'the entire field' of sub-sequent genetics. Two important objections to the eugenics of this earlier moment show, he claims, that any contemporary or future eugenics would be unlikely to make the mistakes of its predecessor: first, the available tech-nology was then inadequate to deliver the intended programmes; second, it was 'state-sponsored and coercive'. These, clearly, are hardly the senti-ments of an opponent of eugenics. Rather, a 'kinder and gentler' eugenics of the present is, for Fukuyama, an ultimate extension of his belief in the virtues of the free market modified by minimal state intervention. In conclusion, Fukuyama argues that democratic countries must regulate the use and development of biotechnology, 'setting up institutions that will discriminate between those technological advances that promote human flourishing, and those that pose a threat to human dignity and well-being'.[2] Somewhat contradictorily, however, the prime motive force of the new, 'kinder and gentler' eugenics will be the sovereign individual consumer, in the form of the parental couple, who will decide on the constitution of their children as a matter of individual choice; in this scenario, collective politi-cal regulation is overridden by the rights of the private individual, such that the onus of regulation falls upon those 'opponents of breeding new humans' who 'will have to explain what harms will be produced by the free decisions of individual parents over the genetic makeup of their children'.[3]

Somewhat disarmingly perhaps, Lawrence early declared that his inten-tion in writing was to make folks 'alter, and have more sense'; readers cannot fail to be aware that his work has designs upon them. This *alterability* can be understood in a eugenic context, the strong imperative behind it con-sisting in no less than the improvement of humans: something has gone wrong; we are unsure of our place in nature, struggling to relate to that animal condition which is plainly other than, yet also integral to, ourselves.

Human being *is not* a given. We first 'discover' ourselves, Lawrence writes, 'naked betwixt sky and land, belonging to neither'; man has 'made such a mighty struggle to feel at home on the face of the earth without even yet succeeding' (*STH* 7). Such figures well express the ambiguous condition of thinking matter, our thought dependent *upon* matter, yet perpetually falsifiying our relation to it. In this sense, perhaps it is indeed our nature to go wrong, to be unnatural, or at least to possess a nature which is 'not yet fixed'. Like Hardy's heroes and heroines, we 'struggle hard to come into being'; risking a paraphrase of Beauvoir, we are not born human, but learn what it is to become it.

Yet intellect, apparently the cause of all the trouble, also persuades us that the struggle might be worthwhile. Lawrence's early rationalism, embodied in a text like the *Origin of Species*, persuaded him that there were no limits to the imaginative reach of a reason which must, argued Darwin, at moments of extremity, transcend imagination itself. If reason for Lawrence therefore consisted in the 'thought-adventure', making alteration for the better seem possible, it must be a dialectical reason, always willing to turn the critical gaze upon its own claims. To fail in the latter is to produce a didactic science, obscuring politics behind the appearance of objective knowledge. Just as he could excoriate the crude epistemology of Trotter's eugenics, so Lawrence would have identified the delusion in Fukuyama's belief in science as 'the only important social activity that by common consensus is both cumulative and directional', its 'progressive conquest of nature' made possible 'not by man, but by nature and nature's laws'.[4] Lawrence cannot, by the same token, have been unaware of the deep irony of basing his own, new theory of human being on the principles of a 'pure science'.

In this chapter, I examine two closely-interrelated ways in which Lawrence's 'philosophical' writing pursues the question of the alterability of the human. The first is a concern with the human as an individual organism. Lawrence insisted, in the infamous 'solar plexus' philosophy, that we re-read our own physiology, and adjust our ideas and our actions accordingly. The second concerns the human as a collective or gregarious entity, gathered together in cultures or, in the essentialist discourse of eugenics, 'races'. Eugenics provided a framework within which a writer such as Lawrence could move easily from the dynamics of individual human bodies to the dynamics of different cultures; yet, at the same time, he remained deeply critical of the science, and the ideological assumptions, that seemed to make eugenics possible. Lawrence looked at individuals and cultures in order to represent the possibility that the 'human' might be other than what it was; such alterability makes the human being simultaneously a political, and a posthuman, subject.

A crucial third term in Lawrence's work, however, positioned between these extremes of the individual and the collective, is the human sexual relationship. Sexuality is the primary mode of the 'hard struggle to come into human being' in novels such as *Sons and Lovers* and *The Rainbow*. The former focuses on the struggle of a single protagonist, Paul Morel, to come into sexual maturity, while the latter examines patterns of relationship and reproduction across generations of the Brangwen family. The reputation of these texts has been that they signify Lawrence's most *humanistic* fictional achievement, wedged between the sometimes overwrought mannerisms of his two earlier novels and a move towards greater abstraction in the later fiction, signalled first in *Women in Love* and extended in the generic variations and uneven qualities of 'political' novels such as *Aaron's Rod*, *Kangaroo* and *The Plumed Serpent*. In revisiting *Sons and Lovers* and *The Rainbow* in this chapter, I will try to unsettle this connection between the human and the humanistic, suggesting ways in which the human condition explored is *already*, as it were, a posthuman one. As Donna Haraway and Katherine Hayles insist, the question of what kind of posthumans we might become is open and political, requiring to be fought for. For Lawrence, as for Haraway and Hayles, I suggest that the openness of the question follows from the unresolved, perhaps unresolvable nature of human kinship with living matter and inert matter. Lawrence condemned Trotter's conception of the human as a clockwork machine that can be 'wound up in the head'. But there are many ways of being a machine, some hardly machine-like at all: 'our machines', Haraway reminds us, 'are disturbingly lively, and we ourselves frighteningly inert'.

2. The solar plexus

At a first glance, Lawrence's theory of the solar plexus seems to have little to do with the alterability of the human subject. It is difficult not to see in it a form of biologistic essentialism, asserting an unchanging material base for the human consciousness as a corrective to the (equally human) tendency towards idealism and the distortion of our natures. I have argued that the foundation of a 'posthuman' Lawrence is his critique of Cartesian dualism: human being is a condition of the material whole, not to be falsified by the 'superstition' of a body with a mind in it, and the guarantee of that wholeness is the 'pristine' first consciousness,

> That active spontaneity which rouses in each individual organism at the moment of fusion of the parent nuclei, and which, in polarized connection with the external universe, gradually evolves or elaborates its own individual psyche and corpus, bringing both mind and body forth from itself (*FU* 242).

Yet Lawrence, it is well-established, is a dualistic thinker: the self evolves in 'polarized connection' with the world. Accordingly, when we try to pose the *question* of human consciousness as Lawrence saw it, we are immediately thrust into a complex debate around the relative claims of wholeness and of dualism. The infant, he asserts, in the first of many formulations of the theory, is 'awake and alive' in body *before* the brain is able to produce thought. This condition of 'first-consciousness' *is* a form of 'knowledge', but it is located in the upper (breast or cardiac plexus) and lower (bowels or solar plexus) nerve centres rather than in the brain. We are, then, 'creatures of duality, in the first place'; our experience of oneness or wholeness is subsequent (*SM* 55–6).

When Lawrence came to re-work this material in *Education of the People* and *Psychoanalysis and the Unconscious*, there is a much simpler emphasis on the primacy of the solar plexus, because it is there, Lawrence maintains, under the navel, that the 'first fused nucleus of the ovule' remains, from the origin of the foetus through to maturity. This combines, however, with a more elaborate diagram of pre-cerebral knowledge: growth involves the elaboration of a polarized circuit, the 'lumbar ganglion' at the back of the body counterbalancing the solar plexus at the front, this 'abdominal plane' then 'immediately' complemented by a corresponding development in the region above the diaphragm, where the thoracic ganglion in the shoulders counterbalances the cardiac plexus. In this fourfold diagram, the 'cross of all existence and being', the horizontal divides the lower 'subjective' from the upper 'objective' region, and the vertical divides the frontal 'sympathetic' from the rear 'voluntary'. The entire field of knowledge described is still entirely pre-conscious or in Lawrence's term 'unconscious'; the child's first relationship with its mother does not involve the 'so-called *human* relations'; it is a 'vitalistic circuit' which is 'neither personal nor biological' (*FU* 229).

Any reader attempting to track these theories in Lawrence's work will soon realise that the dualism itself is not as simple as it first seems. Humans may be physically dual in the first place, but the duality that really matters is, it seems, the one that later accompanies the emergence of mind. This is further complicated by the fact that Lawrence's use of the term 'mind' registers, in its inconsistency, ongoing scientific disputes over the nature of consciousness. The Crèvecoeur essay, for example, is strictly anti-Cartesian in positing the 'oneness and wholeness of full mental consciousness' as subsequent to the development of the pristine consciousness: 'mind' is a whole bodily condition of human being. In *Psychoanalysis and the Unconscious*, however, mind becomes conflated with an account of the development of the *brain*, the 'terminal instrument of the dynamic consciousness'. Figures of instrumentation are carried over from *Education*, where the brain was a 'switchboard' keeping the pre-conscious centres in 'a circuit of communication'; in *Psychoanalysis* it is a 'telegraph instrument', printing off 'glyphs and graphic representations which we call percepts, concepts, ideas'. These call to mind Bergson's version of our *mistaken* view of mental activity as representational, for example in the faculty of memory, though they also accord with his view of the intellect as something which must interrupt and falsify the experience of being and duration. For Lawrence the 'brain' becomes the 'mind', 'instrument of instruments', authoritatively taking the 'creative flux' and turning it into fixed ideas: 'mentality, being automatic in its principle like the machine, begins to assume life' (*FU* 247). The final version of *Studies*, from which all explicit traces of the solar plexus philosophy have been removed (filtered, perhaps, into *Education*, and the two books on the unconscious), presents the issue more starkly:

> Nowadays men do hate the idea of dualism. It's no good, dual we are. The Cross. If we accept the symbol, then, virtually, we accept the fact. We are divided against ourselves. . . .
> Blood-consciousness overwhelms, obliterates, and annuls mind-consciousness.
> Mind-consciousness extinguishes blood-consciousness, and consumes the blood.
> We are all of us conscious in both ways. And the two ways are antagonistic in us.
> They will always remain so.
> That is our cross (*SCAL* 83).

Here 'blood-consciousness' has come to stand in for the previous elaborate schemas of the pristine domain; 'mind-consciousness' is now the idealising activity orchestrated by the brain.

Lawrence's argument, continually redrafted and assuming various forms across the decade from 1913 to 1923, seems to combine or fluctuate across three positions. On the one hand, the mind affects the organism to its detriment: we have succeeded in reducing and mechanizing ourselves, by allowing mind-consciousness to gain the upper hand over a period of 2,000 years. 'We have so subjected the centres of sensual cognition that they depend automatically on the upper centres', they have 'collapsed', and are 'waiting to be worked according to some secondary idea'. On the other hand, the self has a pristine integrity that cannot be falsified: 'The quick of the self is *there*. You needn't try to get behind it'; 'you can't make an ideal of the living self . . . (*P* 712–13). Finally, 'man is an ideal animal: an idea-making animal'; he '*can't* live by instinct, because he's got a mind' (*PII* 626, 624). Can ideas, then, physically affect or change the body, or not? If the pristine self is inviolable, why worry? Conversely, if it is our nature to be 'ideal', and thus to work detrimental effects within our own natures, what can we do about it? Alternatively, doesn't the *idea* of the mind as a machine instal or hypostatize the very dualism that Lawrence sought to contest? Are we biologically dual, or are we simply burdened with an idea of dualism which limits our thinking about the human?

Such questions cannot simply concern the internal consistency or otherwise of Lawrence's theory; the stakes are higher, for he claims, we remember, to be doing 'pure science, establishing 'what the unconscious actually is'. It is here, then, in the solar-plexus theories, that the advocate of a post-human Lawrence is most aware of the shadow of the Sokal affair. What, in other words, if the solar plexus theories are simply *wrong*? Critics have already colonized this territory. James Cowan notably asserts that, whatever we might think of the theory as a metaphorical description of human physiology, it is literally 'anatomical nonsense'. There are, Cowan insists, only two broad divisions of the nervous system, central and peripheral; there are no such single structures as the 'lumbar' and 'thoracic' ganglia, so that only the solar and cariac plexuses can be located anatomically.[5] Arguments for the extraordinary interdisciplinary synthesis of Lawrence's writing on the pristine unconscious in the case of *Studies* (a work, after all, of literary criticism) shrink under this evidently hard epistemological scrutiny. Nor does a knowledge of the Lawrentian *bricolage* informing the solar plexus theory – part derived from the ancient Hindu model of the chakras, part from a medical book he had borrowed from Edith Eder in 1918, 'a book which describes the human nervous system, and gives a kind of map of the nerves of the human body . . .' – inspire confidence (*LIII* 243–5). He was, he confessed, in a typical act of distancing from professional academic discourse, an 'amateur of amateurs', no '"scholar" of any sort', proceeding by hints, suggestions and 'intuition' (*FU* 11–12). The theory thus occupies a kind of limbo, too fanciful to be defended on the grounds of hard anatomy, yet too realist in its motivation to be defended purely as metaphor.

Let us however re-frame the theory's inconsistencies in terms of their relation to positions encountered in materialist debate. Lawrence accepts the evolutionary narrative that the emergence of human intellect is a scientific fact. He also knows that dominant versions of materialism are vulnerable, in the domain of logic, in their explanantions both of the emergence of animate organic life and of the emergence of intellect. Finally, a historical sense persuades him that the 'human' cannot remain untouched by sweeping movements such as Christianity, industrialism, the rise of nation-states, or war. The fact that such positions co-exist *within* the framework of scientific debate, as well as within Lawrence's own idiosyncratic philosophy, suggests a different model of 'science' from that endorsed by Cowan. In one sense impeccably orthodox in its version of scientific truth, Cowan's argument is also epistemologically vulnerable. The body, he claims, works *this* way, and science can only ever be right or wrong about it. He accuses Lawrence of attributing complex effects to structures that 'merely transmit impulses which mediate relatively simple involuntary functions'. As I suggested in Chapter 1, it is only, paradoxically, from within humanist criticism that one is most likely to encounter an image of science occupying a world of unequivocal fact – an image, in other words, unlikely to be shared by scientists themselves, whether of the nineteenth or of the twenty-first centuries. Bergson, as Schwartz puts it, did not dispute the adequacy of science to provide practical and reliable knowledge of function, but challenged the 'cognitive distortion that proceeds from the methods of the natural sciences'.[6] Consciousness, Bergson maintained, could not be explained as the cause-and-effect *outcome* of material structures and stimuli, if it had simultaneously produced and participated in that explanation; nor could this explain the distinctive qualities of consciousness, or the apparent transition from matter into consciousness. Lawrence's formula for this was to refuse to look for the phenomena of physics in human beings; matter could be a determining realm or base, yet at the same time unfixed and unpredictable in its effects, and immersed in relationship with its environments.

It is important then to return to the apparently deterministic biologism of the 'pristine self'. This aspect of the theory seems uppermost in *Psychoanalysis and the Unconscious* and *Fantasia of the Unconscious*, where it was deployed as a means of challenging the Freudian definition of the unconscious and the discipline of psychoanalysis. 'What the unconscious actually is', we remember, is the same as 'first consciousness'. With this contradiction, Lawrence insists that aliveness is not a condition of our mental awareness of it; we are unconscious of most of our consciousness, as in the case of the 'blood' that 'thinks' or, in the later essay 'Introduction to Pictures' (1928), in the claim that 'All the cells of the body are conscious' (P 767). Psychoanalysis, he argues, is not interested in this pristine unconscious; Freud's definition, typified by the incest motive, is of a part of mental consciousness that is 'unwilling to expose itself to full recognition' and is therefore repressed, 'recoiling back' into the affective self where it wreaks destructive effects (*FU* 209).

Lawrence's clear admiration for Freud's journey, 'like some supreme explorer' disappearing into the 'cavern' of dreams and sleep, is counteracted by the fact that it is, in a sense, the ultimate logical conclusion of a scientific idealism traceable through Plato, Descartes and on, as my reading in Chapter 3 suggests, into Spencer. Freud seems to wish to dig deeper than the intellect, to an unconscious which is by definition the very obverse of mental consciousness; yet in doing so, he intellectualizes it *as* an intellectual entity: the ultimate idealism is one in which the very *antithesis* of idealism is intellectualized as ideas which cannot be admitted. A similar paradox is identified by Terry Castle in her reading of psychoanalysis as a product of the late eighteenth-century, romantic 'spectralization of the other', based on a Lockean epistemology which conferred greater reality on mental images than on human subjects. Even as psychoanalysis promises to liberate us from the tyranny of the spectral, it 'recreates the habit of spectralization in a new and intensified form . . . (P)sychoanalysis seems both the most poignant critique of romantic consciousness to date, and its richest and most perverse elaboration'.[7] What stays in place in the Freudian dispensation is the bourgeois ideology of modern science, retaining its capacity to reinvent and master the real on its own terms, while disguising this impulse to control behind a methodology of 'humility' or passive openness to the evidence of material nature. Lawrence's alternative 'true' unconscious could only, therefore, be constituted by the first fused nucleus of any individual human being, lying beyond or prior to discourse and idealization: like Elizabeth Costello's frogs, the pristine self lies outside of representation – 'How can you postulate that which is *there*?' (*P* 713).

Having established the material *there*-ness of the solar plexus, Lawrence's task is to show how an alert materialist science is characterized by its *lack* of determinism, in contrast to the fixed affects achieved by the internalizing of a psychoanalytic, self-fulfilling category such as the incest motive. The relative freedom of such an indeterminate self might now be compared with the posthuman conception of autopoietic volition. In the rest of this section I will highlight four aspects of this indeterminacy. First, closely related to Bergson's sense of experiential duration, there is the insistence that the nature of any new creature 'does *not* follow from the natures of its parents'. At stake here is the naturalistic logic of the complete *sufficiency* of material explanation, such that new life can be nothing more or other than the recombination of already-existent elements. 'Granted the whole cause-and-effect process of generation and evolution', Lawrence maintains, 'the individual is still not explained'; there is in the individual 'something entirely new, underived, underivable, something which is, and which will remain forever, *causeless*' (*FU* 214). The individual is in this sense a third thing, occupying what he was later to call the 'fourth dimension'; against the expected charge of mysticism (and 'I don't like mysticism' [*FU* 23]), the newness of the individual is a 'hard physiological fact'. Shunning recourse to popular vitalism and its extraneous and unanalysable qualities, Lawrence insisted that he argued on the ground of logic: is it more occult to say that the renewal of a material universe is dependent upon the creation of new individuals, or that new individuals are products of an already-existent material universe? Since *Hardy*, he had sought thus to examine the inscription of a human political economy of 'self-preservation' in biological science; he knew, also, that the logic of this apparently pure materialism required, for its perpetuation, the granting of a single, inexplicable material origin.

Second, 'No human being can develop save through the polarized connection with other beings' (*FU* 244–5). The fourfold diagram of the pristine unconscious is already a model of a *dynamic* state, consisting of vital internal polarities between the upper and lower and voluntary and sympathetic modes. But, while the solar plexus emphasizes the new-found isolation of this organism, the individual is 'never purely a thing-by-himself'. When the child takes the mother's breast, drawn by a 'vital magnetism', a 'lovely, suave, fluid, *creative* electricity' flows in a circuit between the 'great nerve centres' or 'poles of passional unconscious' in the 'two now separated beings' (*FU* 220-1). Harmony and separation, relatedness and individual selfhood are 'synchronized' in the activities of 'love' and 'creativity', the production of self implicit in the latter utterly dependent upon the polarization with others implicit in the former. The human is not given, but forged by the maintenance of vital flows between circuits both within and between material bodies; for, in a formula which echoes Haeckel,

> There certainly does exist a subtle and complex sympathy, correspondence between the plasm of the human body, which is identical with the primary human psyche, and the material elements outside. The primary human psyche is a complex plasm, which quivers, sense-conscious, in contact with the circumambient cosmos. Our plasmic psyche is radio-active, connecting with all things, and having first-knowledge of all things (*SM* 176).

'What', Lawrence asked, in the more knockabout mode of the final version of *Studies*, 'is the breath of life? My dear, it is the strange current of interchange that flows between men and men, and men and women, and men and things. A constant current of interflow, a constant vibrating interchange' (*SCAL* 109). This radically materialist arrangement of flows across polarized circuitry – and 'There are lots of circuits' – is particularized as '*creative*' in order to distinguish it from the 'sundering' electricity of the material universe; again, we must not look for the phenomena of physics to be found in human beings.

Third, in common with other living things, we 'have the instinct of turning right away from *some* matter, and of blissfully ignoring the bulk of most matter, and of turning towards only some certain bits of specially selected matter . . .' (*SCAL* 149). While 'matter gravitates because it *is* helpless and mechanical', humans, further distinguished in this from other living creatures by their possession of intellect, 'are tricksy-tricksy, and they shy all sorts of ways'; if you *do* gravitate helplessly, it is because the 'main-spring of your own individuality must have broken', and you have lapsed into 'mechanization' (*SCAL* 150). Here we are afforded a glimpse of intellectual function as no longer simply a source of mismatch and idealizing 'mechanization' in itself, but rather as a key factor in the maintenance of a creative, and therefore dynamic, human balance with the environment. 'Man is given mental intelligence in order that he may effect quick changes, quick readjustments, preserving himself alive and integral through a myriad environments and adverse circumstances which would exterminate a non-adaptable animal'; in 'Introduction to Pictures' this condition is reconfigured as 'vital sanity': 'the human body preserves itself continually in a delicate balance of sanity' (*RDP* 115; *P* 765–6). While closely related to the evolutionary logic by which the intellect is defined as an instrument of survival, such reflections at the same time demonstrate striking associations with a posthuman mode of thinking which positions active organic self-fashioning at the crux of a mode of development whose relation to evolution might be far more tenuous. Lawrence's 'human' approximates here both to the homeostatic condition of delicately preserved equilibrium and to the more creative-reflexive condition of an autopoiesis embodied, like Maturana's frog, in the ability to *construct* environment through the selection of some parts of matter and the 'blissful ignoring' of many others.

Finally, Lawrence tries to spring the trap of determinism through a crucial hesitation over the term 'human' itself. Overlaying the identification of an individual human essence in the first fused nucleus is a sense that this entity does not in itself constitute humanness. Lawrence's perhaps-notorious views on children are germane to this argument. Why, he maintained, have children, if we do not know how to live ourselves? The procreation of humans in this sense represented a consistent deferral of the responsibility of being, transferring that responsibility onto children who might be able to realize a condition that eludes us. The goal of life, as he had stressed in *Hardy*, was to 'flower' into individual being – not, in other words, self-preservation either at the individual level or, in the sense of Dawkins' selfish gene, at the level of species. Thus, 'newness occurs not in children, but in mature, consummated men and women' (*SM* 104). This debunking of the romantic mythology of childhood is of a piece with his consistent satirizing of a return to a pristine state of 'Nature', for example in Crèvecoeur. The human becomes a term of fugitive value rather than normative definition, a state to be achieved through strenuous striving towards integrity and balance. Will Brangwen's human-ness can be as 'unresolved' at nearly fifty as it was at twenty: to see him is, for Birkin, to call the meaning of the human into question, presented as he is with an 'unfused', 'disunited', 'strange', 'inexplicable' and 'almost patternless' collection of 'passions and desires and suppressions and traditions and mechanical ideas'. 'It's harder', wrote Lawrence, 'to be a human being than to be a president or a bit of fluff. You can be a president, or a bit of fluff, or even a nose, by clockwork. Given a role, a *part*, you can play it by clockwork. But you can't have a clockwork human being' (*PII* 290).

Or can you? 'Clockwork' takes us back to the critique of Trotter's crude behaviourist eugenics. In all of the previous instances, Lawrence questions the logical limitations of such a one-dimensional model of cause and effect in favour of a more complex and unpredictable, interactional version of the human. This might be Hayles' 'cyborg' or 'man-machine', as she summarizes its emergence in the history of post-1945 cybernetics,

> responding flexibly to changing situations, learning from the past, freely adapting its behaviour to meet new circumstances, and succeeding in pre-

serving homeostatic stability in the midst of even radically altered environments. Nimbleness is an essential weapon in this struggle, for to repeat mindlessly and mechanically is to let noise win. Noise has the best chance against rote repetition, where it goes to work at once to introduce randomness. But a system that *already behaves unpredictably* cannot be so easily subverted. If a Gibbesian universe implies eventual information death, it also implies a universe in which the best shot for success lies in flexible and probabilistic behaviour. The Greek root for *cybernetics*, 'steersman', aptly describes the cybernetic man-machine: light on its feet, sensitive to change, a being that both is a flow and knows how to go with the flow.[8]

In the next chapter I will explore more fully how far the Lawrentian-posthuman discourse of 'flows' might be articulated with the notion of the machine, drawing on the direct confrontation of this humanist taboo in the philosophy of Deleuze and Guattari. But the mechanical is not quite so clearly ambivalent in Lawrence. We remember that, since the triumph of idealism, it is possible, or even probable, to *endure* in human life as a machine. Human being can be achieved, but also lost: Poe's Roderick Usher represents the continuation of the 'instrumental consciousness' once the 'rich centrality of self is broken' – a consciousness in which the blood maintains its own 'sympathies and responses to the material world' and the nerves 'vibrate all the while to unseen presences, unseen forces' (*SM* 126). It is tempting to review yet again Lawrence's hostility to Trotter's clockwork eugenics when we read his view that most miners are 'complicated machines' or 'implements' for cutting coal and voting on a ballot paper, leaving among them – possibly – only 'two or three living individuals' (*PII* 290–1). How was Lawrence able to justify the politics of this position, in which a only few rare exceptions contain the seeds of new human possibility: 'We have got to discover a new mode of human relationship . . . we have got to get a new conception of man and of ourselves' (*P* 615)? It was in the study and experience of other cultures that Lawrence was able to pursue the question: what other forms of human flesh might there actually be?

3. Cultures

> You say nature is always nature, the sky is always the sky. But sit still and consider for one moment what sort of nature it was the Romans saw on the face of the earth, and what sort of heavens the medievals knew above them, and your sky will begin to crack like glass. . . .
>
> We are at the phase of scientific vision. This phase will pass and

this vision will seem as chimerical to our descendants as the medieval vision seems to us.

Review of *A Second Contemporary Verse Anthology*

If only nations would realize that they have certain natural characteristics, if only they could understand and agree to each other's particular nature, how much simpler it would all be.

Twilight in Italy

The writing Lawrence began in continental Europe in May 1912, after leaving Britain for the first time, marks an intriguing conjuncture as well as a new departure. For the first time, he could begin to assess how far the human, in other cultures, might be genuinely different. For the first time too, writing became work, informed by the pressure of making a living. The critical tradition sees this moment as inaugurating the Lawrentian 'savage pilgimage', the restless search for a mode of human being other than that embodied in Western cultures of modernity. Certainly, one of the most arresting features of this early travel writing, which culminated in *Twilight in Italy* (1916), is a sometimes-awed apprehension of cultural otherness.

The essays are also, however, exercises in racial theorizing, and in this sense Lawrence brought *to* his experiences, as if in recognition of a new-found professionalism, a quasi-scientific approach to race drawing from the eugenicist debates with which he was familiar. The essays exemplify a deeply embedded disposition towards individual and racial evaluation grounded in physical appearance; Lawrence proceeds like the Edwardian musuem ethnographer, for whom 'the man himself in his everyday life, is the best illustration of his own place in history, for his physical aspect, the expression of his face, the care of his person, his clothes, his occupations . . . tell the story with much clearness'.[9] The Bavarian peasant is a 'hot welter of physical sensation'; the Italian Bersaglieri have 'strange hard heads, like young male caryatides' (*TI* 92, 150). Paolo and Maria, the peasant couple in whose farmhouse Lawrence briefly stays as a guest, are placed with a breathtaking interpretative economy. Paolo's head was 'hard and fine, the bone finely constructed, though the skin of his face was loose and furrowed with work'; he is 'finished', 'statuesque' and 'inaccessible' in his being, but 'the mind was unintelligent, he could not grasp a new order' (*TI* 156–8). Maria, from the plain rather than the hills, reminds Lawrence of 'oxen, broad-boned and massive in physique, dark-skinned, slow in her soul', yet with an 'attentive and purposive intelligence'. However apparently essentialistic, and often embodied in the explicit taxonomy of 'types', the judgements nevertheless take surprising turns: while Paolo has 'an almost glass-like quality, fine and clear and perfectly tempered', yet 'brittle', Maria was 'coarser, more vulgar, but also . . . more human, more fertile' (*TI* 156–8). Lawrence thus unsettles the discourse of race even as he deploys it; individual characteristics make it possible to differ, as it were, from oneself: "you have not an English face; no, never"', observes the wife of a Metz barber to Lawrence (*TI* 16). Yet, again, the opening gesture of *Twilight in Italy* is to assert the significance of racial theorizing over and against a universalized conception of human nature: 'if only nations would realize that they have certain natural characteristics, if only they could understand and agree to each other's particular nature, how much simpler it would all be' (*TI* 91).

Another strategic advantage of the travel writing was its effect of grounding ambitious historical and cultural theories in the evidence of these actual encounters. In Chapter 3, section 1, I summarised the sweeping narrative history of Christianity in *Twilight in Italy*, highlighting Lawrence's view that Christian religious belief eventually 'expressed itself in science'. In the chapter 'The Lemon Gardens', this historical narrative is wedged between parts of an anecdote concerning the aged *padrone*, who comes to beg Lawrence's help in fixing a new door-spring. With delicate humour, Lawrence ironizes both parties in the encounter: the padrone with his 'wrinkled, monkey's face', representative of the dark, arrested Italian consciousness, and with his abject approach to a superior English being; and Lawrence himself, 'feeling uncomfortably like Sherlock Holmes', and with a sense of 'the honour of mechanical England in my hands'. Bearing the burden of such responsibility with dignity, Lawrence deciphers the laconic American instructions for the door-spring – ' "Fasten the spring either end up. Wind it up. Never unwind." ', diagnoses the problem and rectifies it.

> There was a moment of anxiety, the screw was fixed. And the door swung to. They were delighted. The Signore Gemma, who roused in me an electric kind of melancholy, clasped her hands together in ecstasy as the door swiftly shut itself. '*Ecco!*' she cried, in her vibrating, almost warlike woman's voice: '*Ecco!*' Her eyes were a-flame as she looked at the door. She ran forward to try it herself. . . .
>
> I must try also. I opened the door. Pouf! It shut with a bang. We all exclaimed with joy (*TI* 123).

The satire is affectionately poised: if Italian credulity is mimicked, so too is Lawrence's authoritative position and with it the legitimacy of science. Like his younger counterparts, the padrone now wishes to grasp the practical benefits of a science Italy had thus far relinquished: 'He wanted machines, machine-production, money, and human power' (*TI* 131). Yet Lawrence, despite his abomination of England's mechanical conquest of the world and of 'her horrible destruction of natural life', cannot renege on or wish away the knowledge he knows he has: 'it is better', we remember, 'to go forward into error than to stay fixed inextricably in the past' (*TI* 132). This knowledge allows him both to fix the door-spring and to condescend towards the padrone and his wife in the narrative. The overarching historical meta-narrative nevertheless insinuates them all as actors in a drama bigger than themselves, so that 'we all exclaimed with joy' might be moment of dramatic unity as much as an extension of irony.

The consequences of such ambivalence for Lawrence's conception of posthuman possibility will be the main concern of this section of the chapter. Lawrence recognizes in himself a certain deep cultural affiliation with industrialism and the idea of rational scientific progress. At the same time, so compelling was his critique of industrial capitalism, the 'base forcing of all human energy into a competition of mere acquisition' (P 138), that, as his 'travel' writing unravels over the next eighteen years, his chosen places – Italy, Mexico, Australia, America – come to bear the heavy weight of his desires for an alternative. How far does such weight compromise an understanding of those precise, 'natural', national characteristics of other cultures? In a complementary sense, postcolonial theory now brings to bear on Lawrence the idea that the cultural other is an inevitable construction of the desires, as well as the inverted mirror-image, of colonial interests. 'In studying primitive societies or in inventing versions of them', writes Marianna Torgovnick with Lawrence in mind,

> Westerners pretend to learn about or to create alternate, less oppressive ways of knowing, all the while establishing mastery and control over those ways of knowing. Primitive societies and systems of thought which might critique Western ones are instead processed in Western terms. Thinkers like Lawrence yearn for, but lack the ground for, radical critique.[10]

Lawrence might thus have been less eager to find precise differences than to have confirmation of some authentic, cross-cultural 'primitive' or 'savage' mode of alternative human being. As Howard Booth puts it, 'assumptions remained in place about the right of the Western subject to develop fantasy constructions of the "other"', and so Lawrence 'never found a stance that transcended the prevailing colonialist discourses'.[11] For Torgovnick, Lawrence's typical modernity, which 'we' broadly share, needs to be stripped of its 'humanist' pretensions and seen for what it is: as 'needing the primitive', and inventing a primitive to fit that need.

The problem with Torgovnick's position is twofold. First, it returns us to the anthropomorphic *reductio* confronted by Coetzee's Elizabeth Costello, though here transposed from a general human to a cultural dilemma. If it is impossible to step outside of modern Western preconceptions, such that even our proposed alternatives are structured by those preconceptions, then it is not only Lawrence that lacks the ground for radical critique – the lack is, rather, an entire and inevitable cultural condition. Second, the position underestimates the extent to which the *precariousness* of a politics of cultural observation and knowledge are already explicitly acknowledged, both in Lawrence's thinking and in the discourses on culture surrounding him. Eugenics was not the only discourse framing Lawrence's thought about cultures and the potential alterities of the human. Another, equally pervasive, and attractive to the modernist temperament, was the rise of cultural anthropology as embodied in the works of, for example, J.G. Frazer, E.B. Tylor, and Jane Harrison. Edward Said's work has consistently shown that this discourse was equally tainted by the interests of power, its ideological pull lying precisely in the claim to the *scientific* study of evolving cultural forms.[12] Yet an ambivalence about science, of the kind dramatized in *Twilight in Italy* and in the encounter with the padrone, is evident, as I attempt to show, in works such as Tylor's *Primitive Culture* (1871) and Harrison's *Ancient Art and Ritual* (1913), which Lawrence came to know and value.

Let us first examine an arresting change of emphasis on the 'savage' in the first and final versions of *Studies in Classic American Literature*. The revisions are made to the chapter on Herman Melville's *Typee* and *Omoo*, where Lawrence is discussing Melville's representation of Typee, a 'primeval' South Sea Island community, hitherto undiscovered, whose members are feared to be cannibals. This becomes the occasion for general reflections on the 'savage'. In the first version, Lawrence argues that it is absurd to speak of savages as children. Reversing the chronology, it is the people of the North, 'starting new centres of life in ourselves', who have 'become young'; savages, by contrast, are defined as 'old grotesque people', 'remnants' of a world civilization based on 'sensual knowledge' and living on in a dream-like state – 'infinitely sophisticated souls' continuing 'almost mechanically' long after their creative moment has gone:

> Any man reading the Bushman folk-lore, as we have it now literally rendered, must feel horror-struck, catching the sounds of myriad age-long contractions and age-long repetitions in human communication, communication become now unintelligible. . . . The ideographs are so complicated, the sound-groups must convey so many unspeakable, unfeelable meanings, all at once, in a stroke, that it needs myriads of ages to achieve such unbearable concentration. The savages are not simple. It is we who are simple. They are unutterably complicated, every feeling, every term of theirs is untranslatably agglomerate (*SM* 223–4).

Replacing this material in the final version of *Studies*, and in the radically different, laconic and acerbic style of that version, is a repeated emphasis that 'we can't go back' to the savage condition. Despite their efforts to be 'renegade', moderns such as Melville and Gauguin discover that there is a gulf separating them from the South Sea Islanders; without despising him or feeling inferior, 'one' realizes that the Islander is 'centuries and centuries behind us in the life-struggle, the consciousness-struggle':

There is an invisible hand grasps my heart and prevents it opening too much to these strangers. They are beautiful, they are like children, they are generous: but are more than this. They are far off, and in their eyes is an easy darkness of the soft, uncreate past. In a way, they are uncreate. Far be it from me to assume any 'white' superiority. But they are savages. They are gentle and laughing and physically very handsome. But it seems to me, that in living so far, through all our bitter centuries of civilisation, we have still been living onwards, forwards. God knows it looks like a *cul de sac* now. But turn to the first negro, and then listen to your own soul. And your own soul will tell you that however false and foul our forms and systems now are, still, through the many centuries since Egypt, we have been living and struggling forwards along some road that is no road, and yet is a great life-development. And our own soul says inside us that on we must still go (*SCAL* 127).

The revisions show Lawrence wrestling with the politics of modernist primitivism. In the first case, the challenge to evolutionist progressivism is paramount: *we* are simple, the *savage* is unutterably complicated and sophisticated. The second version preserves only a trace of this corrective force – the savages are 'more than' children – and erases the attribution of intellectual complexity, urging us instead to check any sentimental impulses we might be tempted to adopt towards savagery. Searching for a way to describe a superiority which is not superiority, and which does not tie in with a teleology of linear progress – 'far be it from me', the road which is 'no road' or becomes a *cul de sac* – his concept of 'life-development' cannot quite cast off the shadow of an 'onwards, forwards' momentum.

What did Lawrence know about cultures? From what kind of position does he write? For today's reader, it is 'turn to the first negro, and the listen to your own soul' that is most likely to persuade us that the position was one of fatuous ignorance. At the same time, Lawrence shows an intense wariness of what it means to adopt '"white" superiority'. Realizing that he is acceding to some version of this superiority, perhaps in and by the very act of writing about and conceptualizing the 'savage', the adoption of a note of reluctant but robust resignation in the revised version is significant. We cannot, Lawrence argues, un-know that broad narrative of human history, the unravelling of modernity, by which some cultures have transformed themselves through reason, science and technology. To maintain that we should 'go back' would be an act of intellectual irresponsibility, sentimentalizing, idealizing and falsifying the savage-as-other. Better, in this sense, to risk acknowledging some limited form of superiority than to 'revert' to a condition which might, in any case, be the invented product of our desires.

Far more risky, however, would be the unequivocal assumption that this history gives 'us' a superiority of intellect and being over the primitive. In the actuality of *reading* translations of Bushman folk-lore, Lawrence 'catches' the sounds of an untranslatably complex and concentrated ideographic language. In a similar modernism, Ezra Pound and the Imagist poets were drawn to oriental ideographic forms of language as offering a radical alternative to the modes of subjectivity and temporality embedded in European grammars. Strictly, according to his own theory, it would seem that Lawrence's exoticization of the Bushman could never be verified: if Bushman language is incommunicable and unintelligible, how *can* we know that it contains a complexity that we cannot know – how can we know that we have not invented such complexity for our own purposes? The claim mirrors his reading of the old spinner woman in *Twilight in Italy*, where Lawrence was at pains to emphasize a fundamental relativity separating them; he addresses her and they speak, but from different, incommensurate mental worlds: 'we divided the gift of speech, that was all' (*TI* 30). This untranslatability becomes the very basis from which he allows himself to claim a profound knowledge of the nature of the woman's otherness. Her eyes, 'wonderful', 'clear' but 'unthinking' and 'unconscious', have 'no looking in them' and thus do not see him as an individual: 'she saw merely a man's figure, a stranger standing near . . . (A) piece of the environment' (*TI* 106–7). The absence of objectification or of an awareness that 'there is that which is not me' is rendered briefly in free indirect, internal narration:

> She knew that I was an inhabitant of lands which she had never seen. But what of that! There were parts of her own body which she had never seen, which physiologically she could never see. They were none the less her own because she had never seen them (*TI* 107).

From such a perspective, then, the woman, as she tells him of a sheep that has died, cannot understand that *he* cannot understand her; lacking the sense of cultural relativity that would follow from objectification, she 'only thought me different, stupid'. The woman proceeds 'as if she were talking to her own world in me'; the profound irony of this phrase is that it may register precisely what Lawrence himself does even as he thinks he is avoiding it.

Across the range of Lawrence's writing on cultural otherness, we find a sustained dialectical movement between the two versions of the 'savage' I have highlighted. On the one hand, the primitive or savage world comprises a complexity we have lost, highlighting the epistemological limits of our own science. On the other hand, the explanatory power of science and the kind of cultural 'superiority' it confers upon us cannot be gainsaid. Lawrence's emphasis on linguistic untranslatability and relativity suggests that our scientific world view is, like any cultural frame of reference, heavily deterministic, and in this sense he is acutely aware of the implications of such determinism. How could any construction of the other, whether as complex or as child-like, be anything but a mode of cultural imperialism?

We return to the sense of a political gamble undertaken by Lawrence's writing on cultures, of the kind implicit in the audacity to *know* the Italian spinner woman in such paradoxical depth, and to extend this into a mode of pronouncement on racial differences which to us looks like a dangerous essentialism. To question and even invert the evolutionary narrative of linear progress, and to insist upon the complex sophistication of the primitive and savage even when the grounds of proof are by definition beyond us, is to prise open the possibility that the human might be radically other than that defined by Western humanism and the liberal, industrial-capitalist order to which it is allied. In this light, the risk is to endorse an element of hierarchical difference rather than to posit a universal conception of human nature which might, in actuality, be a more stealthy imposition of Western ideology. Acknowledging the particular superiority conferred by science – the ability to fix door-springs, or to build industrial economies – then constitutes the platform from which the alternative superiority of the other, its 'unthinkable complexity', can begin to be thought.

We must, Lawrence argues with a disarming directness in *Mornings in Mexico*, leave off trying 'to render the Indian in our own terms':

> It is almost impossible for the white people to approach the Indian without either sentimentality or dislike. The common healthy vulgar white usually feels a certain native dislike of these drumming aboriginals. The highbrow invariably lapses into sentimentalism like the smell of bad eggs.
>
> Why? – Both the reactions are due to the same feeling in the white man (*MM* 54).

Racism (connoted by 'vulgar' and 'dislike') and sentimentalism are two sides of the same imperialist coin. Lawrence does not however place the same emphasis on each. Racist dislike, he claims, is a 'quite natural' and 'instinctive' reaction to differences of colour which it is 'only honesty' to admit to. 'Instincts' could of course, in evolutionary terms, be acquired, and Lawrence knows that racist reflexes are embedded in himself and in his culture. Heavier critique is reserved for sentimentalist primitivism, a lie or 'mental trick' by which you 'fool yourself and others into believing that the befeathered and bedaubed darling is nearer to the true ideal gods than we are'. Quite explicitly, Lawrence reveals here the ideological construction of the Cowboys and Indians mythology, both sides of which need to be 'debunked', with a reminder that 'Indian bunk' is not the Indian's 'invention' but ours. The 'we' in question includes 'anthropologists and myth-transcribers', whose 'creeping sentimentalism' of the savage 'makes one shrug one's shoulders and wish the Indians to hell, along with a lot of other bunk' (*MM* 54).

This abrasive rhetoric – Lawrence at his intolerantly racist and anti-intellectualist worst? – can nevertheless be viewed as part of the strategic gamble I have argued for. Lawrence strives to expose the scientific-academic as ideological, chancing an alliance with reaction and the 'amateur' in order to set in relief the subtler, more deeply embedded, because professionally respectable, racism of anthroplogical primitivism. In *Apocalypse*, he identified such racism as a form of scholarly and scientific collusion in the academic German phrase *Urdummheit*, which he translates as a dismissive reference to 'primal stupidity'. *Urdummheit* might be 'just the fellow who is different from me', but for the academy he is the speaker of any language that is not 'Oxford or Harvard or an obsequious imitation of one of these' (*A* 36–9).

If we look at the kinds of anthropology Lawrence might have been drawing upon, we find comparable and important ambivalences. In November 1913, he recorded a debt to Jane Harrison's newly-published *Ancient Art and Ritual* – 'stupidly put' by a 'school-marmy woman', but 'it lets one in for an idea that helps one immensely' (*LII* 114). This central idea was no doubt Harrison's thesis concerning the common origins of art and religious ritual in ancient, and particularly Greek, cultures. But certain aspects of Harrison's *polemic* are perhaps even more resonant in Lawrence's work. The early stages of the book contain trenchant critiques both of Platonic idealism and of a Kiplingesque cultural imperialism, insinuating the close ideological links between the two. We must, Harrison argues, grasp the 'wrong-headed' falsehood of Plato's theory of art as imitation, which condemns the artist to the copying of natural objects which are themselves shadowy copies of higher realities. Why should art be imitation? The theory, Harrison claims, fails utterly to account for art as a 'widespread human energy'. Just as it is irrelevant to the artistic ritual of the Huichol Indians, practical, emotional, and 'making or doing or enriching the object or act desired', so the modern challenge of photography exposes the irrelevance of imitative, realist painting (*AAR* 8–10).

The critique of Platonic mimeticism thus opens up a parallel between the motivations and interests of 'primitive' art and advanced, experimental modernist art of the early twentieth century. A naïve mimeticism, Harrison implies, can only be what lies behind the imperialist misreading of primitive religion as the 'heathen in his blindness' bowing down to 'gods of wood and stone'. Modern science allows us to examine how art actually did arise, drawing on anthropological research to show, for example, that it is based on a religion of action rather than of obeisance. Paradoxically, then, to examine primitive culture scientifically is to reveal a *relativistic* as well as hierarchical mode of difference: Harrison's research shows for example that 'science . . . has dwarfed actual human life almost to imaginative extinction' (*AAR* 109). Science 'deals with abstractions, concepts, class names, that we may handle life on the side desirable to us', abstractions being things (in a distinctly Bergsonian sense) '*dragged away* consciously by the intellect, from actual things objectively existing' (*AAR* 122–3). However, just as we find in ourselves 'instincts kindred' with those of the savage, so we find the origins of abstraction in the re-enactments characteristic of ritual: the more the savage re-enacts a *particular* battle, the more the battle is likely to become generalized and thus resemble a transformation 'we think of as characteristically and exclusively intellectual'. On this subject of abstraction, Harrison is at her most ambivalent: it is still the case that what constitutes abstraction for we moderns is 'foreign' to the 'mental habit' not only of the savage but of the peasant of today, for whom the 'faculty of conception' is 'but dim and feeble': 'his actual function is to perceive the actual fact year by year, and feel about it' (*AAR* 36). What is intriguing is precisely the delicate counterbalancing of this scientific condescension, clearly predicated upon a Spencerean model of human cultural evolution, with a genuine cultural relativism. Harrison warns that we assume scientific triumphalism, particularly if it is based on an unexamined, Platonic-realist epistemology, at our peril.

E.B. Tylor's *Primitive Culture* (1871), which Lawrence came to know by March 1916, seems less equivocal in its embodiment of a confident Victorian scientificity. Its ethnography is firmly declared as a philosophy of history dependent upon the laws of causality and evolution. In amassing data on primitive cultural practices and beliefs, especially those relating to language, Tylor, like Harrison, aimed to show the ineluctable evolutionary traces of modern cultural forms. 'The nobler tendency of advancing culture, and above all of scientific culture', he writes, 'is to honour the dead without grovelling before them, to profit by the past without sacificing the present to it' (*PC* 157). Yet Tylor still worries that many of our ideas exist 'rather by being old than by being good', condemning the savage as 'firmly, obstinately conservative': 'we listen with pity to the rude Indian as he maintains against civilized science and experience the authority of his rude forefathers . . .', 'we smile at the Chinese appealing against modern innovation . . .', and so on (*PC* 156). To the envisaged objection that his science necessitates writing 'soullessly of the soul, and unspiritually of spiritual things', Tylor responds in familiar ideological terms: the anatomist 'does well to discuss bodily structure independently of the world of happiness and misery which depends upon it'; science is in any case as natural as breathing, so that the man who criticizes the idea of laws of human conduct is an 'inductive philosopher' without knowing it.

Behind the pitying smile of condescension, however, *Primitive Culture* is at the same time a surprising source of primitivist sentiment, lamenting the loss of cultures in a way that inevitably unsettles its own scientific authority. 'The growth of myth has been checked by science', writes Tylor; 'it is dying of weights and measures, of proportions and specimens – it is not only dying, but half-dead, and students are anatomizing it' (*PC* 317). The sciences, he declaims, highlighting a language of imperialism, have 'seized whole provinces of the ancient Animism, setting force for life and law for will':

> No indwelling deity now regulates the life of the burning sun, no guardian angels drive the stars across the arching firmament, the divine Ganges is water flowing down into the sea to evaporate into cloud and descend again into rain. No deity simmers in the boiling pot, no presiding spirits dwell in the volcano, no howling demon shrieks from the mouth of the lunatic.[13]

If this is what Lawrence meant by the sentimentalism of anthropology, it is at least instructive to compare Tylor's emphasis, encapsulated in his series of chapters on Animism by the phrase 'we have lost something...', with Lawrence's reminder, in his last work *Apocalypse*, that 'we have lost the cosmos'. 'With us', he insists, 'all is personal', and 'even the universe of the scientist is little more than an extension of our personality':

> Our sun is a quite different thing from the cosmic sun of the ancients, so much more trivial. We may see what we call the sun, but we have lost Helios forever, and the great orb of the Chaldeans still more. We have lost the cosmos, by coming out of responsive connection with it, and this is our chief tragedy. What is our petty little love of nature – Nature! – compared to the ancient magnificent living with the cosmos, and being honoured by the cosmos! (*A* 21–2).

Combined with his own developing experience of other cultures, anthropologies such as those of Harrison and Tylor provided Lawrence with a strong sense of the possibility of alternative modes of thinking and being human. Unlike the futuristic politics of eugenics, anthropology claimed to ground itself in the real historical existence of these alternative modes, whether lapsed, or abiding within non-industrialized cultures. It also managed a precarious balance between evolutionary progressivism, according to which such existences were regarded as inevitably superseded, and a cultural relativism, which granted the dignity of a certain autonomy to the 'savage' or 'primitive'. Lawrence subscribed to this relativism, for example, when he urged his readers to consider how their world differed from that of the Romans or of the medievals, maintaining that our 'phase of scientific vision' will pass just as surely as its predecessors had: nature is *not* always 'nature', the sky is *not* always 'the sky'.

As in the solar plexus theory, so Lawrence's 'racism' must be carefully defined in terms of a dialectic between essentialism and relativism. His insistence on 'natural' national characteristics extended even to the determining physicality or 'magnetism' of place itself: 'every people is polarised in some particular locality, some home or homeland' (*SM* 20). Place in this sense could override established nature: migrants to or colonizers of America develop a 'new molecular disposition' in their 'nerves, bones and sinews' (*SM* 29). Racial identities were therefore the basis of a recognition of difference, and of the impossibility of any *universal* human essence or nature. Lawrence's thoroughgoing relativism was grounded in the belief that human identity was a highly specific but overdetermined condition, within which concepts of race and culture blend into each other. What is 'natural' to us as racial beings is, for Lawrence, as much a fact of the historical growth of cultures as it is of the physical properties of heredity or place, such factors fusing into a complex determinism.

Lawrence may not, in his time, have been unique in this. In comparing nineteenth-century with contemporary postcolonial uses of the term 'hybridity', for example, Robert Young suggests that in the racial theory of the earlier period the term is 'contradictory, disruptive and already deconstructed'.[14] Just as nineteenth-century humanists generated convenient caricatures of science, postcolonial criticism gestures towards the 'pseudo-scientific' racialisms of that period, risking, Young argues, the glib dismissal of something which was never simply biologically essentialistic in the first place:

> Today it is common to claim that in such matters we have moved from biologism and scientism to the safety of culturalism, that we have created distance and surety by the very act of the critique of essentialism and the demonstration of its impossibility: but that shift has not been so absolute, for the racial was always cultural, the essential never unequivocal.[15]

Lawrence's racism, the recognition of radical, 'natural' cultural difference, works to repudiate the totalitarian alternative of a common 'humanity' defined by the West and masking its own interests. There are important connections here with a line of critique which runs, say, from Adorno and Horkheimer's analysis in Enlightenment thinking of the elision of difference through abstraction – 'Bourgeois society is ruled by equivalence. It makes the dissimilar comparable by reducing it to abstract quantities'[16] – to a post-colonialism necessitating the transition towards a thinking of the posthuman.

In an example of the latter, Bill Readings brings Jean-François Lyotard's concept of the *différend* to bear on Werner Herzog's drama of the relationship between the Australian state and the Aboriginal community in the film *Where the Green Ants Dream*. The film, Readings argues, demonstrates the injustice done to Aborigines by attempting to resolve territorial disputes with a mining company through recourse to a universal conception of humanity embodied in the subject form 'we'.

> The Aborigines 'belong' (to) a land which cannot be abstracted, transferred, translated (*trans-latio*, lift across, move, transfer); it is not a land

on which humans live, which they exploit, but a land to which humans and non-humans belong in ways that cannot be mapped conceptually.[17]

No 'we' can judge this case on the grounds of an abstract human nature; the unavailability of such a conception in the Aboriginal world-view marks that cultural untranslatability or recalcitrance which is implicit in Lyotard's *différend*, 'a case of conflict between (at least) two parties that cannot be equitably resolved for lack of a rule of judgement applicable to both arguments'. Lyotard finds in paganism, by contrast, a 'tolerance of difference' which is suppressed in the 'self-authorising' republican 'we' of American and French revolutionary discourse; Readings begs his reader's forbearance in withholding from Aborigines the attribution of humanity, because 'by considering them "human" (exemplars of an abstract nature that we share) we victimise them, make them more like us than they are'.[18]

Lawrence's account of Benjamin Franklin's frontier encounter with native Indians is directly comparable. Franklin, the 'virtuous little automaton', creates a 'barbed-wire fence' of Puritan virtues and then proceeds to apply them as standards of the ideal or 'dummy' citizen to the indigenous Americans he meets. In the first and final versions of *Studies*, Lawrence quotes from Franklin's disdainful account of a visit to a Pennsylvanian Indian settlement for the purposes of drawing up a treaty. With 'suave complacency', Franklin notes the drunken behaviour of the Indians – 'there was no appeasing the tumult, and we retired to our lodgings' – and their demands for more rum. Lawrence turns Franklin's satire back against him, echoing the observation that rum might be Providence's way of 'extirpat(ing) these savages in order to make room for the cultivators of the earth':

> 'This is good, that is bad. Turn the little handle and let the good tap flow,' saith Benjamin, and all America with him. 'But first of all extirpate those savages who are always turning on the bad tap' (*SCAL* 26).

From the basis of this critique of the Enlightenment, imperialistic ideal of the good citizen, Lawrence was able to build a model of cultural otherness which was not restricted to human evolutionism, even as it continued to draw on the latter for its historical account of modernity. The characteristics he found in or attributed to the people of his chosen places – Italians and Mexicans, in particular – do not simply refer 'back' down the evolutionary ladder, but constitute the seeds of a posthuman condition which might obtain once our present 'phase of scientific vision' has passed. Moving beyond scientific orthodoxy meant in this sense retaining science's intense engagement with the material world while at the same time re-evaluating modes of knowledge, complex and sophisticated, which had been deemed, at best, and according to the logic of the *différend*, untranslatable, at worst superseded. In like manner, Bergsonian philosophy, and the posthuman sci-

ences of the mind and of information, challenge the logic of realist epistemology from within the framework of science. 'We are apt to assume', writes
Lawrence, 'that there is only one mode of science – our own', the conquest
of science insinuating not only the displacement of 'the old hermetic science
and alchemy and astrology' but also its fallaciousness (*SM* 163). The whole
effort to deconstruct this polarized, either–or triumphalism is signalled in a
Janus-principle which he called the Holy Ghost: 'you've got to learn to
change from one consciousness to the other, turn and about. Not to try to
make either absolute, or dominant. The Holy Ghost tells you the how and
when'; 'the only thing you can do is to have a little Ghost inside you which
sees both ways, or even many ways' (*SCAL* 100; *MM* 55).

Italy and Mexico are of crucial significance in Lawrence's work in this
respect. Italy informs one of his most infamous and anthologized irrationalist declarations:

> My great religion is a belief in the blood, the flesh, as being wiser than
> the intellect. We can go wrong in our minds. But what our blood feels
> and believes and says, is always true. The intellect is only a bit and a
> bridle. What do I care about knowledge. All I want is to answer to my
> blood, direct, without fribbling intervention of mind, or moral, or what
> not . . .
>
> That is why I like to live in Italy. The people are so unconscious. They
> only feel and want; they don't know (*LI* 503–4).

From first observations on the preferences of the local theatre audience for
D'Annunzio over Ibsen in *Twilight*, through to his 1928 introduction to the
novel *The Mother* by the contemporary Sardinian writer Grazia Deledda,
Lawrence elaborates this theory of the 'unconscious' Italian, whose blood
reigns over the intellect, in terms of a philosophy of the Italian language
embodied collectively in the creative work of Italian writers. D'Annunzio's
language, Lawrence claims, achieves a 'physical' effect on the 'blood', satisfying the child-like Italian's desire for sensuous gratification over intellect;
much of it might be rhetorical 'bosh', but the hearer is emotionally fulfilled.
Giovanni Verga achieves a 'revolution' in style appropriate to the subjectivity of the Sicilian peasant. In its wryest and most laconic form, Lawrence's
theory of the Sicilian makes a direct physical correlation between climate
and human orientation: 'in the sun, men are objective, in the mist and
snow, subjective. Subjectivity is largely a question of the thickness of your
overcoat' (*P* 229). Like the Greek, Lawrence claims, the Sicilian is incapable
of what we understand as introspection, 'our sort of subjective consciousness', because his consciousness, 'so to speak, doesn't have any inside to it.
He can't look inside himself, because he is, as it were, solid' (*P* 228; *PII* 284).
The Sicilian's 'solidity', his inability to conceive of himself as a subject or
'soul' ('in our sense of the word'), is a condition of language, in which the

subject–object relation, crucial to dualism and science, does not occur. Lyotard's *différend* becomes appropriate: the Greeks, such as Socrates, are translated into 'another thing, our own thing', being so 'peculiarly *objective*' that 'we could never get him if we did not translate him into something else, and thus "make him our own"' (*PII* 286).

Translation then always involves appropriation, the transformation of an experience into the structures of 'our own'. Verga, having listened to the 'ungrammatical and disconnected' narrative of a sea-captain, develops a language of the 'emotional' mind which, however 'muddled', has 'its own rhythm, its own commas and colons and full-stops'. In a distinctly Bergsonian reading of this 'activity of the mind', Lawrence argues that it completely dispenses with time as a form of measurement: only 'afterwards' can the logical and temporal sequences be deduced, 'as historians do from the past'. In the Introduction to his translation of *Cavalleria Rusticana*, Lawrence decides that the only way to describe this style is to enact it, in the 'curious spiral rhythm' of the mind as a bird repeatedly swooping towards and retreating from the 'point of pain or interest', 'destroying the time-sequence entirely' (*P* 249–50), as if to parallel the active, practical orientation of primitive orientations towards the universe as described by Harrison.

Finally, in the introduction to Grazia Deledda's *The Mother*, a more prosaic account of Italian takes us directly back to the observations of *Twilight in Italy*. As if to confirm Lawrence's sense that Sardinia embodies the 'mystery of an unevolved people', Deledda strives to 'create the passionate complex of a primitive populace'. But there are the inevitable losses in translation: Italian is an 'instinctive' language in which a 'natural mist or glow of sensation' prevails over exactitude. This quality cannot be conveyed in the northern languages, where 'every word has its fixed value and meaning, like so much coinage' (*P* 263–6).

Is there any alternative to seeing Lawrence's views on Italy, its language and its relation to the blood as, themselves, the insulting epitome of cultural imperialism? Let us consider the convergence of Lawrence's primitivist Italian with ideas of the contemporary posthuman. We have seen the latter rooted in a critique of the Cartesian dualism of body and mind, and of the installation of intellect as an 'evolutionary upstart' reigning over a prior bodily condition of complex totality. Following from this dualism are fundamental humanistic assumptions through which we claim to know the world – principally, the distance between subject and object, and the model of time as a condition of linearity which explains progressive development. Renewing Bergsonian philosophy's critical analysis of these assumptions, posthuman science proposes a changing epistemology: perception and memory are not representational; the subject is embodied in the material world, autopoietically constructing and shaping even as it is constructed and shaped; a circular rather than linear temporality, threatening to evolutionism, best describes the unpredictabilities of organic development; finally, all of these call into question the decisive separation of the human from the material whole.

All of these are present in Lawrence's contestatory version of the primitive, which similarly figures the possibility of a radically different epistemology, and thus a different humanness. Inevitably, as we have seen, the politics of this primitivism are not straightforward; evolutionism is still in place, so that Sardinia is 'unevolved' and Verga's Sicily 'incredibly backward'. But such temporalities are themselves under intense scrutiny. Consistently, Lawrence's emphasis is also that it is 'we', not 'the savage', who are simple. Verga's mistrust of intellectualism must be carefully distinguished from a simplistic primitivism; he was not seeking the brute or cave-man, the 'animal man', because he knew that these lay close beneath the surface of contemporary man (*P* 243).

Again, these ambivalences, and the glimpsing between them of a conception of the posthuman, are not without foundation in the anthropology that Lawrence took *to* his cultures. Even Tylor stressed the rationality and effectiveness of the animistic world-view, which could so successfully account for the 'plain evidence of man's senses' that it had endured well within the higher developments of education and philosophy. The savage may have never 'learnt to make that rigid distinction between subjective and objective ... to enforce which is one of the main results of scientific education'; at the same time, however, it would be an 'extreme mistake' to assume that theories of a continuity between humans and animals were the product of advanced science only (*PC* 445). In a revealing contradiction, the sense of 'absolute psychical distinction' between man and beast is seen as a 'purely civilized' one (*PC* 467). More searchingly, Jane Harrison finds that in order to understand the fine distinction the Greeks made between art and ritual (Lawrence could have derived his emphases on Greek untranslatability, and on the connections between Greek and 'savage' thinking, directly from Harrison), an alternative human nature needs to be predicated. We are accustomed, Harrison maintains, to the hierarchical division of the human constitution into faculties, with Reason as 'head and crown'. This psychology is, however, a 'convenient and perhaps indispensable mythology'; more fruitful would be to see the human, not as 'a bundle of separate faculties' but as '*a sort of continuous cycle of activities*' (my emphasis; *AAR* 17). This cycle of unhierarchized 'knowing, feeling and striving' co-exists with the notion of art as *presentation*, the making or being of a thing, rather than *re-presentation*, which is based on a reductive modern mistranslation of the Greek *mimesis* as an art of 'mere copying'. A line can thus be traced between two critiques of realist epistemology: the Platonic 'misconception' of art as imitation, and the challenge to representationalism – the sense that the mind screens images of what it sees, knows or remembers – in Bergsonism and in the posthuman science of dissipative structures of cognition.

Lawrence's Italian posthuman begins to resemble a more generally primitive posthuman, working against cultural specificity. Clearly, the argument from language allows him to collapse together Sicilian, Sardinian and Northern Italian into one 'Italian' consciousness, for example. Yet the language of physicality or organicism constantly blurs the boundaries between natural and cultural, literal and metaphorical. 'Blood' is a particular and notorious case in point. If sun can physically alter the constitution of the blood, so too, it seems, can language; for the Italian, there is 'the physical effect of the language upon the blood', while for 'us', European culture is an organic condition of 'our very blood and bones' (*P* 215).

Contemporary postcolonial theory obliges us to consider the inevitably *metaphoric* significance of blood and organicism in such pronouncements. Yet the clear orientation of Lawrence's thinking, as in the 'pure science' of the solar plexus, is that we must move beyond a merely *linguistic* relativity in order to consider the conjunction of language and embodiment which makes up a 'culture'. Fully persuaded of the inherent metaphoricity of language, Lawrence's own hesitancy over this issue is sometimes apparent: the Sicilian consciousness doesn't have an inside, '*so to speak*'; the Sicilian is, '*as it were*, solid'. Yet his specific materialism seems to depend upon the wager of overriding such hesitancies. If a European culture of scientific rationality could be granted historical and material reality, embodied in human flesh and blood, so too could a non-European culture of otherness known in popular currency as 'primitive' and 'savage'. The crucial point of such distinctions is that human being not only conceives of itself differently, but *is* different. It may nevertheless be that 'blood' in this sense has a weakened metaphorical (or strengthened literal) connotation, standing for a general condition of materiality: 'what our blood feels and believes'; 'the blood, *the flesh*' (my emphasis). As we know, there was ample ground in Lawrence's materialist formation for the conviction that the human is rooted in instinctive modes of bodily knowledge, expressed in reflex and habitual behaviours which occur independently of conscious decision. These, precisely, are the kind of theories which are renewed in posthuman conceptions of complex embodiment.

If we turn briefly to Lawrence's account of Mexico in *Mornings in Mexico* (1927), we find some confirmation of a generalised version of the primitive. Rosalino the *mozo* has 'black', 'visionless' eyes of 'incomprehension', and an irritating resistance to conceptual meaning – although he is, we learn, something of an exception to the Mexican Indian race, being 'just a bit aware that there is another being, unknown, at the other end of his glance'; 'usually, these people have no correspondence with one at all' (*MM* 33). This is a version of the Italian spinner woman's creaturely, 'tiger'-like vision, which 'cannot see, except with the light from within itself', and of the implicit logic of the *différend* or lack of correspondence: 'there was nothing between us', Lawrence had written of 'Il Duro', 'except our complete difference' (*TI* 178). Like his Italians, Greeks and Singhalese, Lawrence's Mexicans have a 'complete absence of what we call "spirit"', which goes – 'perhaps' – with their 'beautiful, suave, rich skins . . . ; a sort of richness of the flesh' (*MM* 31).

Lawrence's Mexico also embodies familiar paradigms of primitive consciousness and conceptions of time and space. In the chapter 'Market Day', the initial stimulus is meteorological, a 'restless morning' in which a centripetal wind makes everything – clouds, mountains, dust, hawks – appear to be 'slowly wheeling and pivoting upon a centre' (*MM* 45). This prompts a brief excursus upon the 'strangeness' of thinking in straight lines when we know that 'space is curved, and the cosmos is sphere within sphere'; what was presented in Verga's prose as the notation of the 'emotional mind' is here read in the context of a cosmology legitimized by contemporary physics. The linear, progressive thinking of scientific modernity is revealed to be both unnatural and violently imperialistic: 'The straight course is hacked out in wounds, against the will of the world'. This alternative conception of time then informs what happens in the Indian marketplace. People throng to the market along the big valley road, 'almost straight', 'on a strange current of haste', but, once there, they turn capitalist logic upside-down: the rationale is not to commingle in order to buy and sell, but to buy and sell in order to commingle, to 'exchange, above all things, human contact':

> They have been part of a great stream of men flowing to a centre, to the vortex of the market-place. And here they have felt life concentrate upon them, they have been jammed between the soft hot bodies of strange men come from afar, they have had the sound of strangers' voices in their ears, they have asked and been answered in unaccustomed ways (*MM* 51).

Lifted free from any conception of utility, and from the idealized objectification of things which is expressed in the notion of *commodity*, it is thus significant that the Indians' intense physical contact is neither fixed nor even tangible: 'no goal', 'no abiding place', 'nothing but the touch, the spark of contact': '*Only that which is utterly intangible, matters*' (*MM* 51–2; my emphasis). It is a Bergsonian *durée* that the Indian experiences, dissolving subjectivity into 'flow' or process.

Closely associated with this deconstruction of time is Lawrence's account of ritual dance. Here, the ideas assimilated from Jane Harrison's *Ancient Art and Ritual* seem to stand confirmed, in a conception of the aesthetic at odds with Western entertainment-as-spectacle, precluding Platonic mimeticism and disavowing the subject–object relation crucial to science. 'We', argues Lawrence, sit in the theatre as 'a little democracy of the ideal consciousness', safely distanced from images which, Platonic realism tells us, are reflections of our own shadowy perceptions of ourselves. Cinema, he maintains, is the logical extension of this form of spectacle, firmly ensconcing us as gods presiding over the abstract machine and safely detached from the 'solid stuff of earth' (*MM* 53–4). The Indian dance banishes spectacle: it is not representational, and there is 'no division between actor and audience'. Like the Italian's experience of D'Annunzio in the theatre, the dance affects the 'human bloodsteam', is 'generic' and 'non-individual'. Again, however, what distinguishes this physicality is that it is barely tangible, a 'very soft, subtle, delicate' form of '*being*' rather than representing.

With a reflexive subtlety, Lawrence acknowledges that his own otherness places him at a disadvantage: 'It means nothing at all' modulates into 'What are they doing? Who knows?', as if to revisit the encounter with the Italian spinner – meaninglessness might be a quality attributed to what we do not understand, but it cannot be assumed on behalf of the other. Lawrence thus seems to draw on his anthropological knowledge, of Greek drama but primarily of animistic religion, to augment his reading of Mexican Indian culture. His account of animism reveals our 'God' to be an instance of the subject–object relation, harking back to the interpretation of Christianity underpinning his interpretation of Italy; there is never a 'distinction' between 'God and God's creation, or between Spirit and Matter':

> The Indian does not consider himself as created, and therefore external to God, or the creature of God. To the Indian there is no conception of a defined God. Creation is a great flood, for ever flowing, in lovely and terrible waves. In everything, the shimmer of creation, and never the finality of the created (*MM* 61).

The version of animism in the centrepiece chapter on the Hopi Snake Dance seems closest to an alert, materialist science, appropriately accompanied by a polemic on 'our' science as a 'religion of conquest'. For the Indian, again, there is no God-as-Maker, but a 'great living source of life: say the Sun of existence: to which you can no more pray than you can pray to Electricity' (*MM* 74). This suggested parallel with contemporary materialism – the materialism of, say, Frankstone – is quickly modified: this is not a 'oneness' of strict causality, because 'all lives', and life is a definition of the separation and multiplicity of living things – 'The law of isolation is heavy on every creature'. To the Indian, 'the so-called mechanical processes do not exist'; the orientation of the human towards the world then *affects*, as in autopoiesis, the world itself. While the subjugation and conquest of matter produces one kind of world, the 'profound respect' and 'desperate courage' of the Hopi produces another; while the Hopi possess the 'strange inward sun of life', we 'die of *ennui*'.

To summarise. It became crucial for Lawrence to stress that there were other ways of being human than those imagined by Western, Enlightenment cultures. At the same time, his writing on anthropomorphism and scientific idealism showed an acute awareness that any such pronouncement on cultural otherness must be compromised by the very fantasies and ideas it sought to contest. His resolve, in the face of the double bind which so oppresses Coetzee's Elizabeth Costello, was to transmit this otherness in the terms of *relationship*, rather than of objective knowledge taking place in the abstract space between subject and object. As in his account of the otherness of animals, so Lawrence's account of other cultures tries to evade idealism by embracing relationship as a dialectic. Such relationship is, for example, prone to a dynamic in which antagonism can be honestly articulated, and yet quickly change into its opposite, a passionate and even sentimentalized endorsement of the other. What matters is the movement of sympathies itself, the record of an engagement which guards against hypostatization. Is the 'modern' superior to, advanced beyond, the 'primitive'? Yes, in a concrete historical sense, but also emphatically no; the former's progress is also degeneration. Are 'European' and 'primitive', conditions of physical and biological being? Yes, but also no. Are cultures inalienably different, and literally untranslatable to each other? Yes, and no.

Mornings in Mexico can starkly demonstrate one side of this dialectic in a way which differentiates it from Lawrentian versions of Italy. The early chapters are characterized by a world-weary tone of contempt and mockery for the individual Indian and for his race. Rosalino is a 'dumb-bell', of which there are many in the land; the Aztecs are, as far as we know, 'an unlovely and unlovable lot'. 'We don't belong to the ruling race for nothing', Lawrence wryly declares, as they march back into the yard of Valentino Ruiz after a literally fruitless search. Democracy in Mexico is 'farcical', exemplified by two men canvassing for votes in a shed.

> My dear fellow, this is when democracy becomes real fun. You vote for one red ring inside another red ring and you get a Julio Echegaray. You vote for a blue dot inside a blue ring, and you get a Socrate Ezekiel Tos. Heaven knows what you get for the two little red circles on top of one another. . . . Suppose we vote, and try. There's all sorts in the lucky bag. There might come a name like Peregrino Zenon Cocotilla (*MM* 25).

At its lowest ebb, Lawrence's apparently vulgar racism descends into the gesture of foreigners with funny names. Yet, as in *Twilight*'s padrone anecdote, the satire points in both directions; if the Mexican is too childish to understand democracy, democracy is too stupid to realize its own inappropriateness to the culture.

However seriously misguided this might be as an underestimation of Mexico's ability to generate its own democracy, let alone of the emancipatory significance of revolutionary politics in early twentieth-century Mexican history, Lawrence's account bears further analysis. 'My dear fellow' mimics the voice of white aristocratic superiority both to democracy and the Mexican. From the beginning of the text, the question of a superiority conferred by evolutionary principle has been subjected to intense satirical interrogation through the theme of mimicry. The ability of the parrots to mimic both Rosalino and the dog Corasmin, with a sound that 'penetrates one straight at the diaphragm, belonging to the ages before brains were invented', leave Lawrence genuinely perplexed, and calling into question the evolutionary narrative (*MM* 11). '*Is it possible?*', and again, 'Is it possible that we are so . . . ridiculous?': what does the parrot *know*? Is its intelligence superseded, or is it simply *incommensurate*, a way of knowing whose unconscious kinship with our own is registered in the vibration of the diaphragm, and which contests the notion of mimicry as the reflex response of an automaton? The logic of the latter is carried over (in a move of dubious legitimacy, perhaps) to the relation between the Mexican and the white man or 'white monkey', as Lawrence has it from the Mexican perspective. The white monkey has a lot of 'curious tricks', 'semi-magical secrets of the universe' of a conceptual and technological nature. The 'horrible puzzles' of exactitude in time and space are mirrored in capitalism, whose principles of accumulation and investment imply a past and future inimical to the Mexican sense that 'Tomorrow is always another day, and yesterday is part of the encircling never'. Nevertheless, the white monkey has the 'keys of the world', and 'the black-eyed Mexican has to serve the great white monkey, in order to live'; if one of the white monkey's tricks is 'pretending to think', then the Mexican will go along with that trick too, for 'one may as well amuse oneself that way as any other' (*MM* 36).

It is part of Lawrence's refusal to idealize the Mexican that the latter is fully capable of being corrupted by the values of capitalist modernity; it is also a measure of the vulnerability of capitalist democracy that it can be mimicked so easily by the Mexican peasant, from the position of a culturally specific intelligence. Democratic modernity would include the peasant within an abstract definition of humanity, flattening out difference in order to prepare the ground for the inequalities generated within the neutral spaces of capital. Lawrence's sometimes open scorn for the Mexican claims the honesty of an experienced, interpersonal 'strangeness', set against the systematic exploitation hidden within humanistic abstractions.

Sketches of Etruscan Places (1927) exemplifies the other side of this dialectic, betraying more of a politicized idealization than any of Lawrence's other cultural writings. From the outset, it is clear that the significance of the Etruscans is inseparable from their destruction at the hands of a violent imperialism in the form of 'those pure, clean-living, sweet-souled Romans, who smashed nation after nation and crushed the free soul in people after people' (*EP* 9–10). Again and again, Lawrence's construction of the Etruscans flaunts its role as wish-fulfilment. 'It must have been a wonderful world', he opines, 'that old world where everything appeared alive and shining in the dusk of contact with all things . . .' (*EP* 124). History is romance and poeticized evocation: '(T)his is the Tyrrhenian sea of the Etruscans, where their shipping spread sharp sails, and beat the sea with slave-oars, roving in from Greece and Sicily . . .' (*EP* 25). In such a world, the women 'must have had' that 'very attractive look of noiselessness and inwardness', and in the evening they would 'drift in' wearing loose smocks, joining the men, 'naked, darkly ruddy-coloured from the sun and wind', and 'somebody, surely, would be playing on the pipes; and somebody, surely, would be singing, because the Etruscans had a passion for music, and an inner carelessness the modern Italians have lost' (*EP* 115).

Alongside this narrative mode, there is however a more sharpened sense of what Roman cultural imperialism had meant. Lawrence first notes in the Etruscan tombs the widespread evidence of a 'phallic consciousness', phallic sculptures and images and, acompanying them, representations of the Ark, 'womb of all the world'. He finds in the sacred object called the *patera* or *mundum*, the saucer with a raised knob in the centre, the image of the first fused nucleus or, here, 'life-electron' which we have seen at the heart of his solar plexus theory: 'the indivisible God of the beginning, and which remains alive and unbroken to the end, the eternal quick of all things' (*EP* 36). In such symbols we see the reason for 'the utter destruction and annihilation of the Etruscan consciousness'; 'you cannot', he notes, 'dance gaily to the double flute and at the same time conquer nations or rake in large sums of money'.

> The new world wanted to rid itself of these fatal, dominant symbols of the old world, the old physical world. The Etruscan consciousness was rooted, quite blithely, in these symbols, the phallus and the arx. So the whole consciousness, the whole Etruscan pulse and rhythm, must be wiped out (*EP* 20).

Etruscan phallicism must however be carefully reinterpreted so as to avoid any possible identification with the bullying of Roman imperial power. It thus becomes a form of 'natural proportion': 'we begin', he writes, 'to realise that it is better to keep life fluid and changing, than to try to hold it fast down in heavy monuments. . . . Give us things that are alive and flexible, which won't last too long and become an obstruction and a weariness' (*EP* 32–3). Just as the geopolitical situation overridden by Roman 'oneness and uniformity' was a delicate web of identities, an 'endless confusion of differences', so Etruscan artefacts come to embody a natural resilience paradoxically located in the frail and the fugitive: 'Brute force and overbearing may make a terrific effect. But in the end, that which lives lives by delicate sensitiveness' (*EP* 36). The tombs themselves partake of the 'true Etruscan quality', 'ease, naturalness, and an abundance of life, no need to force the mind or the soul in any direction'.

We are reminded of the Mexican context in which only 'that which is intangible, matters', and of the more general context of animistic religion framing Lawrence's Mexicans and Etruscans. *Etruscan Places* is however more concerned to highlight the difficulty of the relationship between animism and 'what we feebly call Nature'. In so doing, and despite the perennial obstacle of untranslatability ('the Etruscan language is a mystery'), Lawrence comes closest to spelling out how a re-thinking of *organicism*, glimpsed in the Etruscans, might be the root of a new conception of the human. It is true that an organic, holistic anti-Cartesianism is again encoded in the old pagan dictum on which he draws to characterise Etruscan animism: 'every part of the body and of the *anima* shall know religion, and be in touch with the gods' (*EP* 50); to the Etruscan, 'all was alive; the whole universe lived; and the business of man was himself to live amid it all'. This vitalistic rhetoric, which threatens at times to engulf the argument, extends to a reverential evaluation of a state of being; the Etruscan, we are regularly reminded, lived a life of rich plenitude: 'It is as if the current of some strong different life swept through them, different from our shallow current today: as if they drew their vitality from different depths, that we are denied' (*EP* 56).

How much there is in this of a present-centred 'fantasy' is clearly a moot point. The argument is at its most convincing, however, when trying to show that the 'strong different life' might be characterized by an *epistemology* capable of challenging the conventional humanistic languages of the aesthetic and the scientific. The challenge of Etruscan art to Western aesthetics is seen to be twofold: first, it is fugitive and unfinished; second, the vigour of Etruscan life shows through so powerfully that the issue of form becomes irrelevant – 'there is more life in these Etruscan legs, fragments as they are', Lawrence concludes of a painting of a man, 'than in the whole bodies of men today' (*EP* 53). Lawrence's account of the young German archaeologist guide shows how this is more than an unreflective theory of romantic organicism. Disenchanted with the young man's summary dismissals or simplistic, literal readings of the painted images, Lawrence approaches some heraldic beasts – a pale man on a dark horse followed by a galloping bull; a 'queer galloping lion' with the head and neck of a goat emerging from its neck, and with a serpent's head at the end of its tail. To his enquiry concerning its meaning, the guide gives his characteristic shrug of the shoulders: ' "Nothing!" '. Lawrence is scandalized: the Chimaera not only has an 'exact esoteric meaning', but this meaning belongs to an un-anthropomorphic animism whose subtleties the guide appears completely oblivious to. Animism starts from an impersonal, creaturely materialism which sidesteps the superstition of a personal god, the consequence of the latter being to 'deny the physical universe true existence'. In their 'complex animals', the Etruscans sought to embody 'all those physical and creative powers and forces which go to the building up and the destroying of the soul', and such animals inevitably include the human:

The human being, to the Etruscan, was a bull or a ram, a lion or a deer, according to his different aspects and potencies. The human being had in his veins the blood of the wings of birds and the venom of serpents. All things emerged from the blood-stream, and the blood-relation, however complex and contradictory it became, was never interrupted or forgotten. There were different currents in the blood-stream, and some always clashed: bird and serpent, lion and deer, leopard and lamb. Yet the very clash was a form of unison, as we see in the lion which also has a goat's head (*EP* 122–3).

The epistemology is of 'things mentally contradictory fusing together emotionally, so that a lion could be at the same moment also a goat, and not a goat', and so with the human, sharing a blood-stream with the natural order and thus possessing a 'myriad manifold consciousness, storming with contradictions and oppositions that are eternal, beyond all mental reconciliation'. At stake is the ability to think the human in terms of multiplicity and synchronicity, to reconsider organicism not as wholeness but as an 'unthinkable' agglomeration of contradictory states which together constitute only a 'potential'. This for Lawrence is *both* a child-like vision of 'wonder' *and* a 'sensual knowledge of true adults' which is beyond the reach of the young German; he is, of course, 'a scientist' and a 'modern', adhering only to the obvious or the 'A.B.C. of facts', and 'when he doesn't want a thing to have a meaning, it is ipso facto meaningless'. Reacting against his estimation of the Etruscan's 'crude incapacity to think', Lawrence presents the 'boy' as himself unable to think difference.

Anne Fernihough and Amit Chaudhuri have each noted the profound importance of Lawrence's carefully discriminated position on organicism. Reading *Etruscan Places*, Chaudhuri observes: 'the organically-whole image is exactly what Lawrence wishes to undermine'. This is placed in the context of a Derridean, deconstructed subjectivity in which nothing is ' "anywhere ever simply present or absent" '; Chaudhuri alerts us, with a reference back to Lawrence's Mexican market-place, to the importance of a non-individualistic politics inscribed in Lawrence's language of 'flows' and 'forces', 'touch' and 'contact'. Reflected also in Chaudhuri's study of Lawrence's methods of poetic assembly and *bricolage*, this non-organicism constitutes a profound challenge to humanistic readings of Lawrence. Organicism, Chaudhuri claims, was associated by Lawrence both with 'will-to-power' and with 'mainstream literary discourse'.[19] Elsewhere in his study, however, Chaudhuri upholds the view that 'Lawrence's turning towards nature was also a turning away from man and industrial society'; the word 'machine' is said to stand for 'a wholly abhorrent way of life, . . . anti-life and anti-man', placing Lawrence in the tradition of 'many other modernists'.[20] Yet, if Lawrence found in the animism of the Etruscans a repudiation of modern science, he equally repudiated any 'feeble' sentimentalized view of 'Nature' which was simply the obverse of science. The 'storming of contradictions and oppositions . . . beyond mental reconciliation' in the Etruscan human bears a strong comparison with the function of the contemporary, post-human cyborg, which embodies the 'unthinkable' combination of the organism and the machine – the posthuman who is simultaneously both and neither. In the next section, as a prelude to my final chapter, I suggest that Lawrence's most evidently humanistic fictions do not simply repudiate the industrialized human, and that the notion of the full, rich life, glimpsed in his chosen 'primitive' cultures, might translate back into a posthumanist projection of ordinary life in which the taboo surrounding the machine is confronted.

4. Sensual riches: the posthuman in *Sons and Lovers* and *The Rainbow*

How might an analysis of 'primitive' sensuality connect with the revolu-tionary movement into a posthuman future? Let us set the foregoing discussion of Lawrence's particular cultural primitivism alongside Terry Eagleton's account of Marx's challenge to the diminishing of the role of the senses in modern aesthetics. Born as a 'discourse of the body' in Alexander Baumgarten's *Aesthetica* (1750), and implying a newly scientific approach to the concrete evidence of the senses, aesthetics becomes, Eagleton argues, progressively 'anaesthetic' as it is subject to various revisions, in the think-ing of Kant, Schiller, Schopenhauer and Kierkegaard, who edge it towards the idealization of beauty and away from a sensuous, bodily materialism. What if it were possible, he asks, to strip aesthetics back to 'the standpoint of the body itself'; or, more precisely,

> What if an idea of reason could be generated up from the body itself, rather than the body incorporated into a reason which is always already in place? What if it were possible, in a breathtaking wager, to retrace one's steps and reconstruct everything – ethics, history, politics, rationality – from a bodily foundation?[21]

This is the project that Eagleton locates within Marx's critique of capitalism. Marx calls for a '*real* science' to be based on sense perception, but only where the latter is understood as a complex mutual interaction between body and world. As in both primitivist and posthuman models, Marx conceives of the human body as, in the words of Habermas, 'oriented towards action'; antici-pating the posthuman concept of distributed cognition, Marx sees the pro-duction through work of technology and social life as the human body's extension of itself, for example in the notion of agriculture as 'a conversion of the soil into the body's prolongation'.[22] This of course forms the basis of the dilemma of thinking matter: such distribution becomes a form of dis-embodiment or abstraction, encapsulated in the power of the language-using human to 'extend its body into a web of abstractions which then violate its own sensuous nature'. Capital is the most contentious and pow-erful of these modes of abstraction, reducing labour to repetitive mechanism for the purposes of bare survival alone and the capitalist himself to a mere cypher whose sensuousness is displaced onto the abstract power of capital itself. A gothic vocabulary of the monstrous is appropriate to a relation in which both owners and producers of the means of production are reduced to the living dead; 'if communism is necessary', as Eagleton puts it, 'it is because we are unable to feel, taste, smell and touch as fully as we might'. Marx's aestheticism thus lies in striving to restore these powers as an end in themselves, beyond utilitarian justification:

> (T)he society that is *fully developed* produces man in all the richness of his being, the *rich* man who is *profoundly and abundantly endowed with all the senses*, as its constant reality.[23]

Sons and Lovers, completed in 1912, before Lawrence had barely begun to experience the richness of cultural otherness, maps out the possibilities of a sensuous 'richness of being' for the industrial working class. 'Rich' is a key word in the novel. Mrs. Morel returns from the market 'rich in spirit', having successfully haggled with the 'pot man' over a dish decorated with corn-flowers which delights Paul: ' "I *love* cornflowers on things!" ' (*SL* 100). Paul, returning from his work at the factory, feels 'rich in life and happy'; his mother's belief in his potential makes her feel that life is 'rich with promise' (*SL* 222). If wealth in this sense is about worldly possibilities opening out for this class, it is also closely associated with a love of the natural world. Lawrence however strives to avoid the strict hypostatization by which working-class proximity to nature is set against bourgeois alienation from it. The beauty of nature is readily available to Paul and his parents, but it is not simply *there*; rather, it is to be achieved or won, in part by a kind of persistence and determination which is rewarded, sometimes by chance, in the social and economic sphere, and in part by a deep, thoughtful *attention* to nature and our relation to it. Mrs. Morel's principal access to nature is through her garden, and, in the scene in which she rapturously discovers three scyllas nestling hidden under a gooseberry bush, we are reminded of the fortunate circumstance that the garden has come through a house move perhaps prompted by William's death: 'The garden was an endless joy to her. Paul was thankful for her sake at last to be in a house with a long garden that went down to the field' (*SL* 200). Paul's access to natural beauty devel-ops through his cultivation of friendship with the Leivers family; he accom-panies Mr. Leivers in his milk float, for example, on the drive up to Willey Farm: 'Tiny buds on the hedges, vivid as copper-green, were opening into rosettes; and thrushes called, and blackbirds shrieked and scolded. It was a new, glamorous world' (*SL* 174).

This application of 'glamour' encapsulates, for today's reader of Lawrence, a sense of the Ruskinesque critique at stake. The term is generated by human interaction with nature, not by a consumerist, image-driven culture of modernity: ' "Who ever would want Streets of Gold" ', exclaims Emily in *The White Peacock*, ' "... when you can have a field of cowslips!" ' (*WP* 208). Coming into possession or appropriation of this glamour nevertheless requires both aspiration and critical vigilance. It is not easy for the human as 'thinking matter' to emerge into a state of conscious fulfilment: how do we come into flower, if intellect makes the meaning of this in the human realm endlessly problematic? Intellect cannot be relinquished, by some dubious recourse to a romanticized oneness with nature which would at the same time surrender the definition of rationality into the hands of the dominant, scientific-capitalist order. The conflict between Gertrude and Walter Morel is physical in its effect – when they are together, 'both felt an oppression on their breathing' – but, when Morel goes to bed, his wife can enter into a fuller state, enjoying herself alone, 'working, thinking, living' (*SL* 63). She joins the Co-operative Women's Guild, sometimes presenting a paper for discussion, thereby attracting the deep respect of her children; Paul is thus not the only one to combine 'thinking' with 'working' in pursuit of the full life. As we have seen, this thinking, in the novel as a whole, is dramatized in the question of how to sustain an appropriate approach to 'man's place in nature', avoiding two modes of idealism, the mystic-sentimentalist on the one hand, and the instrumental-rationalist on the other.

Sons and Lovers and *The Rainbow* can be seen as ontogenetic and phylogenetic versions of this human struggle into riches or a fullness of being. 'How to act,' asks Ursula Brangwen, 'that was the question? Whither to go, how to become oneself, ... how to know the question and the answer of oneself ...' (*TR* 264). In each novel, the problem of 'mating' embodies the struggle, with its suggestion of a process of creaturely instinct lurking beneath human social and intellectual life. If Miriam realizes that 'she could never be properly mated', so too Paul wrestles with the 'complication of sex' in him, 'like so many young men of his age' (*SL* 326, 319). Humans must mate – at least, species-wise, for the time being – but development and complexification make the conditions of human mating obscure. How does a sensitive, artistic and intelligent soul, intimately attached to his mother as both 'son' and 'lover', achieve the sexual relationship he needs? Hinting at the cyclical, seasonal rhythms to which, modernity tells us, humans are not tied, the conflict between Paul and Miriam starts anew every spring, a season they come to 'dread'. Miriam's piety and mystic-reverential approach to nature do not allow Paul the 'great hunger and impersonality of passion'; he must always be brought back to 'a deliberate, reflective creature'.

There is an inevitable suggestion of retrospect in this dilemma of human development. For Mrs. Morel, children playing outside the house 'had the feel of wild creatures singing'; when they come in, she 'understood'. The element of the unstateable yet certain, a knowledge of the not-known, picks up on her earlier feeling that, in Paul's state of infanthood, the 'navel string . . . had not been broken'. Did the child, she wonders, 'know all about her? When it lay under her heart, had it been listening then?' (*SL* 51). Paul's growth, conventionally understood, is a movement away from this state of knowing creatureliness: intellect, sexuality, and the attempt to merge these in human relationship, as well as the world of work, loom ahead, as elements in Lawrence's sense of becoming human, and of making oneself at home on the earth. On entering the factory, 'already he was a prisoner of industrialism', a fate seemingly associated with Paul's ability to think, for he 'wished he were stupid' as a consequence.

Yet Wordsworthian shades of the prison house do not begin to close around the growing boy, and *Sons and Lovers* does not become the occasion of a critique of the industrial system. Rather, the factory becomes a fertile ground for Paul's maturation. His work environment is largely feminized, and he becomes popular with the warehouse girls, who are protective of him. He works well and is successful; the shop floor also becomes a testing-ground of his burgeoning masculinity, as the affair with Clara develops and, in a Darwinian drama of sexual jealousy, Baxter Dawes confronts Paul over it. For all the love of nature which is the substance of his love with Miriam, Paul is not an opponent of industrial modernity: the town is ' "all right" ', rather we need to ' "find out what the idea is" '; he is, we remember, drawn towards its 'humming, glowing' promise at the novel's close. He also likes the pits, ' "here and there" ', connecting with a portrayal of his father at work which runs counter to the humanist image of mining as an alien and dehumanizing activity typical of industrialism. Towards the end of his life, Lawrence returned to both of these points in the essay 'Nottingham and the Mining Countryside'. Industrial England had missed its opportunity to build mining villages 'like the lovely hill-towns of Italy', failing to develop an urban and civic consciousness: the English 'don't know how to build a city, how to think of one, or how to live in one' (*P* 134, 139). The pit 'did not mechanize men'; his father, Lawrence argues, loved it, partaking in a 'very highly developed' community of instinctive and intuitional contact, 'very real and very powerful'. The advanced character of this sensuous fulfilment is expressed in two characteristics which are certainly aligned with Lawrence's primitivism and also, I would argue, with his posthumanism: first, the collier's sense of life as a 'flow' rather than as 'facts', so that he has to 'change' his flow when he emerges from the pit into the daylight world; and second, his 'instinct for beauty'. In a reprise of how to know flowers, the collier extends his perception of the life-flow to the flow-er, embodying a principle of 'contemplation' rather than the instrumentality of 'possession' and showing a '*real* awareness of the presence of beauty: 'the human soul needs actual beauty even more than bread' (*P* 135–8).

Lawrence is, then, able to build in *Sons and Lovers* a model of the human in which the non-utilitarian values of communal relationship and aesthetic contemplation are not entirely distinct from industrial civilization. Ambivalences in the discourse of mechanism contribute to a sense of the human delicately poised between an instinctive organicism and an equally instinctive gravitation towards the machine. Without doubt, the 'deathly' potential of the mechanical is in evidence. While Clara is spinning, her arm 'moved mechanically, that should never have been subdued to mechanism'; when her relationship with Paul starts to wane, a 'mechanical' element creeps in to spoil their lovemaking. In situations of tension or conflict, the human organism switches into a condition in which instinct and automatism are impossible to tell apart: Paul 'mechanically' resumes his painting after hearing of his father's pit accident; in attacking Miriam, 'these things came from him mechanically', his words 'jetted off' like 'sparks from electricity'; Dawes 'mechanically' shakes Paul's hand when he is visited in hospital.

At the same time, the condition can be one of fulfilment, especially when associated with the absorption of satisfying work; following his mother's death and the break-up with Clara, Paul 'was most himself when he was alone, or working hard and mechanically at the factory. In the latter case there was pure forgetfulness, when he lapsed from consciousness' (*SL* 454). Such lapsing from consciousness, we realize, is far more prominent as a desideratum for Paul, symbolically expressed in sexual consummation, and coming to stand for a more general alternative to the constraints of human individuality. ' "To be rid of our individuality, which is our will, which is our effort – to live effortless, a kind of conscious sleep – that is very beautiful, I think – that is our after-life – our immortality' (*SL* 332). In a scene of climactic intensity, Paul wakes after an intercourse with Clara 'strong and blind and ruthless in its primitiveness'. Momentarily disorientated, and seemingly unable to distinguish between near and far, he wonders 'what was near his eyes, curving and strong with life in the dark, and what voice it was speaking'. The grass, the screaming of the peewits in the field and the warmth of Clara's breathing merge into a material whole 'bigger than themselves', in which they 'knew they were only grains in the tremendous heave', 'blind agents of a great force' (*SL* 397–9). The experience is of an impersonality, in which, in the terms of the letter to Garnett, Clara figures as the 'inhuman' material woman: for Paul, it was 'not Clara', but 'something that happened because of her'.

It is a condition, then, of the rich sensuous life, that one should be capable of lapsing out into an intense unconscious materiality, beyond the consciousness that defines us as human. At the same time, only the most strenuous extension of rationality can convince us of why it is necessary to know how not to know, and of how to discriminate between different kinds of knowing. If it is our nature to be enmeshed in a materiality which includes both organic and inorganic matter, it cannot *not* be our nature to conceptualize this. We need therefore to keep this conceptualization open and flexible, dialectical and reflexive; to avoid, in Birkin's terms, imprisoning ourselves within a 'false, limited set of concepts'. Within the temporal limits of the early life of Paul Morel, the difficulties of achieving such fulfilment are registered as Paul, alone and unmated after losing his mother, Miriam and Clara, heads for the town. *The Rainbow* explores them through the sweep of generational change, from the fecundity of the nameless Brangwens of the early nineteenth century, whose knowledge is of the 'intercourse' between themselves and the physical universe, to Ursula, the New Woman, whose inconclusive relationships culminate symbolically in miscarriage.

The Rainbow is also charged more fully, as the letter to Garnett indicates, with the task of extending a mode of characterization, or a re-definition of the human, into the 'allotropic' realm of the inhuman. Within what Middleton describes as a changing 'history of consciousness', an emphasis on unconscious and instinctive humanness remains persistent across the generations, augmented by a particular propensity of the Brangwens for a sensuous intelligence which often puts them at odds with institutionalized education and its modes of evaluation. Tom Brangwen, as youngest son and his mother's favourite, is a reworking of Paul Morel as well as of Cyril and George Saxton. He is sent to Grammar School, where 'his mind simply did not work'; fatalistically, he feels 'guilty of his own nature, as if his being were wrong'. Yet he 'loved anyone' who could enlighten him through feeling, and again 'loved' one school companion, a 'frail, consumptive' boy who remains unnamed. In the next generation Anna, though not Tom's natural daughter – a point to which I will return soon – has an 'instinct to avoid thinking, to avoid it, to save herself', while her own daughter Ursula is not ' "thorough" ': 'If a thing did not come to her instinctively, she could not learn it' (*TR* 251, 310).

In all three characters this mode of consciousness accompanies an acute perception of the difficulties of becoming human. As Middleton suggests, Tom does not fit prevailing images of the rational masculine subject, and this is conveyed in painful detail in the travails of his tense and lonely early manhood before meeting Lydia: impelled into adopting yet more familiar subject positions, in this case drunkenness and debauchery, Tom develops a condition of bodily conflict, with a strained light in his eyes and a knitting of the brows (*TR* 21). Yet even after his successful 'mating' with Lydia and the crucial entry into another circle of existence after two years of marriage, the uncertainties are not dispelled. Tom's pain at Anna's early marriage is bound up with his own continuing sense of being unachieved, wondering 'if he should ever feel arrived and established . . . .' Anna too in her marriage remains 'not quite fulfilled', channelling her existential question through the image of the setting sun: '"What is it that you keep so busy about, that you will not let us alone?"' (*TR* 181). Ursula comes to realize, in the manner of many Lawrentian protagonists, that she must take on the responsibility of her own life, though the question of 'whither to go, how to become oneself' abides. Precisely at a moment of significant achievement, when she leaves Brinsley School with a Skrebensky-like pride in her work and comradeship, Ursula finds the enigmatic continuity of a dissipative structure most pressing:

> In every phase she was so different. Yet she was always Ursula Brangwen. But what did it mean, Ursula Brangwen? She did not know what she was. . . .
> That which she was, positively, was dark and unrevealed, it could not come forth. It was like a seed buried in dry ash (*TR* 405).

Even as *The Rainbow* examines the possibility that human flowering might be achieved through 'mating', it seems increasingly to undermine such a possibility; or, at least, to question how reproduction itself might relate to the more complex process of human relationship. Nowhere is this more evident than in the words, 'She was his mate', which close the extraordinary chapter 'Shame', summarizing the relationship between Winifred Inger and Ursula's Uncle Tom. Children for this couple are an extension of their shared 'worship' of the machine, freeing them from the 'clog and degradation of human feeling'; Brangwen decides that he wants 'to propagate himself', to counter an increasing apathy and inertia by letting 'the machinery carry him' (*TR* 325–7). As I suggested in Chapter 2, Lawrence uses a breathtaking narrative shorthand to condemn the dangers of a dogmatic, because excessively abstract and idealized, materialism, by 'mating' Brangwen's industrialist instrumentalism with Inger's secular humanism and 'perversion'.

There seems little equivocation over the machine in this portrayal. Yet it enables us to prise apart an *in*human mechanism (transgressively associated with some of the things that we prize as most human or humane, such as the birth of children, or humanistic studies) from a posthuman condition which also partakes in crucial ways of mechanism or automatism in a different guise. Like Paul Morel and her grandfather, Ursula experiences sexual maturation as a systemic dysfunction requiring adjustment; when Skrebensky leaves for the war, her sexuality becomes a kind of disease, making her morbidly sensitive even to the touch of coarse wool on her skin (*TR* 309). As we have seen, the matings of the two prior Brangwen generations have hardly constituted a solution to this problem, or to their uncertainties about what it might be to become an achieved human being. But they do signal modes of relationship whose *unconscious* dimensions constitute a rich sensuous life increasingly unavailable to humans evolving towards the cerebral and the disembodied.

The extremely moving account of Tom Brangwen's courtship with Lydia is a case in point. It begins with the first glimpsing of Lydia on the road and the 'involuntary' exclamation, ' "That's her" ' (*TR* 29). As he meets her and begins to know her, still in a very reserved and formal way, a 'daze' comes over Tom's mind: 'somewhere in his body, there had started another activity'. He becomes conscious only of a 'fate' approaching, knowing that 'he did not belong to himself'. Although Tom takes a long time to decide, Lawrence characteristically makes this a brisk period of narrative time, and Tom is, within a few pages of the chapter, walking to the vicarage to make the proposal. Following an initial equivocation – yes, no, I don't know – Lydia comes to kiss him and accept, 'curiously direct and as if without movement, in a sudden flow'. The kiss makes something 'break' in the man's 'brain', and he is plunged into 'darkness'; then, sitting with her in his arms, 'he went utterly to sleep, asleep and sealed in the darkest sleep, utter, extreme oblivion' (*TR* 44–5).

The scene blends a sparing and intensely practical dialogue of arrangement between Tom and Lydia, discussing for example their ages and the question of the child Anna, with a narrative discourse of sensual encounter which still, almost a century after the novel's publication, has the capacity to startle with its unfamiliarity. How does Lydia move without moving? In what sense does Tom fall asleep? While acting out one of the most intense yet common scenarios of human experience, Lawrence's people are *post*-human in the sense that they operate in a seemingly unrecognizable cognitive world. The reader is challenged, rather, to reassess the scene's intense realism from the perspective of a posthuman epistemology: Lydia is not so much an entity as a 'flow' moving through a line of force and Tom is an embodied intelligence whose 'sleep' is the body's unconscious adjustment to the momentous, sensuously charged nature of this life-changing event.

A historical interpretation is no doubt available for the absence of a more familiar discourse of romantic love in such an account. Later in the novel, after the famous corn-gathering scene in which Will and Anna work up to the point of a rapturous embrace, the 'shock' to Will of his physical passion for Anna leads, seemingly involuntarily, to the simple conclusion that they must marry. Similarly, after Ursula and Skrebensky's 'superb consummation', there is the latter's ' "I suppose we ought to get married" '. While Lawrence carefully re-calibrates the relationship between sexual passion and marriage from one generation to the next, it is marriage that in each case continues to regulate and enclose the relationship. Tom and Lydia are, historically, the least able to articulate their love outside of marriage, either verbally or physically.

There is, however, a more profound motivation underpinning the refusal of romantic love across Lawrence's work as a whole. According to this, the all-too-human discourse of love partakes of the modern culture of objectification and commodification – connecting it, in other words, to the scientificity of Christianity – leading to a narrowly idealized concept of human relationship and of the 'loved' other. Tom and Lydia's connection thus sustains the principle of the marriage of 'the Alfred Brangwen' and the 'woman from Heanor' of the 1840s, 'two very separate beings, vitally connected, knowing nothing of each other, yet living in their separate ways from one root' (*TR* 15). 'What did it matter who they were, whether they knew each other or not?', records the narrative, with its implication of Tom's thought processes as he encounters, with wonder, the violent and unpredictable oscillations between love and antagonism in the early stages of his marriage; 'They did not think of each other – why should they?' (*TR* 60, 90). Similarly, in the relentless oscillations of Anna and Will's marriage, 'They fought an unknown battle, unconsciously' (*TR* 156).

The aspiration of Lawrence's work in such instances is to suggest that the alternatives to romantic love and marriage, however apparently located in the past, are not thereby atavistic but alert, advanced, progressive. They suggest a model of the human in which a Cartesian supremacy of the intellect is held in check by a more complex sense of material embodiment and relatedness. When Anna goes back to her mother for advice and reassurance, she is told that the love between two people is 'a third thing you must create', one not constrained by humanistic idealizations of the individual ego; Ursula similarly is able to derive from her grandmother a 'great relief, to know the tiny importance of the individual, within the great past'. As a particular kind of ratiocination takes hold historically, married love partakes of the same necessary abstraction as Christianity, science and industrial capitalism, as another dogmatic idealization of rational human perfectibility. Arguing with this, *The Rainbow* does its work on the richness of ordinary lives by attributing to them an alternative mode of intelligence which is sensuous, bodily, and which does not discount the automatisms tabooed by humanistic definition. Lydia's time in England immediately after the death of Paul Lensky can be described as a kind of unconsciousness within which she is aware of people only as 'looming presences', while for the young Ursula even her mother can count only as 'a condition that happened to endure' (*TR* 203).

Such apparently *in*human perceptions are tied to the economy with which the novel observes and summarizes humans as creatures and mechanisms. The heavy and uncouth Alfred, Tom's brother, adheres to the draughtmanship which crushes the bowels within him, until he becomes 'set and rigid, a rare-spoken, almost surly man' (*TR* 15). Anticipating the visits of Will following his placement in Ilkeston, Anna first remembers his 'very curious', animal-like head (*TR* 100). Once the courtship is under way, Will's 'inhuman', hawk-like qualities become more evident, and in his wood-carving he produces beautiful things, working 'swiftly and mechanically' in

a 'tense, electric darkness' (*TR* 108). Glimpses are caught of people, sometimes in extremity, whose unfamiliarity places them momentarily beyond
the human. When Anna hears of her father's death, she presses back her
head and rolls her eyes, 'as if something were reaching forward to bite at
her throat', a physical reflex fighting against the feeling that the event is
dragging her back to her youthful love of Tom. At the same tragic moment,
the young Ursula sees her uncle Tom in his grief, his face with its unseeing
eyes adopting a 'bestial look of torture' (*TR* 234).

Such quick physical assessments of human identity become very characteristic of Lawrence's work, whether in the observation, as we have seen, of
cultural others or of fictional characters. What can appear to be a crude
determinism must, I suggest, be re-evaluated along the lines of a posthumanism in which neither the creaturely nor the mechanical is in itself
a reductive category, and in which the concept of the cyborg expresses a
rational deconstruction of the two. Something of the contestatory value of
Lawrence's approach is highlighted by the logic of another case for the
restoration of the aesthetically sensuous, Susan Sontag's 'Against Interpretation' (1964). Sontag finds the overweening influence of Platonic
mimeticism at the heart of the preoccupation with interpretation in modern
aesthetics; interpretation is 'the revenge of the intellect upon art', seeking
always to excavate below the text or manifest content to find the true
sub-text or latent content, rendering art thus 'manageable, conformable'.
The argument is not simply for greater sensory stimulation, because modern
culture effects an unprecedented bombardment of the senses; rather, if we
are to 'recover our senses', to see/hear/feel 'more', the 'more' for Sontag must
be a function of discrimination, achieved through the 'transparence' of the
art work, the 'luminousness of the thing itself'. Prefacing her argument is
an epigraph from Wilde: 'It is only shallow people who do not judge by
appearances. The mystery of the world is the visible, not the invisible.'[24]

Lawrence's 'judging by appearances' in *The Rainbow* is also, of course, as
is commonly observed, a mode of depth psychology, interpreting certain
humans in a way that they could never articulate for themselves: bodily dis-
positions are the expression of a whole state of being. Intellect, if not scrupu-
lously attentive to the question of its own limits, can override the simplicity
or transparency of its own embodiment; thus the emphasis on 'what the
woman *is*' rather than on what she thinks herself to be. But such embodiment is also a condition of complexity, *un*thinkable in the sense that, as the
realist novel tended to show, we conceive of ourselves as conscious egos
operating in terms of systemic moral values. Tom Brangwen is 'startled' to
find that he has been with a prostitute, and undergoes a searching reassessment of the meaning of women in his life: the curious retrospect shows the
mind catching up with the body. But in this way too, the body can become
a site of indeterminacy, a sensitive and flexible cyborg with the potential for
unpredictable change. Alongside the Alfred Brangwens, humans whose

embodiment becomes a fixed destiny, there are those, like Paul Lensky, who are ' "alive and changing – never fixed . . . like a running stream" ' (*TR* 165).

The discourse on 'riches' in *The Rainbow* joins up precisely with this condition, even where it coincides with that sense of uncertainty or the 'unestablished' illustrated earlier. At his daughter's wedding, Tom gazes spellbound at the royal-blue stained-glass window, 'unwearyingly rich and splendid'. This richness he then immediately associates with the 'unfinished and unformed' lives of Lydia and himself, in a vitalistic discourse on 'sporting' bodies and the fires 'glowing' in their 'meshes'. It is significant here too that Tom's deep chagrin is at the 'loss' of a daughter who is not, biologically, his. The very moving treatment of Tom's relationship with Anna has, at its outset, his response to Lydia's asking if he would love her daughter: ' "I love her now" '. No determinism of 'blood' or heredity prevents Tom from becoming closer to Anna than to any of his own subsequent children. When he takes the distressed child into the barn during Lydia's labour, an enigmatic formulation seems to encompass the deep posthuman susceptibility to creative adjustment: 'all wonder', Anna watches Tom preparing the feed for the cows, and 'A new being was created in her for the new conditions' (*TR* 75). Later in life, in the midst of her struggles with Will and personal unfulfilment, Anna becomes pregnant again, and settles into a new sense of being 'a rich woman enjoying her riches', in which she becomes a 'door and a threshold' through which 'another soul was coming' (*TR* 182). Later still, Ursula is transported in the early days of her courtship with Skrebensky, their intimacy described in physical terms which insistently challenge the discourses of romance and humanism. While driving a cart, Skrebensky deftly unbuttons her glove with a free hand which was 'intent as a living creature skilfully pushing and manipulating in the dark underworld'; they walk, with their bodies 'moving in complex unity' (*TR* 276, 278). Ursula's hands are soon to be transformed into metal blades of destruction, but for now, she feels 'rich and augmented', as if 'she were the positive attraction and he the flow towards her' (*TR* 280).

Two final examples might summarize Lawrence's model of sensuous riches and its accompanying projection of a posthuman future in *The Rainbow*. In his tipsy and mischievous wedding speech, Tom Brangwen tests out his curious conundrum that the marriage of a man and a woman constitutes an 'angel'. ' "Bodies and souls, it's the same" ', he says, but the combination is in any case ' "more than a human being" ' (*TR* 129). At the novel's close, as Ursula watches for a 'new creation' and finds a rainbow on the face of the earth, it is the in the colliers *below* this conventional image that she finds 'the swelling and the heavy contour' of newness. In other respects, there is nothing idealized in this depiction of the industrialized human: 'sordid', 'hard-scaled' and 'separate', the bodies of the colliers are stiff and their eyes unchanging, 'the eyes of those who are buried alive' (*TR* 458). Yet, as I have tried to show in this chapter, Lawrence's 'human' can comprise any degree of mechanism; the colliers are 'living still', and the rainbow can arch in their blood and quiver in their spirit, promising 'new, clean, naked bodies'. Any such utopian posthuman futurity can only be established by stripping away the illusions of humanist idealism; 'sordid' British workers or 'dumb-bell' Mexican Indians are identified in order to find, within them, forms of wealth unthought of by the dominant culture. To be 'more than a human being' might thus involve the embrace of machines as well as angels. In the next chapter, I examine the place of the machine in Lawrence's posthuman.

7
Machines

1. Luddite Lawrence

> Let us smash something. Ourselves included. But the machine above all.
>
> *Studies in Classic American Literature*

In the previous chapter, I began to trace out connections between the posthuman cyborg and Lawrence's conception of 'non-human human being'. In each of these versions of the human, the mechanical is delicately poised with the creaturely. A rationalist and materialist tradition, informing what Lawrence saw as the 'adventure' of thought, made it possible for him to align our moments of mechanism with organicist notions of instinct and intuition, conditions which make for the sensual 'riches' of human life. Such a sensuality disdains the Cartesian notion of a separate intellect, seeing intelligence instead as a whole condition of embodiment. In the theory of the solar plexus or 'pristine' unconscious, in the cultural alterity of Italians and Mexicans, in the lives of the British industrial working class, and in the striving of the Brangwens for integrity and fulfilment, Lawrence figured a challenge to dominant, liberal-humanist definitions of the human. A 'transvalued' discourse of mechanism can in Nietzschean terms be seen as a significant resource for Lawrence in his confrontation of humanist taboos.

Let us nevertheless acknowledge that there is, after all, a Luddite Lawrence, one whose overwhelming desire was to smash the machine. 'The machine', he writes in his essay on Dana's *Two Years before the Mast*, is 'the great Neuter', the 'eunuch of eunuchs', which in the end will 'emasculate(s) us all'. In switching on electricity, or even in turning on a water tap, we 'intervene' machinery between ourselves and the physical world, 'numbing' and 'atrophying' our senses (*SCAL* 117). The machine, he writes elsewhere, has 'killed the earth for us', making it 'a surface, more or less bumpy, that you travel over' (*PII* 511). There is a fatal correspondence or equivalence between ideas and machines: the 'ideal world' is 'invented exactly as man invents machinery', and 'the moment man learned to abstract, he began to make engines that would do the work of his body' (*P* 704, 29). Where contemporary posthumanism might see in the latter a benign understanding of the principle of distributed cognition, offering an escape from the narrowly conceived humanistic self, Lawrence remained wary of the death of the self, coincident with the demise of an animistic and holistic way of thinking nature associated with the 'great god Pan'. Man, he writes, is 'not a little engine of cause and effect', the body is 'not an instrument', but thinking, or the power of idealism, can make him so: the 'death products' of science and machinery, we remember, emerged out of the 'long slow death of the human being' that set in after the Reformation (*P* 757, 618; *A* 26).

Smash the machine, then, before it kills us. Is it possible to reconcile the Luddite with the posthuman Lawrence? It has been observed that the first Luddite rebellion (occurring, ironically enough, in Nottinghamshire in 1811) was directed not against the introduction of new machinery but against the abuse of old: the Nottinghamshire 'stockingers' or framework knitters found that the superseded 'wide frames' were being used by the owners, employing unapprenticed labour, to produce cheap and shoddy goods which, within the already-dire circumstances of the war economy, were ruining the market. Only later, in the 1812 uprisings in Yorkshire (against shearing machines), and Lancashire and Cheshire (against power looms), and again in the more famous 'Captain Swing' riots of the early 1830s, did Luddism come to be principally associated with the smashing of labour-saving new machinery whose devastating effect had been to threaten and remove the livelihoods of many.

Arguably, however, current popular usage of the term 'Luddite' occludes a key aspect of this history. The most recent (2002) *Concise Oxford English Dictionary* defines Luddite as, first, 'a member of any of the bands of English workers who opposed mechanization and destroyed machinery in the early 19th. century' and, second, as 'a person opposed to industrialization or new technology'. The latter encapsulates current usage in its emphasis on an opposition which is individual and temperamental, as if based on an irrational hatred of the machine. The former historical definition does nothing to suggest that Luddism consisted in an opposition, not to the machine *in itself*, but to the socio-economic consequences of the uses to which it was put.

If Lawrence was a Luddite, it may be in this precise historical sense of a critique of the *deployment* of technology, which can be carefully discriminated from a fear of the machine as constituting a threat to human *being*. Such a position calls to mind Raymond Williams's critique of 'technological determinism', a concept by which technology is seen to emerge from a value-free process of scientific discovery, but then takes on a determining logic in its irrevocable effect on the human. This, Williams observes, is a deep-seated approach to machinery which it is 'very difficult to think beyond'; a necessary alternative is to restore intention and agency, seeing technology as 'looked for and developed with certain purposes and practices already in mind'.[1]

In the *Study of Thomas Hardy*, Lawrence addressed himself to the question of technology in relation to ideas of work and its place within a utopian society where human being might be realised to the full. Quite explicitly, he distances himself from an opposition to the machine-in-itself. There is now, he notes, a 'railing against the machine, as if it were an evil thing', connecting with intellectual discussion of a 'return to the medieval system of handicrafts' (*STH* 36). Both of these ideas he finds 'absurd': machines can help fulfil the 'dream' or 'joy' of every man, which is to be released from labour. As he looks around his room, Lawrence is 'glad' of the functionality and 'essential simplicity' of machine-made things: the bedstead, books, chairs, bottles. He has 'no business to ask machines to make beautiful things', but is gratified that they can make the 'perfect', 'convenient' mechanical instruments. In this sense the machine has arisen to 'take the place of the human machine', prompting Lawrence to 'do honour' to it and its inventor: 'It will produce what we want, and save us the necessity of much labour. Which is what it was invented for.' He realises however that such honourable intentions have now been thoroughly appropriated by the capitalist economic order: the machine is put to 'pitiable misuse', a 'muck-rake for raking together heaps of money'. Human greed transforms the machine from a 'means to freedom' into a 'means to more slavery' (*STH* 36).

This chapter's main developing concern will be with the relationship between machines and the culture of capitalism in Lawrence. I want however to pause for a moment at the view that the machine has arisen to '*take the place of the human machine*' (my emphasis). Given what we know of the 'deathly' opposition of machinery and the human in Lawrence, is this phrase anything other than an unfortunate contradiction? In its context it relates, we find, to a preceding argument about human fulfilment *in* work, where work, regardless of its nature ('the doctor, the teacher, the lawyer, just as much as the farm labourer or the mechanic'), is 'the approximation to a perfect mechanism, more or less intricate and adjustable' (*STH* 34). This is the mode of total and impersonal absorption in some activity that we find in Paul Morel or Will Brangwen; the 'certain keen, definite satisfaction' deriving from it is a condition of 'perfect' mechanism: 'when a man is working perfectly, he is the perfect machine', merely 'the mode where certain mechanical forces meet to find their resultant'. This state, Lawrence goes so far as to argue, is 'almost the deepest craving' in man; it is overridden only by the fact that it is *also* 'a state which every man hopes for release from', for in the final analysis 'A man is not a machine: when he has finished work, he is not motionless, inert. He begins a new activity' (*STH* 34).

It is customary to associate Lawrence with a critique of industrialism which is rooted in a group of nineteenth-century thinkers – principally Coleridge, Carlyle and Ruskin – whose distinctive characteristic, as Colin Clarke sees it, was to use the language of organicism 'in a rhetoric of sheer rejection'.[2] For Raymond Williams, Lawrence's social writings bear a 'remarkable' resemblance to the work of Thomas Carlyle in particular, while Anne Fernihough observes that it is 'easy' to see how Carlyle's attack on utilitarianism, and on the assumption that 'human beings are as straightforward and as orderly as the machines they tend', fed into Lawrence's concern with organic spontaneity and unpredictability. Lawrence had read widely in Carlyle and Ruskin by the age of 22; we know of the early significance for him of Carlyle's satire on scientific principles, *Sartor Resartus* (1836). His Carlylean organicism is reflected for Williams in the recurrent anti-industrialist key words *'mechanical, amorphous, disintegrated'*. It is certainly possible to see in Carlyle a strong source of the view that the machine, far from remaining a mode of external convenience for human life, enters into, shapes and redefines the human itself, as this much-cited extract illustrates:

Not the external and physical alone is now managed by machinery, but the internal and spiritual also . . . Men are grown mechanical in head and in heart, as well as in hand. . . .

Mechanism has now struck its roots down into man's intimate, most private sources of conviction; and is thence sending up, over his whole life and activity, innumerable stems – fruit-bearing and poison-bearing. . . . Intellect, the power man has of knowing and believing, is now nearly synonymous with Logic, or the mere power of arranging and communicating.[3]

It is a question, however, how far this organicism – so voracious that it metaphorizes mechanism itself as a plant that bears dubious fruit – might map onto the precarious balancing, or play of contradictions, we find in Lawrence's continuing account of the human and the machine. The decisiveness of 'a man is not a machine' does not erase the deep 'craving' for, and satisfaction gained from, man working as 'the perfect machine'. In the latter, we glimpse the optimism of a rationalist tradition in which the machine is a source of emancipation and pleasure, founded perhaps on a confidence that the political control of technology is there to be struggled for and won, its deathly grip on the human not simply a foregone conclusion inscribed in the determining structure of the machine itself. In 'honouring' the machine, and in separating function from appropriation, Lawrence is in fact closer to the utopian socialism of William Morris; and in borrowing this quotation again from Raymond Williams's argument in *Culture and Society*, it is worth noting that Williams is at pains to point up the superficial and misleading nature of the habitual reaction, ' "Morris – handicrafts – get rid of the machines" '. Morris writes:

If the necessary reasonable work be of a mechanical kind, I must be helped to do it by a machine, not to cheapen my labour, but so that as little time as possible may be spent on it. . . . I know that to some culti-vated people, people of the artistic turn of mind, machinery is particu-larly distasteful . . . (but) it is the allowing machines to be our masters and not our servants that so injures the beauty of life nowadays. In other words, it is the token of the terrible crime we have fallen into of using our control of the powers of Nature for the purpose of enslaving people, careless meantime of how much happiness we rob their lives of.[4]

In Morris here, and in the arresting echo of it in Lawrence's study of Hardy, there is an important but subtle modification of the prominent narrative critique of industrialism as alienating and dehumanizing. Krishan Kumar's analysis of ideas of industrialism in the nineteenth century complements this task: without seeking to 'score points' off the nineteenth-century social critics, who form the bedrock of a progessive socialist analysis of the evils of the British Industrial Revolution as an actual historical phenomenon, Kumar notes how the rapid pre-eminence of an *image* of industrialism deriving from this mode of critique comes effectively to define and delimit the 'model and type of industrial society "as such" '.[5] Within such a critique, a historical shorthand of binaries or polarities of development emerges out of the hypostatized image of 'industrialism': pre-industrial and industrial; *Gemeinschaft* and *Gesellschaft*; folk and urban; sacred and secular.

Accordingly, critical questions concerning mechanism cannot disregard the binary opposite of organicism by which it is held in place. How secure was this binary, for Lawrence? Anne Fernihough proposes, for example, an astute uncoupling of Lawrence from Carlyle. Given their shared anti-mechanism, Carlyle's stance derives, Fernihough argues, from the idealist transcendentalism of a German philosophical tradition that included Kant and Novalis. In Carlyle's version, the world of the machine has replaced the world of the invisible, where ultimate truths are to be found; his repudia-tion of the machine is actually a repudiation of 'the material world itself', as a mere veil clothing the truths of the transcendent. Such a metaphysics, notes Fernihough, was not for Lawrence an alternative to science and tech-nology, but on the contrary a product of exactly the same kind of instru-mental logic: if abstraction is responsible for the machine, still more is it responsible for the simple dichotomy that separates the material from the immaterial. However paradoxical and contradictory it was to become, Lawrence's commitment was to a rationality whose function was constantly to call to account such 'fixities' of thought as the binaries structuring our understanding of the human. If the machine was an ambivalent category, so inevitably too, as Amit Chaudhuri has recently argued, was the organ-ism. Let me close this section with Lawrence returning, in his long essay *Education of the People*, to the status of the machine in contemporary thinking about democracy and social life. While the passage culminates in a simple choice, 'mechanical or organic', I want to go on to suggest that the conceptual formation of this dichotomy may be less straightforward than it seems. Lawrence's focus is the concept of 'system'. There are those, he asserts, who in crying out against the present political system call it 'the Machine which devours us all', and call for an end to *all* system. This apparent organicism is, however, misplaced and unelaborated: such people confuse the issue, for the choice is not between system and no-system – 'there must be a system' – but between mechanical system and organic system. 'All life is organic', but those humans 'collectively active in organic life-production' must be 'organized', whereas those active 'purely in material production' must be 'mechanized':

> Obviously a system which is established for the purposes of pure material production, as ours today, is in its very nature a mechanism, a social machine. In this system we live and die. But even such a system as the great popes tried to establish was palpably not a machine, but an organization, a social organism. There is nothing at all to be gained from disunion, disintegration, and amorphousness. From mechanical systematization there is vast material productivity to be gained. But from an organic system of human life we shall produce the real blossoms of life and being (*RDP* 111).

2. Mechanical and organic

Lawrence's work strives, with an ever greater intensity of focus, to uncouple the machine and the system from the logic of capitalism. For Anne Fernihough, what is radical about Lawrence's project is the attempt (comparable to those of Marx, Nietzsche and Heidegger) to 'abolish transcendence' and 'rewrite philosophy from the beginning, from the material here and now'.[6] Let us assume that this act of rethinking, of stripping back, must include critical attention to the mechanical–organic binary and all its accretions. When we look at the history of these terms, we find that the polarity is a late one; what are now antitheses may once have been synonyms.

Raymond Williams pays close attention to the terms, from the outset of his project of historical semantics in *Culture and Society* (1958) through to the more developed form of *Keywords* (1983). In the earlier book, Williams notes that the Greek equivalent of our 'organic' meant 'tool' or 'instrument', and was 'equivalent to our "mechanical"'. In sixteenth-century English, 'organic' and 'mechanical' are still synonyms, but the Greek root of 'organic' contains a 'derived sense' of 'physical organ' which perhaps facilitates the later, eighteenth-century development of a separation along the lines of the 'biological' and the 'physical'. Burke and Coleridge begin to use 'organic' to refer to institutions and societies, and they exploit one of the senses of 'mechanical' – that which implied 'artificial' – to help bring about the now-familiar dichotomy. This dichotomy then proceeds to split the 'organ' family itself, such that the 'organ of sense' connotation gives rise to 'organic' and 'organism', while the 'organ as instrument' connotation gives rise to 'organize' and 'organization'. Burke could use 'organic' and 'organized' as synonyms, but a more familiar opposition is established by the middle of the nineteenth century.

Keywords substantiates this account in certain key respects. The *instrumentality* of 'organ' in English from the thirteenth to the sixteenth century is again underlined, but the transformations of 'organic' are much more explicitly tied to the Romantic movement, particularly Coleridge and Carlyle, and the influence of the developing natural history and biology upon it. Coleridge, for example, makes a distinction between organic – 'the whole is everything and the parts are nothing' – and the inorganic – 'the whole is nothing more than a collection of the individual parts' – which is exacerbated by developments in 'mechanical' that are tied to perceptions of the Industrial Revolution. While in the sixteenth century 'machine' still carried its Latin association with any contrivance, structure or framework, it moves progressively closer to the generalized application of 'power' developing in the new science of mechanics. From the early nineteenth century, the familiar distinction between 'mechanical and 'organic', previously 'very close in meaning', emerges, as the new 'machines' proceed to work on their own and replace human labour, suggesting a Godless universe and 'an association with the older (and socially affected) sense of routine, unthinking activity – thus action without consciousness'.[7]

In such semantic histories it is possible to see the source of Colin Clarke's important judgement that, while Lawrence drew the mechanical–organic antithesis from romanticism, it was precisely the 'great Romantics' who 'make it possible for him ultimately to qualify and subtle-ize that antithesis'.[8] In Lawrence's discussion of 'system' we can glimpse a dialectic between, on the one hand, the overt organicism which depends upon a stabilizing concept of mechanism, and, on the other hand, a much more uncertain, overlapping and sometimes synonymous history of the kind suggested by Williams. If his first aim is to detach 'system' from a caricature of 'the Machine which devours us all', then both system and machine benefit from this gesture: the orientation of the argument is to protect or rescue both systematicity and mechanism from superficial, reflex reactions. After all, we 'live and die' within a 'social machine', and from such a system we derive 'vast material productivity'. When, nevertheless, Lawrence asserts the possibility of alternative kinds of system, he runs together terms – 'organization' and 'social organism' – which according to Williams were pulling apart through Romanticism, with 'organization' becoming attached to the negative connotations of mechanism. This is reinforced by a reiterated emphasis on the necessity of system: 'nothing at all to be gained from disunion', and so on. In *Women in Love*, the Crich father and son introduce industrial systems, Christian-democratic and instrumentally profit-driven respectively, whose mechanism is in each case a state of 'chaos'; in his essay, however, Lawrence reminds that there is also the chaos that issues from a sentimentalized lack of system. In the apparently clinching organicist gesture, 'real blossoms of life and being', this can only be achieved through 'organic system'; such a concept, in holding within it 'organization' and 'organism', cannot completely erase the suggestion of mechanism from its 'system'.

My suggestion is that the relationship between mechanical and organic was, for Lawrence as it was historically, dynamic and unstable. In any such deconstruction of terms, we are drawn away from questions of absolute referentiality and towards the interests and ideological forces by which binary differences are held in place. The question of how far the human might *be* mechanical and how far organic subsides, to be supplemented by the question of what interests might be served by the maintenance of the mechanical–organic binary itself: what is it there to do, and where does it come from?

For Gilles Deleuze and Félix Guattari, such instabilities around the mechanical and the organic are called into play by Samuel Butler's utopian/dystopian novel *Erewhon* (1872, revised in 1901). In Chapter 5, I drew attention to a striking anticipation of the contemporary posthuman in the evolving machines of Butler's *Life and Habit* (1910). In Butler's novel, the English narrator travels to a colony on a distant continent to start a new life. While exploring there, he stumbles upon a remote and undiscovered state, Erewhon, whose palpably civilized inhabitants nevertheless embrace a socio-political Luddism. In a collective gesture of knowing how not to know, all machines have been eradicated, and education is furthered at Colleges of Unreason. Enquiring into this condition of 'apparent retrogression in all arts, sciences and inventions', he learns that Erewhon had, some four hundred years previously, developed a highly sophisticated mechanical knowledge, and was 'advancing with prodigious rapidity', when one of its prominent thinkers persuaded the state that, at the present rate of advance, the machines would soon 'supplant' the human race if they were not immediately destroyed. The destruction took in all machinery constructed in the previous two hundred and seventy-one years, and was followed by a civil war between the 'machinists' and 'anti-machinists', from which Erewhon had eventually emerged in its present form.[9]

Deleuze and Guattari's interest centres wholly on the 'Book of the Machines', the narrator's translated *resumé* of the work which led to the revolution in Erewhon. The burden of this work is that, in the light of evolutionary history and the practically unthinkable emergence of thinking matter from 'a hot round ball with a crust gradually cooling', there is no reason to suppose that life might not thence evolve in the direction of machines with a consciousness far superior to our own. The rationale involves Butler's narrator in an extended rehearsal of materialist accounts of consciousness or, more accurately, of materialist challenges to the absolute separation of consciousness from the non-conscious. ' "Where does consciousness begin, and where end? . . . Who can draw any line?" ' How can we say that a steam engine does not have ' "a kind of consciousness? . . . Is not machinery linked with animal life in an infinite variety of ways?" ' (*E* 141). A machine, argues the writer, returning to the earliest derivation of the word, is only a ' "device" '; the shell of a hen's egg is no less of a 'device' than her nest is. Conversely, how can we say that a plant that traps and eats flies but nothing else, or a potato in a cellar that sends shoots towards the light, does not have a kind of cunning – ' "What is consciousness if this is not consciousness?" '. If such actions are 'chemical and mechanical', is not every sensation thus chemical and mechanical? It may even be possible to grant reproductive capacity to the machine; by an unusual sleight of hand which again anticipates the posthuman theory of distributed cognition, the 'system' is not confined to the concept of internal reproductive organs but extends outwards in a web of relationships. Thus, just as the humble bee is part of the reproductive system of the red clover, so the human and other machines are part of the reproductive system of any machine. The incredibly rapid advance of machines, within the 'last five minutes' of deep evolutionary time, convinces the writer that their hegemony is inevitable; already, more humans are locked into a 'state of bondage' to their machines than they are involved in tending each other, and 'man's very soul' has become a 'machine-made thing'.

For Deleuze and Guattari, the significance of Butler's narrative is that it quickly moves beyond the poles of a familiar argument, according to which *either* organisms are deemed to be perfect machines *or* machines are never more than parts of an organism. The 'Butlerian manner', they insist, carries 'each of the arguments to an extreme point where it can no longer be opposed to the other, a point of nondifference or *dispersion*' (*A-O* 284). At this point, then, 'it becomes immaterial whether one says that machines are organs, or organs, machines':

> In a word, the real difference is not between the living and the machine, vitalism and mechanism, but between two states of the machine that are two states of the living as well (*A-O* 285–6).

We could gloss the obscurity of 'Butlerian manner' by noting that Butler has the arguments of the writer undermine themselves. If the machine is so pervasive as to have entered and re-shaped the human, then it cannot be annihilated (a fact the writer is obliged to acknowledge with the rather weak admission that we should 'destroy as many of them as we can possibly dispense with'); if its evolution is towards the vital and the animate, and in this sense also towards a complexity which is strictly unforeseeable ('new channels dug out for consciousness'), then in this manner it ceases to *be* mechanical, or remains so only in so far as the organic and the mechanical become interchangeable. Thus, in a dialogical irony which Deleuze and Guattari curiously fail to recognize, Butler has the narrator briefly invoke an extract from the writer's single, significant 'machinist' opponent – only for this opponent to confirm the implications of the writer's stance: man is a 'machinate mammal', machines 'are to be regarded as the mode of development by which human organism is now especially advancing, every past invention being an addition to the resources of the human body' (*E* 160–1).

For Deleuze and Guattari, this deconstruction of 'mechanical' and 'organic' is not simply revealing of language, as a system of differences, and its problematic relationship to our understanding of the world. It represents also the possibility of moving beyond the limits set on our thinking of consciousness and human nature by a division along the lines of 'vitalism' and 'materialism'. Butler, they claim, opens out the vitalist argument '*by calling in question the specific or personal unity of the organism*', and opens out the mechanist argument 'even more decisively' by '*calling in question the structural unity of the machine*' (*A-O* 284). Both parts of the mechanical–organic polarity predicate forms of structural *unity* which police our thinking about human and political possibility; originating in the era of bourgeois revolution and Romanticism, the polarity organizes an ideology of the human subject which becomes the crucial, *explicit* humanism of capitalism. In order to dismantle this structure, Deleuze and Guattari devise a contestatory vocabulary of the human which seems to come firmly down on the side of the machine: we are desiring-machines, bodies without organs. While addressing the taboos of organicism, it is also true that Deleuze and Guattari's machines no longer coincide with their traditional, industrial-scientific predecessors. How and why does D.H. Lawrence emerge as a significant figure within this philosophy?

3. Deleuze and Guattari's Lawrence

> . . . (T)hose who are best at 'leaving', those who make leaving into something as natural as being born or dying, those who set out in search of nonhuman sex . . .
>
> *Anti-Oedipus*

It is at first difficult to recognize in Deleuze and Guattari's anti-capitalist philosophy anything closely resembling a 'humanistic' impulse. To their endorsement of a schizophrenic model of the human, David Harvey makes a pointed insinuation of irresponsibility: he cites the case of a clinical schizophrenic who had boiled his infant children in molten metal, and the then-Chairman of the Amstrad Corporation, Alan Sugar, opining that if there was a market for mass-produced nuclear weapons, '"then we'd market them too"'.[10] In this light it is worth recording Deleuze and Guattari's condemnation of the unparallelled *cruelty* and *terror* which define capitalism. These qualities, they argue, are intimately tied to the *assimilative* power of the capitalist 'machine': it is 'always capable of adding to its axiomatic in terms of an enlargement of its limits: let's create the New Deal; let's cultivate and recognize strong unions; let's promote participation, the single class . . .'; yet, within this 'enlarged reality', permitting 'increases and improvements of standard at the centre', the 'harshest forms of exploitation' are moved out to the peripheries – 'lack is arranged in the most scientific of ways, final solutions of the "Jewish problem" variety are prepared down to the last detail, and the Third World is organized as an integral part of capitalism' (*A-O* 373).

This argument suggests, in other words, that schizophrenia is a structure integral to capitalism itself. As Hardt and Negri put it,

> Historically, capital has relied on sovereignty and the support of its structures of force and right, but those same structures continually contradict in principle and obstruct in practice the operation of capital, finally obstructing its development. The entire history of modernity that we have traced thus far might be seen as the evolution of the attempts to negotiate and mediate this contradiction.[11]

Harvey's reaction is understandable in its sentiment, but it slightly misconstrues the wider operative sense in which, for Deleuze and Guattari, and echoing Marx's earlier assessment of bourgeois revolution, capitalist schizophrenia is both the worst and the best that can happen to us. While, explicitly, capitalism requires for its sovereignty the force of repression, 'structure', its implicit logic requires the opening of all boundaries. Born of the confluence of two 'decoded' flows, those of money-capital and the 'free worker' in the marketplace, capitalism, unlike previous 'social machines', 'is incapable of providing a code that will apply to the whole of the social field' (*A-O* 33). Thus, as it dismantles traditional structures from the inside, energies and resistances become more uncontainable, 'deterritorialized', and manifest themselves on a thousand plateaus, in a 'new milieu of maximum plurality and uncontainable singularization':[12]

> What we are really trying to say is that capitalism, through its process of production, produces an awesome schizophrenic accumulation of energy or charge, against which it brings all its vast powers of repression to bear, but which nonetheless continues to act as capitalism's limit. For capitalism constantly counteracts, constantly inhibits this inherent tendency while at the same time allowing it free rein; it continually seeks to avoid reaching its limit while simultaneously tending toward that limit (*A-O* 34).

While, therefore, Deleuze and Guattari can generate a revolutionary optimism from capitalism's covert, released and 'decoded' desires, the critical task of their philosophy is also to dismantle the structures through which capitalism protects itself in the appearance of order, stability and tradition. The mechanical–organic binary is one such structure, sequestering a humanism which is crucial to the well-being of capitalism. Mechanism promises the fulfilment of the modern project, the dream of emancipation through technology, but is counterbalanced by the *organic* integrity of the human subject. Paradoxically, then, critiques of mechanism, for example in organicist discourses on industrialism, valuably hold in place this idea of the subject by continuing to reify both sides of the binary.

Lawrence's writing periodically reminds us that, in relation to 'mechanisms' such as the law (a 'very, very clumsy and mechanical instrument'), 'we people' are 'very, very delicate and subtle beings' (*P* 405). Deleuze and Guattari attempt to unsettle the mechanical–organic binary by transferring the properties of delicacy and subtlety to mechanism itself. *Anti-Oedipus* begins with a vision of 'desire' which is impersonal, perhaps even allotropic, but at the same time not generalized – 'what a mistake to have ever said *the* id'. 'It' is, rather, 'machines – real ones, not figurative ones'; organ machines plug into energy-source machines, 'the breast is a machine that produces milk, and the mouth a machine coupled to it'. Machines are defined not as objects or structures, but as couplings, connecting and interrupting flows of desire; the unpredictable *production* of desire, whereby anything becomes possible, is set against the constraining of desire within dominant interpretative frameworks. In *Anti-Oedipus*, the critical focus is on Freudian psychoanalysis and its theoretical cornerstone, the Oedipus complex; in *A Thousand Plateaus*, the perspective widens to take into account models of organic unity such as the tree of life/tree of knowledge. Replacing the hierarchical and gradualist model of the latter, the figure of the rhizome suggests transversal and unpredictable development, as if anything might be connected to anything. Organicism is, in other words, under scrutiny as fully as the instrumental models of capitalist machinery. The 'body without organs' (BwO) is what remains when the idea of 'the organization of the organs we call the organism' has been dismantled; it is 'fluid and slippery', making the impression of human subjectivity as organic depth, centred in the body, merely a kind of side-effect of a play of surfaces in which the body is connected in a 'fusional multiplicity' with the world. Famously, *'There is only desire, and the social, and nothing else'* (*A-O* 29).

Deleuze and Guattari's arguments suggest a new logic of pragmatism. What if we were to think of our bodies, not as organic wholes, but as desiring machines? What if we were to think of such machines merely, as it were, in terms of the flow and interruption of forces? What are the effects of trying to think the human in such a radically different way, beyond the binary of the mechanical and the organic? 'The unconscious poses no problem of meaning, solely problems of use. The question posed by desire is not "What does it mean?", but rather *"How does it work?"'* (*A-O* 109). Yet Deleuze and Guattari dissociate their pragmatism from that linguistic-relativistic version of the postmodern according to which we play our various alternative language games around an inaccessible material reality. The desiring-machine is 'not a metaphor', the BwO and its intensities similarly 'not metaphors, but matter itself' (*A-O* 41, 283). Thinking and being posthuman fuse together; in detaching their ideas from metaphoricity, Deleuze/Guattari signal the need for epistemological reappraisal, suggesting that the human body might actually *be* other than that signified within the dominant symbolic order.

If we are reminded here of Lawrence's insistence on the physical reality of European culture, or the abiding primacy of the solar plexus, beyond interpretation and representation, we are similarly reminded of his complaint that the Freudian unconscious is an *idea* of the unconscious dominated by the incest taboo. Both Lawrence and Deleuze/Guattari express an initial admiration for the Freudian journey towards the unconscious, subsequently tempered by what Freud does with what he finds there. For Deleuze/Guattari, the discovery was of a 'domain of free syntheses where everything is possible: endless connections, nonexclusive disjunctions, nonspecific conjunctions, partial objects and flows' (*A-O* 54). Freud must, however, draw back from this 'world of wild production and explosive desire', into a model of order framed by classical Greek theatre; the production of desire is thereby 'crushed, subjected to the requirements of *representation*, and to the dreary games of what is representative and represented in representation'. In *Anti-Oedipus*, then, they completely concur with Lawrence's view of the Oedipus complex as, in their words, an 'idealist turning-point': Oedipus is a 'sham image', nothing but 'an idea that repression inspires in us concerning desire'. Lawrence, they argue,

> (H)ad the impression – the purely instinctive impression – that psychoanalysis was shutting sexuality up in a bizarre sort of box painted with bourgeois motifs, in a kind of rather repugnant artificial triangle, thereby stifling the whole of sexuality as production of desire so as to recast it along entirely different lines, making of it a 'dirty little secret', the dirty little family secret, a private theatre rather than the fantastic factory of Nature and Production (*A-O* 49).

Even though they endorse the irrationalist-romantic Lawrence of the 'purely instinctive impression' here, Deleuze/Guattari also attribute to him a historicized analysis of Freudian psychoanalysis as an ideological phenomenon. In confining the problems of desire and psychosis within the framework of the parental and familial, psychoanalysis continued the nineteenth-century project of moralizing mental pathology, 'keeping

European humanity harnessed to the yoke of mommy-daddy', and thus 'taking part in the work of bourgeois repression at its most far-reaching level' (*A-O* 50). Underlining his insistence that 'the so-called *human* relations are not involved' in the originary flows and connections of the unconscious, for example with the mother – 'the first relationship is neither personal nor biological' – Deleuze/Guattari's Lawrence endorses a 'nonhuman' sexuality which is sceptical both of the anthropomorphic and of the organicist.

Deleuze/Guattari's machinic and Lawrence's 'pantheism' of 'flows and intensities' are thus brought into connection. Lawrence's deconstruction of the humanist self is crucial to the understanding of such flows: in the essay 'We Need One Another', for example, a complex dialectic picks its way *both* around 'our disastrous modern egoism of the individual' *and* our tendency to idealize people in terms of conventional roles or models which, in the words of Deleuze/Guattari, cut off the flows of sexuality 'like so many tourniquets' (*P* 188–95). For 'we' here might be read capitalism in its fully schizophrenic sense. The atomistic individualism of *laissez-faire* prevents relationship, yet the conformity of relationship – marriage, family, and hence oedipalization – is crucial for the appearance of order. Only with unidealized relationship can we arrive, Lawrence maintains, at de-commodified selfhood in which a human is, for example, 'a fountain of life-vibration, quivering and flowing towards someone', receiving 'outflow' and sending back 'inflow', 'so that a circuit is completed, and there is a sort of peace' (*P* 191). 'It is certain', Deleuze/Guattari discern in Lawrence as well as in Henry Miller and R.D. Laing, 'that neither men nor women are clearly-defined personalities, but rather vibrations, flows, schizzes and "knots"'; the task of schizoanalysis is 'that of tirelessly taking apart egos and their presuppositions', for 'everyone is a little group (*un groupuscule*) and must live as such' (*A-O* 362).

Again we must stress the subtle play of differences within and across these versions of the machine in Lawrence and in Deleuze/Guattari. 'Science', Lawrence argues in *Fantasia of the Unconscious*, is

> wretched in its treatment of the human body as a sort of complex mechanism made up of numerous little machines working automatically in a rather unsatisfactory relation to one another. The body is the total machine; the various organs are the included machines; and the whole thing, given a start at birth, or at conception, trundles on by itself. The only god in the machine, the human will or intelligence, is absolutely at the mercy of the machine (*FU* 55).

Does this leave any room for the desiring machine? The answer must surely run that there are machines and machines. Lawrence's target is the machine as a totalized or totalizing category, a thing containing things, monopolizing what we can say about consciousness just as the machine itself monopolizes 'intelligence'. This is an industrial-instrumentalist version of the machine, appropriated by and at the service of capitalist ideology, and unmasked as such by both Lawrence and Deleuze/Guattari. But the machine is, as it were, the more obvious target; had not the task of such critique been undertaken by nineteenth-century organicists through to the Frankfurt School? The priority is then to unmask the organicism holding this version of mechanism in place, sustaining a reductive because unexamined humanism and blocking the emergence of a posthuman humanism. Machines then become ways of mediating the creative, strictly unpredictable flows of human desire; not totalizing structures, but ways of releasing difference. Should we thus play loose and fast with meaning, machines seeming to gravitate towards their opposite, the stability of the mechanical–organic binary undermined? The history of language reveals this binary to be always-already fluid and open to contestation.

In Lawrence, despite his greater evident proximity to the organicists, Deleuze/Guattari seem to discern, beyond anti-mechanism, a similar unease with this binary as a whole. They detect an anti-mechanistic philosophy of human 'flows', but of flows manifested in 'vibrations' and 'circuits'. In the pursuit of that 'nonhuman' or 'inhuman' which, he knew, was the only means to a fuller and more intelligent humanism, Lawrence could reliquish neither the languages of organicism nor of mechanism. In *A Thousand Plateaus*, this tireless worrying-away at the mechanical–organic opposition is translated into an alignment with their own curious and transgressive conception of identity as *becoming*. In a version of literary history and evaluation first hinted at in *Anti-Oedipus*, the Anglo-American novel, with Lawrence as a principal protagonist, is contrasted favourably with its French counterpart. While the latter is 'profoundly pessimistic and idealistic', spending its time 'plotting points instead of drawing lines', the former, proclaims: 'Go across, get out, break through, make a beeline, don't get stuck on a point. Find the line of separation, follow it or create it, to the point of treachery' (*ATP* 186–7). In this fiction of 'flight' and 'deterritorialization', nothing, least of all the human, remains entirely recognizable. Deleuze/Guattari's sustained critique of *faciality* echoes Lawrence's warnings about the anthropomorphic or all-too-human interpretation of the human itself; the face is a familiar image into which we read humanist presuppositions, blocking the emergence of a more comprehensive, non-human human being. Writers such as Lawrence, Hardy, Melville and Miller 'know how hard it is to break through the wall of the signifier'; beyond conventional representation, however, and beyond the 'black hole' of subjectivity and the dismantling of the face, artistic writing becomes a 'tool for blazing life lines', with Lawrence one of those who 'were able to tie their writing to real and unheard-of becomings' (*ATP* 244).

Two examples are given of this condition of becoming. Lawrence's tortoise poems are studies in anomaly; to the objection, '"Your tortoises aren't real!"', Deleuze/Guattari's Lawrentian answer is: 'Possibly, but my becoming is, my becoming is real, even and especially if you have no way of judging it, because you're just little house dogs...' (*ATP* 244). In moving in his tortoise descriptions from 'the most obstinate animal dynamism' to 'the abstract, pure geometry of scales and "cleavages of division"', Lawrence sets the creaturely into an indeterminate state, freed from the potential impasse of the mechanical–organic binary. Likewise, Lawrence attacks the 'great dualism machines' whose function in the domain of gender is not simply to oppose masculine to feminine but to appropriate the body itself, 'the body they *steal* from us in order to fabricate opposable organisms' (*ATP* 276). This is not a recommendation of Lawrence's fictional technique so much as a social phenomenon comparable with Virginia Woolf's expressed dismay at the idea of writing '"as a woman"'. Writing itself should call into question the anthropomorphic category of 'woman' itself, producing a sense of 'becoming-woman' as 'atoms of womanhood capable of crossing and impregnating an entire social field, and of contaminating men, of sweeping them up in that becoming'.

The challenge of the '*becoming*', in Lawrence as in Deleuze/Guattari, is epistemological – a suspension of categories by which we might begin to know how not to know. As we have seen, evolutionary theory presented this challenge to Lawrence in the starkest form: how can you describe the rabbit, when it is always-already in the process of becoming something else? But the problem is not simply to be circumscribed by the linear temporality of evolutionary change, or by rejecting the 'mechanism' of abstraction in favour of a fluid organicism. In his essay on Dana, Lawrence turns from Luddite tirades against the machine to a consideration of paganism princi-pally because the latter's life-worship is also a mode of epistemological flexibility and ambivalence:

> When we study the pagan gods, we find that they have now one meaning, now another. Now they belong to the creative essence, and now to the material-dynamic world. First they have one aspect, then another. The greatest god has both aspects (*SCAL* 118).

The didactic science of the young German guide in *Etruscan Places* consists, we remember, in a refusal or inability to think multiplicity of identity. While for the Etruscan the lion has a goat's head, and the human has a 'complex and contradictory' blood-stream containing 'the blood of the wings of birds and the venom of serpents', these for the scientist are 'mere crude incapac-ity to think'; he can only see the obvious, for 'that which is unthinkable is non-existent' (*EP* 123). This paganism is further complicated by Chaudhuri's recent point that such images embody for Lawrence a principle of 'vital flow' or contact which is *non*-organicist, the touching of the heterogeneous and incompatible being precisely what is at issue: 'the organically whole image

is exactly what Lawrence wishes to undermine'.[13] The challenge to organicist assumptions in Deleuze and Guattari can provoke, as we have seen, the
scandalized reaction of astute critics such as David Harvey, his sense of
humanism offended by their theory of the schizophrenic. In the next
section, I want to consider together three novels in which Lawrence sought
to extend his critique of the human in ways which readers, perhaps with
some justification, have often found unacceptable. If these are quite clearly
fictions of the posthuman, they are also post-humanist fictions, in which
part of the challenge lies in the abiding presence of what Samuel Butler
called the 'machinate mammal'.

4. *Aaron's Rod, Kangaroo, The Plumed Serpent*: anti-capitalism and the post-humanistic

> The thing called 'Life' is just a mistake we have made in our own
> minds. Why persist in the mistake any further?
>
> *The Plumed Serpent*

My concern in this section is with a number of similarities between these
novels of the 1920s. They represent a departure or leave-taking from the illu-
sionist conventions of the realist novel to which, despite marked stylistic-
modernistic idiosyncracies, Lawrence's earlier fiction had adhered. The
breaking of this illusion is, I would suggest, the formalistic extension of a
challenge to *humanistic* assumptions which Lawrence had begun overtly to
articulate in *Women in Love*. Accordingly, readers and critics have been
dubious about the aesthetic success of these novels, and have shown unease
about their apparent turn against 'Life' and the human/humane.

To some extent, my decision to read the novels as a group reflects comparable reservations. *Aaron's Rod* is the weakest of Lawrence's novels, a lame
and lazy reprise of aspects of *Women in Love*. Sheila McLeod recollects her
teenage response to the novel's central act, Aaron Sisson's abandonment of
his wife and children in order to fulfil the nomadic Lawrentian project of
self-responsibility: far from being interested in the progress of the hero's spiritual condition, her concern lay with the human fate of the family left
behind. In the hastily written *Kangaroo*, the realist contract collapses more
than in any other of his works; this meditation on Australian identity and
politics, in the words of Frank Kermode, 'gropes along' and is 'nobody's
choice for Lawrence's masterpiece'. *The Plumed Serpent* stages an interest in
ritualistic murder-as-sacrifice and a 'marriage' for Kate Leslie with the
Mexican priest-soldier Cipriano in which she is studiously denied orgasm,
in an inhuman 'religion . . . of male supremacy' famously condemned by
Kate Millett.[14]

In each case the exiled, nomadic protagonist finds in an alternative culture
– Italy, Australia, Mexico – a context in which to cease to *care* about con-

ventional human values, to lapse into a state of isolation or, in the key word of *Kangaroo*, 'indifference'. The term is deceptive, however, in that the novels are highly political in orientation; each uses the protagonist's encounter with a charismatic individual 'leader' to focus a debate around alternatives to capitalist imperialism. While Sisson, Lovat Somers and Kate Leslie are all escaping from a condition or culture of instrumental mechanism, the political context of the novels firmly identifies this mechanism with *money*. Thus Sisson meets Rawdon Lilly, a lightly sketched and barely contextualized leadership figure whose nomadic impulse is characterized by Sisson as the ability to 'take a sudden jump' (*AR* 126). Their separate wanderings lead to a reunion in Italy, where the state is being challenged by socialist and anarchist demonstrations. Lilly is a diluted version of Birkin's role as an eloquent seer, but also acts as a sketch for his two successors, Kangaroo and Cipriano. In *Kangaroo*, Lovat Somers, a writer known for his sceptical critiques of democracy, travels to Australia with his wife. There, Somers becomes acquainted with revolutionary, anti-capitalist politicians of left- and right-wing persuasions. The aim of the Diggers, an underground racist and nationalist movement led by Kangaroo, is to allow the Socialist party under Willie Struthers to seize power, and then in turn to effect a coup which would install a true Australian political identity. The logic behind this strategy, that Bolshevism is not an alternative to capitalist materialism but simply its obverse face, also informs the rediscovery of Aztec identity, culture and religion under the Quetzalcoatl movement led by Don Cipriano and Don Ramon in *The Plumed Serpent*. Kate Leslie's profound disillusionment with the alliance of Christian-humanist culture and a specifically American economic imperialism leads into her fascinated-yet-horrified embrace of Quetzalcoatl and of Cipriano.

These explicitly political novels suggest that what is at stake for Lawrence is not the machine as such but its appropriation by capitalism. As Deleuze/Guattari's work implies, a critique of capitalism cannot confine itself to an excoriation of mechanism, but must instead attend to the dichotomy in which the machine is counterbalanced by an idealized human realm of 'life', organicism and nature. The association of the mechanical and unhuman *with* the human, and as a challenge to the *humanistic* human, may come to constitute a deeply paradoxical means of pursuing this critique. In the posthumanism of these novels, we see Lawrence striving, with mixed success, for just such a precarious dialectic. One very familiar framework of interpretation, reinforced by letters of the period, shows that a prominent discourse lay to hand in this respect: the novels demonstrate the pre-eminence of power over love, a Nietzschean emphasis on natural force and difference expressed as a critique of the Christian ethic of love and its corollary in democratic egalitarianism. Rawdon Lilly voices this unequivocally, in his condemnation of a whole 'beehive' of 'dead' and 'stinking' ideals: 'The ideal of love, the ideal that it is better to give than to receive, the ideal of liberty, the ideal of brotherhood of man, the ideal of the sanctity of human life, the ideal of what we call goodness, charity, benevolence, public spiritedness, the ideal of sacrifice for a cause, the ideal of unity and unanimity . . .' (*AR* 326).

The problem for Lawrence is of how to translate the human embrace or exploration of these ideals into fictionalized form. Is it possible that such aggressive life-negation might just be at the service of an 'alive' and 'flexible' posthumanism dedicated to the 'delicate sensitiveness' of the living? The bitterness of tone in much of *Aaron's Rod* seems actively to militate against this. Aaron and the Marchesa del Torre exchange a look of mutual understanding, 'without any moral necessity or any other necessity':

> Outside – they had got outside the castle of the so-called human life. Outside the horrible, stinking human castle of life. A bit of true, limpid freedom. Just a glimpse (*AR* 272).

Such anti-human rhetoric is consistent across the novels. Somers, 'filled with fury', reacts against Kangaroo's monologue on the doctrine of love and the necessity of the 'warm heart': 'No more cloying warmth. No more of this horrible stuffy heat of human beings' (*K* 140). The death of ideals makes Somers wish 'to be clear of humanity altogether, to be alone'. Don Ramon declares that he is 'nauseated with humanity and the human will', to which Kate responds, 'Oh! isn't human life horrible!' (*PS* 80). Such sentiments began, as we have seen, in Ursula and Birkin, whose relationship continues to offer some hope of redemption after the tragic union of mechanisms in Gudrun and Gerald. In *Aaron's Rod*, however, with Aaron remaining isolated at the end, and deprived even of his precious flute, which is destroyed in the bomb-blast, no such redemption seems available. Lawrence tentatively takes up another strand from *Women in Love*, the possibility of the male couple as an alternative to the tainted, idealized love between the sexes. But this is compromised from the start by the manner of its representation of the heterosexual. A pattern develops in which any sexual liaison brings for Aaron a loss of integrity and real physical debilitation, illness: in the case of the affair with Josephine, he succumbs to a life-threatening bout of 'flu, and is saved only by Lilly's body massage and general ministrations. To give oneself to a woman is to betray a weakness in the spine or 'tail', which extends to the legs. The far-fetched and tiresome literalness of this emphasis reaches its nadir in the demonization of Lottie, his wife, as a seductive serpent, when Aaron pays a return visit to the family home.

Again this anti-Enlightenment emphasis presents a challenge to the contemporary reader. The only possibility of redemption seems to lie in the sense that woman has become the main, but invisible victim and vehicle of capitalist ideology. Men may run the machines of the capitalist order, but it is stabilized and sanctioned by the corresponding mechanism of Christian idealization: love, marriage, family, and in particular the elevated status of motherhood. In *Fantasia of the Unconscious*, Lawrence's most sustained critique of the idealization of love and its *physical* effects, the modern mother–child relationship is described as the 'viciousest of circles', the mother acting in her 'new role as idealist and life-manager' to personalize the relationship with the child. The mother thus comes to bear the heaviest symbolic weight of Deleuze/Guattari's 'yoke of mommy-daddy', domesticating sexuality and making the incest motive a self-fulfilling prophecy. In a moment of the uncanny, Aaron gazes with a 'nostalgia which was at least half-revulsion' at his home; the 'horrors of domesticity' and the 'unspeakable familiarity' have 'prevented his thinking' (*AR* 148, 18–19). Aaron is regularly accused, by his wife and Lady Franks, for example, of being unnatural in leaving his family: 'altogether cold and unmanly and inhuman'. Such a conception of human 'nature' is however tied inexorably to the industrial-capitalist machine: Sir William boasts of having 'harnessed' his spirit to 'the cart which mankind is riding in', the 'work of productive labour', and with 'an eye to the market'; he possesses, however, 'the devilish spirit of iron itself, and iron machines'. Provocatively, under cross-examination by the Franks, and browbeaten by their evident clichés, Aaron maintains that his desertion was 'a natural event' (*AR* 173, 176).

There is a sense that breaking the taboos of a humanism coralled by capitalism requires extreme measures. Aaron, 'our hero', is beset by misgivings as he contemplates the snapping of 'all the bonds and ligatures which bound him to the life that had formed him. . . . And why? In God's name, why? What was there instead?' (*AR* 214). Lawrence seems to give up on the novel in the act of writing it. The strategy of making Aaron a musician in order to release him into various cultured upper-middle-class and aristocratic contexts produces a series of strained caricatures – 'this expensive comfort of modern Bohemia', for example. The narrowing of ambition on Lawrence's part may best be explained as a renunciation of aesthetic effect and its *humanistic* consolations in order to focus attention more single-mindedly on the main obstacle to a subtler posthumanism. From the beginning of the novel, where Christmas Eve in the main street means 'people struggling to buy things, to get things', Aaron is aware that 'It's money we live for, and money is what our lives is worth – nothing else' (*AR* 23, 29). He comes to realize that the 'bloody revolution' which might redistribute wealth is, itself, an impulse and construction of moneyed culture. Money, he concludes, observing the deference given to the Franks, is 'the only authority left' (*AR* 165). This gives rise to two startling anticipations of a postmodern critique of globalized capital. Despite re-writing in Aaron's first visit to Italy some of the freshness and perception of human difference of Lawrence's own first experience of cultural otherness – 'a new life-quality everywhere' – the narrative crucially modifies Aaron's view:

> But alas, the one world triumphing more and more over the many worlds, the big oneness swallowing up the many small diversities in its insatiable

gnawing appetite, leaving a dreary sameness throughout the world, that means at last complete sterility (*AR* 185).

Alongside this conception of McDonaldization-as-mechanism, we might set Lilly's Baudrillardian response to Herbertson's harrowing account of the war, where Herbertson has stressed the unprecedented role of machinery in the production of carnage. Just as Jean Baudrillard argues that the Gulf War did not take place, but was experienced as a virtual event mediated by the technologies of global capitalism, so Lilly, to the bewilderment of Herbertson and Aaron, maintains that the war 'never happened', was 'all unreal'. Aaron's commonsense retort – 'Real enough for those that had to go through with it' – prompts a more searching redefinition of the logic of the human. The war, Lilly argues, was 'humanly quite false': no one who was 'awake and in possession of himself' would use poison gases; the war took place 'in the automatic sphere', in other words in a state of mass-suggestion commensurate with the later potential of media technologies (*AR* 118–19).[15]

In a context of capitalist imperialism, producing both the war and the machines to prosecute it, *Aaron's Rod* can summon up few resources of hope for a renewed humanism along recognizable lines. The 'accursed mechanical ideal' gains ground just as surely in Italy as it does in England. In the face of capitalism's *colonization* of the humanistic, it is of greater strategic value, as it were, to affirm the inhuman and the mechanistic *in* the human, even at the risk of appearing to collude thus with capitalism's own internal mechanism. We should not idealize human being so far as to forget that the human is quite capable of *being* mechanized, that human life can be lived as mechanical life, or as the 'fall' into automatism'; to do so is to adopt a dogmatic, unreflexive humanism, conveniently setting aside the close kinship and tenuous divide between thinking and inorganic matter. To a scandalized humanistic Levison, Lilly argues that 'People are not *men*: they are insects and instruments, and their destiny is slavery' (*AR* 327). Yet the conditions for a new dialectical thinking of the human, beyond the givens of a capitalist culture which include democracy as well as love, are underlined in Lilly's next, contradictory breath. 'I should say the blank opposite with just as much fervour'; his future state embodies the unthinkable combination of hierachical dictatorship with the eradication of all '*bullying*', so that 'every man is a sacred and holy individual, never to be violated' (*AR* 328). It seems appropriate to this novel's strategic disregard for its reader's expectations that the reasonable Levison should be mocked ('Bah, Levison – one can easily make a fool of you') and his efforts at rationalizing Lilly's position then be violently interrupted by the anarchist bomb.

Aaron Sisson is left only with the need for a state of isolation, 'alone in possession of onself', through which he is granted a mere glimpse of the significance of the non-human and the posthuman together. Setting out into the Tuscan countryside, he rests to watch the cypress trees 'breathing and communicating, faintly moving and as it were walking in the small wind', and in a moment of 'clairvoyance' perceives:

> (T)hat our life is only a fragment of the shell of life. That there has been and will be, human life such as we do not begin to conceive. Much that is life has passed away from men, leaving us all mere bits. In the dark, mindful silence and inflection of the cypress trees, lost races, lost language, lost human ways of feeling and of knowing. Men can know as we can no more know, have felt as we can no more feel. Great life-realities gone into the darkness (*AR* 309–10).

Kangaroo and *The Plumed Serpent* pursue the possibility of beginning to conceive such posthuman alterities. They do so by fully immersing the protagonist in a culture which seems to offer a more authentic alternative to capitalism, but which by the same token pushes human being into ever greater unrecognizability. 'Culture', as I suggested in the previous chapter, is defined here as an interaction of the social and conventional with the geographical and even geological, producing alternative *physical* states of the human which inevitably call up the category of 'race'. In such states too, the mechanical-organic binary is progressively blurred even as the protagonists see themselves as escaping from capitalist mechanism. Somers and Harriet learn that the heat of the Australian continent 'thins down the blood' of British people over a period of years, an idea which Australians seemed to accept 'as a scientific fact'. Somers is soon musing on whether he wants this to happen to himself, and on the improbability of world brotherhood if 'the very blood is of different thickness on different continents' (*K* 165–6). His own thinking shows a similar kind of cultural biologism – letters from young, upper-middle class Englishmen reveal that 'all their tissues were soft and sweetish' – and the upshot of this for white Australians, who are curiously categorized as 'aboriginals', is a creatureliness inseparable from mechanism and degeneration. Jack Calcott is 'just a trifle less than human', with 'no mind, no spirit, no soul', but only 'a strong body full of energy like a machine that has got steam up, but is inactive'; this exemplifies 'The old psyche slowly disintegrating'. His wife Victoria, by contrast, is 'like a dynamo'; she 'fluttered in the air like a loose live nerve, a nerve of the sympathetic system' and, as a result, 'belonged' to her husband 'as one pole belongs to the other pole in a circuit' (*K* 201–2).

The appeal of this *kind* of mechanism for Somers is what constitutes the 'fern-dark' indifference of Australia, allowing one 'just enough grip to run the machinery of the day' and thereafter to 'let yourself drift, not to think or strain or make any effort to consciousness whatsoever'. Such ambivalence surrounding human mechanism is closely echoed in Kate Leslie's Mexico, a place where the energy is 'switched off' and there is an 'aboriginal, empty silence, as of life *withheld*'. Kate might have wished, in her flight, to escape from all 'mechanical connections' and 'mechanical cog-wheel people', but the alternative she glimpses in the 'black eyes' of the Mexican Indians is sometimes difficult to discern as such. The Mexicans are 'clogged and tangled in the elements, never able to extricate themselves, . . . held down by the serpent tangle of sun and electricity and volcanic emission'; they have been unable to form for themselves the individual 'soul' or integrity of modern ego-consciousness, and so remain a people 'without the energy of *getting on*, . . . their backbones were locked in malevolent resistance' (*PS* 145, 159). Such lumbar malevolence expresses itself in the seemingly automatic and inhuman blood-lust of ritual sacrifice, or simply in the cruelty that Kate observes in two 'ugly boys' who torture a wildfowl chick by the lakeside. Conditioned only to an elemental world that is 'monstrous', the boys are unable to see the chick as a 'soft, struggling thing finding its own fluttering way through life'; Kate 'hates' them physically, with their 'stiff broad American shoulders', 'high chests' and 'prancing, insentient walk', as if 'some motor-engine drove them at the bottom of their back' (*PS* 231–3). Yet precisely in this physique and its 'heavy, dreary nature' we find rein-scribed that 'richness' which is the condition of a genuine human alterity. Of Ramon and Cipriano, Kate is moved to observe: 'They have got more than I, they have a richness that I haven't got.'

It is worth pausing again on the instability of the mechanical and the organic in these accounts. If mechanism with its 'cog-wheel' people is the modern industrial-capitalist condition to be repudiated, there is also in the native people of Mexico and Australia a degenerative, 'dark', life-denying mechanism whose significance is precisely opposite, the denial of an *ideal-ist* mechanism characteristic of modern Enlightenment. Framing these *eval-uative* definitions, there is a more normative sense in which mechanical and organic become interchangeable as descriptions of bodily function. When, Somers muses to himself, man realizes that he has been 'sold' on the modern ideals of 'Love, Self-sacrifice and Humanity', something 'goes wrong with his whole mechanism'; elaborating on this, something 'breaks in his tissue', a 'black poison' enters his 'blood', and he follows a 'natural' course to become a 'creature' of revenge on the system and on himself (*K* 292). Mecha-nism thus sits easily next to tissue, blood, the natural and the creaturely. As if in anticipation of readerly consternation at this semantic fluidity, with its constant requirement to reassess that which might be taken for granted, the later chapters of *Kangaroo* slide into long excurses on the relationship between science and the possibility of thinking 'non-human human being' – passages which constitute some of Lawrence's most sustained speculation on science. The exercise proceeds in terms of an exhaustive negation: man is

(N)ot a creature of circumstance, neither is he a result of cause-and-effect throughout the ages, neither is he a product of evolution, neither is he a living *Mind*, part of the Universal Mind. Neither is he a complicated make-up of forces and chemicals and organs. Neither is he a term of love. Neither is he the mere instrument of God's will. None of these things (*K* 291).

This is not however the occasion of a re-installation of the solar plexus lying beyond all representation; in *Kangaroo*, as I have already suggested, those who deny they have an idea of themselves are held to be more idealist than those who haven't. In this sense the 'automatic side' of life is pervasive; here, as in numerous other occasions in his later writing, Lawrence is at pains not to underestimate the extent to which human life under capitalism is lived *as* mechanism: 'Most people are dead, and scurrying and talking in the sleep of death'. The passage from this to that rare condition in which life, 'wonderful and complex', is a condition of alert relativity – 'the true life makes no absolute statement' – may be difficult to discern. Fully aware that his theories of mass psychology would be both threatening and humiliating in the extreme, Lawrence–Somers returns in a later chapter to try to discriminate between two modes of 'herd instinct': that of the mob, which is automatic and vengeful, and that of vertebral telepathy, the 'true means of communication between animals' and the 'stupendous wits of brainless intelligence' (*K* 329).

While the latter might constitute a version of Deleuze/Guattari's anti-humanistic Lawrentian flows, it also denotes the exhaustion of *Kangaroo's* ambitions as a novel of politics and ideas. Of the political alternatives on offer, Somers might prefer the unsentimental international socialism of Struthers, but the posthuman future does not seem to lie in any political domain at all. Australia may as yet have made 'no great mistake, humanly', but its profound 'indifference', in which 'people hardly matter at all', nevertheless represents the temporal 'running down' of the 'heavy established European way of life' (*K* 379–81). In this sense the novel's centre of value lies less in Australia than in the sea and its life-forms, which consistently pull Somers 'clear' from humanity. To free oneself from the 'horrible stuffy heat' of the human, Somers yearns towards the life of the 'isolated swift fish in the big seas'; the 'swing away into cold separation' of the gannet whose 'desire' takes it plunging in a parabolic movement into the sea, and out with its prey, 'flashing into the air and white space' expresses again the anti-humanistic trajectories endorsed by Deleuze/Guattari. The dialectic remains: Somers can waver, within a page or two, from the shore and the 'other dimension' of the octopus, to the prospect of 'home and tea'. Similarly, in a luminous final chapter, Somers realizes what he loves in the 'flimsy, foundationless', bungaloid human life of the country, and the 'frail *inconspicuousness*' of its landscape; yet the necessity of saying 'adieu' seems determined by his inability to 'give up the flag of our real civilized consciousness' (*K* 383).

Somers leaves; Kate Leslie determines to go, but her final words in response to Cipriano's pleas – 'You won't let me go!' – suggest otherwise. If there is a posthuman refrain in the doctrines of Quetzalcoatl, it is that 'men are not yet men in full, and women are not yet women' (*PS* 223). With more conviction than either of its predecessors, *The Plumed Serpent* adheres to the notion of a religious-political programme and all its attendant paraphernalia – hymns, rituals, the appropriation of churches, the letters to clergy and politicians – in order to bring about a 'new conception of human life'. Kate, like Somers and Aaron Sisson, is the means by which the contradictions of this situation are anxiously rehearsed. How do you prevent a programme and its movement from becoming fixed and idealized? There is certainly, as we have seen, no idealization of the Mexican Indian, whose own mode of mechanism has its hateful side. The Mexican is, it appears, no more exempt than his civilized counterpart from Kate's anti-humanist recognition of the 'incomplete' nature of the human:

> Men and women had incomplete selves, made up of bits assembled together loosely and somewhat haphazard. Man was not created ready-made. Men to-day were half-made. Creatures that existed and functioned with certain regularity, but which ran off into a hopeless jumble of inconsequence (*PS* 115).

Lying awake and anxious at night, Kate has to persuade herself that she is not in the process of subscribing to the return of an evil Pantheism. 'No! It's not a helpless, panic reversal. It is conscious, carefully chosen. We must go back to pick up old threads' (*PS* 147). In the essay 'America, Listen to Your Own', Lawrence had made it explicit that this thread should be that of the Red race or Montezuma, in order to ensure a 'departure from the old range of emotions and sensibilities' (*P* 90–1). Despite Cipriano's vivid condemnation of American capitalist imperialism – 'You are compelled all the time to be thinking U.S.A. thoughts' – Quetzalcoatl is not a form of national socialism: Bolshevists are, as in the two previous novels, only 'the logical children of materialism'. But in this novel the 'conscious' element of the posthuman turn is that it should *be* a programme, a means of doing before being and thinking, just as ritual in Jane Harrison is a mode of action rather than of contemplation or representation. Under the pressure of this necessity, it seems that the novel cannot avoid thinning out into a series of rigidities or postures. Cipriano's education 'lay like a film of white oil over the black lake of his barbarian consciousness' (*PS* 89); the fourth hymn asks how Mexicans can be masters of the machines they cannot make but 'only break'. The people themselves, 'weary' of modernity, seem to say that 'of all things human, and humanly invented, we have had enough' (*PS* 272). But it is questionable whether the reader, by this point, has not become similarly weary of having enough of all things human. Reassessing her feelings after being 'shocked and depressed' by the ritual executions, Kate reflects that Quetzalcoatl requires of her the belief that the individual was an 'illusion and a falsification', possible only in 'the world of machines'. Why then even think of inculcating, as she had before, a 'responsibility' for achieving 'any more perfected being or identity', if the only thing is the 'Morning Star', which can 'only arise between two: or between many'? (*PS* 115, 405). Lawrence's reassessment of this question is reflected in the arresting formal shift of his last novel, *Lady Chatterley's Lover*.

5. 'To live beyond money': *Lady Chatterley's Lover*

Lady Chatterley's Lover is at once the most retrospective and the most futuristic of Lawrence's novels. Retrospective, in that it is a transparent reprise of much of his earlier fiction, but in particular of *The White Peacock*. The gamekeeper, first figured in Annable with his philosophy of the 'good animal', reappears in the form of Mellors. Both embody the principles of regeneration and resistance through the power of bodily instinct. In each, however, such principles are arrived at via education, and a pre-history of class mobility and manipulative power, implicit in their use of the vernacular, which belie their present servile position. In each, then, Lawrence plots the possibility that creatureliness might be an understanding of bodily or creaturely complexity – a mode of the posthuman, requiring advanced thought. Both Annable and Mellors know how not to know, though more persuasively in the latter case: Connie Chatterley has already enjoyed much passion with Mellors before the discovery of his bookshelf prompts another significant stage in their affair: 'So! he was a reader after all' (*LCL* 212).

The novel is also prospective in that it consistently speculates upon a posthuman future in which the human body has become expendable. Around Connie and Mellors' trangressive affair, Lawrence builds an intellectual 'set' at Wragley whose debates regularly return to questions of human evolution and the place of sexual reproduction. Four years before the publication of Aldous Huxley's *Brave New World*, the character Olive Strangeways has been reading 'a book about the future, when babies would be bred in bottles and women would be "immunized"'. In the conversation that follows from this, 'civilization' is defined in terms of the success with which it could help us to forget or even dispense with the body altogether: 'It's quite time man began to improve on his *own* nature, especially the physical side of it' (*LCL* 74–5). Later in the novel, Clifford Chatterley reassures his wife that, 'whatever God there is is slowly eliminating the guts and alimentary system from the human being, to evolve a higher, more spiritual being' (*LCL* 235). By this point, Connie's experiences with Mellors lead her to passionately endorse the opposite, the 'lovely life' of the human body; remembering Mellors' characterization of her 'nicest woman's arse', she can hardly now see her own sexuality as an 'encumbrance'. Yet it has been clear, at the beginning of the novel, that Connie in the early days of her marriage, and before Clifford's injuries, had subscribed to the fashionable evolutionary view that sex was 'merely an accident, or an adjunct: one of the curious obsolete organic processes which persisted in its own clumsiness, but was not really necessary', to the extent that even Mellors' sexual performance is submitted to coldly critical analysis: 'Yes, this was love, this ridiculous bouncing of the buttocks . . . (S)urely a complete evolution would eliminate this performance, this "function"' (*LCL* 12, 172). It seems hardly surprising that, in such a context, Connie and Clifford should have been able to discuss the possibility of having a child by artificial insemination.

If *Lady Chatterley's Lover*, then, marks a return to the redemptive appeal of the natural in *The White Peacock*, it is worth remembering how, as I suggested in Chapter 4, such a 'nature' never entirely coincides with itself. The war, which has returned Clifford Chatterley to Wragby 'more or less in bits', puts nature even more decisively into question. Connie can derive some comfort from walking in the park: she 'kicked the brown leaves of autumn, and picked the primroses of spring', but the very drabness of the prose here indicates that for her it is all 'like the simulacrum of reality', spectral and dream-like:

> The oak-leaves to her were like oak-leaves seen ruffling in a mirror, she herself was a figure somebody had read about, picking primroses that were only shadows, or memories, or words. No substance to her or anything – no touch, no contact. (*LCL* 18).

The Platonic 'simulacrum' reintroduces a critique of realist aesthetics and epistemology – a mimeticism, in other words, which is a form of idealism. Connie sees with a consciousness which feels like a mirror, in a model of representation challenged by Bergson's thought; the fact that she sees *herself* in this mode recalls the critique of Freudian idealism in Lawrence and Deleuze/Guattari. The call then for a return to 'substance' is also an appeal to the flows of 'touch' and 'contact' in the latter's desiring-machines.

To claim as much, however, is to invoke a theoretical comparison which may seem less appropriate to *Lady Chatterley* than to its predecessors. For Colin Clarke, for example, there is a sharp descent in this novel from the 'doubleness' of artistic voice in *Women in Love*, where a constructive ambivalence is maintained concerning a mechanism which might also be the source of 'genuine vitality', to a monologism in which the mechanical is 'flatly opposed to the organic and paradisal'.[16] Certainly, it is difficult not to see in the figure of Clifford Chatterley a reductive symbolic value: emasculated by the war, reliant on his mobile 'engine', throwing himself into uncompromising industrial solutions in the mode of Gerald Crich, and losing Connie to the sexual dynamism of the militant, *déclassé* working man. How convincing then is Clarke's criticism of the novel as the 'art of the cartoon strip'? Given that he finds in *The Plumed Serpent* an 'even more absolute' rejection of the machine-principle, how do we assess the nature of Lawrence's changing approach to the posthuman in his final novel?

It is clear that *Lady Chatterley* represents a certain stripping down of the elaborate cultural and political contexts for the posthuman, and a dismantling of the metafictional devices of *Kangaroo* and *The Plumed Serpent*. The tale hovers between realism and fable, the directness of this form enhanced by the fact that at its core is the simpler, that is, *relatively* unmediated, sexual relationship between two human beings. In this sense it again summarizes a tendency in Lawrence's work to dramatize the cross-class liaison, with sex as the possible means of stepping beyond the symbolic order. But how far are Connie and Mellors antithetical to Clifford and the Wragby set? In the typically Lawrentian dispersal of views across a range of characters – Lawrence's highly rationalistic means of staging debates with himself and his readers – this antithesis is not quite so secure. On her first encounter with Mellors, something about him reminds Connie of Tommy Dukes, an independent-minded brigadier-general who is central to the Wragby set, and who becomes an 'oracle' for Connie. Dukes voices views which are difficult to dissociate from those apparently endorsed by Lawrentian narratives of the posthuman. His contribution to the debate on human evolution is to look beyond the decline of sex to consider what the next, posthuman phase might actually bring – 'a civilization', he hopes, of 'real, intelligent, wholesome' men and women, for at the moment, '*We're* not men – and the women aren't women. We're only cerebrating make-shifts, mechanical and intellectual experiments' (*LCL* 75). This is recognizable as the posthuman refrain of *The Plumed Serpent*, finished off deftly by Dukes with the anti-capitalist aspiration towards a 'democracy of touch, instead of a democracy of pocket'. It 'echoes' inside Connie, who associates a 'democracy of touch' with a 'resurrection of the body'; the narrative, however, quietly tempers her enthusiasm, by pointing out that it comforts her 'as meaningless things may do' (*LCL* 76).

It is revealing, then, to set Dukes' critique alongside the sentiments of Chatterley and to Mellors. Writing to Connie while she is in Venice, Clifford finds Mrs. Bolton a 'queer specimen':

> The more I live, the more I realize what strange creatures human beings are. Some of them might just as well have a hundred legs, like a centipede, or six, like a lobster. The human consistency and dignity one has been led to expect from one's fellow-men seem actually non-existent. One doubts if they exist to any startling degree even in oneself (*LCL* 266).

This disenchantment with the *humanism* of the human is then extended into a defamiliarized vision of a world turned upside-down, where what we see as the surface of things is really 'the *bottom* of a deep ocean', the air we breathe is a kind of water, and humans are 'a species of fish'. The irony of this account becomes apparent when we consider Clifford's own growing absorption in the 'weirdness of industrial activity', by which he becomes 'almost' a creature,

> (W)ith a hard, efficient shell of an exterior and a pulpy interior, one of the amazing crabs and lobsters of the modern, industrial and financial world, invertebrates of the crustacean order, with shells of steel, like machines, and inner bodies of soft pulp . . . (*LCL* 112).

Alternatively, Connie observes her husband as he reads to her with unusual 'clapping' and 'gurgling' sounds: one of those 'strange creatures', she reflects, 'of the afterwards', with the 'sharp, cold, inflexible will of some bird, and no warmth'. Mellors, like Birkin before him, contemplates with calm pleasure the 'extermination of the human species, and the long pause that follows before some other species crops up'. His vision is of an evolution actively distorted by industrial capitalism and, familiarly, with the collusion of bolshevism as its obverse face: 'every generation breeds a more rabbity generation, with indiarubber tubing for guts and tin legs and tin faces. Tin people! It's all a steady sort of bolshevism – just killing off the human thing, and worshipping the mechanical thing. Money, money, money!' He concludes that

> (I)t's a shame, what's been done to people these last hundred years: men turned into nothing but labour-insects, and all their manhood taken away, and all their real life. I'd wipe the machines off the face of the earth again, and end the industrial epoch, absolutely, like a black mistake (*LCL* 217, 220).

Mellors' Luddism has an Erewhonian sweep, seeming to confirm Clarke's diagnosis of a simplified binary of mechanism pitted against organicism. Yet this is surely undermined by the spread of views, which suggest that the discourse on the posthuman is a *shared* area of debate characterized by surprising overlaps, subtle differences and an uncertain distinction between the mechanical and the organic. Even as Mellors condemns the rise of capitalist machinery, his version of evolution shows a curious ambivalence: tin and indiarubber are the same as 'rabbitiness', posthuman prosthetic interventionism is mixed up with creatureliness. So too, as Chatterley commits himself to the industrial subjugation of matter, does he become a crustacean invertebrate, with a machine-like shell and a body of soft pulp – a creature simultaneously lower than the human in the evolutionary order, and yet of the 'afterwards'. While Chatterley himself comes to the uneasy realization that evolution may not be all he thought it was, the vision is tainted by his snobbery and superiority towards the lower orders, and becomes a pretext for a version of transcendence: it is our 'immortal destiny' for the soul at last to shoot up out of the depths, confirming our 'immortal nature'. But if the machine, as Colin Clarke notes of *The Rainbow* and *Women in Love*, is inevitably *within* us, it is within us all, crustacean bosses and labour-insects alike. We cannot, the novel implies, have our anti-mechanism on easy terms, as if from a safe distance. Connie's terror of the industrial masses reminds us of a consistent refrain, especially in the Brangwen sisters of *Women in Love*. She indulges in speculation about the Tevershall coal-miners as peculiar, non-human products of evolution, 'elementals, . . . animas of coal and iron and clay', who might become extinct when the coal that gave rise to them also disappeared. But the narrative intimates how easily evolutionary theory can become fancifully indulgent: she 'was glad to be home, to bury her head in the sand' (*LCL* 160).

Who or what has the last word? The question has a particular resonance for Lawrence's final novel. The case of Tommy Dukes suggests that the answer is consistent with the work that has gone before: there is no last, or final, word. With his notion of humans as 'cerebrating makeshifts, mechanical and intellectual experiments', and his alternative 'democracy of touch', we are invited to think of Dukes as a plausible, 'oracular' spokesperson. Why, then, Connie's insinuation of meaninglessness? The answer here is that, for all his astuteness, what Dukes produces is 'talk'. We are reminded that even the most seductive or convincing of formulations must always be submitted to critique, can never be assumed to be the last word.

Lawrence's novel seems then to embody the true alternative in deeds rather than words: while Dukes talks about a democracy of touch, Mellors and Connie begin to realize it. After Kate Leslie's disillusionment with the individual, and her perplexity at the idea that 'perfected being' is *only* a condition of relationship, between two or many, *Lady Chatterley's Lover* returns to the representative figure of the individual human, in Mellors, in a relationship of duality. Lawrence strives, in this sexual relationship, to figure a model of interpersonal 'tenderness' capable of standing outside of social and political structures. Yet, at the same time, the decision is intensely political, and by political we mean also linguistic and representational. 'It's the one insane taboo left: sex as a natural and vital thing', observes Duncan Forbes (*LCL* 264). Continuing the effort of the later fiction to confront the reader with an unsettling of humanist taboos, the strategy in *Lady Chatterley* is to focus this on the language of so-called obscenity. Words, like machines, mean nothing in themselves, are never 'last', but function only in their appropriations and relations. In Mellors' lexicon, they are transformed in a way which makes them unrecognizable and at the same time *loci* for new modes of thinking. Thus, in response to Connie's assumption that 'cunt' and 'fuck' are the same in their general obscenity,

'Nay nay! Fuck's only what you do. Animals fuck. But cunt's a lot more than that. It's thee, dost see: an' tha'rt a lot besides an animal, aren't ter? – even ter fuck! Cunt! Eh, that's the beauty o' thee, lass!' (*LCL* 178).

Whether such discriminations help the relationship to transcend the phallic worship of which it has been accused remains debateable; we can only say that in Mellors, inevitably the redemptive male to some extent, Lawrence strove for a *difference* at the heart of the familiar: he had 'too much of the woman in him', for the army; he wants men to wear tight red trousers and little white jackets; he has a poise and a 'breeding' which confounds class structures. Finally too, *Lady Chatterley's Lover* is not devoid of a programme; voiced by Mellors, it is given the last word, in the sense that it emerges in the letter to Connie which closes the novel. The only way to 'solve the industrial problem' is to 'train the people to be able to live and live in hand-someness, without needing to spend . . . (T)o live beyond money' (*LCL* 300). Lawrence's last novel thus presents the ideological contest between two versions of the posthuman: one, a capitalist utopia-dystopia characterized by the gradual supercession of the body; and the other, a post-capitalist future in which our bodiliness is renewed and enhanced. The 'machine' haunts both versions, but in a dialectical sense which Lawrence's work had stead-fastly pursued. 'The only difference between a human machine and an iron machine is that the latter can come to an utter state of rest, the former cannot' (*SM* 28). As T.H. Huxley might have put it, this difference, registered in the word 'only', is at once vast and extremely tenuous.

Postscript: On Abstraction

'One contemporary belief likely to stupefy future generations', writes N. Katherine Hayles, 'is the postmodern orthodoxy that the body is primarily, if not entirely, a linguistic and discursive construction.' While a certain version of the cybernetic posthuman strips information of its body, the linguistic turn in the humanities, for example in Michel Foucault's archaeology of knowledge, spins the body into a 'play of discourse systems'.[1] Hayles argues that such 'beliefs' or ideas can only be arrived at through a process of *abstraction*; her narrative of cybernetics in postwar America demonstrates 'how much had to be erased in order to arrive at such abstractions as bodiless information'. Similarly, while far from anti-Foucauldian in her own thinking, Hayles feels that general systemic concepts such as that of the Panopticon lead Foucault to construct the 'body' as an abstraction which diverts attention away from 'actual bodies' and their specificities, as well as their modes of resistance to power.

But what do we mean by 'abstraction' in such contexts, and what is the problem with it? The narrowly literal sense of withdrawing or removing something expands, in 'abstraction', into a quality of idealism, in which the thought processes withdraw, whether through selection or through generalization, from the concrete and complex particularities of life: as Jane Harrison had it, a conscious 'dragging away' by the intellect from 'actual things objectively existing'. Abstraction is, Hayles concedes, a necessary element in all theorizing, but in the case of the posthuman-as-bodiless information, it risks, or enables, the failure to see the trees, 'the infinite multiplicity of our interactions with the real', for the wood. How then do we take account of the 'real'? If we were to use the terms 'material' or 'materialism' to designate this aspiration, how do we prevent materialism from becoming abstraction? What, in fact, would a mode of thought without abstraction look like? Is there a materialism that somehow avoids the inevitable pitfalls of thought – a materialism, as Samuel Beckett might have put it, so material that materialism was not the word?

We are, Lawrence asserted, 'ideal animals – idea-making animals'; there is,

233

moreover, 'a great fascination in a completely effected idealism' (*PII* 626; *FU* 211). An idea, or ideal, is nevertheless, he explains, 'only a fixed, static entity, an abstraction, an extraction from the living body of life' (*P* 711). In the dilemma of thinking matter, Lawrence confronted the unavailability to the conscious mind of its own material ground – a version of what Hayles describes as the now 'familiar story' of how 'deconstruction exposed the inability of systems to posit their own origins'.[2] We are aware of what *is*, but reason, being dependent upon it, cannot embrace its own condition. Lyotard dramatizes the view that this is an absolute horizon: 'after the sun's death there won't be a thought to know that its death took place'.[3] Thought *cannot*, as Hayles also emphasizes, go on without a body. Hence Elizabeth Costello's son comforts her with the thought that 'it will soon be over'; death is the only sure release from the tortured awareness, which she shares with Lawrence, that reason cannot be relinquished, even when it discloses its own limits and impotence.

Lawrence concluded from this dilemma that our goal could only be to know how not to know: that is, how to *be*, to live dynamically 'from the source' rather than from ideas in the head, and so on. But we should not, as I have tried to show, be fooled into thinking of this as a crude irrationalism. 'We have to know all', he maintained, in a typical modernist ploy, 'before we can know that knowing is nothing' (*SM* 214).[4] 'Knowing all' meant continuing to *think together* the ideal and the animal, the thought and the matter, without abstracting one or the other, glimpsing thus the co-existence of the inseparable and the irreconcilable. Another version of the posthuman would, of course, add the machine into this equation.

In her early critical work, N. Katherine Hayles was one of the first to associate Lawrence's work with the context of relativity physics, identifying in his thought a 'both/and' rather than 'either/or' epistemology.[5] We remember, of course, 'I would contradict myself on every page . . .'. In his response to Earl Brewster's suggestion that he set out his philosophy, Lawrence showed the non-philosopher's wariness of dialectic. Yet Lawrence's is a philosophical oeuvre, in which the centrality of the contradictory is consistently evident. The ant is 'more vividly alive' than the pine-tree; the ant and the pine-tree are alive in 'different ways', and therefore 'incomparable, incommensurable'.

> But one truth does not displace another. Even apparently contradictory truths do not replace one another. Logic is far too coarse to make the subtle distinctions life demands (*RDP* 357).

Similarly it was 'no paradox' to say that 'your idealist alone is a perfect materialist' (*P* 711):

> It is obvious that the ideal becomes a mechanical principle, if it be applied to the affective soul as a fixed motive. An ideal established in control of

the passional soul is no more and no less than a supreme machine-principle. And a machine, as we know, is the active unit of the material world. Thus we see how it is in the end that pure idealism is identical with pure materialism, and the most ideal peoples are the most completely material. Ideal and material are identical. The ideal is but the god in the machine – the little, fixed, machine-principle which works the human psyche automatically (*FU* 211).

The emphasis of this book has been that Lawrence started from, and continually aspired towards the possibility of, a materialist knowledge, even as he was apt to condemn materialism-as-mechanism in its popular, non-dialectical sense. 'Ideal' and 'material' hold each other in place, are two sides of the same coin – are, even, 'identical'. Lawrence thinks dialectically about terms which are not, as it were, meant to be recognised as dialectically related. He saw 'materialist' thinkers glimpse the fact that we are 'ideal animals' and wrestle with the consequences of this for materialism itself. In the end, they tended to persevere with an *idea* of matter as a thing-in-itself, consistent and predictable, unrolling 'automatically' in the patterns of the nebular theory of the universe and 'throwing off life as a by-product' in the theory of natural selection (*SM* 178). This was a convenient idea, licensing the control and colonization of the world's resources in the name of scientific 'progress', but it was as deluded, Lawrence felt, as the 'funny sort of superstition' that the human being was a bodily machine with a mind inside it.

Abstraction was also a key term in Lawrence's critical vocabulary. 'We have abstracted the universe into Matter and Force, we have abstracted men and women into separate personalities . . .' (*PII* 512). Here, in his reflections on *Lady Chatterley's Lover*, abstraction in epistemology is in direct connection with abstraction in human sensual life: in each case, *relationship*, with the universe or with each other, is problematized. The symbolic solution of the fiction lay in the domain of sexuality, but we often glimpse in the discursive writing an alternative direction not taken: that of work. If we are living a 'greater and greater abstraction from the physical', then this is expressed in a progressive 'revulsion' from physical labour: the 'aim is to abstract as far as possible', and 'science is our only help' (*PII* 589, 584). Instincts can change, and 'in the most amazing fashion'; one task of a really alert science would be to maintain a full consciousness of this.

Abstraction in this sense lay, Lawrence felt, at the idealist root of a didactic science that was not sufficiently reflexive to recognize the contradictions that informed it, becoming thus a barrier to dialectical thinking. Is abstraction, then, a universal feature of human thought? Lawrence's answer would seem to be yes: while man is 'balanced between spontaneous creativity and mechanical-material activity', his 'tendency' is to allow the desires and impulses to 'automatize into fixed aspirations or ideals'. This is our greatest 'temptation', our 'fall', and 'all our education should be a guarding against it' (*P* 714). But the alertness deriving from such education would also show us that abstraction can itself become an idealized entity. The tendency to associate abstraction with a universal human disposition towards a certain purity or withdrawal of human thought is itself a product of abstraction. Abstraction is also a historical entity, gaining ascendancy as an idealized category under certain ideological conditions.

For Adorno and Horkheimer, abstraction is the 'tool' of an Enlightenment which is 'totalitarian', and as such,

> (T)reats its objects as did fate, the notion of which it rejects: it liquidates them. Under the leveling domination of abstraction (which makes everything in nature repeatable), and of industry (for which abstraction ordains repetition), the freed themselves finally came to form that 'herd' which Hegel has declared to be the result of the Enlightenment.[6]

Presupposing a distance between subject and object, abstraction licenses violent mastery of impersonal forces.[7] Science displaces the 'specific representations' of magic and the unique holiness of the individual creature ('what happens to the enemy's spear, hair or name, also happens to the individual') with abstract identity and universal interchangeability. In his writing on the fiction of Nathaniel Hawthorne, Lawrence likewise thinks dialectically about Enlightenment. Is it not, after all, in the ancient, esoteric model of science that mastery obtains? The alchemist 'sought to perform the supreme act of authority and command . . . (H)e would *compel* the material world to yield up its secret to him' (*SM* 163). But no: this is a unique and individual relationship, in which the magician-scientist and the elements are mutually dependent. The mastery of modern science lies, paradoxically and by contrast, in its humility, impersonality, 'self-abnegation': assuming a passive attitude before phenomena, waiting for the laws of nature to reveal *themselves*, the scientist derives a power based on abstract truth – 'Man submits, and in submission triumphs' (*SM* 165).

Enlightenment abstraction, with its generalized interchangeability of value and downplaying of material instantiation, is given a more precise inflection in the analysis of the German Marxist thinker Alfred Sohn-Rethel. For him, abstraction is the inherent thought-form of a culture of commodity fetishism, with its displacement of use value by exchange value. Abstraction, in its present form, coincides, in other words, with the rise of the money economy. Marx, Sohn-Rethel argues, had shown in the *Critique of Political Economy* (1859) and in *Capital* (1886) that abstraction was in this sense *not* the exclusive property of thought, but was tied to money, whether coinage or banknotes, as 'an abstract *thing* which, strictly speaking, is a contradiction in terms'. Abstraction is therefore intensified in the concept of capital, a society of commodity capitalism constituting a 'purely abstract set of relations'. Sohn-Rethel writes:

Anybody who carries coins in his pocket and understands their function bears in his mind, whether or not he is aware of it, ideas which, no matter how hazily, reflect the postulates of the exchange abstraction. To go about his marketing activities of buying and selling and to take advantage of the power of his money no clearer awareness is required. But to reflect upon the ideas involved, to become conscious of them, to formulate them, to take stock of them and to work out their interrelations, to probe into their uses and implications, to recognise their antithetic contrast to the world of the senses and yet their intrinsic reference to it, etc. – this does not follow automatically from the use of coined money, it constitutes a clearly definable conditioned potentiality inherent in a monetary economy.[8]

Sohn-Rethel speculates on the manner in which capitalism might be able to raise an awareness of its own constitutive contradictions. This, for a thinker interested in revolution, must always exist as an inherent potentiality. But Enlightenment *cannot* recognize itself and the intimate relationship with its other, without losing the promise of domination. It must remain non-dialectical, keeping a safe distance between subject and object. It thus sustains a multiple division of labour: reason and unreason; heads (pure thought) and hands (manual work); science and art; organic and mechanical. 'A particular linguistic structure', writes Raymond Williams, 'the separation and contrast between "nature" and "man"', was 'largely developed in periods of the dominance of idealist and humanist thought.' 'Nature' and 'Man' are thus abstractions, preventing us from fully recognizing a dialectical relation. In the 'actual world' – the world, for posthuman theory, of distributed cognition – we have, Williams maintains, 'mixed our labour with the earth, our forces with its forces too deeply to be able to draw back and separate either out'. But Enlightenment makes it very difficult to see all of our products, and not just the benign ones, *as* products; the slagheaps, polluted rivers and moors, slums and traffic jams, are 'by-products', objects in which we are unable to see ourselves.[9]

For a sense of how the human can become the abstract repository of a wishful, non-dialectical, *humanistic* thinking, we tend to gravitate back towards the writing of F.R. Leavis. The iterative, self-evident value of the human is embodied in Leavis's insistence that science, while 'obviously of great cultural importance to mankind', is simply antithetical to the exercise of human responsibility. 'In the rapidly changing external civilization of the technological age', he writes, it is crucial that a sense of human responsibility for human need and human ends, charged with human experience, must prevail:

To suggest otherwise is to propose leaving the human consequences of the process of change (which more and more manifestly have their own

momentum and internal logic – which is often *anti*-human) to be determined, in so far as human motives are involved and tell, by the crude
promptings of a starved and perverted sense of human nature – the sense
we see being generated around us.[10]

Leavis misrecognizes that his solution in its abstraction is part of the non-
dialectical, Enlightenment problem: 'science' and the 'human' are only
antitheses in that instrumentalist logic which is the very object of his
critique. There is no sense of the capitalist *appropriation* of science, or of a
willingness to recognise it as such.

There is, nevertheless, a peculiar resonance in Leavis's appeal for contestation and shared involvement in the direction of technological change, and
in his determination not to leave the field open to the 'crude', anti-human
promptings of a 'starved and perverted sense of human nature'. In her programme for posthumanism, Hayles is equally concerned to counter a nar-
rowed, recidivist version of the posthuman announcing itself as the bodiless
cybernetic future. This, she reminds us, is a reinscription of the established
exercise of wealth and power, clearing the field of the troublesome particu-
larity of human bodies in order to facilitate the smooth and abstract movement of capital. Disembodied intelligence is a new form of the autonomous,
individual will; mastery through this will is, however, 'merely the story consciousness tells itself to explain results that actually come about through
chaotic dynamics and emergent structures'.[11] Hayles' distributed, dissipative
posthuman may call the concept of human nature into question, while at
the same time enriching human nature as an expression of the relatedness
and undecidability of the cyborg.

My interest here, as the reader may by now have surmised, is in how
Lawrence can come to figure, through his critique of abstraction, in such
apparently diverse critical projects: the passionate anti-scientific humanism
of Leavis, and the embrace, in Hayles, of a dialectical posthumanism firmly
rooted in science, linking modernist relativity physics to the new epistemology of the cyborg. 'Our last wall', Lawrence wrote in concluding 'Reflections on the Death of a Porcupine', 'is the golden wall of money. This is
a fatal wall. It cuts us off from life, from vitality, from the alive sun and
the alive earth, as *nothing* can' (*RDP* 363). In typically dialectical mode,
Lawrence turns the sheer abstraction of money on its head: it is precisely
what Catherine Gallagher calls money's 'attempted disappearing act', from
coins to paper to numbers on a computer screen, and the consequent reduction of human relations and difference to the abstract interchangeability of
capital, that builds a solid wall between humans and life.[12] The critique of
abstraction as a mode of commodity relation is implicit across his work.
Ursula Brangwen's condemnation of her university professors, offering
'commercial commodity that could be turned to good account in the exam-

ination room' (*TR* 404), anticipates Jean-François Lyotard's theory of a post-modern 'exteriorization of knowledge', in which the relationship between suppliers and users of knowledge increasingly resembles that between the producers and consumers of commodities.[13] In 'Democracy', Lawrence maintained, the ideal unit of human subjectivity is the 'possessor of property' (*P* 717). The perilous commodification of love in his fictions is exemplified by Hannelle's 'Captain's Doll', which is eventually displayed in a shop window; Mellors' anti-capitalist programme is a final diatribe against the insidious power of this abstraction.

Lawrence then had little or none of Leavis's implicit faith in the absolute value of the human; he knew how far the concept itself could be colonized and compromised. The human could only be thought in its dialectical relation to the non-human, the material and mechanical, in line with a twentieth-century epistemology stressing the relativity of all things. Nor should this relativity itself lie beyond dialectic, however. If all is relative, then relativity is an absolute. In the example of Jamesian pragmatism, Lawrence had seen how far even relativity itself could be appropriated as a non-dialectical ethic for the marketplace, in which truth is what works, or sells, best. In this case, then, to be dialectical is to hold to the possibility of the absolute; to knowledge, however fragile and provisional. Matter is our ground, to which consciousness is tied, but matter is complex, flowing, unpredictable. The 'special character' of materialism, notes Raymond Williams, 'is its rigorous openness to physical evidence'; but this occurs in strict conjunction with the labour of conceptualization, by which materialism 'defines and redefines its procedures, its findings and its concepts, and in the course of this moves beyond one after another "materialism"'.[14]

Lawrence tried to be vigilant about the lure of the abstract and the non-dialectical in his own writing. Readers will note a distinct shift in his prose from around the writing of the essay 'Democracy' (1919), just after he had discovered in the Russian writer Leo Shestov a loosely disconnected, epigrammatic and indifferent style which he described as 'tweaking the nose of European idealism' (*P* 216). It is evident in the distinction between the two central presentations of the solar plexus theory: the lyrical, even rhythmic and incantatory, yet serious and rationally argued prose of *Psychoanalysis and the Unconscious*, and the knockabout, impatient and irreverent style of *Fantasia of the Unconscious* – 'Help me to be serious, dear reader'. Its implications are most precisely condensed in an essay, 'Climbing down Pisgah' (1924), which derives its theme from *Fantasia*. If humanity is now, with the help of aeroplanes and tractors, laying the 'tin cans' of civilization on Everest, the North Pole and the Sahara, then 'of the thing we call human, I've had enough'. But the essay is also a commitment to the 'venture of consciousness' – 'the joy for ever, the agony for ever, and above all the fight for ever'. The venture is expressed in an extraordinary and enigmatic pronouncement on the laws of science, all of which are 'but the settled habits of a vast living incomprehensibility' which can be broken 'in a moment of great extremity'.

Behind this, the creative scepticism deriving from materialist tradition, and the determination to shake the complacencies of scientific ideology (for a 'self-satisfied rationalism', wrote A.N. Whitehead, 'is in effect a form of anti-rationalism'[15]), combine with a belief in the sheer unpredictability of matter. Human agency is central: it is we who can break and supersede in a moment of great extremity, perhaps. Already we are, 'as human beings, evolved and cultured far beyond the taboos which are inherent in our culture' (*PII* 489). This further, 'extreme' posthuman possibility, whatever future it signals, must be a conscious decision, a decision to fully know how not to know, demonstrating that we are 'meditative fowl who have thought the thing out and decided to migrate' (*P* 740–4). To do so, in other words, we need to retreat from the non-dialectical knowledge of 'One Intelligence', and slide down from Pisgah, the vantage point of the promised land, on the material seat of our pants. We are, after all, only human.

Notes

Introduction

1. Walter Benjamin, *The Arcades Project*, trans. Howard Eiland and Kevin McLaughlin (Cambridge, Mass. and London: Harvard University Press, 1999), p. 626.
2. Neil Belton, 'Candied Porkers: British Scorn of the Scientific', in Francis Spufford and Jenny Uglow (eds), *Cultural Babbage: Technology, Time and Invention* (London and Boston: Faber and Faber, 1997), p. 260.
3. F.R. Leavis, *Nor Shall My Sword: Discourses on Pluralism, Compassion and Social Hope* (London: Chatto and Windus, 1972), pp. 88, 97, 142.
4. See, for example, Herbert Grierson, *The Background of English Literature and Other Essays* (1925; Harmondsworth: Peregrine, 1962), and Basil Willey, *The Seventeenth-Century Background* (1934; Harmondsworth: Peregrine, 1962). For an analysis of Leavis's advocacy of history of science for students of English, see my '"Taking Possession of the Ordinary Man's Mind": Literary Studies and History of Science', *Literature and History*, second series, 1:1 (Spring 1990), pp. 58–74.
5. Roland Barthes, 'From Science to Literature', in *The Rustle of Language*, trans. Richard Howard (Oxford: Basil Blackwell, 1986), pp. 3–10.
6. Leavis, *Nor Shall My Sword*, p. 89.
7. Michael Hardt and Antonio Negri, *Empire* (Cambridge, Mass. and London: Harvard University Press, 2000), pp. 91–2.
8. Donna J. Haraway, 'A Cyborg Manifesto: Science, Technology and Socialist-Feminism in the Late Twentieth Century', in *Simians, Cyborgs, and Women: The Reinvention of Nature* (London: Free Association Books, 1991), p. 154.
9. Belton, 'Candied Porkers', p. 260.
10. See, for example, Roger Ebbatson, *Lawrence and the Nature Tradition: A Theme in English Fiction, 1859–1914* (Brighton: Harvester, 1980) and *The Evolutionary Self: Forster, Hardy, Lawrence* (Brighton: Harvester, 1982).
11. Alan Sokal, 'Transgressing the Boundaries: Toward a Transformative Hermeneutics of Quantum Gravity', *Social Text* 46/47, 14:1/2, Spring/Summer 1996, 217–52.
12. Bruce Robbins, 'Modernism and Literary Realism: Response', in George Levine (ed.), *Realism and Representation: Essays on the Problem of Realism in Relation to Science, Literature and Culture* (Madison: University of Wisconsin Press, 1993), pp. 225–31.
13. Eugene Goodheart, *The Utopian Vision of D.H. Lawrence* (Chicago: University of Chicago Press, 1963).

1 Thinking Matter

1. The phrase is from Pete A.Y. Gunter, 'Introduction' to Bergson, *Creative Evolution*, p. xxvii.
2. Terry Eagleton, *Ideology: An Introduction* (London: Verso, 1991), p. 159.
3. Friedrich Nietzsche, *The Birth of Tragedy* (1872), in *The Birth of Tragedy and The Genealogy of Morals*, trans. F. Golffing (New York: Doubleday Anchor, 1956), p. 111.

4. Winwood Reade, *The Martyrdom of Man* (1872; London: Watts and Co., 1933), p. 331.
5. Friedrich Nietzsche, *The Genealogy of Morals* (1887), in *The Birth of Tragedy and the Genealogy of Morals*, pp. 217–18.
6. See Edward Nehls, *D.H. Lawrence: A Composite Biography*, Vol. III (Madison: University of Wisconsin, 1959), p. 287.
7. A.J. Balfour, 'Creative Evolution and Philosophic Doubt', *Hibbert Journal* October 1911, p. 6.
8. J.M. Robertson, 'The Theism of Earl Balfour' (1923), in *Spoken Essays* (London: Watts and Co., 1925), p. 171.
9. May Chambers Holbrook, in Nehls, *D.H. Lawrence: A Composite Biography*, Vol. III, p. 593.
10. Jessie Chambers, *D.H. Lawrence: A Personal Record* (1935; Cambridge: Cambridge University Press, 1980), pp. 112–13.
11. Aldous Huxley, 'Introduction' to *Letters of D.H. Lawrence* (1932), in Harry T. Boulton (ed.), *The Collected Letters of D.H. Lawrence*, Vol. 2 (London: Heinemann, 1962), p. 1252.
12. Aldous Huxley, *Literature and Science* (New Haven: Leete's Island Books, 1963), p. 24.
13. Linda Ruth Williams, *Sex in the Head: Visions of Femininity and Film in D.H. Lawrence* (Hemel Hempstead: Harvester Wheatsheaf, 1993), p. 45.
14. For this mapping of existentialism, see William Barrett, *Irrational Man: A Study in Existential Philosophy* (New York: Doubleday Anchor, 1962).
15. Nietzsche, *Genealogy of Morals*, p. 179.
16. Theodor W. Adorno and Max Horkheimer, *Dialectic of Enlightenment* (1944; trans. John Cumming; London and New York: Verso, 1995), pp. 3–39, 84.
17. In Sir Compton Mackenzie's novel *The West Wind of Love*, Daniel Rayner, the explicitly Lawrentian figure, declares: 'I want to find people who think here', pointing to the fly of his trousers, to the surprise of passing country-folk. See Nehls, *D.H. Lawrence: A Composite Biography*, Vol. II, p. 27.
18. T.S. Eliot, *After Strange Gods: A Primer of Modern Heresy* (London: Faber and Faber, 1934), p. 58.
19. Huxley, 'Introduction', p. 1259.
20. Eliseo Vivas, *D.H. Lawrence: The Failure and Triumph of Art* (London: Allen and Unwin, 1961), p. 92.
21. Michael Black, *D.H. Lawrence: The Early Fiction* (Basingstoke: Macmillan, 1986), pp. 148–9.
22. Percy Bysshe Shelley, 'A Defense of Poetry', in Harold Bloom (ed.), *The Selected Poetry and Prose of Shelley* (1966; New York: Meridian, 1978), pp. 441–2.
23. Raymond Williams, *Culture and Society 1780–1950* (London: Chatto and Windus, 1958), p. 43.
24. See, for example, John Beer, 'Lawrence's Counter-Romanticism', in Gamini Salgado and G.K. Das (eds), *The Spirit of D.H. Lawrence: Centenary Studies* (Basingstoke: Macmillan, 1988), pp. 46–74, and Robert Montgomery, *The Visionary D.H. Lawrence: Beyond Philosophy and Art* (Cambridge: Cambridge University Press, 1994).
25. Vivas, *D.H. Lawrence: The Failure and Triumph of Art*, p. 92.
26. Michael Black, *D.H. Lawrence: The Early Fiction*, p. 90.
27. F.R. Leavis, *D.H. Lawrence: Novelist* (1955; Harmondsworth: Penguin, 1976), p. 29.
28. Leavis, *Nor Shall My Sword*, pp. 142–3.

29. F.R. Leavis, *Thought, Words and Creativity: Art and Thought in Lawrence* (London: Chatto and Windus, 1976), p. 45.
30. Leavis, *Nor Shall My Sword*, p. 98.
31. Donald R. Benson, 'Facts and Constructs: Victorian Humanists and Scientific Theorists on Scientific Knowledge', in James Paradis amd Thomas Postlewait (eds), *Victorian Science and Victorian Values: Literary Perspectives* (New Brunswick: Rutgers University Press, 1985), pp. 299–318.
32. Benson, 'Facts and Constructs', p. 303.
33. From Nehls, *D.H. Lawrence: A Composite Biography*, Vol. II, p. 119.
34. Vivas, *D.H. Lawrence: The Failure and Triumph of Art*; David Ellis, 'Poetry and Science in the Psychology Books', in David Ellis and Howard Mills, *D.H. Lawrence's Non-Fiction: Art, Thought and Genre* (Cambridge: Cambridge University Press, 1988), pp. 67–97.
35. Francis Mulhern, *The Moment of 'Scrutiny'* (London: New Left Books, 1979), p. 297.
36. Chambers, *D.H. Lawrence: A Personal Record*, pp. 112, 86.
37. John Worthen, *D.H. Lawrence: The Early Years 1885–1912* (Cambridge: Cambridge University Press, 1991), p. 184; Daniel Schneider, *The Consciousness of D.H. Lawrence: An Intellectual Biography* (Kansas and London: University of Kansas Press/Eurospan, 1987), p. 8.
38. Robert Alan Donovan, 'Mill, Arnold and Scientific Humanism', in Paradis and Postlewait (eds), *Victorian Science and Victorian Values*, p. 189.
39. Quoted in Nehls, *D.H Lawrence: A Composite Biography*, Vol. III, p. 472.
40. Francis Fukuyama, *Our Posthuman Future: Consequences of the Biotechnology Revolution* (London: Profile Books, 2002), p. 7.
41. Haraway, 'A Cyborg Manifesto', p. 154.
42. Haraway, 'A Cyborg Manifesto', pp. 151, 154.
43. N. Katherine Hayles, *How We Became Posthuman: Virtual Bodies in Cybernetics, Literature, and Informatics* (Chicago and London: University of Chicago Press, 1999), pp. 2–3.
44. From a website co-authored by Alvin Toffler, and quoted in Hayles, *How We Became Posthuman*, p. 18.
45. Michel Foucault, *The Order of Things: An Archaeology of the Human Sciences* (1966; London and New York, Tavistock/Routledge, 1974), p. 386.
46. Hayles, *How We Became Posthuman*, p. 286.
47. Reade, *The Martyrdom of Man*, p. 330.
48. Hayles, *How We Became Posthuman*, p. 201.
49. Sean Watson, 'The New Bergsonism: Discipline, Subjectivity and Freedom', *Radical Philosophy* 92 (November/December 1998), pp. 6–16.
50. Gilles Deleuze, *Bergsonism*, trans. Hugh Tomlinson and Barbara Habberjam (New York: Zone Books, 1991), p. 25.
51. Watson, 'The New Bergsonism', p. 13.
52. The first example is from the letter to Edward Garnett of 5.June 1914; the second is from the essay 'Why the Novel Matters', *Phoenix*, p. 533; the third is from *The Symbolic Meaning*, p. 135.
53. Leo Bersani, *A Future for Astyanax: Character and Desire in Literature* (Boston and Toronto: Little, Brown and Co., 1976), p. x.
54. Ed Jewinski, 'The Phallus in D.H. Lawrence and Jacques Lacan', *D.H. Lawrence Review* 21 (1989), p. 20.
55. Williams, *Culture and Society*, pp. 199–215.
56. Schneider, *The Consciousness of D.H. Lawrence*, p. 66; Jonathan Arac, *Critical*

Genealogies: Historical Situations for Postmodern Literary Studies (New York: Columbia University Press, 1989), p. 149.
57. Anne Fernihough, *D.H. Lawrence: Aesthetics and Ideology* (Oxford: Clarendon Press, 1993).
58. Fernihough, *D.H. Lawrence: Aesthetics and Ideology*, p. 128.
59. Colin Clarke, *River of Dissolution: D.H. Lawrence and English Romanticism* (London: Routledge and Kegan Paul, 1969), pp. 72, 74.

2 Science, Ideology and the 'New'

1. D.H. Lawrence, *The Prussian Officer and other stories* (1914; London: Granada, 1984), p. 222.
2. J. Morrell and A. Thackray, *Gentlemen of Science: Early Years of the British Association for the Advancement of Science* (Oxford: Clarendon Press, 1981), pp. 11–12, 22, 224.
3. Chambers, *D.H. Lawrence: A Personal Record*, p. 84.
4. John Worthen, *D.H. Lawrence: The Early Years*, pp. 177, 173.
5. Stuart Macintyre, *A Proletarian Science: Marxism in Britain, 1917–1933* (London: Lawrence and Wishart, 1986), p. 106.
6. Graham Holderness, *D.H. Lawrence: History, Ideology and Fiction* (Dublin: Gill and Macmillan Humanities Press, 1982), p. 91. Working-class memoirs of the period show, in a recurrent pattern, the study of natural science and history undermining religious belief; see Macintyre, *A Proletarian Science*, p. 126.
7. Jonathan Rose, *The Intellectual Life of the British Working Classes* (New Haven and London: Yale University Press, 2002), p. 216.
8. Both versions are to be found in D.H. Lawrence, *Study of Thomas Hardy and Other Essays*, ed. Bruce Steele (Cambridge: Cambridge University Press, 1985), pp. 221–9 and 133–42.
9. Chambers, *D.H. Lawrence: A Personal Record*, p. 120.
10. Wallace Martin, *The New Age under Orage: Chapters in English Cultural History* (Manchester: Manchester University Press, 1967), pp. 18–19.
11. Martin, *The New Age under Orage*, pp. 2–3.
12. For an elaboration of this theory of the performative, see for example Judith Butler, *Gender Trouble: Feminism and the Subversion of Identity* (New York and London: Routledge, 1990).
13. Chambers, *D.H. Lawrence: A Personal Memoir*, p. 34. See also H.A. Mason, 'D.H. Lawrence and *The White Peacock*', *Cambridge Quarterly* 7 (1977), p. 225, and the (contrasting) reminiscences of Earl H. Brewster and Witter Bynner in Nehls, *D.H. Lawrence: A Composite Biography*, Vol. II, pp. 60 and 233.
14. See Holderness, *D.H. Lawrence: History, Ideology and Fiction*.
15. Ezra Pound, 'A Retrospect', in *Literary Essays of Ezra Pound*, ed. T.S. Eliot (London: Faber, 1974), pp. 12, 6.
16. For further treatment of the double-bind for women in Lawrence, see Hilary Simpson, *D.H. Lawrence and Feminism* (London: Croom Helm, 1982), and Cornelia Nixon, *D.H. Lawrence and the Turn against Women* (Berkeley: University of California Press, 1986).
17. Sally Ledger, *The New Woman: Fiction and Feminism at the Fin de Siècle* (Manchester and New York: Manchester University Press, 1997).
18. Anne Smith, 'A New Adam and a New Eve', in Anne Smith (ed.), *Lawrence and Women* (London: Vision Press, 1980), p. 13.

19. Smith, 'A New Adam and a New Eve', p. 27.
20. Ann Oakley, *Subject Women* (Oxford: Martin Robertson, 1981), p. 18.
21. Peter Middleton, *The Inward Gaze: Maculinity and Subjectivity in Modern Culture* (London and New York: Routledge, 1992), p. 73.

3 Writing Matter: Science, Language and Materialism

1. Montgomery, *The Visionary D.H. Lawrence*, pp. 42, 35.
2. Marie Cariou, 'Bergson: The Keyboards of Forgetting', in John Mullarkey (ed.), *The New Bergson* (Manchester and New York: Manchester University Press, 1999), pp. 99–117. Cariou provides a particularly succinct summary of Bergson's critique of Zeno on pp. 110–11.
3. Montgomery, *The Visionary D.H. Lawrence*, p. 141.
4. William James, *The Varieties of Religious Experience* (1902; Harmondsworth: Penguin, 1982), p. 456.
5. Gilles Deleuze, *Bergsonism*, p. 13.
6. Quoted in Deleuze, *Bergsonism*, fn. 24, p. 121.
7. Cornel West, *The American Evasion of Philosophy: A Genealogy of Pragmatism* (Madison: University of Wisconsin Press, 1989), p. 67.
8. For a fuller discussion of this point and others in this section, see my 'Introduction: Difficulty and Defamiliarisation – Language and Process in *The Origin of Species*', in D. Amigoni and J. Wallace (eds), *Charles Darwin's* Origin of Species*: New Interdisciplinary Essays* (Manchester and New York: Manchester University Press, 1995), pp. 1–46. See also my Introduction to Charles Darwin, *The Origin of Species* (1859; Ware: Wordsworth Classics, 1998), pp. vii–xxiv.
9. Tess Cosslett, 'Introductory essay', in Cosslett (ed.), *Science and Religion in the Nineteenth Century* (Cambridge: Cambridge University Press, 1984), p. 2.
10. Thomas Vernon Wollaston, 'Review of the *Origin of Species*', from *Annals and Magazine of Natural History* (1860) 5; in David L. Hull, *Darwin and His Critics: The Reception of Darwin's Theory of Evolution by the Scientific Community* (Cambridge, MA: Harvard University Press, 1973), p. 139.
11. John Tyndall, 'The Belfast Address', *Nature* 20 (August 1874), quoted in Cosslett (ed.), *Science and Religion in the Nineteenth Century*, p. 182.
12. Jacques Barzun, *Darwin, Marx, Wagner: Critique of a Heritage* (London: Secker and Warburg, 1942), p. 45.
13. Tyndall, in Cosslett (ed.), *Science and Religion in the Nineteenth Century*, p. 182.
14. The analysis is that of Coleridge, as illustrated by Montgomery, *The Visionary D.H. Lawrence*, pp. 36–7.
15. Tyndall, in Cosslett (ed.), *Science and Religion in the Nineteenth Century*, pp. 182–3.
16. Fernihough, *D.H. Lawrence: Aesthetics and Ideology*, pp. 176–9.
17. Samuel Butler, *Life and Habit* (1910; London: Wildwood House, 1981), p. 196.
18. See my 'Introduction: Difficulty and Defamiliarisation', in Amigoni and Wallace (eds) *Charles Darwin's* Origin of Species*: New Interdisciplinary Essays*, pp. 41–2.
19. An alternative version of the discussion of Lawrence and Spencer in this section is to be found in my 'Against Idealism: Science and Language in Lawrence's Philosophical Writing', *Etudes Lawrenciennes* 19 (1999), pp. 33–54.
20. Sources here are: J.W. Burrow, *Evolution and Society: A Study in Victorian Social Theory* (Cambridge: Cambridge University Press, 1966); John H. Goldthorpe, 'Herbert Spencer', in Timothy Raison (ed.), *The Founding Fathers of Social Science* (Harmondsworth: Penguin, 1969), pp. 76–83; Adrian Desmond, *Archetypes and*

Ancestors: Palaeontology in Victorian London 1850–1875 (Chicago: University of Chicago Press, 1984) and *Huxley: From Devil's Disciple to Evolution's High Priest* (Harmondsworth: Penguin, 1998).

21. Desmond, *Archetypes and Ancestors*, pp. 96–7.
22. Burrow, *Evolution and Society*, p. 206.
23. Ebbatson, *Lawrence and the Nature Tradition*, p. 40.
24. Montgomery, *The Visionary D.H. Lawrence*, pp. 29–30.
25. Ebbatson, *Lawrence and the Nature Tradition*, pp. 38, 34.
26. Montgomery, *The Visionary D.H. Lawrence*, p. 37.
27. T.H. Huxley, 'Science and Culture', in *Collected Essays of T.H. Huxley*, Vol. III: *Science and Education* (London: Macmillan, 1895), pp. 140–1.
28. James Paradis, *T.H. Huxley: Man's Place in Nature* (Lincoln and London: University of Nebraska Press, 1978), p. 6; Adrian Desmond, *Huxley*, pp. 637–8.
29. Belton, 'Candied Porkers'.
30. T.H. Huxley, 'Technical Education', in Huxley, *Science and Education*, pp. 407–8.
31. Paradis, *T.H. Huxley: Man's Place in Nature*, p. 8.
32. T.H. Huxley, *Evolution and Ethics and Other Essays* (London: Macmillan, 1894), p. viii.
33. Huxley, *Evolution and Ethics*, pp. 34, 39.
34. Paradis, *T.H Huxley: Man's Place in Nature*, p. 172.
35. West, *The American Evasion of Philosophy*, p. 55.
36. Chambers, *D.H. Lawrence: A Personal Record*, p. 113.
37. James, *Varieties of Religious Experience*, p. 423.
38. D.H. Lawrence, *Movements in Modern European History*, ed. Philip Crumpton (1921; Cambridge: Cambridge University Press, 1989), pp. 260–1.
39. See Jean Baudrillard, *The Mirror of Production*, trans. Mark Poster (St. Louis: Telos Press, 1975).
40. Michael Payne and John Schad (eds.), *life.after.theory* (London and New York: Continuum, 2003), p. 95.
41. J.M. Coetzee, 'Newton and the Ideal of a Transparent Scientific Language', *Journal of Literary Semantics* 11 (1982), pp. 3–13; 11.

4 Posthuman D.H. Lawrence?

1. Keith Ansell-Pearson, 'Bergson and Creative Evolution/Involution: Exposing the Transcendental Illusion of Organismic Life', in John Mullarkey (ed.), *The New Bergson* (Manchester and New York: Manchester University Press, 1999), p. 147.
2. Watson, 'The New Bergsonism', p. 6.
3. Cited in Adrian Desmond and James Moore, *Darwin* (London: Michael Joseph, 1991), p. xviii.
4. Hayles, *How We Became Posthuman*, p. 157.
5. Deleuze, *Bergsonism*, p. 25.
6. Watson, 'The New Bergsonism', p. 6.
7. Ansell-Pearson, 'Bergson and Creative Evolution/Involution', p. 149; Deleuze, *Bergsonism*, chapter I, 'Intuition as Method'.
8. Watson, 'The New Bergsonism', p. 7.
9. Watson, 'The New Bergsonism', p. 11.
10. Hayles, *How We Became Posthuman*, p. 104.
11. Watson, 'The New Bergsonism', p. 13.
12. Amit Chaudhuri, *D.H. Lawrence and 'Difference': Postcoloniality and the Poetry of the Present* (Oxford: Oxford University Press, 2003), p. 128.

13. Hayles, *How We Became Posthuman*, p. 289.
14. Hayles, *How We Became Posthuman*, pp. 194–203.
15. Quoted in Watson, 'The New Bergsonism', p. 8.
16. Ansell-Pearson, 'Bergson and Creative Evolution/Involution'.
17. Jean-François Lyotard, *The Inhuman: Reflections on Time*, trans. Geoffrey Bennington and Rachel Bowlby (Stanford: Stanford University Press, 1991), p. 45.
18. Ansell-Pearson, 'Bergson and Creative Evolution/Involution', pp. 161, 159. The quotation is from Richard Dawkins, *The Extended Phenotype* (Oxford: Oxford University Press, 1983).
19. Ansell-Pearson, 'Bergson and Creative Evolution/Involution', p. 152.
20. Hayles, *How We Became Posthuman*, p. 149.
21. Lyotard, *The Inhuman*, p. 12.
22. Daniel Dennett, *Kinds of Minds: Towards an Understanding of Consciousness* (London: Phoenix, 1996), p. 30.
23. Lyotard, *The Inhuman*, p. 41.
24. Raymond Williams, *Problems in Materialism and Culture* (London: Verso, 1997), p. 100.

5 Animals

1. Chaudhuri, *D.H. Lawrence and 'Difference'*, p. 60.
2. Donna Haraway, 'A Cyborg Manifesto', in *Simians, Cyborgs, and Women*, p. 150; Chaudhuri, *D.H. Lawrence and 'Difference'*, p. 164.
3. Page references here are to J.M. Coetzee, *The Lives of Animals*, ed. Amy Gutmann (Princeton, NJ: Princeton University Press, 1999). It should be noted, however, that the same narrative constitutes Lesson 3 and Lesson 4 of *Elizabeth Costello* (London: Secker and Warburg, 2003).
4. Hayles, *How We Became Posthuman*, p. 134.
5. D.H. Lawrence, 'The Flying Fish', in *The Princess and Other Stories* (Harmondsworth: Penguin, 1980), p. 110.
6. Raymond Williams, *Problems of Materialism and Culture* (London: Verso, 1997), p. 96.
7. John Worthen, *D.H. Lawrence: The Early Years 1885–1912*, p. 228.
8. In previous editions of *Women in Love*, this chapter is integrated into chapter XXIX, 'Continental'.
9. Butler, *Life and Habit*, p. 42.
10. Butler, *Life and Habit*, pp. 206, 213.
11. Butler, *Life and Habit*, pp. 255, 272, 282.
12. Hayles, *How We Became Posthuman*, pp. 134–5.
13. John Berger, *About Looking* (New York: Pantheon, 1980), p. 26; quoted in Coetzee, *The Lives of Animals*, p. 34.
14. David Ellis, *D.H. Lawrence: Dying Game 1922–1930* (Cambridge: Cambridge University Press, 1998), p. 253.
15. James Wood, 'A Frog's Life' (review of *Elizabeth Costello*), *London Review of Books* 25:20 (23 October 2003), p. 16.

6 Humans

1. Anne Fernihough, '"Go in fear of abstractions": Modernism and the Spectre of Democracy', *Textual Practice* 14:3 (2000), p. 481.

2. Fukuyama, *Our Posthuman Future*, p. 182.
3. Fukuyama, *Our Posthuman Future*, p. 88.
4. Francis Fukuyama, *The End of History and the Last Man* (London: Hamish Hamilton, 1992), p. xiv.
5. James C. Cowan, *D.H. Lawrence's American Journey: A Study in Literature and Myth* (Cleveland: Case Western Reserve, 1970), p. 20.
6. Sanford Schwartz, 'Bergson and the Politics of Vitalism', in Frederick Burwick and Paul Douglass (eds), *The Crisis in Modernism: Bergson and the Vitalist Controversy* (Cambridge: Cambridge University Press, 1992), p. 292.
7. Terry Castle, *The Female Thermometer: Eighteenth-Century Culture and the Invention of the Uncanny* (New York and Oxford: Oxford University Press, 1995), p. 139.
8. Hayles, *How We Became Posthuman*, p. 104.
9. W.H. Holmes, 'The Classification and Arrangement of the Exhibits of an Anthropological Museum', *Journal of the Anthropological Institute* XXXII, 1902, quoted in Annie E. Coombes, 'The Franco-British Exhibition: Packaging Empire in Edwardian England', in Jane Beckett and Deborah Cherry (eds), *The Edwardian Era* (London: Phaidon/Barbican Art Gallery, 1987), p. 162.
10. Marianna Torgovnick, *Gone Primitive: Savage Intellects, Modern Lives* (Chicago and London: University of Chicago Press, 1990), p. 173.
11. Howard J. Booth, 'Lawrence in Doubt: A Theory of the "Other" and its Collapse', in Howard J. Booth and Nigel Rigby (eds), *Modernism and Empire* (Manchester and New York: Manchester University Press, 2000), p. 197.
12. See, for example, Edward Said, *Orientalism* (Harmondsworth: Penguin, 1985).
13. Tylor, *Primitive Culture*, Vol. II, p. 180.
14. Robert J.C. Young, *Colonial Desire: Hybridity in Theory, Culture and Race* (London and New York: Routledge, 1995), p. 27.
15. Young, *Colonial Desire*, pp. 27–8.
16. Adorno and Horkheimer, *Dialectic of Enlightenment*, p. 7.
17. Bill Readings, 'Pagans, Perverts or Primitives? Experimental Justice in the Empire of Capital', in Neil Badmington (ed.), *Posthumanism* (Basingstoke: Palgrave – now Palgrave Macmillan, 2000), p. 125.
18. Readings, 'Pagans, Perverts or Primitives?', p. 115.
19. Chaudhuri, *D.H. Lawrence and 'Difference'*, pp. 164–5.
20. Chaudhuri, *D.H. Lawrence and 'Difference'*, pp. 164–5, 43.
21. Eagleton, *The Ideology of the Aesthetic*, pp. 196–7.
22. Eagleton, *The Ideology of the Aesthetic*, p. 198.
23. Karl Marx, *Economic and Philosophical Manuscripts*, in *Karl Marx: Early Writings*, intr. Lucio Colletti (Harmondsworth: Penguin, 1985); quoted in Eagleton, *The Ideology of the Aesthetic*, p. 202.
24. Susan Sontag, 'Against Interpretation', in *Against Interpretation and other essays* (New York: Dell, 1969), pp. 13–23.

7 Machines

1. Raymond Williams, *Television: Technology and Cultural Form* (Glasgow: Fontana/Collins, 1974), p. 14.
2. Clarke, *River of Dissolution*, p. 16.
3. Thomas Carlyle, *Works of Thomas Carlyle*, Vol. II, pp. 234–6, 245; quoted in Williams, *Culture and Society*, p. 73.

4. William Morris, *How We Live and How We might Live*, repr. Nonesuch Morris, p. 581 and pp. 584–5; quoted in Williams, *Culture and Society*, p. 154.
5. Krishan Kumar, *Prophecy and Progress: The Sociology of Industrial and Post-Industrial Society* (Harmondsworth: Penguin, 1981), p. 53.
6. Fernihough, *D.H. Lawrence: Aesthetics and Ideology*, p. 138.
7. Williams, *Culture and Society*, pp. 263–4; Raymond Williams, *Keywords: A Vocabulary of Culture and Society*, 2nd edition (London: Fontana, 1988), pp. 201–2 and 227–9.
8. Clarke, *River of Dissolution*, p. 137.
9. Samuel Butler, *Erewhon* and *Erewhon Revisited* (London: Dent, 1962), p. 57.
10. David Harvey, *The Condition of Postmodernity* (Cambridge MA and Oxford: Blackwell, 1990, p. 352.
11. Hardt and Negri, *Empire*, p. 327.
12. Hardt and Negri, *Empire*, p. 25.
13. Chaudhuri, *D.H. Lawrence and 'Difference'*, p. 164.
14. Sheila McLeod, *Lawrence's Men and Women* (London: Heinemann, 1985), p. 2; Frank Kermode, *Lawrence* (London: Fontana, 1973), p. 99; Kate Millett, *Sexual Politics*, p. 283.
15. See Jean Baudrillard, *The Gulf War Did Not Take Place*, trans. Paul Patton (Bloomington: Indiana University Press, 1995).
16. Clarke, *River of Dissolution*, pp. 137–8.

Postscript: On Abstraction

1. Hayles, *How We Became Posthuman*, p. 192.
2. Hayles, *How We Became Posthuman*, p. 285.
3. Lyotard, *The Inhuman*, p. 9.
4. 'Typically modernist' may be an exaggeration. Lawrence's strategy is nevertheless reminiscent of T.S. Eliot's account of impersonality in poetry. Poetry, Eliot explains, is neither a turning loose of emotion nor an expression of personality. But, 'of course, *only those who have personality and emotions know what it means to want to escape from these things*' (my emphasis). 'Tradition and the Individual Talent' (1919), in Peter Faulkner (ed.), *A Modernist Reader: Modernism in England 1910–1930* (London: Batsford, 1986), p. 91.
5. See Nancy Katherine Hayles, 'The Ambivalent Approach: D.H. Lawrence and the New Physics', *Mosaic* 15:3 (September 1982), 89–108.
6. Adorno and Horkheimer, *Dialectic of Enlightenment*, p. 13.
7. See also Fernihough's comparison of Lawrence and Heidegger in their critique of the violence of technology as 'the *indexical* trace of a violent, exploitative kind of thinking'. For Heidegger, ' "Science's knowledge . . . already had annihilated things as things long before the atom bomb exploded".' *D.H. Lawrence: Aesthetics and Ideology*, p. 131.
8. Alfred Sohn-Rethel, *Intellectual and Manual Labour: A Critique of Epistemology*, trans. Martin Sohn-Rethel (London: Macmillan, 1978), pp. 19, 59–60.
9. Raymond Williams, *Problems in Materialism and Culture*, pp. 107, 83.
10. Leavis, *Nor Shall My Sword*, pp. 140–1.
11. Hayles, *How We Became Posthuman*, p. 288.
12. Catherine Gallagher, 'Raymond Williams and Cultural Studies', in Christopher Prendergast (ed.), *Cultural Materialism: On Raymond Williams* (Minneapolis and London: University of Minnesota Press, 1995), pp. 315–17.

13. Jean-François Lyotard, *The Postmodern Condition: A Report on Knowledge*, trans. Geoff Bennington and Brian Massumi (Manchester: Manchester University Press, 1986), p. 4.
14. Williams, *Problems in Materialism and Culture*, p. 122.
15. A.N. Whitehead, *Science and the Modern World* (Cambridge: Cambridge University Press, 1927), p. 250.

Bibliography

D.H. Lawrence

Aaron's Rod, ed. Mara Kalnins (1922; Cambridge: Cambridge University Press, 1988)

The Complete Poems of D.H. Lawrence, eds Vivian de Sola Pinto and F. Warren Roberts (Harmondsworth: Penguin, 1980)

Fantasia of the Unconscious and Psychoanalysis of the Unconscious (1923; Harmondsworth: Penguin, 1977)

The Fox, The Ladybird, The Captain's Doll, ed. Dieter Mehl (1923; Cambridge: Cambridge University Press, 1992)

Kangaroo, ed. Bruce Steele (1923; Cambridge: Cambridge University Press, 1994)

Lady Chatterley's Lover and A Propos of 'Lady Chatterley's Lover', ed. Michael Squires (Cambridge: Cambridge University Press, 1993)

The Letters of D.H. Lawrence, Vol. I (September 1901–May 1913), ed. James T. Boulton (Cambridge University Press, 1979)

The Letters of D.H. Lawrence, Vol. II (June 1913–September 1916), eds George J. Zytaruk and James T. Boulton (Cambridge: Cambridge University Press, 1981)

The Letters of D.H. Lawrence, Vol. III (October 1916–June 1921), eds James T. Boulton and Andrew Robertson (Cambridge: Cambridge University Press, 1984)

Mornings in Mexico and Etruscan Places (Harmondsworth: Penguin, 1981)

Movements in Modern European History, ed. Philip Crumpton (1921; Cambridge: Cambridge University Press, 1989)

Phoenix: The Posthumous Papers of D.H. Lawrence, ed. Edward D. McDonald (1936; Harmondsworth: Penguin, 1980)

Phoenix II: Uncollected, Unpublished and Other Prose Works by D.H. Lawrence, eds Warren Roberts and Harry T. Moore (1968; Harmondsworth: Penguin, 1978)

The Plumed Serpent (Quetzalcoatl), ed. L.D. Clark (1926; Cambridge: Cambridge University Press, 1987)

The Prussian Officer and Other Stories, ed. John Worthen (1914; London: Granada, 1984)

The Rainbow, ed. Mark Kinkead-Weekes (1915; Cambridge: Cambridge University Press, 1989)

Reflections on the Death of a Porcupine and Other Essays, ed. Michael Herbert (1925; Cambridge: Cambridge University Press, 1988)

Sketches of Etruscan Places and Other Italian Essays, ed. Simonetta De Filippis (Cambridge: Cambridge University Press, 1992)

St. Mawr and Other Stories, ed. Brian Finney (Cambridge: Cambridge University Press, 1983)

Studies in Classic American Literature, eds Ezra Greenspan, Lindeth Vasey and John Worthen (Cambridge: Cambridge University Press, 2003)

Study of Thomas Hardy and Other Essays, ed. Bruce Steele (Cambridge: Cambridge University Press, 1985)

The Symbolic Meaning: The Uncollected Versions of Studies in Classic American Literature, ed. Armin Arnold (Arundel: Centaur Press, 1962)

Twilight in Italy and Other Essays, ed. Paul Eggert (Cambridge: Cambridge University Press, 1994)

The White Peacock, ed. Andrew Robertson (1911; Cambridge: Cambridge University Press, 1983)

Women in Love, eds. David Farmer, Lindeth Vasey and John Worthen (1920; Cambridge: Cambridge University Press, 1987)

Other primary sources

Bergson, Henri, *Creative Evolution*, trans. Arthur Mitchell (1911; Lanham: University Press of America, 1983)

Bergson, Henri, *Matter and Memory*, trans. Nancy Margaret Paul and W. Scott Palmer (London: Allen & Unwin, 1911)

Blatchford, Robert, *God and My Neighbour* (1903; London: Clarion Press, 1907)

Burnet, John, *Early Greek Philosophy*, 3rd edn (London: A. & C. Black, 1920)

Burrow, Trigant, *The Social Basis of Consciousness: A Study in Organic Psychology Based upon a Synthetic and Societal Concept of the Neuroses* (London: Kegan Paul, 1927)

Butler, Samuel, *Erewhon and Erewhon Revisited* (London: Dent, 1962)

Butler, Samuel, *Life and Habit* (1910; London: Wildwood House, 1981)

Campbell, R.J., *The New Theology* (1907; London: Mills and Boon, 1909)

Chambers, Jessie, *D.H. Lawrence: A Personal Record* (1935; Cambridge: Cambridge University Press, 1980)

Coetzee, J.M., *Elizabeth Costello: Eight Lessons* (London: Secker & Warburg, 2003)

Coetzee, J.M., *The Lives of Animals*, ed. Amy Gutmann (Princeton, NJ: Princeton University Press, 1999)

Darwin, Charles, *On the Origin of Species by means of Natural Selection, or, The Preservation of Favoured Races in the Struggle for Life*, ed. Jeff Wallace (1859; Ware: Wordsworth Editions, 1998)

Dickens, Charles, *Hard Times* (1854; Harmondsworth: Penguin, 1975)

Haeckel, Ernst, *The Riddle of the Universe*, trans. Joseph McCabe (1899; London: Watts & Co., 1929)

Harrison, Jane Ellen, *Ancient Art and Ritual* (1913; Bradford-on-Avon: Moonraker Press, 1978)

Huxley, T.H., *Collected Essays, Vol. III: Science and Education* (London: Macmillan, 1895)

Huxley, T.H., *Evolution and Ethics and Other Essays* (London: Macmillan, 1894)

Huxley, T.H., *Man's Place in Nature and Other Essays* (London: Dent, 1906)

James, William, *Pragmatism*, ed. Bruce Kuklick (1907; Indianapolis: Hackett, 1981)

James, William, *Principles of Psychology*, 2 vols (London: Macmillan, 1890)

James, William, *The Varieties of Religious Experience*, ed. Martin E. Marty (1902; Harmondsworth: Penguin, 1982)

Nietzsche, Friedrich, *The Birth of Tragedy and the Genealogy of Morals*, trans. F. Golffing (New York: Doubleday Anchor, 1956)

Phelips, Vivian (Philip Vivian), *The Churches and Modern Thought: An Inquiry into the Grounds of Unbelief and an Appeal for Candour* (1906. 4th edn; London: Watts & Co., 1934)

Reade, Winwood, *The Martyrdom of Man* (1872; London: Watts & Co., 1933)

Robertson, J.M., *Spoken Essays* (London: Watts & Co., 1925)

Spencer, Herbert, *First Principles* (1862. 6th edn; London: Watts & Co., 1937)

Trotter, Wilfred, *Instincts of the Herd in Peace and War* (1915. 2nd edn; London: T.F. Unwin, 1919)

Tylor, E.B., *Primitive Culture*, 6th edn, 2 vols (London: John Murray, 1920)

Wells, H.G., *Ann Veronica* (1909; London: Virago, 1984)

General bibliography

Adorno, Theodor, and Max Horkheimer, *Dialectic of Enlightenment*, trans. John Cumming (London: Verso, 1995)

Alldritt, Keith, *The Visual Imagination of D.H. Lawrence* (London: Arnold, 1971)

Amigoni, David, and Jeff Wallace (eds), *Charles Darwin's Origin of Species: New Interdisciplinary Essays* (Manchester and New York: Manchester University Press, 1995)

Anderson, Perry, *English Questions* (London: Verso, 1992)

Ansell-Pearson, Keith, 'Bergson and Creative Evolution/Involution: Exposing the Transcendental Illusion of Organismic Life', in John Mullarkey (ed.), *The New Bergson* 146–67

Arac, Jonathan, *Critical Genealogies: Historical Situations for Postmodern Literary Studies* (New York: Columbia University Press, 1989)

Badmington, Neil (ed.), *Posthumanism* (Basingstoke: Palgrave – now Palgrave Macmillan, 2000)

Balfour, A.J., 'Creative Evolution and Philosophic Doubt', *Hibbert Journal*, October 1911

Barrett, William, *Irrational Man: A Study in Existential Philosophy* (New York: Doubleday Anchor, 1962)

Barthes, Roland, *The Rustle of Language*, trans. Richard Howard (Oxford: Basil Blackwell, 1986)

Barzun, Jacques, *Darwin, Marx, Wagner: Critique of a Heritage* (London: Secker & Warburg, 1942)

Baudrillard, Jean, *The Gulf War Did Not Take Place*, trans. Paul Patton (Bloomington: Indiana University Press, 1995)

Baudrillard, Jean, *The Mirror of Production*, trans. Mark Poster (St. Louis: Telos Press, 1975)

Beckett, Jane, and Deborah Cherry (eds), *The Edwardian Era* (London: Phaidon/ Barbican Art Gallery, 1987)

Beer, Gillian, *Darwin's Plots: Evolutionary Narrative in Darwin, George Eliot and Nineteenth-Century Fiction* (London: Ark, 1985)

Beer, Gillian, *Open Fields: Science in Cultural Encounter* (Oxford: Clarendon Press, 1996)

Beer, John, 'Lawrence's Counter-Romanticism', in Gamini Salgado and G.K. Das (eds), *The Spirit of D.H. Lawrence: Centenary Essays* (Basingstoke: Macmillan, 1988), 46–74

Bell, Michael, *D.H. Lawrence: Language and Being* (Cambridge: Cambridge University Press, 1991)

Belton, Neil, 'Candied Porkers: British Scorn of the Scientific', in Francis Spufford and Jenny Uglow (eds), *Cultural Babbage: Technology, Time and Invention* (London: Faber & Faber, 1997)

Benjamin, Walter, *The Arcades Project*, trans. Howard Eiland and Kevin McLaughlin (Cambridge, Mass. and London: Harvard University Press, 1999)

Bersani, Leo, *A Future for Astyanax: Character and Desire in Literature* (Boston and Toronto: Little, Brown, 1976)

Black, Michael, *D.H. Lawrence: The Early Fiction* (Basingstoke: Macmillan, 1986)

Bonds, Diane S., *Language and the Self in D.H. Lawrence* (Ann Arbour, Michigan: UMI Research Press, 1987)

Booth, Howard J., 'Lawrence in Doubt: A Theory of the "Other" and its Collapse', in Howard J. Booth and Nigel Rigby (eds), *Modernism and Empire* (Manchester and New York: Manchester University Press, 2000), 197–223

Burns, Aidan, *Nature and Culture in D.H. Lawrence* (Basingstoke: Macmillan, 1980)

Burrow, J.W., *Evolution and Society: A Study in Victorian Social Theory* (Cambridge: Cambridge University Press, 1966)

Burwick, Frederick, and Paul Douglass (eds), *The Crisis in Modernism: Bergson and the Vitalist Controversy* (Cambridge: Cambridge University Press, 1992)

Butler, Judith, *Gender Trouble: Feminism and the Subversion of Identity* (New York and London: Routledge, 1990)

Castle, Terry, *The Female Thermometer: Eighteenth-Century Culture and the Invention of the Uncanny* (New York and Oxford: Oxford University Press, 1995)

Chaudhuri, Amit, *D.H. Lawrence and 'Difference': Postcoloniality and the Poetry of the Present* (Oxford: Clarendon Press, 2003)

Clarke, Bruce, 'A Different Sun: The Allegory of Thermodynamics in D.H. Lawrence', in Michael Bell and Peter Poellner (eds), *Myth and the Making of Modernity: The Problem of Grounding in Early Twentieth-Century Literature* (Amsterdam: Rodopi, 1998), 81–98

Clarke, Colin, *River of Dissolution: D.H. Lawrence and English Romanticism* (London: Routledge & Kegan Paul, 1969)

Coetzee, J.M., 'Newton and the Ideal of a Transparent Scientific Language', *Journal of Literary Semantics* 11 (1982)

Connerton, Paul, *How Societies Remember* (Cambridge: Cambridge University Press, 1989)

Cosslett, Tess (ed.), *Science and Religion in the Nineteenth Century* (Cambridge: Cambridge University Press, 1984)

Cowan, James, *D.H. Lawrence's American Journey: A Study in Literature and Myth* (Cleveland: Case Western Reserve, 1970)

Danius, Sara, *The Senses of Modernism: Technology, Perception, and Aesthetics* (Ithaca and London: Cornell University Press, 2002)

Deleuze, Gilles, *Bergsonism*, trans. Hugh Tomlinson and Barbara Habberjam (1966; New York: Zone Books, 1991)

Deleuze, Gilles, and Felix Guattari, *Anti-Oedipus: Capitalism and Schizophrenia*, trans. Robert Hurley, Mark Seem and Helen R. Lane (1972; London: Athlone, 1984)

Deleuze, Gilles, and Felix Guattari, *A Thousand Plateaus: Capitalism and Schizophrenia*, trans. Brian Massumi (1980; London and New York: Continuum, 2003)

Desmond, Adrian, *Archetypes and Ancestors: Palaeontology in Victorian London 1850–1875* (Chicago: University of Chicago Press, 1984)

Desmond, Adrian, *Huxley: From Devil's Disciple to Evolution's High Priest* (Harmondsworth: Penguin, 1998)

Desmond, Adrian, and James Moore, *Darwin* (London: Michael Joseph, 1991)

Doherty, Gerald, 'White Mythologies: D.H. Lawrence and the Deconstructive Turn', *Criticism* 29:4 (1987), 477–96

Dollimore, Jonathan, *Radical Tragedy: Religion, Ideology and Power in the Drama of Shakespeare and his Contemporaries* (Brighton: Harvester Press, 1984; 3rd edn Basingstoke: Palgrave Macmillan, 2003)

Drain, Richard, 'Formative Influences on the work of D.H. Lawrence' (unpublished PhD dissertation, Cambridge, 1962)

Eagleton, Terry, *Ideology: An Introduction* (London: Verso, 1991)

Eagleton, Terry, *The Ideology of the Aesthetic* (Oxford: Basil Blackwell, 1990)

Ebbatson, Roger, *Lawrence and the Nature Tradition: A Theme in English Fiction, 1859–1914* (Brighton: Harvester Press, 1980)

Ebbatson, Roger, *The Evolutionary Self: Forster, Hardy, Lawrence* (Brighton: Harvester Press, 1982)

Eliot, T.S., *After Strange Gods: A Primer of Modern Heresy* (London: Faber & Faber, 1934)

Ellis, David, *D.H. Lawrence: Dying Game 1922–1930* (Cambridge: Cambridge University Press, 1998)

Ellis, David, and Howard Mills, *D.H. Lawrence's Non-Fiction: Art, Thought and Genre* (Cambridge: Cambridge University Press, 1988)

Fernihough, Anne, *The Cambridge Companion to D.H. Lawrence* (Cambridge: Cambridge University Press, 2001)

Fernihough, Anne, *D.H. Lawrence: Aesthetics and Ideology* (Oxford: Clarendon Press, 1993)

Fernihough, Anne, '"Go in fear of abstractions": Modernism and the Spectre of Democracy', *Textual Practice* 14:3 (2000)

Foucault, Michel, *The Order of Things: An Archaeology of the Human Sciences* (London and New York: Tavistock/Routledge, 1974)

Fukuyama, Francis, *The End of History and the Last Man* (London: Hamish Hamilton, 1992)

Fukuyama, Francis, *Our Posthuman Future: Consequences of the Biotechnology Revolution* (London: Profile Books, 2002)

Goode, John, 'D.H. Lawrence', in ed. Bernard Bergonzi, *The Twentieth Century* (London: Barrie & Jenkins, 1970)

Goodheart, Eugene, *The Utopian Vision of D.H. Lawrence* (Chicago: University of Chicago Press, 1963)

Greenslade, William, *Degeneration, Culture, and the Novel 1880–1940* (Cambridge: Cambridge University Press, 1994)

Grierson, Herbert, *The Background of English Literature and Other Essays* (Harmondsworth: Peregrine, 1982)

Haraway, Donna J., *Simians, Cyborgs, and Women: The Reinvention of Nature* (London: Free Association Books, 1991)

Hardt, Michael, and Antonio Negri, *Empire* (Cambridge, Mass., and London: Harvard University Press, 2000)

Harvey, David, *The Condition of Postmodernity* (Cambridge MA and Oxford: Blackwell, 1990)

Hayles, Nancy Katherine, 'The Ambivalent Approach: D.H. Lawrence and the New Physics', *Mosaic* XV:3 (Sept. 1982), 88–108

Hayles, N. Katherine, *How We Became Posthuman: Virtual Bodies in Cybernetics, Literature, and Informatics* (Chicago and London: University of Chicago Press, 1999)

Head, Dominic, 'Coetzee and the Animals: the Quest for Postcolonial Grace', in Andrew Smith and William Hughes (eds), *Empire and the Gothic: The Politics of Genre* (Basingstoke: Palgrave, 2003), 229–244

Heywood, Christopher (ed.), *D.H. Lawrence: New Studies* (London: Macmillan, 1987)

Hinz, Evelyn J., 'The Beginning and the End: D.H. Lawrence's *Psychoanalysis* and *Fantasia*', *The Dalhousie Review* 52 (1972), 251–65

Holderness, Graham, *D.H. Lawrence: History, Ideology and Fiction* (Dublin: Gill & Macmillan, 1982)

Hough, Graham, *The Dark Sun: A Study of D.H. Lawrence* (London: Duckworth, 1975)

Hull, David L., *Darwin and his Critics: The Reception of Darwin's Theory of Evolution by the Scientific Community* (Cambridge MA: Harvard University Press, 1973)

Huxley, Aldous, *Literature and Science* (New Haven: Leete's Island Books, 1963)

Jewinski, Ed, 'The Phallus in D.H. Lawrence and Jacques Lacan', *D.H. Lawrence Review* 21 (1989), 7–24.

Johnson, Mark, *The Body in the Mind: The Bodily Basis of Meaning, Imagination and Reason* (Chicago: University of Chicago Press, 1987)

Jones, Greta, *Social Darwinism and English Thought: The Interaction between Biological and Social Theory* (Brighton: Harvester Press, 1980)

Kalnins, Mara (ed.), *D.H. Lawrence: Centenary Essays* (Bristol: Bristol University Press, 1986)

Kermode, Frank, *Lawrence* (London: Fontana, 1973)

Kinkead-Weekes, Mark, *D.H. Lawrence: Triumph and Exile 1912–1922* (Cambridge: Cambridge University Press, 1996)

Kumar, Krishan, *Prophecy and Progress: The Sociology of Industrial and Post-Industrial Society* (Harmondsworth: Penguin, 1981)

Leavis, F.R., *D.H. Lawrence: Novelist* (Harmondsworth: Penguin, 1976)

Leavis, F.R., *Nor Shall My Sword: Discourses on Pluralism, Compassion and Social Hope* (London: Chatto & Windus, 1972)

Leavis, F.R., *Thought, Words and Creativity: Art and Thought in Lawrence* (London: Chatto & Windus, 1976)

Ledger, Sally, *The New Woman: Fiction and Feminism at the Fin de Siècle* (Manchester: Manchester University Press, 1997)

Levine, George (ed.), *Realism and Representation: Essays on the Problem of Realism in Relation to Science, Literature and Culture* (Madison: University of Wisconsin Press, 1982)

Lyotard, Jean-François, *The Inhuman: Reflections on Time*, trans. Geoffrey Bennington and Rachel Bowlby (Stanford: Stanford University Press, 1991)

Lyotard, Jean-François, *The Postmodern Condition: A Report on Knowledge*, trans. Geoff Bennington and Brian Massumi (Manchester: Manchester University Press, 1986)

Macintyre, Stuart, *A Proletarian Science: Marxism in Britain, 1917–1933* (London: Lawrence & Wishart, 1986)

Martin, Wallace, *The New Age under Orage: Chapters in English Cultural History* (Manchester: Manchester University Press, 1967)

Mason, H.A., 'D.H. Lawrence and *The White Peacock*', *Cambridge Quarterly* 7 (1977), 216–31

McLeod, Sheila, *Lawrence's Men and Women* (London: Heinemann, 1985)

Middleton, Peter, *The Inward Gaze: Masculinity and Subjectivity in Modern Culture* (London and New York: Routledge, 1992)

Millett, Kate, *Sexual Politics* (London: Sphere Books, 1971)

Milton, Colin, *Lawrence and Nietzsche: A Study in Influence* (Aberdeen: Aberdeen University Press, 1987)

Montgomery, Robert, *The Visionary D.H. Lawrence: Beyond Philosophy and Art* (Cambridge: Cambridge University Press, 1994)

Morrell, J., and A. Thackray, *Gentlemen of Science: Early Years of the British Association for the Advancement of Science* (Oxford: Clarendon Press, 1981)

Mulhern, Francis, *The Moment of 'Scrutiny'* (London: New Left Books, 1979)

Mullarkey, John (ed.), *The New Bergson* (Manchester and New York: Manchester University Press, 1999)

Nehls, Edward, *D.H. Lawrence: A Composite Biography*, 3 vols (Madison: University of Wisconsin, 1959)

Neilson, Brett, 'D.H. Lawrence's "Dark Page": Narrative Primitivism in *Women in Love* and *The Plumed Serpent*', *Twentieth Century Literature* 43:3 (1997), 310–25

Nixon, Cornelia, *D.H. Lawrence and the Turn against Women* (Berkeley: University of California Press, 1986)

Oakley, Ann, *Subject Women* (London: Martin Robertson, 1981)

Paradis, James, *T.H. Huxley: Man's Place in Nature* (Lincoln and London: University of Nebraska Press, 1978)

Paradis, James, and Thomas Postlewait (eds), *Victorian Science and Victorian Values: Literary Perspectives* (New Brunswick: Rutgers University Press, 1985)

Payne, Michael, and John Schad (eds), *life.after.theory* (London and New York: Continuum, 2003)

Pick, Daniel, *Faces of Degeneration: A European Disorder, c.1848–c.1918* (Cambridge: Cambridge University Press, 1989)

Pinkney, Tony, *D.H. Lawrence* (Hemel Hempstead: Harvester Wheatsheaf, 1990)

Pound, Ezra, *Literary Essays of Ezra Pound*, ed. T.S. Eliot (London: Faber, 1974)

Ragussis, Michael, *The Subterfuge of Art: Language and the Romantic Tradition* (Baltimore and London: Johns Hopkins University Press, 1978)

Raison, Timothy (ed.), *The Founding Fathers of Social Science* (Harmondsworth: Penguin, 1969)

Readings, Bill, 'Pagans, Perverts or Primitives? Experimental Justice in the Empire of Capital', in Badmington (ed.), *Posthumanism*, 112–28

Robbins, Bruce, 'Modernism and Literary Realism: Response', in Levine (ed.), *Realism and Representation*, 225–31.

Rose, Jonathan, *The Intellectual Life of the British Working Classes* (New Haven and London: Yale University Press, 2002)

Rylance, Rick, 'Ideas, Histories, Generations and Beliefs: The Early Novels to *Sons and Lovers*', in Anne Fernihough (ed.), *The Cambridge Companion to D.H. Lawrence* (Cambridge: Cambridge University Press, 2001), 15–31

Sagar, Keith, *D.H. Lawrence: A Calendar of His Works* (Manchester: Manchester University Press, 1979)

Sagar, Keith (ed.), *A D.H. Lawrence Handbook* (Manchester: Manchester University Press, 1982)

Sayer, Derek, *The Violence of Abstraction: The Analytic Foundations of Historical Materialism* (Oxford: Basil Blackwell, 1987)

Sayers, Janet, *Biological Politics: Feminist and Anti-Feminist Perspectives* (London: Tavistock, 1982)

Schneider, Daniel, *The Consciousness of D.H. Lawrence: An Intellectual Biography* (Kansas and London: University of Kansas Press/Eurospan, 1987)

Sewell, Elizabeth, *The Orphic Voice: Poetry and Natural History* (London: Routledge & Kegan Paul, 1961)

Smith, Anne (ed.), *Lawrence and Women* (London: Vision Press, 1980)

Simpson, Hilary, *D.H. Lawrence and Feminism* (London: Croom Helm, 1982)

Sohn-Rethel, Alfred, *Intellectual and Manual Labour: A Critique of Epistemology*, trans. Martin Sohn-Rethel (London: Macmillan, 1978)

Sokal, Alan, 'Transgressing the Boundaries: Toward a Transformative Hermeneutics of Quantum Gravity', *Social Text* 46/47, 14:1/2 (Spring/Summer 1996), 217–52

Sontag, Susan, 'Against Interpretation', in *Against Interpretation and other essays* (New York: Dell, 1969), 13–23

Soper, Kate, *What is Nature?* (Oxford and Cambridge MA: Blackwell, 1995)

Torgovnick, Marianna, *Gone Primitive: Savage Intellects, Modern Lives* (Chicago and London: University of Chicago Press, 1990)

Vivas, Elisio, *D.H. Lawrence: The Failure and Triumph of Art* (London: Allen and Unwin, 1961)

Wallace, Jeff, 'Against Idealism: Science and Language in Lawrence's Philosophical Writing', *Études Lawrenciennes* 19 (1998), 33–54

Wallace, Jeff, 'Language, Nature and the Politics of Materialism: Raymond Williams and D.H. Lawrence', in W. John Morgan and Peter Preston (eds), *Raymond Williams: Politics, Education, Letters* (Basingstoke: Macmillan, 1993), 105–28

Wallace, Jeff, ' "Taking Possession of the Ordinary Man's Mind": Literary Studies and History of Science', *Literature and History*, 2nd series, 1:1 (Spring 1990), 58–74

Wallace, Jeff, 'Turning Descartes Upside Down: on Katherine Hayles, *How We Became Posthuman*', *Comparative Criticism* 23 (2001), 349–59

Watson, Sean, 'The New Bergsonism: Discipline, Subjectivity and Freedom', *Radical Philosophy* 92 (November/December 1992), 6–16

West, Cornel, *The American Evasion of Philosophy: A Genealogy of Pragmatism* (Madison: University of Wisconsin Press, 1989)

Whitehead, A.N., *Science and the Modern World* (Cambridge: Cambridge University Press, 1927)

Willey, Basil, *The Seventeenth-Century Background* (Harmondsworth: Peregrine, 1962)

Williams, Linda Ruth, *Sex in the Head: Visions of Femininity and Film in D.H. Lawrence* (Hemel Hempstead: Harvester Wheatsheaf, 1993)

Williams, Raymond, *The Country and the City* (St Albans: Paladin, 1975)

Williams, Raymond, *Culture and Society 1780–1850* (London: Chatto & Windus, 1958)

Williams, Raymond, *Keywords: A Vocabulary of Culture and Society*, 2nd edn (London: Fontana, 1988)

Williams, Raymond, *Problems in Materialism and Culture* (London: Verso, 1997)

Williams, Raymond, *Television: Technology and Cultural Form* (Glasgow: Fontana/Collins, 1974)

Worthen, John, *D.H. Lawrence and the Idea of the Novel* (London: Macmillan, 1979)

Worthen, John, *D.H. Lawrence: The Early Years 1885–1912* (Cambridge: Cambridge University Press, 1991)

Young, Robert J.C., *Colonial Desire: Hybridity in Theory, Culture and Race* (London and New York: Routledge, 1995)

Index

abstraction, 174–5, 177–8, 186, 203, 206, 233–40
Adorno, Theodor, 19, 177, 236
animism, 176, 181, 184, 187–90
Ansell-Pearson, Keith, 102, 110, 114–15
anthropology, 170, 174–6
anthropomorphism, 119–23, 130–5, 143–4, 184–5
Arac, Jonathan, 32
Arnold, Matthew, 23–6, 47
autopoiesis, 104, 112, 116, 163, 165, 180

Balfour, A.J., 15–16, 23
Barrett, William, 242 n.14
Barthes, Roland, 3, 7
Barzun, Jacques, 68
Baudrillard, Jean, 96, 222; *The Gulf War Did Not Take Place*, 222; *The Mirror of Production*, 96
Baumgarten, Alexander, 190
Beauvoir, Simone de, 157
Beckett, Samuel, 233
Beer, Gillian, 8
Beer, John, 242 n.24
behaviourism, 121, 154
Bell, Clive, 59
Belton, Neil, 3, 5–6, 86–7, 89
Benjamin, Walter, 1, 5
Bennett, Arnold, 43; as 'Jacob Tonson', 42
Benson, Donald, 23–4
Berger, John, 144
Bergson, Henri, 6–7, 11–16, 30–1, 56, 61, 63–6, 69–70, 72, 74, 79, 95, 102–3, 107, 109–12, 114, 116–17, 135, 146, 154–5, 159–60, 162, 174, 178–9, 180–1, 183, 228, 245 n.2; *Creative Evolution*, 11–14, 56, 64–6, 70, 79, 102; *Matter and Memory*, 13–14, 64, 110–12
Bergsonism, New, 7, 30–1
Berkeley, George (Bishop), 64
Bersani, Leo, 31

Black, Michael, 20, 22
Blake, William, 59, 122
Blatchford, Robert, 37–9, 40–1, 43; *Clarion, The*, 43; *God and My Neighbour*, 37–9, 40–1
bolshevism, 226, 230
Booth, Howard, 169
Brewster, Aschah, 1
Brewster, Earl H., 17, 24, 234, 244 n.13
British Association for the Advancement of Science (BAAS), 35–6, 68
Brontë, Emily, *Wuthering Heights*, 127
Burke, Edmund, 87, 153, 207–8
Burnet, John, *Early Greek Philosophy*, 61–5
Burrow, J.W., 73, 245 n.20
Burrow, Trigant, 16
Burrows, Louie, 51
Butler, Samuel, 66, 70, 105, 109, 135–6, 209–11, 218, 230; *Erewhon*, 209–11, 218, 230; *Life and Habit*, 66, 70, 105, 109, 135–6
Butler, Judith, 244 n.12
Bynner, Witter, 244 n.13

Campbell, R.J., *The New Theology*, 37, 38–41, 76
capitalism, 48, 53, 96, 149–50, 169, 183, 186, 190–1, 204, 207, 211–13, 219–32, 236–9
Capra, Fritjof, 30, 112
Cariou, Marie, 63
Carlyle, Thomas, 205–6, 208
Carpenter, Edward, 43
Castle, Terry, 162–3
Cézanne, Paul, 32, 58–61, 64–5
Chambers, Jessie, 16, 24–6, 35–7, 39, 42–3, 51, 57, 92
Chambers, Mary, 25
Chaudhuri, Amit, 113, 119–20, 189–90, 206, 217–18
Christianity, 15–16, 25, 36–41, 59–60, 62, 140, 143, 151, 168, 184, 198, 219–20

Clark, Andy, 113–14
Clarke, Colin, 32, 205, 208, 228–9, 230–1
Cocker, Edward, 2
Coetzee, J.M., 97, 119–23, 129–30, 134–5, 144, 146–7, 149–51, 163, 169, 185, 234, 247 n.13; *Elizabeth Costello/The Lives of Animals*, 119–23, 129–30, 134–5, 144, 146–7, 149–51, 163, 169, 185, 234, 247 n.13; 'Newton and the Ideal of a Transparent Scientific Language', 97
Coleridge, Samuel Taylor, 21, 78, 205, 207–8, 245 n.14
Connerton, Paul, 113
Coombes, Annie E., 248 n.9
Cosslett, Tess, 67
Cowan, James, 161
Crèvecoeur, Hector, 159, 165
Cripps, J.L. Redgrave, 48
Cubism, 58–9
cyborg, 26–7, 136, 165–6, 190, 199, 238

Dana, Richard, 202, 217
D'Annunzio, Gabriele, 146, 179, 184
Darwin, Charles, 4, 12–13, 16, 46, 66–72, 74, 79, 81–2, 84, 87, 91–2, 97, 104–5, 135, 138, 157, 193; *The Origin of Species*, 12–13, 16, 66–72, 74, 157
Dawkins, Richard, 114–15, 165, 247 n.18
Dax, Alice, 42, 53
deconstruction, 31
Defoe, Daniel, 2
Deledda, Grazia, 179–80
Deleuze, Gilles, 30, 66, 110, 112, 114–15, 166, 209–18, 221, 225, 228; *Anti-Oedipus*, 30, 209–16; *Bergsonism*, 30, 66, 110; *A Thousand Plateaus*, 213, 216–17
democracy, 149–50, 185–6, 231, 239
Democritus, 69
Dennett, Daniel, 117
Derrida, Jacques, 189
Descartes, René, 28–30, 69, 77, 101, 104–5, 108, 110, 113–14, 122, 135, 154, 158–9, 162, 180, 188, 198, 202
Desmond, Adrian, 73, 86, 89, 245–6 n.20, 246 n.3

Dickens, Charles, *Hard Times*, 1–2, 5, 25, 43, 57, 75, 89
Diogenes, 87
dissipative structure, 112
distributed cognition, 113–14
Doherty, Gerald, 31
Donovan, Robert Alan, 25
Dostoyevsky, Fyodr, 106
Driesch, Hans, 46
dualism, 28–9, 77, 82, 101, 104, 113, 158–60, 180, 217

Eagleton, Terry, 13, 190–1
Eastwood Congregational Literary Society, 37
Ebbatson, Roger, 73–4, 81
Eder, David (MD), 45–8, 52, 56, 65, 91, 154
Eder, Edith, 161
Einstein, Albert, 16, 25, 95
Eliot, George, 72
Eliot, T.S., 19–20, 22, 24, 249 n.4
Ellis, David, 12, 148
Ellis, Havelock, 45
Enlightenment, 13, 39, 220, 224, 236–8
Euclid, 2
eugenics, 44–8, 91, 152–8
evolution, 11, 45–8, 61, 66–72, 89, 92–3, 101–2, 115–18, 153, 178, 186, 217, 228–30, 240
existentialism, 18–19

Fabian Society, The, 42
Fernihough, Anne, 32, 69, 120, 154, 189, 206–7, 249 n.7
Foerster, Heinz von, 121
Forel, Auguste, 48
Foucault, Michel, 4, 29, 113, 233
Fourier, Charles, 5
Frankfurt School, 18–19, 21, 177, 216, 236
Franklin, Benjamin, 178
Frazer, J.G., 16, 170
Freud, Sigmund, 16, 30, 48, 84, 107, 135, 162–3, 213–15, 228
Frobenius, Leo, 16
Fukuyama, Francis, 26–7, 29, 116, 155–7
Futurism, Italian, 106–8, 111–12

Gallagher, Catherine, 238
Galton, Francis, 44, 156
Garnett, Edward, 20, 106–7, 194–5, 243 n.52
Gauguin, Paul, 170
Ghiselin, Brewster, 14, 17
Gingrich, Newt, 29
Goethe, Johann Wolfgang von, 42
Goldsmith, Oliver, 2
Goldthorpe, John H., 245 n.20
Goodheart, Eugene, 8
Greek philosophy, early, 61–5, 69, 71, 74, 102, 181
Grierson, Herbert, 241 n.4
Guattari, Félix, (see Gilles Deleuze, *Anti-Oedipus* and *A Thousand Plateaus*) 30, 114–15, 166, 209–18, 221, 225, 228
Gunter, Pete A.Y., 12

Habermas, Jurgen, 190
habit, 105, 113, 135–6
Haeckel, Ernst, *The Riddle of the Universe*, 16, 40, 73, 80–5, 87, 92, 97, 164
Haraway, Donna, 4, 27, 32, 102–4, 108, 117, 119, 135, 158
Hardt, Michael, 4, 8, 26, 102, 212
Hardy, Thomas, 216
Harrison, Jane, *Ancient Art and Ritual*, 16, 170, 174–6, 180–1, 183, 226, 233
Harvey, David, 211–12, 218
Hawthorne, Nathaniel, 109, 236
Hayles, N. Katherine, 27–30, 32, 103–5, 112–14, 116, 121, 137, 155, 158, 233–4, 238
Hegel, G.W.F., 236
Heidegger, Martin, 18, 207, 249 n.7
Helmholtz, Hermann von, 81
Hemingway, Ernest, 122
Herzog, Werner, 177–8
Holbrook, May Chambers, 242 n.9
Holderness, Graham, 51
Holmes, W.H., 248 n.9
homeostasis, 112, 165–6
Horkheimer, Max, 19, 177, 236
Hughes, Ted, 122
Human Genome Project, The, 155
humanism, 2–8, 20–4, 26, 29, 47, 86, 103–4, 113, 119–20, 133–4, 150–1, 155–6, 166, 177, 190, 193, 200–1, 202, 211–12, 218–27, 229–30, 237–8
Humboldt, Alexander von, 97
Hutchings, Edwin, 113
Huxley, Aldous, 6, 17–21, 26–7, 87, 227; *Brave New World*, 227; *Literature and Science*, 17
Huxley, T.H., 1, 5–6, 8, 16–17, 36, 68, 79, 85–92, 97, 125, 127, 232; *Evolution and Ethics*, 91; *Man's Place in Nature*, 1, 5–6, 8, 16–17, 36, 86–91, 127, 232; 'The Progress of Science', 91; 'Science and Culture', 86; 'Technical Education', 87

Ibsen, Henrik, 42–3, 179
idealism, 59–60, 63–4, 76–8, 126–7, 139–41, 143, 158, 160–1, 174, 198, 201–3, 206, 219–21, 224–8, 233–6, 239
Imagism, 172
Impressionism, 59
instinct, 135–6

Jackson, Holbrook, 42
James, William, 16, 35, 61–5, 85, 91–7, 104, 124, 239; *Pragmatism*, 16, 35, 61–5, 92, 94–6; *Principles of Psychology*, 92–4; *Varieties of Religious Experience*, 96
Jeffers, Robinson, 122
Jennings, Blanche, 51, 53
Jewinski, Ed, 31
Johnson, Mark, 113
Johnson, Samuel, 65
Jones, Ernest, 48
Jung, Carl, 16

Kant, Immanuel, 14, 190, 206
Keats, John, 72
Kermode, Frank, 218
Kierkegaard, Søren, 18, 190
Kipling, Rudyard, 174
Köhler, Wolfgang, 121
Kumar, Krishan, 206

Labour Party, The, 42
Lacan, Jacques, 31
Laing, R.D., 215
Lamarck, Jean-Baptiste, 46, 72–3, 105

Lavoisier, Antoine Laurent, 81
LAWRENCE, D.H., *Aaron's Rod*, 158, 218–19, 220–3; 'America, Listen to Your Own' 226; *Apocalypse*, 58, 62, 116, 174, 176; 'A Propos of *Lady Chatterley's Lover*', 50, 58–61, 235, 240; 'Art and the Individual', 41–2; 'Climbing down Pisgah', 239–40; *The Captain's Doll*, 239; *A Collier's Friday Night*, 42; 'Democracy', 142, 239; *Education of the People*, 155, 159–60, 206–7; *Etruscan Places*, 186–90, 217; *Fantasia of the Unconscious*, 66–8, 155, 161, 163, 215, 221, 239; 'The Flying Fish', 122; *The Fox*, 138, 141–7; 'Hymns in a Man's Life', 25; 'Introduction to Pictures', 162, 164; 'Introduction to These Paintings', 58, 73, 76, 95; *Kangaroo*, 14, 70, 123, 135, 141–6, 158, 218–20, 223–6, 229; *Lady Chatterley's Lover*, 126, 227–32, 235, 239; '. . . Love Was Once a Little Boy', 148–9; *Mornings in Mexico*, 115, 173, 179, 182–6; *Movements in Modern European History*, 96; *Mr. Noon*, 42; 'Nottingham and the Mining Countryside', 193–4; 'Odour of Chrysanthemums', 34; *The Plumed Serpent*, 158, 218–20, 223–4, 226–7, 229, 231; *Psychoanalysis and the Unconscious*, 84, 158–60, 162, 233–5, 239; *The Rainbow*, 2, 20, 34–5, 52–7, 73, 89–90, 106, 131, 158, 195–201, 204, 231, 238–9; *Reflections on the Death of a Porcupine*, 147–51, 164, 234, 238; Review of Frederick Carter, *Dragon of the Apocalypse*, 19; Review of *Second Contemporary Verse Anthology*, 166–7; *Sons and Lovers*, 22, 36, 40, 49–53, 73, 124, 130, 136, 158, 191–5, 204; *St. Mawr*, 119–20, 130, 137, 141, 147; *Studies in Classic American Literature*, 155, 160–1, 164, 170–1, 178–9, 202; *Study of Thomas Hardy*, 58, 73, 79, 96, 105, 115–16, 125, 128, 157, 163, 165, 204; *The Symbolic Meaning*, 16–17, 83, 85, 109, 159, 164–5, 170–1, 176, 179, 234–6, 243 n.52; 'Thought' (poem), 111; *The Trespasser*, 22; *Twilight in Italy*, 59,

117–18, 167–70, 172, 179–80, 182, 185; *The White Peacock*, 48–9, 120, 123–30, 192, 195, 227–8; 'Why the Novel Matters', 101, 243 n.52; 'The Wild Common' (poem), 80–1; *Women in Love*, 26, 34, 49–50, 53, 80, 95, 118–19, 123, 128–37, 144, 147, 165, 195, 209, 218, 220, 228, 231
Leavis, F.R., 3, 22–4, 26, 31–2, 47, 90, 104, 116, 237–9
Ledger, Sally, 52–3
Liberalism (and Christianity), 38–41
literary studies, 2–4, 7–8
Locke, John, 162
Luddism, 202–4, 209, 217, 230
Lyell, Charles, 71
Lyotard, Jean-François, 114, 117, 177–8, 180, 234, 239; *The Inhuman*, 114, 117, 234; *The Postmodern Condition*, 239

Macintyre, Stuart, 37, 244 n.6
Mackenzie, Sir Compton, *The West Wind of Love*, 242 n.17
Malthus, Thomas, 72–3, 140–1
Marinetti, Filippo Tommaso, 106–8
Martin, Wallace, 43
Marx, Karl, 190–1, 207, 212, 236
Marxism, 43, 190–1, 236–7
Mason, H.A., 244 n.13
materialism, 2, 5–6, 8, 14–16, 24–6, 63–4, 69, 76–8, 80–5, 88–9, 102, 107–8, 112–13, 126–7, 152–4, 161–2, 164, 182, 184, 196, 210–11, 233–6, 240
Maturana, Humberto, 104, 112, 116, 137–8, 165; 'What the Frog's Eye Tells the Frog's Brain', 137–8
Mayer, Julius Robert, 81
McCabe, Joseph, 81, 83
McLeod, A.W., 108
McLeod, Sheila, 218
Melville, Herman, 170–1, 216
memory, 109–13, 135–6
Mendel, Gregor, 46
Merz, John Theodore, 23
Middleton, Peter, 57, 195
Mill, John Stuart, 15
Miller, Henry, 215–16
Millett, Kate, 218

modernism, 14, 52, 79, 132–3, 147, 154, 171, 174–5, 234, 238
money, 48, 219, 221, 227–32, 236–9
Montgomery, Robert, 62, 64, 82, 242 n.24, 245 n.14
Moore, James, 246 n.3
Morel, Ottoline, 62
Morris, William, 42, 205–6

Nagel, Thomas, 'What Is It Like to Be a Bat?', 121
Negri, Antonio, 4, 8, 26, 102, 212
Nehls, Edward, 242 n.6, 243 n.33 and 39
New Age, The, 16, 35, 39, 41–8, 65, 91, 154
New Theology, The, 35–41
New Woman, The, 35, 52–7
Newman, John Henry, 23, 26
Newton, Isaac, 97
Nietzsche, Friedrich, 14, 18–19, 42–3, 62, 120, 123, 136, 143, 154, 202, 207, 219; *The Genealogy of Morals*, 18–19
Nixon, Cornelia, 244 n.16
Norris, Christopher, 96–7
Novalis (Friedrich von Hardenburg), 206

Oakley, Ann, 55
Orage, A.R., 42–5

Paley, William, 67
Paradis, James, 86–7, 89–90
Parmenides, 63, 69, 75, 83
Pearson, Karl, 47
Penty, A.J., 43
Phelips, Vivian (Philip Vivian), 37–41
Philpotts, Eden, 45
Plato, 42, 59, 162, 174–5, 181, 199, 228
Poe, Edgar Allan, 166
Popper, Karl, 70
postcolonialism, 169–70, 177–8, 182
Post-Impressionism, 59
postmodernism, 7, 111, 239
post-structuralism, 3–4
Pound, Ezra, 52, 172
pragmatism, 66, 94–6, 104, 230
psychoanalysis, 162–3, 213–15
Pythagoras, 63

racial theory, 167–90
Radford, Dollie, 152, 155
Ragussis, Michael, 31
Rationalist Press Association, The, 38, 81
Ray, Thomas S., 103
Reade, Winwood, 14, 16, 30
Readings, Bill, 177–8
Reid, Rev. Robert, 15, 37, 39, 44, 81
relativity, 16, 94–7, 146
Renaissance, 4, 59–60
Ribot, Théodule, 136
Robertson, J.M., 15–16
Robbins, Bruce, 7–8
Romanticism, 20–2, 31–2, 89, 162, 208, 211
Rose, Jonathan, 39
Ruskin, John, 42, 192, 205
Russell, Bertrand, 62

Said, Edward, 170
Saleeby, Caleb, 45
Sapir, Edward, 19, 97
Sartre, Jean-Paul, 18
Schiller, Friedrich, 190
Schneider, Daniel, 25, 31, 32
Schopenhauer, Arthur, 14, 16, 42, 124–5, 190
Schwartz, Sanford, 162
Shelley, Mary, 2
Shelley, Percy Bysshe, 21, 23
Sherren, Wilkinson, 39
Shestov, Leo, 239
Simpson, Hilary, 244 n.16
Slate, Ruth, 39
Smith, Anne, 244 n.18, 245 n.19
Smuts, Barbara, 146–8
Snyder, Gary, 122
socialism, 37–9, 41–8, 142, 219
Social Text, 7
Social Darwinism, 91, 125
Socrates, 180
Sohn-Rethel, Alfred, 236–7
Sokal, Alan, 7, 96, 161
Sontag, Susan, 199
Spencer, Herbert, 11–13, 15–16, 68, 81–2, 87, 92–3, 97, 105, 114, 125, 132, 154, 162, 175; *First Principles*, 12–13, 36, 72–80

Spinoza, Baruch, 4, 81
structuralism, 3–4, 113
Sugar, Alan, 211–12

technology, 34–5, 103
Thales, 62
Thomson, J. Arthur, 46
Toffler, Alvin, 243 n.44
Tolstoy, Leo, 106
Tonson, Jacob (Arnold Bennett), 42
Torgovnick, Marianna, 169–70
Trotter, Wilfred, *Instincts of the Herd in Peace and War*, 152–5, 165–6
Turgenev, Ivan, 106
Two Cultures, 6, 86
Tylor, E.B., *Primitive Culture*, 16, 170, 175–6, 181
Tyndall, John, 23, 68–9, 78, 87, 92–3

utilitarianism, 1–2

Varela, Francisco, 105, 112, 116
Verga, Giovanni, 179–81, 183
vitalism, 102, 114, 159, 188, 211
Vivas, Eliseo, 20–2, 24
Vivian, Philip (Vivian Phelips), 37–41
Vries, Leonard de, 46

Watson, Sean, 30–1, 104, 110, 112, 247 n.15
Watts and Co., 38
Weismann, August, 46
Wells, H.G., 43, 53–6; *Ann Veronica*, 53–6
West, Cornel, 66, 72, 92, 104
Whewell, William, 36, 86
Whitehead, A.N., 16, 240
Whitman, Walt, 43
Whorf, Benjamin Lee, 19, 97
Wiener, Norbert, 112
Wilde, Oscar, 199
Willey, Basil, 241 n.4
Williams, Linda Ruth, 18
Williams, Raymond, 21, 31, 118, 125, 203–5, 207–8, 237, 239
Wollaston, Thomas, 68
Wood, James, 150–1
Woolf, Virginia, 217
Wordsworth, William, 89, 193
Worthen, John, 25, 37–8, 126

Young, Robert J.C., 177

Zeno, 63–4, 245 n.2
Zola, Emile, 16